No Such Thing

Krissy Lanier

Contents

For those of you who needed to know what happened to Summer
and Kash, this is for you.

Prologue

I F THE SEA COULD talk, she would tell you—with certainty—that the shore is a place where you go to *feel*. It's where you are pulled when you need—desperately—to cry without inhibitions. To taste assuming tears, unable to decipher them from the drops of the ocean.

If the sea had eyes, she would have seen this story unfold, and if she could speak, she would tell you how a woman arrived here on this remarkable piece of land—where sea meets sand. A woman who followed her dreams and her intuition to where she had always been called. And she followed—without expectation—a man, a man who welcomed her with a smile that soothed the unease of change.

The sea has secrets, for the sea bears witness to the minuscule movements on the sand, otherwise unseen.

Intentional brushes of pinky fingers, though brief, they are felt.

The glimmers of a glance under hooded eyelids.

Nervous laughter.

Deep breaths.

If the sea had eyes, she would see it all.

And if she could speak, this story is one she would be dying to tell you.

CHAPTER 1

Summer

APRIL

Have you ever walked outside on the first warm day in spring—when the air feels different for the first time after winter—and you breathe deeply with your eyes closed, as memories weave their way through your mind? You recall images from the past so quickly that you can't catch them, but you know you're reminded of something real because you feel it in your bones.

Maybe the flickering of maple tree buds falling whimsically to the earth remind you of a face you barely recognize—a face that once belonged to you. You see it in your mind's eye, the little child—you—peeling back the ends of the bud, exposing the sticky insides, just enough so that it adheres to the bridge of your nose, conjuring up a memory of a laugh that's foreign and faint. There's joy in the recollection—a welcomed change from the otherwise retched memories from a childhood you'd rather keep forgetting.

But a life where you hide from the past is not a life worth living. I know this all too well. I'm reminded, stepping out of my apartment and onto the sidewalk amongst the falling propellers, that I'm still susceptible to being triggered into the past. But I'm much better off now, stronger than I once was. It took effort and it was hard work, but I did eventually move away from simply surviving.

I pick up my pace as I head toward the ocean. I can hear the rumble of the waves, fierce and unforgiving, crashing against the Santa Monica sand. As I get closer to the pier, the sun begins to fully awaken. It was only just beginning to stretch as I began my walk.

I have been using walks as a form of therapy for years now—a way to clear my head, focus on breathing, gratitude, and being present. Until last year, living in the past was my way of life. Slowly, I started working to heal from my past trauma and began actually living my life. No more running, no more hiding.

My childhood, which was riddled with abuse, led into adolescence that was filled with abandonment and unease; being labeled a foster child—an orphan—seemed to be my only identity. Because of that, I was a shell of a person. I ended up homeless and weak, unable to stand on my own two feet, with no one to turn to or nowhere to go. I fell headfirst into a dark hole that seemed impossible to crawl out of. But I did crawl out…or more like claw my way out, digging my nails into the dirt and not giving up until I was on solid ground. The sturdiness I finally found underneath me was no accident. It was not luck. It was a result of the hard work I put into turning my life around, making it what I felt like I deserved.

I was the one who did the work.

I did have some help…from my family. From the family I chose.

Seven is quite a young age to start learning the lesson that adults aren't people you can depend on. But that's what my childhood was, one lesson after another of who not to trust. By the time I was removed from my parents custody at eleven, I had already been conditioned to cower, to close my eyes to the horrors that surrounded me. I learned that I never truly could hide; flinching didn't stop the pain that would inevitably come. So, I went into foster care with an armor that only strengthened as the adults around me continuously let me down.

As I shuffled around my foster family's home for seven years, I switched between indifference and desperation on a daily basis. I was either brushing off the horror that was my life, acting like it didn't bother me at all, or I was carrying myself in such a way that made me hope, deep in my soul, that I was worthy enough for the Brickmans to adopt me. There was a time in my life when the thought of having a family who despised me was better than no family at all.

There's a complex—a difficulty—that people have with believing a woman who claims to be assaulted. When it happened to me by my foster brother, Jason, I didn't even try to cry for help. Not during. Not after. Not ever. He had once been my best friend—my only friend. But that all changed one night during my senior year when he attacked me. Afterward, Jason turned on me, telling me that no one would believe me, and I knew he was right. Because that's how I had been conditioned to think: that there was no one in my corner. Jason lied and told his parents that I was the aggressor, and after he spewed the false truth to his parents, I saw it on their faces: the complete ease with which they cut the strings from me—strings that were already quite tattered and worn. I watched as the life I was living, though horrid, slid out of my grasp. Gone was any chance of a family. So before the Brickmans could send me away, I ran, never looking back. It was then that I told myself that I was better off with no family at all. That it was just me against the world. And the years that followed were what you would expect of a person with no family, no support system, no hope of a better future.

Homelessness. Drugs. Instability. Shelters. Hunger. They say that those who wander are not lost, but boy, was I lost.

Ten years.

A decade.

It's a long string of years to be untethered to the earth. No anchor. No light.

The streets of Louisville sank their teeth into my fragile exterior, taking no time at all to get to the part deep inside me that I once thought of as strong and impenetrable. But the streets ravaged me from the inside out, ruining any soft spirit that once dwelled in my heart.

I did what I had to survive. And I barely made it out of that hell. I hung on for dear life until I eventually made my way off of the streets. I had run myself into the ground, and after suffering a seizure on a park bench in Louisville due to dehydration and malnutrition, I found myself finally being led to peace. Because of the kindness of some beautiful people, I found myself in a facility that helped get me back on my feet. And from there, I eventually left Kentucky and moved to Austin, Texas, with their support and guidance, which is where I lived for two years, where I found myself. Where I found *home*. Where I found my *family*.

I approach the surf, the sun at my back, making its way higher into the sky, little by little. The beach is nearly vacant as I walk closer to where the waves are breaking. I take a seat in the sand that's neither hot nor cold as it hangs on to the last breaths of night before the sun begins to scorch it. I let the grains slide through my fingers, the gentle breeze blowing the tiny specks away from me. A gust pulls a strand of hair from my braid, briefly masking my face. I move it out of the way, taking a deep breath of sea air. I have come to adore the early mornings at the beach. These moments here have become my sanctuary, the place where I connect with myself.

Summer James, you are worthy of goodness.

This new mantra is believable, more so than my old one was. My therapist, Janie, makes me come up with a statement that feels impossible to believe but one that is necessary for me to grasp. One that I have to repeat over and over to train myself to believe it until it feels like it's imprinted into me.

Summer James, you are more than the sum of your past.

It took me many years, but I finally made it—to this place where my childhood and adolescent years don't define me anymore. Though those experiences may be etched into my DNA, into every fiber of my being, I know now that I am not what happened to me. I am no longer a person who doesn't feel worthy, someone who's a victim of their circumstances. Someone who's all alone, left to fight the world by herself. At my core, I am strong. I have overcome a lot. With the help of a few amazing people, I have risen above.

When I left Kentucky and started working at Sullivan's, the famous piano bar in Austin, I would never have imagined that I'd find my home located within the mahogany walls of that beautiful establishment. Amongst the twinkling fairy lights and amidst the wondrous sounds of the piano keys, I found myself. And I found my family. Silvia, Maverick, Farrah, and Kash entered my world and burrowed themselves into the fabric of my heart, never to leave, and I couldn't be more grateful for them.

Now that I'm no longer in Austin, I have to work to keep our relationships alive. These people are too important to me to let distance come between us. I FaceTime with Silvia every week while I sit on the sun-soaked balcony of my apartment. "Dear, you look fabulous," she always says, and, "How are you holding up?" Silvia is like a mother to me, or maybe more like a fun, sweet aunt. I can't really tell which vibe she gives because my experience with either of those figures was nonexistent up until now. My childhood was filled with lonely days and empty nights as my momma and dad slowly sank into their toxic web of turmoil. And there were never any extended family members to help pick up the pieces. My foster mom was cold and looked down on me—she was Lady Tremain, and I was Cinderella. But Silvia loves me like her own flesh and blood; it's a love that surrounds me even though she's thousands of miles away.

Maverick took a chance on me and gave me an opportunity to bartend at his bar, the one he built with his heart. He let me in and gave me a chance, even though I had nothing to show for myself at first. "I always saw something in you, Summer, from the second I met you." His belief in me is a massive reason why I believe in myself now. I don't talk to him as often as Silvia, but since I've moved away, he has remained a constant in my life. He is always sending me pictures of the bar and silly GIFs, and sometimes, we call one another just to say hello.

Farrah, the sister I never had. We met at Champlain Bridge, the facility that provided me the boost I needed to climb out of the hole I was in. She was struggling with some mental health issues, and her husband, Joey, got her the help she desperately needed at that time. She's a spunky and freckled spirit with auburn hair and curvy hips that she swings as she walks, her personality radiating off of her as if it has a mind of its own. Farrah and Joey recently had a baby, little Junie, who is about to start walking; I can tell by the way she shakes her two legs when she pulls herself up. Farrah and I FaceTime multiple times a week and text every day. She calls me Auntie Summer when Junie's on the call with us, and it melts my heart into a puddle on the floor every time.

I miss them, I do. More than anything.

My heart shattered into a thousand pieces when the Uber drove me away as my little family waved to me from the sidewalk outside my old apartment. I was leaving Texas behind as California stretched out in front of me, holding my dreams in its sunny grip. Though I was going to miss them immensely, I was leaving for myself, to go after what was calling me. It was bittersweet, as they say.

I had gotten on the plane feeling as if my life was starting over, the fire inside me reigniting, the tears in my eyes not brought on by a broken heart, but from the overwhelming sensation of it being put back together.

And I wasn't leaving my whole family. As I headed to California, I was also heading toward Kash.

CHAPTER 2
Kash

THE SUN SNEAKS THROUGH the blinds, piercing its way in while the shades attempt to block it. The light rattles me from sleep. Setting an alarm isn't necessary as I'm always awake before it goes off at six thirty, even with my late nights at the bar. I stretch, and with the gesture comes a guttural noise that's almost primal. In my opinion, there's no other way to wake up. I swing my legs over the bed and rise, walking to the window, raising the blinds. Just over the building next to mine, I can see the ocean, waves crashing aggressively on the shore, and as I stare, I know she's out there somewhere…although I can't quite spot her.

Summer.

I know she's out there because though she is shocking, surprising…astonishing even, she is equally predictable. Her patterns, her thoughts, her routines—I can predict them to a T. Since she moved into my apartment a year and a half ago, I have learned Summer's movements, her habits, her flaws—as she calls them—and my ability to memorize her is never quite extinguished. She wakes at six most mornings and rarely misses a walk along the beach. She taps her finger in the pattern of a heartbeat when she's concentrating on something. Sighs accompany all of her emotions—happy, sad, angry—and she rereads books that touch her heart, underlining the words that speak to her.

After many years of front-lining at Sullivan's in Austin, I opened my own piano bar, Two WhisKEYS. I once worked in finance during the day and dueled at Maverick's piano bar at night…until my life became *not enough.* I toyed with my dreams for a long time, but nothing came of it until the night Summer and I sat on the steps in front of her apartment and made a deal, shaking on something that seemed, at the time, so trivial: two young people wishing on fallen stars.

But here we are, Summer and I, living under the same roof and working under the same canopy, attempting to chase similar dreams.

But in all honesty, my dreams have been met. What I wanted, before I even knew Summer, has come to fruition: a quiet life, a bar that's all mine where I can sing and play piano, living where the sound of the waves can both lull me to sleep and pull me from my dreams. I have it…all I ever wanted.

Well, almost.

I don't have her.

CHAPTER 3

Summer

THE DISTANT HOLLER OF a pier employee pulls me from my thoughts. I get up from the sand, brush the tiny specks off my pants, and rest my hands on my hips as I continue to gaze out into the sea. I glance at my phone to check the time—it's 6:47 a.m., and my stomach growls, warning me it's time to head back to the apartment to eat something. *Kash will be up. We can eat together*, I think to myself as I begin to head back toward Ocean Avenue.

Kash Holden.

Where would I be without him? It hurts to even think about, but so often, I do—imagine the life I would be leading had I never left Kentucky in the first place and never met him. Kash continuously pulls me out of my shell, gently probing me to do the things I so desperately need to do to heal the parts of me that I thought would always be broken. I have confided in him, cried on his shoulder, let him see the deepest and darkest parts of my soul. And he never wavers. He never turns his back. Day in and day out he encourages me to remain on the solid ground I finally found myself on, not allowing me to slip back into darkness.

Janie has questioned my feelings for Kash multiple times, pushing me to talk about the topic, which is completely outside of my comfort zone. "He's my best friend," I always tell her. But she continues to respond with a half smile, without showing her teeth, like she doesn't believe me in the slightest. She seems like she's anticipating a confession of love for him, and if that's the case, she will be waiting for an eternity. "When pigs fly, I'll cross that line and ruin the strongest friendship I have had," I said to her at our last session a few weeks ago, scoffing a bit. She had shaken her head at me sweetly and said, "Never say never, Summer."

Her words gave me pause.

I should know better than anyone to never say never because I *have* seen a pig fly—the one that set me free. So, maybe the phrase I uttered to Janie was just a ruse, a distraction from the truth. But even if that were the case, I can't face starting something with Kash and then it failing. I can't do that to myself because, if I do, the mere thought of losing him feels equivalent to what it would be like to lose a limb.

I pick up my pace as I get closer to the apartment. I'm nearly running as a memory pokes its way to the surface. Flashbacks of people who were once the center of my universe being plucked from my life.

Abandoned by Momma and my dad. Alienated from my best friend, Meg. Given up on by my boyfriend, Dan. Ridiculed and assaulted by Jason. Dropped like a bad habit by Piper.

I clung to these people at different times of my life, and though I tried to hang on, they slipped through my fingers like the sand in my hands. At one point or another, each of those people was a saving grace in my life, until the tables turned. Support and love never last for me. It never has.

I can't let that happen with Kash. I do love him; I can admit that now, and because of that, I have to protect him from what could happen if he gets too close. And in doing so, I'm protecting myself, too.

Before I even push the door all the way open, I can smell breakfast cooking. The aroma causes my stomach to rumble in such a way that it physically aches.

"Morning, Summer!" Kash yells as he hears me returning home.

I cross over the threshold of the kitchen. "Hi," I say, grinning. "It smells unbelievable in here." Walking to the stove, I take a peek at what he's putting together—an egg scramble sauteing in one pan and sausage just beginning to brown in the other. "There better be feta in that," I joke, hip-checking him.

"Would I dare make eggs without feta?" Kash winks at me, using the spatula to rotate the combination of eggs, feta, tomatoes, and spinach in the pan. "How was your walk?"

I take a seat at the round kitchen table and pull my hoodie over my head. "It was invigorating, as always." It's true, but I have to force a smile, pushing away the lingering heaviness that came with my thoughts this morning.

Kash serves the food onto plates and then brings them to the table, taking a seat across from me. He looks at me with concerned eyes. "Maybe it was, but there's something else written on your face." He waits a beat, either to give me a chance to reply or because he has more to say and he's trying to find the words.

I open my mouth to say something without thinking, but at the same time, he continues, simply asking, "Are you ok?"

I pull my leg up onto the seat, hugging it close to my body. I stare at him across the table, my eyes darting to all the points on his face that I adore, searching for the words I should say. He pulls his hair into a bun, never taking his eyes off me, while he waits for me to respond.

Oh, nothing, Kash. Janie is convinced I love you and that I'm just too afraid to admit it, and that's what I was thinking about this morning at the beach. And how everyone I have ever loved has left me until now. I worry. I'm scared.

You mean everything to me.

I can't lose you.

I take a shallow breath and give him a real smile, anything to avoid telling him the actual thoughts in my head. "I'm ok," I say, but it comes out in a whisper, certainly revealing the lack of truth within them. "Honest," I add for good measure.

CHAPTER 4

Kash

S HE'S LYING THROUGH HER teeth, but she's giving me that look
I know all too well, the one that says *Don't push this*, so I let
it be. I give her a friendly smile and jostle her hand that rests on
the table. "Glad you're ok," I say, knowing she trusts that she can
always come to me when she needs to, when she's ready.

"What's on the agenda today?" Summer asks in between bites.

"I have to head into the bar early. I have a lot of inventory to go
through and some orders to place."

"Do you need help?" she asks.

I pause before responding because although I don't need help, I
wouldn't mind the company. "Only if you're free."

"I'll be there." She flicks her hand at me like it's no big deal.

Friends helping friends.

———

I let myself into Two WhisKEYS through the back door. Walking into the bar always sets me at ease. It's been nearly two years, and I still haven't been able to come down from the high that opening this place has brought me. Quitting my job in finance in Austin and taking a leap to move to California to open this piano bar was a risk—a big one. But it was a risk that was worth it, and I've never regretted it.

My dad used to paint unimaginably vibrant images of the West Coast in my mind. He had lived here, in Venice, just down the road when he was in his twenties, playing guitar on sandy strips of sidewalk as people on skateboards and rollerblades whizzed by him. He bartended, too, making just enough money to survive, but he didn't need much, he had told me. "California is for dreamers," he said, and in all these years, I never could let that idea go. He planted a longing deep inside me with his stories of the Pacific Ocean and all the shore entailed.

When he died in a horrible car accident when I was a child, the longing turned to a desperation to come here, to try to feel him, to see what he saw, to smell what he smelled. And all these years, I've dreamed of being here, until I finally took the leap. So when I got here and was able to snag this space right before it was even for rent, it seemed like utter fate, a move from God, and my father, I suppose.

I walk to the other side of the bar, where the wall of glass doors opens up completely, inviting in the crashing waves and the wafting of briny air and sunscreen. I step through the open wall onto the paved path in front of the bar; just beyond it, there's the sandy beach. I stare out at the backdrop that has become my security, my therapy, my calm. The Ferris wheel on the pier begins its slow spin, warming up for a day of carrying eager tourists in its buckets, around and around.

"Morning, Kash!" The greeting pulls me from my thoughts, and I turn to see Jim Clarence opening the door to his business next door.

"Hey, Jimmy! Another beautiful day," I shout in his direction.

Jimmy owns the taco bar next door; he has for two decades. He's in his sixties and looks like a person who would own a bar on the beach. His skin is leathery and sun-kissed, as if he never goes indoors. His hair is white, the color of fresh snow. If I try to picture him as a younger man, I imagine his hair to be blonde—a true California man. He's always wearing bright board shorts and a white tank top, or he's shirtless. His wardrobe works with the vibe over at J's Tacos. There certainly isn't a *No Shoes, No Shirt, No Service* sign on his door.

I love Jimmy; I admire him. I can't help but imagine that he is my dad from an alternate universe had he never left California to chase a pregnant woman who was carrying his child and, with that, his entire heart. My dad left California to be a father, and he was the best one in the world. But my heart aches when I think about the path he took and how it led to his demise on a Texas highway. I carry guilt, even though I know I shouldn't, for being the reason Dad left this paradise and was never able to come back.

Everyone told me I left Texas too quickly. They supported me, but they hated to see me go without much of a warning. But for me, it was a long time coming. I had been called here long before I actually left, called to much more than a dream of owning my own bar. It was the desperate longing to connect with my dad, silly as it may seem.

"You're in early this morning, son," Jimmy says, walking over toward me, and I take a few steps in his direction. He pulls his sunglasses down from his forehead.

"I have a lot to catch up on," I say with a soft laugh. "Figured I'd come and open the windows and chip away at the to-do list."

"Ha. It never ends, does it?" he says, patting my back. "But who would want it to end? Am I right? We live the best life out here on the beach, don't we, fella?"

I smile at him genuinely. "We sure do."

"Summer asked me to play guitar for some of her songs this week. Did she run that by you?" Jimmy asks, not seeming too concerned, just curious.

She hadn't, but it doesn't matter either way. This bar feels just as much hers as it is mine at this point.

"No, but that sounds awesome. It's been a while since you've played!" I say, my voice sounding ecstatic.

"I'm stoked," he says, smiling and flashing his teeth.

I reach out my hand to give Jimmy a shake. "I gotta get in there and get started. Talk to you soon, big guy." My left hand reaches out to grab his shoulder, and we embrace in a quick hug.

"Have yourself a sunny day, Kash."

With that, Jimmy turns and heads back toward his establishment, and I take a few steps back into mine. There's a pep in my step, a direct effect of what this place does to me—filling me with pride. I head past the tables and stacked chairs and round the glossy bar toward my office in the back. My plan is to get some orders put in before Summer arrives. Boxes of inventory are stacked by the back door, and there's a food delivery scheduled for a few hours from now. The two of us can get all that organized before we open tonight. I sit down at my desk and jostle the mouse to put in an order for napkins, cleaning supplies, and some other miscellaneous items. I finish the task just as Summer makes her way through the back door.

CHAPTER 5

Summer

"**D**ID YOU MEAN TO order these?" I ask Kash, holding up some plastic cups, a smirk on my face.

"Are you kidding me?" he says, grabbing the packing slip. "They charged me for twenty-four glass tumblers but sent twenty-four plastic ones." He rolls his eyes, tossing the sheet into the box, placing one hand on his hip; the other, he runs through his slick black hair, annoyed.

"I'll call them right now," I offer, taking the slip from the box. I head toward the office.

"Thanks!" he yells. "If they do this one more time, I'm getting a new vendor."

"I'll let them know," I respond lightly. I hear Kash let out a chuckle. He never stays mad for long; it's one of his traits I have learned to love and appreciate. He tends to let things roll off his back quickly and moves on from minor annoyances with grace. I've learned a lot from him in that way because that's not something

I'm particularly good at. We make a good team, though. He tells me to chill out, and I do the work when something needs to be sorted out—when something rolls off his back, but I can't get it to slide off mine.

———

At four o'clock, I glance around the bar. Everything looks ready for the night. The doors aren't unlocked yet; we have another hour before the night begins, but the windows are wide open, and the tables and chairs are set just right, facing the elevated platform where two shiny pianos rest, facing one another.

Most nights, there's a mic stand in the front where I stand, singing mostly covers but also my own songs. I sing while Kash plays the piano sometimes, or other times, it's some of our regular musicians. Finn Gable is a twenty-something with fiery red hair and bright green eyes. His voice is mesmerizing, and the regulars here love him. He's an avid surfer and usually comes right in from the water on nights he's performing. He matches the vibe here, that's for sure. Diego Ramos is another regular. He's from Puerto Rico and is learning English partly from studying words in music videos. He's paying his way through school, desperate to do something in the musical field. He's a phenomenal pianist but also plays the guitar next to me while I sing some nights. The patrons also love him immensely. It makes me smile that Kash has been able to mirror what Maverick does at Sullivan's in Austin, bringing in talent that makes people come back for more.

I pull myself from my thoughts. "I'm going to sit outside and call Farrah before the night gets going," I say over my shoulder.

"Tell her I said hi," Kash says as he tinkers with the piano.

I step out into the California air. The sun is beginning its slow descent out over the ocean. Just over twelve hours ago, when it was just rising, I was sitting out there on the sand, and I'll do it all over again tomorrow. There's comfort in that routine for me, even if it cuts down on hours that I could be sleeping. I have always relied on the stars to set me at ease, but now the rising and setting of the sun has become a new center of gravity for me, a truth that will never waver. I hear the distant sounds of screams, loud at first, then fading as the rides down on the pier spin in rhythmic motions, the people on them enjoying their evening.

I get a whiff of the flowering bougainvillea plants that are located between Two WhisKEYS and Jimmy's restaurant next door, the scent lingering in my nose as the breeze picks up off the shore. I pull out my phone, go into my recent FaceTime calls, and press Farrah's name, listening to the familiar sounds of the call connecting. I smile before she answers. I can't wait to see her and little Junie.

"Say, hi to Auntie, June Bug!" Farrah squeals into the screen, and I giggle.

"Hi, little one!" I boast. "And hi to you, too, Momma!" I say to Farrah.

She lets out a dramatic sigh as she shifts Junie in her arms and moves the phone to a better angle. "Hi, Summer! What's up?"

"Nothing much—Kash and I just finished getting ready for the night. I decided to come out and get some air and check in before things get crazy." I take my gaze out over the horizon. "What are you up to tonight?"

"My mom is watching Junie so Joey and I can head to Sullivan's for a date night," Farrah tells me.

"You didn't want to pick a different place for a date?" I ask, laughing.

"Silas is playing tonight for the first time in a long time. I didn't want to miss it."

Silas Dade. I miss him, too, just like I miss the rest of the Sullivan's crew. He and Kash used to be the regular musicians at Sullivan's, always dueling to perfection but also letting one another shine in the best possible ways. They were captivating together. When Kash broke the news to everyone that he was moving, we were all heartbroken to see them separate. Since then, Silas still plays there once in a while, but he has been working on opening a small music school, which is amazing.

I owe a lot to Silas. Before I moved to California, he helped me perfect the first song I ever wrote. He helped me write the melodies, and we practiced tirelessly for six weeks until I finally performed it at Sullivan's one night with him playing the piano and my family cheering me on in the audience. It was completely out of character for me, but I'm so glad I did it because it was the catalyst that brought me here to Santa Monica.

That night after my performance, Kash walked me home and invited me to come and stay with him in California, to take a leap toward doing something for myself and my dreams for once. I contemplated the offer for some time, and after getting the support I desperately needed from Silvia, Farrah, and Maverick, I knew there was no other choice. They all allowed me to see the situation clearly. They didn't give me a chance to feel guilty for leaving the life I had started to build. They let me fly. And so, it didn't take me long to accept Kash's invitation. It was a decision that I've never regretted, not for a second. Kash says it, too, whenever we sit on our balcony on breezy nights, the moon ornamentally hovering above us, and we contemplate how we ended up here in this place.

"Can you even believe we did this? Can you believe we live here?" he'll say, grounding me into a place of gratitude.

Junie lets out a happy squeal as she reaches for the phone where my face is smiling at her.

"Tell Silas hello for me, and give him a big hug," I say.

"I will. So you guys are working tonight?" Farrah asks.

I nod. "Almost every night," I reply with a laugh. It's true; Kash and I practically live at the bar, but we wouldn't have it any other way.

Farrah laughs and rolls her eyes playfully. "You two need to have a life outside of that place, too, you know," she offers without much force. She just feels the need to say it; I can tell.

I shrug, squinting into the lowering sun.

"I'm just saying," Farrah adds, "how are either of you going to meet anyone?"

"We have friends," I say, a tad bit annoyed.

"I mean people to date, Summer."

I give her a pointed look before glancing back over my shoulder into the bar. Kash is in there straightening a picture on the wall that probably doesn't need to be fixed, the muscles in his forearms flexing under his sleeve of tattoos. I smile in his direction, him unknowingly under my gaze. There's a flutter in my chest, brief but noticeable. I think of Farrah's words, but I know deep in my bones that if I didn't meet another man for the rest of my life, I would be OK.

"Hello?" Farrah is trying to get my attention, but I don't feel like having this conversation, so I change the subject abruptly, a skill I'm quite good at.

"Anyways…," I drag out the word and widen my eyes, giving her the clue that I want to talk about something else. "I hope you and Joey have the best time tonight! Don't call your mom every five minutes, OK?" I laugh.

She laughs, too. "Promise!"

We say our goodbyes, and I tell her that I'll talk to her tomorrow. It's time to get inside and make sure we're all set. I'm bartending tonight, saving my voice for tomorrow. Jimmy is going to play guitar next to me, and I'm really looking forward to it.

When I walk back inside the bar, I see that the rest of the staff have begun to arrive. "Hey, Summer!" Janelle Dagger, or Nel, as we endearingly call her, yells from behind the bar. Nel is a regular bartender and a good friend of mine. She's a quiet woman with a fierce heart. I am always mesmerized by how put together she is—her smooth, dark skin is always flawless, and her thick, short curls that round her face always look styled to perfection. Me, on the other hand? I'm lucky if I get my long, dark hair into a braid of the French variety. Usually, it's in a bun, pieces either falling out from the wind or because I just can't be bothered to do it right.

Farrah jokes that Nel replaced her since Nel and I bartend together now, instead of Farrah and I like we did at Sullivan's. I joke back with her, too—"Well, yeah. I had to replace you because I'm not there with you anymore. But at least Nel doesn't pressure me to go on a date with a different person every night of the week." She used to really put pressure on me to try and make things happen with Kash—until I put a halting stop to it, begging her to let it be, explaining to her that I couldn't, in any way, lose Kash. She backed off last year, and I'm glad. I'm not sure I would be able to hide behind my lies with much conviction these days.

"Hey, Nel!" I announce, pulling her in for a hug. "How's Sienna doing? Is she feeling better today?" Nel's two year old daughter is typically a spunky and energetic toddler but a stomach bug has sucked the energy right out of her, alarming Nel quite a bit.

"She's so much better today, but it's so scary when she gets sick!" I watch her shoulders relax. "We lost a lot of sleep this week. But her fever broke yesterday, and her appetite is back! Thanks for asking," she says, putting her hand on my shoulder with gratitude.

"Of course!" I say. "It must be hard to see her so sick."

"It was, but we're on the up and up." She winks at me and goes to empty the dishwasher, steam billowing up into the air as she opens the door. "Ahhhh," she sighs dramatically. "This is the closest I can get to a sauna these days." Nel laughs as the hot dishwasher steam wraps around her face. I join in her laughter and begin assisting her with the finishing touches behind the bar.

A few more minutes until the crowds will be making their way in. After all this time, the anticipation each night is still indescribable.

By ten, the evening is in full swing, and the background noise is lulling me into a sense of peace that only this place can give me. The sounds of clinking glasses, the hum of conversations that I can't make out, and the melodious beats coming off the piano keys feel so much like home that I can't pinpoint any difference between the feeling I have in these walls and the feeling I have when I'm in our apartment. Finn and Diego are dueling together, playing popular songs from all genres and decades, sending the patrons into squeals of excitement at each song transition.

I know better than anyone that songs are a quick way to travel back in time, the beats and lyrics powerfully moving us, whether we like it or not, to go back to another place altogether. In what seems like another life, music could trigger memories that would suck me from the present and drop me into the past. I would black out and have no idea how much time had passed when I snapped out of those episodes. But things have changed over the last two years. And I'm reminded of this when Diego pulls a request out of the jar and announces their next song: "Sweet Home Alabama." I smile to myself as I maneuver around Nel, who is grabbing a bottle of Pinot Grigio from the cooler. As the song plays, I vividly see the images of a moment long gone flying through my mind.

A happy moment.

A moment when I felt entirely content.

"Come on, Summer, stop talking to Kash and come dance with us!" Farrah yells, trying to pull me out of our conversation. I let out a laugh accompanied by a friendly eye roll and follow her toward the dance floor. Farrah's stunning wedding dress has begun to blacken at the bottom, where it has been dragging through the dirt and grass around her beautiful lakeside venue. But she couldn't care less.

We move to the front of the dance floor and start dancing as Farrah yells the lyrics at the top of her lungs. I laugh at her, choking back tears that are nagging me to be released. Happy tears. Tears of immense gratitude. She grabs my hand and spins me around, and I begin singing the lyrics along with her as we dance our hearts out until we are both sweating and out of breath.

I glance playfully over my shoulder, looking for Kash, and there he is on the edge of the dance floor, an endearing smile spread across his face as he pulls his dark hair into a bun, getting it off of his sweaty forehead. I shudder, a chill moving through my body, as I smile back at him, remembering when, just moments ago, Kash had wrapped me in an embrace and allowed me to experience dancing on a dance floor for the first time in my life. It was that moment when I realized that I loved him. I love him deeply, but it comes with a heaviness—the feeling that he is completely unattainable. Or maybe it's me that is…utterly unreachable.

I smile over at Diego and Finn up on the elevated floor and shake my head at the happy memory swimming around in my mind.

How things have changed.

My attention is pulled toward two women sitting at the bar in front of me. "Just take a look at him. Those tattoos. Oh my God. He must be a bad boy."

I glance up to where the pair is looking to see Kash climbing up onto the stage. I let out an audible chuckle, which causes them to turn and look at me with wide eyes, momentarily halting their conversation

Kash, a bad boy? What a comical thought. I don't relay the truth; I just continue mixing drinks and allow the two women to think what they want.

They quickly forget my intense laugh and resume talking about him as if I can't hear them, as if they are the only people in the bar.

The blonde one agrees with the brunette. "Totally a bad boy. He is so your type. I dare you to ask for his number tonight!" They both laugh obnoxiously, and I turn my back to them to put a bottle of tequila back on the shelf, rolling my eyes and steadying my breath.

These girls are not Kash's type. They are too done up, attention seekers, completely unwholesome.

The complete opposite of me.

I wipe my damp hands on my jeans and head over to two men who just sat down at the bar. "What can I get ya?" I ask, a genuine smile on my face, placing a cocktail napkin in front of each of them.

"Kash's favorite whiskey," says the older of the two gentlemen.

"Same," the other adds.

"You friends of Kash?" I ask as I begin to prepare their order.

"Oh, no. We're just visiting. We had dinner next door, and the owner sent us over here, said it's the best bar in California. Jimmy, I think, was his name. He told us to get Kash's choice whiskey," the older gentleman offers.

"Ah, good ol' Jimmy," I say with a laugh. "He is the best!"

"I'm Tom, and this is my son, Andy. We're here visiting some family in Malibu and decided to make our way down PCH to see what the view was all about." He laughs, leaning back in his stool, crossing his arms over his chest.

"It sure is quite the view, especially when you have never been to California before," Andy adds.

"Absolutely. It truly is breathtaking!" I offer, sliding their drinks over to them.

"Where y'all from?" I ask.

"Y'all? You definitely aren't from California," Tom says with a jolly smile.

I let out a laugh as my head falls back. "Guilty as charged. I'm from Kentucky originally, and I lived in Texas for a few years before I moved here."

"Oh, cool. We live close to Kentucky—in Indiana," Andy says, unknowingly causing a memory to flutter beneath the surface of my consciousness.

I try not to give it the time of day, the visions of when I ran away, leaving Kentucky in the rearview mirror as I hitchhiked to Indiana. My breath suspends in my lungs, and I work hard to bring the air in and then let it go. A thought is intangible. It doesn't have power over me—these are ideas I am constantly working to believe. But memories still tug at me sometimes, no matter how much I attempt to stifle them.

The smell of smoke makes its way so far into my nose that my brain feels like it's clouding over, suffocating. I can hear the voices of the people who live in this strange house through the thin walls. They talk and yell and swear, and occasionally cough so loudly it sounds like their lungs are going to land in a splatter on the floor in front of them. The clutter that surrounds me in my borrowed room makes me feel like I am caged in against my will.

Social services left me here at this house earlier this morning, calling it respite care, as if I am supposed to know what that means, as if I'm supposed to just accept it. My foster family, whom I have lived with for two years, has gone away for Thanksgiving, leaving me home in Kentucky so they could have some family time without their foster child.

I sneak out in the dead of night, afraid of the darkness but equally afraid of the horrors within these strange walls.

My fight or flight senses are activated, causing me to run.

"And we're going to the Warner Bros. Studio tomorrow!" Tom says, utterly thrilled at the plan.

Their glasses look like they have barely taken a sip, telling me that I didn't zone out for long at all.

Progress. It's been a long road, but every little bit of growth matters.

I busy my hands, wiping down the counter. "You better be planning on sitting on the Friends' couch!" I make them promise. Andy shakes his head, and a quiet laugh escapes. "What? Not a fan?" I joke.

"We are more excited about the Batmobiles," Andy says earnestly.

I put my hands up in defense. "Got it." I smile. "Enjoy your drinks. My name's Summer. Let me know if you need anything."

"Will do. Thanks, Summer," Tom says as I walk toward the other end of the bar to check in on a few regulars who have shown up. As I reach the end of the bar, Finn and Diego finish up a song and begin engaging with the crowd. I'm only half listening as I fill drink orders when I hear them call my name.

"Oh, Summer! We need you for this next one," Diego says, his Spanish accent lingering poetically through the bar.

I roll my eyes and shake my head, but my smile tells them I'm not going to say no. "What's it going to be?" I yell, cupping my hands over my mouth.

"'Empire State of Mind,'" Finn says into the mic. "We need you to show up, Alicia Keys. Come on, girl."

"Oh, please," I mutter under my breath as I walk out from behind the bar and start toward the stage. I hear Nel hollering behind me, cheering me on like she always does when the guys make me come up for one song.

I get up on the stage and adjust the mic they brought out. I look up to see Kash leaning against the wall that leads to the kitchen, his arms crossed over his chest and a smile so sincere I can see the dimple on his right cheek.

I smile back at him, my muse.

CHAPTER 6

Kash

Sometimes, it still surprises me how much Summer has changed. It had once taken me months to convince her that she was capable of singing her own song on the Sullivan's stage, and now, here she is, leaving her post behind the bar without much coaxing to sing a song with the guys. She seems like a natural, as if she's been doing this all her life. I stop what I'm doing—checking in with patrons—and lean against the wall to watch her. As the sounds of the intro begin floating around the room, she closes her eyes and sways with the music. You can tell she really feels it. Her eyes remain closed as she sings her part, opening them toward the end and glancing around the bar, making eye contact with people sitting at a table up front.

Soon enough, the song is over, and she gives the audience a quick wave and a gratuitous smile, looking down at her feet as she makes her way down the steps and back toward the bar. I watch her the whole time, holding my breath. She even walks differently than she once did: a confident yet humble stride where there once was unease. I take my gaze down to the floor and allow my breathing to slow back to normal. *Shake it off, Kash,* I think to myself. *Get back to work.*

The bar is packed tonight, like usual, and the sounds that surround me set my soul at ease—the hum of conversations, the crescendo of the pianos dueling with each new song, and the mesmerizing sound of laughter and singing amongst the crowd. I'm proud of this place; there is no better word I can find to describe what I feel.

Are you proud of me, Dad? A lump forms in my throat with the thought. I find myself talking to him a lot these days, looking for a sign of approval…or proof that he sees me, that he's guiding me. I feel him, I do, but it doesn't seem like it's enough.

I pull myself away from my thoughts and head to the bar to check in with Nel and Summer. "Great song, Summer," I say to her with a wink.

She laughs, rolling her eyes. "Thanks," she responds, wiping down some melted ice from the counter.

Nel gently grabs her arm. "Girl, you are amazing, and you know it."

Summer ignores her and asks two women at the bar if they are ready for another round. The women nod but seem distracted. I head behind the bar to help Nel and Summer out, and I hear Summer chuckle.

"What's so funny?" I ask her.

She nods her head inconspicuously toward the women she's serving. "Don't look now," she starts, "but those two over there were ogling over you earlier. They think you're a *bad boy*." She wiggles her eyebrows and bumps me with her hip.

My cheeks turn crimson beneath my five o'clock shadow. "Are you blushing, Mr. Holden?" Summer smiles at me while carrying two tumblers back to the women. "Here you go, ladies. Can I get you anything else? Maybe a chat with Kash himself?"

My eyes go wide as the ladies giggle. Summer smiles at me, proud of her joke. Why does she do this to me?

I make my way toward them and hold out my hand to greet them, uninterested in conversing in the way they want to but never wanting to come off as rude to a customer. "Nice to meet you…," my voice trails off as I wait to hear their names.

"Grace," says the brunette, extending her hand. "And this is my friend, Hannah," she adds, gesturing toward the blonde, who is batting her eyelashes at me.

I stifle a groan, shaking both of their hands. "Are you having a nice night?" I ask.

"Oh, for sure. This place is great!" Grace says, beaming.

"First time here?"

They both nod, a thrill in their eyes.

"Awesome. Well, I hope you enjoy your night. I know Summer and Nel will continue to take good care of you." I put my hand up to wave and shift my weight on my heel, preparing to walk away. But Grace stops me.

"Wait, you and Hannah should go on a date or something." Her eyes are wide and adoring, and I can smell *dare* all over the exchange. I see Summer stiffen in my peripheral vision as she pours a glass of Chardonnay.

"I'm sorry, ladies, I'm not looking for dates at the moment, but it was lovely to meet you." I give them a charming smile, not wanting to make Hannah feel bad. Thankfully, it seems that they are just drunk enough not to be offended by my lack of interest.

Their giggles are at my back as I walk away, along with the sounds of Hannah whispering loudly, most likely chastising Grace for humiliating her.

I walk out from behind the bar, not wanting to engage in conversation with Summer about the women so we don't make them uncomfortable. I head toward the stage where Finn and Diego are singing "Sweet Caroline" as the song's about to end. I need to sit on the bench and play something. I need an outlet. After the song ends, I walk onstage to chat with them as they go on their second set break. When they come back from break, I'm going to play "Piano Man" solo—our most requested song. Though it's predictable to hear that song at a dueling piano bar, I don't mind. I have so many great memories of performing it both here and in Austin. As I adjust the piano a bit, preparing to perform, I'm taken back to the night I was certain that I loved Summer—entirely.

After the song wraps up, I tell the audience we're taking our first set break, but we'll be back for more songs soon. As I'm talking, I look up, past the audience and toward the bar to try and spot Summer, but I can't see her. As I hop off the stage, Silvia tells me she went to take a break—she needed to get some fresh air. I sneak out through the kitchen door and see her there in the alley, her hands on her hips as she looks out onto the main street. At the sound of my voice, she spins around quickly, startled out of her thoughts.

Just like Silvia said, Summer tells me she just needed some air, but I can tell she's lying. I can see it in her eyes—the sadness, the weight of the world…the panic. She thinks she's broken, but that isn't what I see when I look at her. I see strength behind her eyes. I see a desperate need to heal. I see her heart pulsing through her Sullivan's T-shirt in exasperated beats, begging for a reprieve. It's not that I want to save her. She is saving herself. But I want to love her. I want to be there for her. I want her to let me love her. I know from this moment on that there is no one but her.

The night wraps up like it always does—full of camaraderie and cleaning. My ears are ringing from the bustling evening noises, so the quiet is appreciated.

"Let's help Jimmy clean up next door when we're done," Summer suggests as she stacks some chairs against the wall.

"For sure," I reply. "I wonder if he has any tacos left." I let out a soft laugh. "Are you guys coming with us?" I direct my question to Nel, Diego, and Finn.

"Not me; I gotta get home to Sienna. Rob texted me and said he feels like the bug has hit him now, too," Nel says with dismay.

"Hopefully it doesn't hit you!" Finn says.

"Fingers crossed," Nel responds, making the gesture.

"I have to head home. I'm hitting the waves at dawn tomorrow," Finn says, smiling from ear to ear.

"Tired," Diego says, shaking his head.

As the dining area morphs into its overnight setup, I glance around quickly, taking inventory and making sure everything is as it should be. The floors are gleaming (thanks to Eddie, our busboy), the chairs are stacked (group effort), the bar is shining and neat (thanks to Nel and Summer), and the overnight lights are dimmed. The place is ready for us to shut the doors and lock up until tomorrow night. Summer and I begin shutting and locking the windows that open up to the ocean as we say goodbye to the rest of the staff.

When we head out the door, the air is warm, but the breeze off the ocean cools my skin. The sounds of our feet slapping against the concrete, mixed with the crunching of sand, accompany the comfortable silence as Summer and I head to Jimmy's. I hold the door open, letting the last of Jimmy's patrons out, and Summer steps over the threshold into the restaurant.

"Oh, look who it is!" Jimmy announces from the back of the dining area. "My favorite people on the planet."

"Hey, Jimmy," Summer greets, walking toward him.

"How was the night?" I ask.

"Oh, you know. Busy enough to make this old man tired," he responds, a sparkle flickering in his bright blue eyes. "Hope you had a good night for yourselves."

I shake his hand and pat his back, a gesture so familiar to the two of us. "It was a good night, thanks." I smile at him, and Jimmy tells us to take a seat at a table.

"I'll bring you some food. I got lots of fixins' for you folks to make some tacos for yourselves."

"Thanks, Jimmy!" Summer says, walking to a table and falling into a seat.

Jimmy's restaurant is perfectly unique. The walls are white but splashed with neon throughout. Surfboards hang on the walls, and the bar has a tiki hut appearance, making it look as if it belongs outdoors. Sand is strewn around the floor from sun (and moon) bathers coming in right off the beach. Jimmy likes it that way. "If I could feel the sand beneath my feet all the time, I would," he always says.

But my favorite feature of his place is the photo wall. When you walk in the door, the wall on the left is covered, floor to ceiling and end to end, with photographs—some framed, some thumbtacked, some Polaroids. Some are new—celebrities that make an appearance, regulars who want to be on the wall. And some are old, weathered on the edges, the brightness fading from the passage of time and the glare of the California sun through the massive windows. I make my way over to the wall, and my eyes hover over a few of the photographs. There's one with Bill Clinton standing next to Jimmy—Jimmy's squinting his eyes, and his mouth is wide as if he's mid-sentence. I chuckle to myself.

"You could stand there all week and not see every picture on that wall," Jimmy says as he puts the spread down on the table where Summer sits. "You're always over there, Kash. What are you looking for?"

I shrug my shoulders and contemplate his question. *What* am *I looking for?* "I'm just drawn to it, I guess." My voice sounds far off from my ears.

I feel Jimmy approaching me to my right, but I don't take my eyes off the wall, staring at nothing in particular.

He speaks so only I can hear. "Photographs can bring on emotions we can't comprehend, my boy—even if we don't know who's in them. It's a moment suspended in time, a time that's passed us by. It's either beautiful or heartbreaking, depending on how you look at it." My breath catches in my throat, and I turn my gaze to meet Jimmy's. He turns from the wall and meets my eyes, his eyes glossed over.

"So, then, what emotion are you feeling?" I ask him.

He takes a minute, my question lingering between us. "Oh, son, you know me—my heart is a mass of mush and sentiment." He lets out a soft laugh. "I try to live my life to the fullest every day; that's what makes the most sense to me—seizing each moment. It helps me feel like I'm not missing anything. These pictures remind me that I'm living. But looking at this wall also reminds me that time is fleeting. It's here one second, and then it's gone. Knowing that should be enough for all of us, you know what I mean? Enough to not take it for granted. Enough to make sure that we do the things we set out to do in this life."

We stare at each other for a few heartbeats, mine pounding in my ear as his words sink their way into my being. As my gaze lands on Summer, Jimmy's words seem to mean something new all of a sudden.

"You take what I say and don't forget it," Jimmy says softly, his hand on my shoulder.

"Promise," I whisper.

CHAPTER 7

Summer

M Y BODY IS EXHAUSTED as I walk into our apartment and place my bag on the table. The longing to melt into the fabric of my bed is all-encompassing.

"Want to sit on the balcony for a few minutes?" Kash asks.

I look at the clock on the microwave above the stove. Two o'clock in the morning. "Umm…"

"I know, it's really late. I just figured we could wind down for a few."

"You know what? Yes, I could use some water and some more fresh air," I say, smiling sleepily at Kash.

We each grab a glass of water and head out onto the balcony. We sit down in our little wicker chairs and listen for a moment—to the lull of the waves and the whisper of the breeze through the trees. As I let my head fall back against the chair, I take my gaze up to the sky, to the brightest star. When I was a child, I used to talk to that star, pretending it was my momma watching over me. Watching me from up there after she'd left me for good, dying alone under a highway overpass, while I wallowed in self-pity from my foster home with a white picket fence. I haven't spoken to that star in ages. I still love the vast expanse of the sky, velvet and never-ending, always there—the stars like little beacons of hope. But I don't talk to Momma anymore, and I haven't been able to pinpoint why.

One time, back in Austin, Kash and I sat in a park counting the stars, and we learned from each other that we both talked to that star when we were kids, thinking it was our parents. That conversation shifted something in me. It connected me to Kash in a way that I had never connected with anyone else. I had felt seen; I had felt heard.

"Do you still talk to that one?" I ask, not looking at him but keeping my eyes on the brightest star. "Do you still pretend it's your dad?"

I feel Kash look at me, and my eyes shift to meet his. He drags out a sigh before answering. "No." I nod once, inviting him to go on. "I feel his presence everywhere now. Not just up there," he adds, nodding his head toward the sky. "It's like I moved here, and he was instantly always with me." He shifts his body, placing his left ankle over his opposite knee. "I'm always talking to him, and sometimes it's comforting, but other times it creates this longing inside me that I can't soothe."

"Your dad would be so proud of you," I say, stifling a lump in my throat.

Kash nods his head, seemingly agreeing with me. "Jimmy said something tonight that made me think of my dad."

"What did he say?"

"Something about time and how if we aren't careful, it just passes us by. Like, if we are living scared, we aren't living."

"I know all about that," I whisper. "I have to tell myself that every day."

"Well, it's better to tell yourself every day than to forget and stop trying to live." I look at him sincerely, wondering what else he is thinking, what's bringing on this heaviness. He leans forward, placing his elbows on his knees, and takes his gaze up to mine. His expression is pained. "Do you feel like something is missing, Summer?"

"Um…I—"

Kash cuts me off. "Do you ever feel like you're holding back from something you really want? Not allowing yourself to get it?"

I stare at him, unblinking.

Yes, it's you, Kash. It's you that's missing.

I keep that thought to myself. It sounds as if my heart is inside my ears as I attempt to respond without giving away too much. "I lived like that every day for my whole life up until I moved to Austin, and even when I lived there a bit. And maybe still now." I say the last part quietly, afraid I'll let the truth slip out if I'm not careful. He stares at me, with what seems like the weight of the world on his shoulders. He looks as if he might cry. I tap my finger on the table, a nervous habit, as I take shallow breaths. *What is he trying to get at?*

He leans back in his chair and rakes his hands through his hair, looking out toward the ocean. "And have you ever wanted something so bad but you were too afraid of what would happen if you went after it? Because the thought of losing it terrifies you more than anything?" He continues to stare out at the water, but eventually, he looks over at me.

I nod, tears forming at the back of my eyes. "Yes," I whisper. My chest feels so tight, and I'm frozen in the little wicker chair, unable to take a full breath.

"Summer…I—" We're interrupted by the sound of Kash's phone vibrating in his pocket. He takes it out and glances at it. "It's Jimmy," he says, confusion and maybe a little worry written on his face.

I straighten my spine as Kash answers the phone. "Jimmy?" I watch him as he listens intently to whatever Jimmy is saying on the other end of the line.

"Where was this…?"

There's a pause on Kash's end as he listens.

"Ok…um…I'll meet you down there in ten minutes…yup, bye." He hangs up the phone and gets up from the seat.

"What's going on?" I ask, following him back into the apartment.

"Jimmy said he found a girl sleeping in the alley between his restaurant and Sally's Ice Cream." He grabs his keys off the table.

"A girl?" I ask, almost to myself. "How old?"

"A teenager."

"I'm coming with you," I say, taking steps toward the door.

"You don't have to, Summer. It's really late."

"I know I don't *have* to, Kash. But I want to."

He gives me a quick nod, and we head out the door to find Jimmy.

We walk swiftly toward the restaurants, toward the beach, walking in silence. Our conversation on the balcony was halted by a pause button, and my brain is going back and forth trying to figure out where the conversation was heading and what we are about to find with each step we take.

A girl asleep in the alley? My stomach lurches.

As Kash and I approach the space between Jimmy's restaurant and Sally's shop, I attempt to mentally prepare myself for what we are walking into. I head into the alley and see Jimmy sitting on the ground, his forearms resting on his knees with a soft and friendly expression on his face, despite looking weary and tired. Beside him sits a young girl with a backpack on her back, her blonde hair pulled into a sleek ponytail. She looks clean and put together, and so I gather she hasn't been out here for long.

"Well, hello again, my friends," Jimmy says, getting up from his spot on the ground. He approaches us, putting space between himself and the girl. "I can't get her to talk, and you know me, I haven't let up. I think she thinks I'm crazy." His words are soft, and as he finishes, I look over Kash's shoulder at her. She's looking down at the pavement, moving sand around with the sole of her gently worn white Converse sneaker.

"What should we do?" Kash asks.

Jimmy begins responding, but I'm not listening. I'm watching her, my eyebrows knotted, Jimmy's voice sounding like it's coming through janky headphones.

"Let me talk to her," I say, cutting off Kash's attempt at a response.

They each give me a single nod, and I briskly pass them, heading toward her. I take a seat next to her on the opposite side from where Jimmy sat. At first, I don't say anything, attempting to let her get accustomed to my presence. I glance out in the direction of the water and take some leveled breaths. In my peripheral vision, I see her eyes glance over at me, but she doesn't turn her head.

"It's tough being your age, isn't it?" I say, breaking the silence, not expecting her to answer but trying to connect. "I know it was for me, at least." A shudder runs down my spine at the image that plays across my mind. She probably thinks I'm just making this up to get her to talk, but that is so far from the truth. "What are you, fifteen? Sixteen?" I ask gently.

I wait a beat, and then another, until she slowly turns her head toward me, giving me a single nod. "Sixteen," she whispers.

I nod agreeably. "Yeah, you're in the trenches," I say with a sigh. She doesn't say anything, and the sad look on her face is breaking my heart.

"It's time to start picking your head up, Summer, don't you think?" Cassie, my foster mother, tries to sound like she is being helpful, but instead, her annoyance is shining through. Two months have passed since my momma left the earth tragically, and eight weeks is considered enough time for me to have grieved and moved on. Oh, Summer, you barely saw her anyway. Chop, chop, onto bigger and better things—that's what everyone around me seems to be saying. But I can't. I'm sludging through life as if wading through waist-deep mud—tired and depressed, the weight of my forced smile pulling me down.

Sixteen is anything but sweet.

I feel myself falling—down, down—to the depths of something that I can't identify, but it frightens me nonetheless.

"I ran away a few times when I was younger," I say, seemingly to myself, but I want her to know, so she doesn't feel alone. "I was a few years younger than you when I first did it, though." I look over at her, hoping she'll look at me, and when she does, I lean back on my hands. "Turns out that you can't do much living out there with nothing to live off of, huh?"

Kash briskly walks around the corner toward Two WhisKEYS, his phone to his ear, and Jimmy is pacing on the sidewalk, pretending he's not listening to me, but I know he's straining to hear every word.

"I'm Summer," I say softly. "What's your name?" For the first time since I sat down, her eyes meet mine. She looks scared, as if she doesn't believe she can trust me. And I get it. With all of my being, I understand. I've been there myself, not feeling like I had anyone in my corner, no one I could trust. Skeptical of everyone. I give her a sympathetic look. "You can trust me," I whisper the words as I place my hand on her knee.

She bites her bottom lip, tears brimming at the corners of her eyes. She looks away briefly toward the water and then takes her gaze back to me. "Stella," she whispers. "My name's Stella."

"It's nice to meet you, Stella." I smile at her softly, but she doesn't invite me in enough to return the gesture. She keeps her eyes on me, steady, as she takes in my presence and the words that are left unsaid. "I want to help you." I glance over at Kash and Jimmy. "*We* want to help you. Will you let us?"

There's a pause as I hang on the moment, waiting for her to respond, knowing that helping her and doing what she wants are completely different things. I swallow my dread, knowing that wherever Stella ends up tonight will be far from ideal in her mind.

"I'll be right back," I say as I stand up. "Don't worry. It will be OK." I give her a sympathetic look and hope she believes me, even though I don't even trust my own words.

As I head back toward the guys, I spot the moon in the blackness of the night sky. Glancing at my phone, I notice the battery's almost dead and see that it's 3:34 a.m. My body is sluggish, begging for sleep, but my mind is alert and on edge as I try to sort through how to handle this situation we are in.

"The police are coming," Kash says, sliding his phone into his back pocket and running his hand through his tousled hair, a gesture he does when he's stressed.

"The police?!" I hiss, trying to be quiet so Stella doesn't hear me. "Why did you call the police?" I ask, attempting to hide the annoyance in my tone.

Kash puts his hand on my shoulder and gives me a weary look, but I pull away. "Summer, what else did you want me to do? Do you have another idea?" His words come out leveled and calm, the complete opposite of how I feel.

Do I have another idea? I guess I don't, but my desperate need to protect her, Stella, a girl I only met ten minutes ago, is overpowering any sense of logic.

"No," I whisper, looking over at her sitting on the ground. She looks terrified, and in her expression, I see myself at that age. I see a darkness that will only get worse, my own experiences of loss and turmoil clouding my vision. Though I don't know her story in the slightest, I know she's suffering.

I walk over to her and sit back down. "Stella, the police are going to come and help us sort this out and make sure you get to where you need to be safe, OK?" I try to sound positive and uplifting, hoping she will give me a little more to go off of so I can help her.

She whips her head up from her bent knees. "No, please don't!" The panic in her voice guts me. "They will take me back there. I can't go back there!"

"Where?" I ask softly, placing my hand on her back.

"The Girls Home." Stella begins to sob, quietly at first, as she attempts to hide her pain, I assume.

The Girls Home is a group home for female foster youth located about two miles inland from here. I've passed it many times on my walks. I always pretended it didn't exist, afraid of the memories that might poke through the walls I'd built up. Pretending it was just another random building was much safer for me than investigating what it truly was: a home for girls like me—for girls like the old me.

In another life, I ran away to avoid moving into a home like that. I was eighteen, though, technically an adult, and social services needed to move me out of the Brickmans' home because they were ending their foster care license after I'd lived with them for seven years. I would have to stay in the group home until I graduated high school. They didn't say it, but I knew that after graduation, I would be out on my own. So, I took matters into my own hands and ran away. Sometimes, I think that was the biggest mistake I've ever made in life, as it led to me living on the streets for the better part of ten years.

I shake away the negative thoughts. I've learned to accept the roads I took as paths that led me to my present.

And my present is peace.

My present is *home*.

"OK, shhh." I try to soothe Stella. "Is it OK if I hug you?" I ask. She nods but doesn't move, and I carefully wrap her in my arms, resting my chin on her shoulder. "It's the middle of the night. The most important thing is that you are safe and cared for. Let me talk to the police and see if we can get this figured out. How does that sound?" She pulls away from me, wiping her tears.

By now, the police have shown up; a tall and lanky woman with a pointed nose stands before us, her legs apart and her hands on her hips. The look on her face is poised and professional but not cold. The other officer, a burly man with a goatee, stands beside her, the same look resting on his face. He's talking with Kash as I approach.

"She is adamant that she doesn't want to go back to that place," I say, trying to sound strong and in control, but my voice cracks at the end.

The officers look at me. "Do you have another plan for her?" the woman asks, slight impatience seeping into her tone. "All teenagers think they know what's best for themselves." She's trying to prove a point, but my determination to protect Stella shakes me to my core. In taking care of her, it's like I'm taking care of myself at that age. I have to help her. I suck air into my cheeks, attempting to gather the courage to make it right.

The man speaks up. "Someone from the home put in a call to us about three hours ago. We have had cruisers out scouring the area for her since then," he reports.

"So?" I say, sounding childish, but I can't help it. My desire to take Stella back to our apartment is overpowering my ability to look rationally at the reality of the situation.

"So?" the woman asks, a little surprised. "So, she will be returned to the place where she lives, to the people who have custody of her. She is a child, ma'am."

My shoulders slump, knowing that there really is nothing I can do right now at four o'clock in the morning, running on zero sleep.

"OK, let me just talk to her for a second?" I say, backing up toward Stella. Everyone nods at me.

I take a seat next to her and inhale slowly.

"I'm going back, aren't I?" she says, defeat in her voice.

"Yes," I respond. "But I know where the building is. I'll come visit you as soon as I can, OK?" Stella's lip trembles, and it's almost as if I'm inside her body, feeling her pain, as a lump forms in my own throat.

There is an ache in my chest that I'm struggling to soothe. When I couldn't seem to find balance as a teen, there wasn't anyone there to comfort me, to guide me. My thoughts—as dark as they were—never brightened with connection, or a hug, or someone just validating my feelings. I don't know Stella. But I don't want that same fate for her.

"It's OK. You must have your own life. You probably don't have time for a dumb kid like me," she says as if she really feels every word she uttered from her lips.

"I wish someone—*anyone*—offered to make me a priority when I was a kid," I say. "If I tell you that I'm going to visit you, I mean it—honest."

Stella gives me a weak smile through her tears. I smile back at her. I know she probably doesn't believe me; why would she?

But I will make her believe me if it's the last thing I do.

I open my mouth to speak but snap it shut abruptly. I feel the urge to process what just happened. However, I can't find the words. And a cloud hangs over Kash and me—a cloud that holds the words *he* left unsaid just one hour ago. The weight of it hangs over us, as if it's ready to release. Neither of us can deny the heaviness there. But now isn't the time to bring that up again. The combination of events that occurred over the last hour silences me as I listen to the rhythmic beat of our footsteps crunching against the sand as we head back to our apartment.

Kash breaks the silence just as we turn onto our little street. "Are you OK?"

Am I OK? It's a loaded question because, really, I'm fine…or I was fine until the bar closed and the night was supposed to end, but it didn't. "Um…," I attempt to gather my thoughts—compartmentalize my emotions—but the harder I try, the more I struggle. My worries surrounding Stella. My curiosity about what Kash had to say. It's a lot to grapple with. I give Kash a sideward glance. His hands are in his pockets, and he's looking at me, worry etched into the lines on his forehead. "Yeah, I'm fine," I blurt out, not wanting him to be concerned. I shake my head—mostly to myself. "Well, I'm a little shaken up, honestly."

Kash makes a noise, almost as if he's processing his own thoughts. I turn my head toward him. "Go ahead. Tell me what you're thinking." His voice is gentle and assuring.

"I sat there next to her…to Stella…and felt like I was her…and like she was me…," my voice trails off at the end. Kash doesn't respond. I'm sure he probably senses that I have more to say. "I mean, it makes sense, right? When I was her age, I was in foster care, too. So…yeah…," I speak fast now, on the verge of sounding manic.

Kash stops on the sidewalk and places his hand on my shoulder. "It makes sense, Summer." His voice is low—captivating me. I nod, looking away from his intense gaze. "You'll go visit her, right? And I'm sure she'll be grateful for it, just like you would have been."

"That's what I said to her!"

He gives me a warm smile. "You'll make a friend out of Stella, and she will be better for it, I can tell you that."

There's no denying the new rhythm my heart begins to beat in, igniting a feeling inside that can't be ignored.

CHAPTER 8

Stella

FROM A STARS' EYE VIEW

THE RED AND BLUE lights from the police cruiser are a stark contrast to the darkness of night that envelopes the beach town. The sullen child stands, her hands crossed over her chest, protecting her heart as best as she possibly can. She doesn't want to go back to the place where she was. The place where she lays her head at night. She feels bad, though. The way her social worker smiled at her when she first arrived at the group home gave her the impression that she should feel lucky to live there. But none of the girls there seem to feel lucky. That's not the term she would use to describe them—not at all. Not with their angst and eye rolls and their basic hatred and mistrust toward anyone over the age of twenty-five. Thankfully, they are kind to her, though, as if they share an unexplained bond and must look out for one another.

So, no, she wants to tell her social worker that she's not lucky and that she wishes she would stop smiling as if her existence is made up of rainbows and butterflies with pretty wings. But that's the thing with grownups. They forget what it was like when they were young and their emotions swarmed and bubbled, so much so that they couldn't find ways to suppress them or deal with them. So, these grownups smile and beam at her as if to say, "Look, isn't this fabulous?" It's what all the adults around her have done since the day she lost everything: the parents who loved her, her cozy house on an idyllic street in Ventura, and life as she knew it.

She doesn't know what she thought would happen when she snuck out after evening rec time. She didn't have any sort of logical plan of where to go. She had no one to call. Santa Monica wasn't where her roots intertwined with the soil. If she thought about it, she realized that now she didn't have any roots at all, for they had been ripped from the ground the day that life as she knew it had ended. She is just a shell now, periodically checking to make sure her heart is still beating.

She had left the group home, walking swiftly south toward the beach before finding a quiet street in between some shops. She sat on the curb, her head falling into her hands. She wanted to scream; she wanted to blame someone—anyone—for what had happened to her. But no screams emerged. It was impossible to yell when you couldn't catch your breath. When she finally picked her heavy head up, her eyes caught the colorful mural on the wall just up ahead. The mural was filled with water animals, but the dolphins were the ones that caught her eye. It seemed as though they were looking in the direction just up ahead, pointing her there, and so, she followed where the dolphins were guiding. With no plan, she walked until she got to the pier. She was tired, and so she found a little alley in between two quaint restaurants. She would sleep there, and in the morning, she would make her next decision.

But she had been found, and just like that, she was heading back to the group home. She slips into the back of the cruiser as the lights are turned off and the driver—a stoic woman in uniform—pulls away from the curb.

Though her heart is breaking, the universe shines down on her, smiling.

CHAPTER 9

Kash

It's Monday, the only day of the week that I have off. The bar is closed on Mondays, and though I try to sleep in, seven thirty seems to be as late as my body will allow. It's been a few days since Jimmy found that young girl alone outside his restaurant. And a few days since I became dangerously close to crossing the invisible line between Summer and me. Since that night, I have been out of sorts and having trouble getting back to a place of equilibrium.

"Morning," I say through a yawn as I approach Summer in the kitchen. She's sitting on the counter, a paperback open in her lap, a bowl of cereal that's growing soggy next to her. "Is there something wrong with the table?" I ask, humor in my tone.

She barks out a laugh and shovels a spoonful of soggy cereal into her mouth. "I always see people in movies sitting on the kitchen counter. I thought I would try it out and see what the fuss was all about." There's a sparkle in her eye. Her hair says, *I just woke up, leave me alone*, but that glimmer in her eye makes her seem completely alive.

"And is it living up to your expectations?" I ask, moving closer to the stove, and to her. I'm right in front of her now. Any closer and my torso will be touching her knees. A desperate need to take her face in my hands stirs in me, something that I haven't felt yet with her. I have desired her, I've needed her for so long, but it was so much deeper than just a physical reaction—until now. Now, the physical desire struggles to take over.

My words float through the air unanswered, and time seems to stop briefly as Summer glances up at me. Is that fear on her face? I can't quite read her now, so I quickly stop myself from getting any closer.

What am I doing?

I still haven't been able to find the right moment, or the right words for that matter, to try and tell Summer about my feelings, and trying to gauge where she's at has been damn near impossible. But now is not the time. I can feel it in the air, hovering between us like a dense fog.

I slap my hand on the counter next to Summer's cereal bowl and force a smile across my face. "So, what's got you up so early on our day off?" I ask jovially, hoping to curb the awkwardness I just caused. I back away from the counter, head to the fridge, and pull out the creamer. I grab a coffee mug from the cabinet and fill it from the pot Summer has already brewed.

"Nel and I are driving up north a bit," she says, her mouth full, as she hops down off the counter. She dumps what's left of her cereal in the trash and rinses the bowl in the sink before placing it in the dishwasher.

"Oh, really? That's fun. Where are you heading?" I ask.

"Malibu. We are going to the beach."

My forehead wrinkles in confusion, and a smile spreads across my face. "We do live at the beach, you know," I joke. "Finn, Diego, and I are going to surf and play volleyball. You and Nel could join us."

She lets a laugh escape. "I know, I know," she says, batting her hand at me. "We just need a change of scenery. You know what I mean? And besides, you guys wouldn't stand a chance playing against me." She playfully nudges me in the arm and throws a wink my way as she grabs her book off the counter and places it in her bag that sits on the kitchen table. She puts her hands on her hips and blows a piece of hair out of her face with a forceful breath. "You're being weird," she says lightly. "Is everything OK?"

Shit, I'm trying to act normal—nonchalant—but clearly it's not working. I cross my arms across my chest. "Nothing," I say.

"Nothing? What do you mean? I asked if everything was OK." A look of concern sweeps across her face.

I'm an idiot.

"Oh, shit, sorry. I meant everything is good. *Nothing* is wrong." The smile I'm portraying feels too big for my face.

She stares at me, as if she's reading every twitch and movement of my entire body, her eyes darting from my eyes to my mouth, to my shoulders, back and forth. "OK," She whispers and doesn't take her eyes off of me.

My insides are reeling. I don't understand why this is so difficult. But actually, I do know why.

"It's too bad you and Summer aren't into each other like that," *Farrah says as she wipes down the bar one last time for the night. "You guys would just be so perfect together!" Her voice carries through the space*

of the empty Sullivan's dining room, just like it always does. I don't know what to say in response. I have only recently been hanging out with Summer and have been treasuring every moment. I haven't let myself think about anything more than what it is right now, but Farrah laying this hard truth on me makes me disappointed that the choice has already been made and I wasn't even aware of it until just now. "She made me promise that I wouldn't meddle." The boisterous laugh that erupts from her causes me to chuckle, too, but not because I find it particularly amusing. It's quite the contrary, actually.

"We are building a great friendship," I respond because I don't know what else to say. I force a smile, too, hoping she believes me.

Farrah nods. "She's a good friend," she says, and I can tell she means it. "She's had it rough, Kash." The words sound heavy as they come out of her mouth. "Her memories are ferocious and fierce. They take a lot out of her."

"I know. I've been seeing that for myself."

Farrah gives me a sad smile. "She deserves to look back on the past and be happy about it, but that's not the case for her now. It's important to me that I give her some happy experiences and moments for her to look back on fondly in the future." She looks as if she might cry, and I feel my throat tightening up, unsure of what to say.

"I'll do the same. Thanks for telling me that," I say, allowing the sadness to be present for a moment.

Farrah smiles at me. "You're a good guy, Kash." I smile back at her and read between the lines. I know what she's trying to tell me, and I can't decide if it should make me feel good or bad. The unspoken truth of Farrah's words is that I'm good enough for Summer, but she'll never be able to let herself trust in us.

"Kash?"

Summer pulls me from my thoughts as she stands by the kitchen table, staring at me.

I sigh audibly. "Sorry, I guess I'm a little tired…a little out of it today."

"OK, fine. Do you want me to tell Nel that we'll stay in Santa Monica today? That Kash needs us desperately?" Summer winks at me, and we both laugh.

"Nah, you girls have fun. Want to meet for dinner? The guys and I can get us a table at Jimmy's, and you and Nel can join us when you get back?"

"Sure, that sounds good. It might just be me, though. Nel will want to get home to Sienna. Rob is taking her to the aquarium today."

"Sounds good. Have fun," I say.

"You too," Summer adds as she gathers her things and heads for the door. She looks over her shoulder at me briefly, and I can't quite read her expression, but it seems as if there are words she's left unsaid. Words she wants to share but doesn't.

Then again, maybe it's just wishful thinking. Maybe I'm just so desperate for her to let me in completely that I'm making all this up in my head.

———

It's around ten o'clock when I arrive at the volleyball pits on Santa Monica Beach. I'm meeting the guys at ten thirty, so I have some time to enjoy the warm spring air. I adjust my backpack straps as I stroll down the sandy sidewalk. I run my hands through my hair and it stays in place, already slicked with sweat, and my phone starts vibrating in my back pocket. My mom is calling. Taking a seat on the curb, I answer the call.

"Hey, Mom, what's up?" I say into the phone.

"Hi, darling!" she says. "How are you doing on your day off? Did you sleep in? I'm afraid you're really overworking yourself."

I smile, despite myself, and shake my head. She is always worrying. "I didn't sleep in, but I'm rested and feeling just fine." I let out a laugh to reassure her that she has nothing to worry about.

"OK, I believe you," she responds with a laugh.

"How are you?"

"I'm good, I am." Her voice is energetic. "I had lunch with Aunt Samantha yesterday. She sends her love."

"How is she?" I ask.

"Good, good, just fine. But I have something to ask you if it isn't much trouble."

"Of course. What is it?" I ask, my brows furrowing, slightly concerned.

"I was thinking about paying you a visit. Would you be OK with that?"

"Mom! Absolutely. I have been asking you to come since I moved here."

Although I've gone to see her in Waco, Texas twice since moving here two years ago, my mom has yet to make it out here. Sometimes, she claims that she's got too much going on, and other times, she insists that she doesn't want to impose. But I know that she's apprehensive about coming here and facing the memories. Much like I do, my mom, Jacqueline Holden, feels guilty for taking my dad away from California.

She told me once, when I was in my teens, that Dad was magnetic, that his laugh could move mountains, and that she loved him from the second she saw him—his shaggy dark hair falling over his eyes as he emerged from the surf carrying his board. "I'll never forget the color of his hair or the unique shade of green in his large eyes. How he was when I met him is how he stays, emblazoned in my memory. It's as if he will always be the young man he was when we first met." She said these words with tears brimming heavily in her eyes. I've remembered every conversation my mom has had with me about my dad. And I'm thankful for that since my own memories have begun to fade. It's become difficult to hear his voice—a crushing and heartbreaking realization of time marching on without him.

"When are you thinking?" I ask, pulling myself from my sorrow.

"Oh, I'm not sure. Maybe next month?"

I smile to myself, glancing out at the waves crashing against the shore. "Perfect."

"Now, I want you to tell me what hotel I should stay at, you hear? I will not come into your and Summer's home and turn it upside down. I will not have any part in that." She sounds adamant, not wanting to impose, even though she wouldn't be—at all.

I roll my eyes to myself. "OK. We will get that all sorted out this week. How does that sound?"

"It sounds fabulous, my love." I can hear the smile in her voice.

"Great. I gotta go. I'm meeting up with the guys from the bar for some beach shenanigans," I add with a laugh.

"Oh, tell them I say hello and have a good time. I'll talk to you soon."

"Bye, Mom," I say softly and pull the phone from my ear to see her end it before I have a chance to press the button myself.

Another smile spreads across my face. I'm thrilled that my mom has decided to make the trip out here. Summer and I can get everything situated this week for her flight and hotel.

Then Finn calls out, pulling me from my thoughts. "Kash! My man!" He's dripping ocean water from his wetsuit, his hair slicked down to his freckled face.

"You already surfed?" I laugh, getting up from the curb.

"Yeah, but you know me. I could surf twenty-four seven if the world would let me. I'll get back in later with you and Diego." We shake hands and go in for a quick one-armed hug, then turn back toward the volleyball nets, where I see Diego approaching from the direction of the pier.

"Amigos!" he yells, waving over to us.

"Hey, Diego!" I say back, high-fiving him once we reach him. We exchange quick greetings and fill each other in on our mornings before placing our stuff down out of the way and approaching the empty volleyball net.

We mess around for a bit, volleying the ball back and forth and joking with each other as we wait for more people to join in for an actual game.

"How are the surf lessons with the kids going?" I ask Finn as I serve up a ball and send it his way.

He laughs and shakes his head. "I don't know what I'm doing."

I chuckle, and so does Diego, who's on my side of the net. "You're the best surfer around. Are you sure you're not just being hard on yourself?" I say as sweat begins to bead on my forehead and drips down my spine. I put my hair up in a bun and toss my T-shirt onto the pile of my belongings.

"No, I'm aware that I'm the best," he jokes. "But I am also aware that I'm not a teacher. I'm trying, but I just wish the kids could get into my head and understand what I'm saying. You know what I mean?"

"I guess," I respond. "I've never taught piano or singing, but I imagine it must be extremely hard to teach someone who doesn't know anything about the thing you're almost a professional at."

I push the ball over the net with effort, stumbling in the sand. The sun is beginning to strengthen, and all three of us continue to sweat profusely.

"What about you, Diego? How's school going?" Finn asks, picking up the ball and tossing it over the net toward us.

Diego smiles. "Bueno, my friends, bueno." He reaches the ball and volleys it back to Finn. Though his English is constantly improving, Diego still holds some insecurities while interacting with others. I give him a lot of credit for going out on a limb, putting himself out there, and going after something that both scares and invigorates him.

"Man of few words," Finn laughs, and Diego and I join in.

An athletic-looking group approaches us, wanting to get in on a game, two guys and two women. We introduce ourselves and then get started on a more competitive game. I appreciate the distraction as thoughts of Summer have begun to trickle into my mind, and all the things we've left unspoken are festering at the forefront of my conscience.

Summer, Summer, Summer.

It's noon by the time we finish up our game and head into the water on our boards to cool off and catch a few waves. I'm sitting up on my board, out past where the waves are breaking, just floating, my hands submerged beneath the surface of the cool water. The sun creates fractals of light against the constant motion of the waves, a sight that gives me pause—it's beautiful and overwhelming all at once—the enormity, the danger, the unknown; it all takes my breath away.

A wave jostles me a bit, and after steadying myself, I glance to the right toward Venice Beach. Specks of people move about their day, enjoying their surroundings—the paradise right in front of them.

Do you see me, Dad?

The random thought briefly startles me. As I continue to stare at the expanse of beach, I picture him running out to this very spot where I sit, contemplating my existence. I continue to picture him for some time, as a young man, about the age I am now, doing this very thing I'm doing in this very spot, some thirty-five years ago. The image is foggy on the edges, like an old sepia-tone photograph. I take my gaze to the sky, squinting into the sun's rays. The star is up there, invisible to me, but still there. Just like him, I suppose—or at least I hope.

"You haven't attempted a single wave, bro," Finn says, paddling out to me and lifting himself into a sitting position. We both face the shore, watching Diego catch a wave and dive into the surf. We chuckle at his graceful tumble into the water.

"Yeah, I know," I say, my voice sounding distant.

"You alright?" Finn asks, flipping his wet hair out of his face.

I force a smile and turn my head to face him. "Yeah, I'm good." I don't, in any way, want to get into my feelings right now, especially not out here on a surfboard, a good distance off the shore. There are more exciting things to do out here, especially with an adventurer like Finn. "Let's catch a wave," I say, paddling in a bit, looking back toward the sea in search of a worthwhile wave. Finn follows my lead, and just like that, I let my heaviness drift out with the tide.

CHAPTER 10

Summer

THE WIND WHIPS MY hair with gusto as Nel and I cruise north up the Pacific Coast Highway toward Malibu in her white Jeep Wrangler. It's a beach mobile—that's for sure—with its rusted hubcaps and obvious lack of safety. The roof is off, and the doors, if you could call them that, leave little protection from the asphalt. I stick my hand out and let the pressure from the wind push against it and whoosh through my fingers. Resting my head back on the headrest, I close my eyes, letting the sun warm my face.

Nel drives relaxed, her slim arm hanging out of the open space—like mine—while the other rests loosely, holding the steering wheel at six o'clock. Her left knee is bent, her bare foot on the seat. She sings along to the song on the radio, "Night Changes" by One Direction, while I hum quietly next to her.

The Pacific Ocean stretches out in front of us, as far as the eye can see. I lean forward in my seat, looking across Nel's body and down the cliff on the other side of the road. She follows my glance briefly, then turns to smile at me.

"Taking in the scenery?" she asks, smiling at me before moving her eyes back to the road in front of her.

"Yeah. It still amazes me, even after all this time," I say, my voice elevated over the sound of the wind rushing through the Jeep.

"It hasn't been that long, Summer," she says. "Only a year since you moved here."

"A year and a half," I say, laughing.

Nel chuckles. "Yeah, well, it still amazes me, and I've lived here my whole life."

I nod, appreciating the words she's saying.

Nel and I had stopped for breakfast along the pier before we headed out, and it's nearly ten in the morning when she pulls the Jeep into a sandy parking spot along County Line Beach.

"Oh, girl, we are getting seafood at Neptune's Net before we leave here," Nel says to me as she hops down from the driver's seat.

"Sounds good! I haven't been there yet," I say with my hands on my hips, looking down the rocky cliff that drops to the shore.

"Really?! Oh, you are going to love it!" Nel pulls her bag out of the backseat, and I follow her lead, grabbing mine that was resting in Sienna's car seat.

"Do you want a chair?" she yells over to me from the trunk. "I always have two in here for Rob and me. You never know when you're going to end up at the beach." A smile radiates from her face.

"Sure, I'll take one. Thanks!" I say, grabbing a light blue chair from her hand.

We head toward the stairway leading down to the sand and walk silently, Nel in front and me behind. My flip-flops crunch on the sand that covers the sea-soaked wooden steps as we make our way to the bottom. The beach is nearly vacant. A few families are dispersed along the shore, and some lone surfers are bobbing in the water. I glance down the coastline and marvel at the way the sea ebbs and flows, its edges catching the rays from the sun. The rolling hills behind us are casting shadows on the homes on the other side of the street.

"How about here?" Nel asks, choosing a spot midway between the water's edge and the entrance to the beach.

I don't mind at all where we sit—I'm just happy to be here—so I agree, and we set up our area. Chairs unfolded, towels sprawled out in front of them, and our bags at our sides. We collapse into our chairs simultaneously while letting out dramatic sighs and then simultaneous laughs.

"This is the life," I say, reclining my chair just a tad.

"It sure is," Nel agrees.

"How's the family?" I ask, turning to look at her. "Is Sienna completely better after being sick?"

"Oh, yeah, she's great. You know kids. They rebound fast."

I nod my head. I don't really *know* kids, but it seems to make sense. They are energetic adventure seekers. Of course, they are experts in rebounding. They can't waste time being sick.

"And Rob?"

"He's good. He's working so much, but he takes good care of us." She winks at me and moves her arms behind her head.

Rob is a resident in the pediatric trauma wing at UCLA Medical Center. He, of course, works long hours without an end in sight. They need to rely on Nel's mom a lot when she's working at the bar, but despite their busy schedules, they seem intensely happy.

"I'm glad he and Sienna can just have a daddy-daughter day. He needs that. I know he hates missing things with her."

"Oh, I'm sure!" I say. "It must be so hard to be working so much when you have a tiny person at home. He's such a good dad." I smile at her, and she beams back at me.

We each gaze out at the water in comfortable silence for a bit.

"Serious question," I say.

She glances over at me, curious.

"How many sharks do you think are out there right now?" I let out a laugh, and Nel does, too.

"Oh my God. That freaks me out," she squeals. "The fact that you can barely see a few feet in front of you? Nope. No, thank you!" She laughs with her mouth open. "That's why I love having the excuse that I don't want to get this mane wet." She flicks her wrist at me. "That ocean water and this perfection?" She pretends to model her beautiful head of hair. "No, I'm just kidding. But seriously—let the sharks be. Right? That's their home. This is ours, with the other creatures with legs."

I shrug my shoulders. "I agree. It's a bit unnerving not knowing what's around you when you're out there. But I like being in the water. Floating around in something so vast? It's pretty powerful."

Nel acknowledges my words with a caring look, but she doesn't say anything.

"When I was a kid, I used to pretend I was at the ocean." I stop for a second, not really wanting to make things heavy but also wanting to open up more to Nel, so I continue. "I used to distract myself by pretending when things got bad." The words come out soft, almost like a whisper. Nel furrows her brow as she listens. "I'd never been to the ocean before, but it was my safe place, so when I finally saw it…and when I eventually moved here, it was like finally experiencing a safe haven, one I never have to leave. I owe Kash more than I can ever give him for offering me a place here."

She sends me a soft smile. "I think you gave him enough just by agreeing to come."

"Huh?" I'm a bit flustered by her words. "What do you mean?"

She gives me an *oh, come on, Summer* kind of look. "Girl, are you kidding?" Her words are soft and kind, not aggressive or rude. I look out at the ocean and take a deep breath, letting it out abruptly. "You're holding yourself back, Summer. Why?" She puts her hand on my arm gently.

"It's not like that with Kash. It can't be." My words sound so final.

"And that's because…," Nel says, dragging out the last word and waiting for me to explain.

"Because I need him." The sentence comes out more rude than I mean it to. "I need him to be there for me, the way that he always has been—as my best friend. I can't lose him, Nel. Why doesn't anyone understand that?" I feel my emotions bubbling under the surface; the lump in my throat is building.

"Who is 'anyone'?" Nel asks softly. "Where is this coming from?"

I look at her, tears brimming my eyes. "Kash, my therapist, Farrah, Silvia…you." I feel like a child unable to control my emotions, but how many times am I going to have to keep saying this?

"I'm going to go out on a limb here, Summer. And maybe you'll get mad at me for asking, but as your friend, I feel the need." I stare at her, hanging on her every word. "Do you like Kash? Are you just too afraid to do anything about it?"

I shake my head. "No. I don't *like* Kash." I let my head fall, and Nel begins to speak.

"OK, but Summer—"

"I love him." I cut her off abruptly with words that squeak out from my mouth, causing an ache in my chest that throbs, the feeling of my heart breaking a little bit more—as it has day after day for quite a while now.

"Oh my God, Summer." Nel has moved to the edge of her seat, her whole body facing me, both her hands resting on my knees. I feel the panic rising and suddenly feel like I'm gasping for air. "Take a breath, love. In and out." Nel's soothing voice rushes through my ears, and I allow it to comfort me. I do what she says, what Janie always tells me to do.

Breathe. In and out.

I feel Nel's warmth surround me as I let myself focus on the sounds of the waves crashing and the distant sounds of children's laughter.

Breathe. In and out.

"I already feel like I know what my biggest regret in life is going to be." My words come out dull and tired. It's as if I'm not speaking to anyone in particular. It's as if I'm coming to terms with a fact that I need to accept. Nel doesn't say anything. She just waits patiently for me to go on. "It's getting to the end and realizing that I didn't enjoy the ride because I was too caught up in nurturing my fears."

Nel's face is kind and caring. It doesn't hold pity; at least, I don't think that it does. She stands up and reaches out for my hand and pulls me up from my seat. She hugs me, nestling her head onto my shoulder. The tears flow out of my eyes, without any sort of effort.

After a few moments, Nel pulls away and takes my face in her hands. "There's nothing I can say to just magically make you see that loving someone and being loved is a gift, not something to be feared." Her words could not be any truer. "But I will ask you this—what's worse, Summer? Loving him and losing him? Or loving him and never letting him love you back in the first place, ever?" I stare at her unblinking. "And not for anything, but we are talking about Kash here. Kash Holden, the kindest human alive. Do you really believe that, in any circumstance, he would ever leave you?" She speaks to me with urgency now, like she's desperate for me to hear and believe what she's saying. But she doesn't know everything. Where I have been. What I have seen. I can't expect her to. "Don't miss the ride, Summer."

"I'm also protecting him. I—"

Nel cuts me off. "I'm stopping you right there." She shakes her head. "I can't listen to you do this, Summer. I love you. I do. So much. I know you have a past. I know it haunts you still, even though you wish it didn't. I know you work hard, all the time, to be better, but I refuse to listen to you degrade yourself and shut yourself off from the happiness you deserve." She's adamant, her emotion surfacing. "If anything, I think you're doing the opposite of protecting him. I think you break his heart every damn day."

I suck in a sharp breath, and a sob escapes. Nel looks at me with care, her honesty hovering over us like a dark cloud. She pulls me in again. "Just think about what I said. Will you do that?"

I nod, unsure if I can but desperate to try.

I close my eyes, giving myself a minute to settle my nerves and reground myself, the sun warming my face.

Sure, Farrah and Joey's wedding may have been the moment in time where something settled deep in the corners of my heart, an awareness that my feelings for Kash were more than friendly; they were deep and difficult to understand. Although that's when I figured it out, I admit there's a part of me that knew much earlier than that.

The way he never judged or pitied me when I shared the darkest secrets of my life with him.

The way he encouraged me to take risks, to do something solely for myself for the first time.

The way his face looked while he sang on stage at Sullivan's, like the lyrics were always his own. He felt them, so I did.

And the way my breath caught in my chest when our fingers brushed against one another while lying beneath a black, starry Texas sky.

But it took a long time for me to allow myself to see the truth—that my feelings for him were stronger than I realized. I hadn't allowed myself to go there. And I still don't—clearly.

"Here, read this," Nel says, tossing a fashion magazine into my lap. "Think about something mindless for a while." She winks at me, and I pick up the magazine and begin thumbing through it. It smells like department store perfume. I glance at the insane outfits and models with—what I would call—pained expressions, letting my mind wander from my thoughts. We spend the rest of the morning like this, reading magazines and commenting on the ridiculous things we find.

Before long, I begin to feel overheated and walk down to the water's edge. A wave wraps around my ankles, and the sensation seems to cool my entire body, if only slightly. I put my hands on my hips, using my senses to save this moment somewhere in my memory so it will stay for keeps. I always find it amazing that whenever I stare at the ocean—no matter where I am—it always feels familiar, like an old friend.

I head back to Nel. "I'm hungry," I say as I approach her.

Nel smiles. "Neptune's Net?" she asks excitedly.

"Sure," I say, letting out a laugh. We gather up our belongings and make our way back up the stairs to the Jeep before walking over to the restaurant.

Seeing the front of the restaurant brings back memories that aren't mine. I've seen the outside of the iconic building in so many pictures since I moved to California—it's as if I have actually been here before. I see the sign along the walkway first: *Neptune's Net – live seafood & market.* The green hills behind the building roll up and away as if trying to reach the top of the sky. Motorcycles are parked outside, and patrons sit at tables on the front patio eating fried food; the smells wafting to my nose make my stomach ache with hunger.

The inside is, somehow, exactly like I imagined. The wooden beams up above our heads match the color of the picnic tables scattered throughout the restaurant. I eye a table by the window that overlooks the water with a picturesque view. It's no wonder this place is so popular with tourists. It's casual but gorgeous.

"Do you want to order and then grab a table outside on the patio?" Nel asks.

"Yeah, that would be perfect," I say, feeling much lighter than I did an hour ago.

We stare at the menu. I have no idea what to get—everything looks delicious.

"I don't even know why I'm looking. I know what I want," Nel says. "Clam chowder and a clam strip basket." She clasps her hands together giddily.

"Yum!" I respond. "Would you judge me if I got, like, three things," I say jokingly, and Nel laughs. After looking at the menu for another minute, I decide on fish and chips with some clam chowder, too, because I've never had it, and it sounds amazing.

We order at the window and wait for our names to be called before we gather up our food and head out to the patio in search of a table. Just as we walk out, we see a couple getting up to leave, so we snag their table as a busboy comes and wipes it clean for us. We sit down with our trays, admiring our food, practically drooling.

"This is an amazing view," I say when I finally look up from my food and out at the water and pop a crispy fry with ketchup into my mouth. My taste buds seem to scream with pleasure as the food makes its way down to my growling stomach. I groan and roll my eyes to the back of my head.

Nel lets out a gentle laugh as she savors her first bite of chowder and mimics me. We don't have time for conversation as we shovel food into our mouths, every so often shifting our gazes back out to the water. Once I start to feel a bit full, I slow down and stretch my arms up with a sigh.

"Oh, did Kash tell you about what happened the other night outside Jimmy's place?" I ask.

Nel looks at me with interest. "No," she says, her mouth full.

"Jimmy found a teenage girl with a backpack sitting out there around two in the morning. She had run away from The Girls Home a few miles inland. Do you know the one?"

Nel shakes her head. "No, I don't think I do. What happened?"

"Kash called the police, and they ended up taking her back there. But, you know me, I wanted to protect her. I felt like I knew exactly how she was feeling. My heart broke for her as she got in the police cruiser. She didn't want to go back."

Nel looks sympathetic. "Wow. That is really tough, Summer. How are you handling that?"

"Me? I'm fine. It's her I'm worried about. I'm going to go visit her tomorrow morning before I head into the bar."

"That's really amazing of you, Summer," she says with a smile. I shrug my shoulders. I don't need to be told that. It's not amazing. It's necessary. Stella feels scared and alone. "Let me know how she's doing."

"I will," I say, as I pop another unnecessary french fry in my mouth even though I'm stuffed to the brim. "Jimmy and I are playing tomorrow."

"Oh, sweet! Are you bartending, too?"

I shrug. "Probably. I don't think we're doing a whole set. I think I'll bartend with you for an hour or so, then hit the stage."

"Can't wait!" Nel says.

* * *

After lunch, Nel and I make our way back to the beach and spend another two hours there—napping, reading, and chatting. I take a dip in the waves to cool off while Nel opts to stay on the shore, all in the name of protecting her mane.

I text Kash on the drive home, and he lets me know that he and the guys have just come out of the water and are heading to Jimmy's. I let him know that I'll meet him there once Nel and I get back to Santa Monica. We pull up just before five thirty, and she drops me off at the edge of the pier on Ocean Avenue. As I walk past Two WhisKEYS toward Jimmy's, I take notice of how my skin feels sunkissed and my body is spent from a day in the sun. I'm looking forward to some shrimp tacos and a spicy margarita, Jimmy's house favorites.

I push open the door and hear Diego celebrating my arrival. "Hola, bonita!" he says, getting up from his seat at the bar and approaching me, swinging me around before placing me back down on the ground.

"Hey, Diego," I say happily, my voice sounding tired.

"Hey, Summer," Kash says, smiling from ear to ear. "You look relaxed, like you had a great day in the sun." He pulls out a barstool for me and opts to stand as the place is beginning to fill up with people coming in from off the beach. He picks up his Corona and takes a sip.

Jimmy walks over from the other end of the bar and greets me joyously. "My favorite lady!"

"My favorite guy," I respond, giving him a warm, genuine smile. "You know what I'm ordering, Jimmy, right?"

"Shrimp tacos, light on the spice—add the spice to the margarita." He laughs as he begins gathering the things he needs to mix my drink. "Am I right?" He winks at me.

"You know it!"

I take a sip from the water Jimmy's bartender, Mo, placed in front of me, desperate to rehydrate. "Did you guys have fun today?" I ask Kash, Diego, and Finn.

"We got slaughtered in the pits by a bunch of professionals," Finn says, tipping his head back, taking a sip of his Budweiser. He places it back down on the bar. "We really could have used you out there, Summer."

I smile, lifting my brows for a moment as the memory of me playing volleyball in high school whisks through my mind's eye. The smell of the gym, the squeak of sneakers against the shiny wood floors, the grunts of me and my teammates exerting all our effort, the sweat falling to the ground. My heart racing, feeling like it's about to burst—not only from overexertion but from the utter sadness that no one was there to watch me. I found bits and pieces of myself on that court, though, pieces that I'm grateful still linger—the parts that are strong-willed, the parts that are determined, the parts that don't take failing as an option.

"Sorry," I say to Finn. "I'll be there next time, and we can get your revenge." I shove him playfully in the side.

"Oh, thank God." He plays into the dramatics by grabbing his heart, causing the rest of us to laugh.

The scene around me is a comforting one. This small strip of beach has become home—Two WhisKEYS, Jimmy's restaurant, the speckles of sand outside, mine and Kash's little apartment, the lull of the waves that never fail to comfort me. Even the conversations around me from strangers wrap me in an ease that I once never understood.

"Jimmy, cards?" Diego asks, hopeful.

Jimmy looks at Diego mischievously. "What about cards, son?"

"Por favor?" Diego responds with a smile.

"You gotta give me more than that. Come on. You've been practicing your English. Don't be afraid to make a mistake." Jimmy wipes down the melted ice on the counter while he talks.

"We play cards, Jimmy? Please?" There's a glimmer in Diego's eye that does us all in, and we begin to clap. Kash slaps him on the back playfully.

Diego has come out of his shell quite a bit over the last few months, getting more comfortable with his English and putting himself out there more. We tease him in good fun, and I think sometimes he pretends he doesn't know the words because he's afraid of messing up. He's guarded—I can sense the type a mile away, and I'm glad he found us.

"You earned it." Jimmy gives Diego a wink while placing the deck of cards in front of him. Diego takes them out of the pack, shuffles them, and begins dealing them out. I know what we're playing—the mindless game, Trash, that we always play when we're together. I can tell it means a lot to Diego. To sit with others—friends—who don't speak the same language but with whom you have infinite things in common. To sit with friends who are becoming like family. I know the feeling well, and because of that, though I'm tired beyond belief and would be content just sitting here at the bar, I grab my cards and lay them out, giving Diego a smile. His appreciation of my participation is evident.

The guys and I play Trash while we make jokes and talk about the bar. It's almost nine o'clock when a yawn escapes me, and I attempt, feebly, to stifle it.

"We've been sitting here almost three hours!" I say, surprised at how fast the time has flown by. I'm desperate for the sanctuary of my bed, but at the same time, I long to stay here with the guys for hours more.

"Time flies when you're having fun," Finn says, dealing out another round of cards.

Time flies when you're hopelessly attempting to catch it mid-flight.

"You're telling me!" Jimmy chimes in as he walks behind my stool on his way back from clearing a table. "I have the time of my life most days, and I look back on my life and forget that I'm not twenty-five anymore." He chuckles to himself and makes his way back behind the bar.

This conversation is all in good fun, but as I tend to do, I ruin it with my deep, analytical wonderings. "Isn't that kind of sad to you, Jimmy? Feeling like time just went on by…too fast?"

He looks at me for a brief moment, and the look on his face tells me that he has something profound to say. "Oh, Summer. You have it all wrong." His voice is rich with warmth, and I take my attention away from the game at hand.

"What do you mean?" My words come out soft.

Jimmy smiles, his kind eyes sparkling. "Time is time, honey." He puts both hands on the bar in front of where I sit and looks meaningfully into my eyes. "It doesn't speed up. It doesn't slow down. It's all an illusion. People get all hung up on attempting something that no one has been able to do—stop time. And in the process, they forget to live. It's a tragedy, really. In this day and age, people are waiting for the next best thing rather than appreciating what's right in front of them."

He pauses, gauging my reaction to what he's saying. I can't seem to find the right words. My breaths are shallow, in and out in slow bursts. I feel Kash shift next to me, and I glance over at him. He is also hanging on Jimmy's every word.

"Are you hearing me, Summer?" I nod, and he goes on. "Don't be sad if time starts to feel like it's going fast. It just means you're living life and enjoying all it has to offer. Be grateful for that—for having something worth gripping onto with all your might."

I look at the clock. 3:17 a.m. Time inches by ever so slowly as the moon makes its way across the night sky, inching down, seemingly burying itself beneath the earth. I know this is going to be another dreadful night of little to no sleep. I stare at the swirls on the textured ceiling above my borrowed bed before glancing over at Claire, sleeping peacefully in hers—untouched by the horrors of the universe.

Time ticks by as restlessness burrows in the marrow of my bones, wracking my nerves. A tear escapes and slides down my face as if in slow motion, mirroring the pace of dread settling deep in my soul.

I muster a smile at Jimmy and feel a sense of gratitude for the speed at which time is going at this point in my life. Because according to Jimmy, it must mean I'm actually *living* now.

———

I find myself walking faster than I intended, heading toward The Girls Home. I already walked this morning, so I don't need more exercise, but the desperation and anxiety that linger with the anticipation of this visit are causing my legs to be quite restless. *What am I going to find behind the doors of that place? Will I be triggered? How is Stella? Is she ok? Will she be happy to see me? Mad?* My mind has been racing since I woke up this morning. Kash left early for the bar, as he tends to do, and I can't help but feel that something was bothering him. I'll have to check in with him when I get to work later. This visit to The Girls Home is triggering feelings in me that aren't welcome, but I won't let that stop me from what I set out to do, and that's to help Stella. How? I'm not quite sure yet, but the need to check on her is pushing me along faster and faster toward the building.

The Home is inconspicuous, set along a residential street, blending in with the other larger homes around it. A hideout is what comes to mind, a place where you go when you don't want to be found—or *someone* doesn't want you to be found. The latter makes more sense. Girls are brought here, typically against their will, by social services in an attempt to keep them safe, give them shelter. It's the Band-Aid approach to a much bigger problem—stemming from broken families—families much like the one I once had.

I entered foster care when I was eleven. I know now that I was removed from my parents for a reason, but at the time, it made no sense to me. I was abused by my father and neglected by my mother—reasons for me to be removed that made sense to those who were supposed to be helping me. But the abuse I endured in my foster home—abuse of the emotional variety—was just as bad. It makes me wonder, is that how Stella feels within these four walls, made to feel like she has to feel lucky for being saved even though resentment is all she can identify with?

I look up at the front of the building. It's picturesque with gray shingles and white shutters. White pillars support the front porch, and flower boxes line the dark, modern windows. The door is inviting, a mix of modern and farmhouse. My eyes scan the brick walkway leading up to the steps toward the door. As I make my way up the stairs, I give myself a silent pep talk, trying to prepare myself for what's behind these doors and how it will make me feel to be on the other side of them. I made a call this morning to confirm it was OK for me to stop by, and the woman who answered, Lisa, told me ten was a good time. So, here I am at 9:59.

I reach the landing, and the aesthetically pleasing sign next to the doorbell reads: *please ring for assistance.* I lift my index finger and press the little black button. I hear the echo of it ringing on the other side of the door, and I wait, my stomach lurching, for someone to greet me.

The door is opened by a smiling face, a woman, short in stature with a stocky build. Her thin blonde hair is pulled into a ponytail, and she's wearing athletic attire. "Hi," I say. "I called this morning. I'm here to visit Stella."

"Yes, yes, come in," the woman says, moving to the side to allow me to step in. "I'm Lisa. It was me you spoke to." She stretches out her hand to shake mine. "I just need you to sign in, but I haven't gotten the guest book set up for the day. Will you give me a moment? I'll be right back."

"Sure," I say through a smile.

I clasp my hands in front of me as I wait, glancing around the foyer and up the staircase. There's a large living area to my left, and from what I can see, it looks like a rec room of sorts with a TV mounted on the wall, a ping pong table, and a large sectional couch. Leaning back on my heels, I attempt to get a better view and see a table against a window that has assorted art supplies organized in bins and trays. To my right is a dining area with a large table that has a bench on one side and chairs on the other. It looks like it could hold twelve people. The stairs are wood with a gray and white patterned runner leading up to an open landing and, most likely to the bedrooms. The walls are painted a light gray and large black and white photographs from various places around the world hang on them.

Lisa returns with a small wooden podium and a book and pulls me from being nosey. "Can you sign your name and the time of arrival here," she says, pointing to the spot in the book after she sets it up.

"Yup, no problem," I say, adjusting my crossbody bag. I take the pen from her hand and sign the book. "It's quiet in here," I note.

Lisa smiles. "Some of the girls are up in their rooms, and a few are out on the back patio. I'll go get Stella. Would you like to have a seat on the couch?"

"Sure," I say, heading toward the rec room. I had explained who I was to Lisa on the phone and gave her my phone number. She had to call the police station to confirm my identity with the officers who wrote the report the night Jimmy found Stella. She then called me back and asked me a few questions that made me uncomfortable—*Do you know any family members of Stella's? How long do you plan to stay?* —and some others. I know they need to take safety precautions, of course, but it all felt clinical, and for that, my heart ached.

"Summer?" I hear Lisa's voice as she heads into the room. I get up from the couch and see her and Stella making their way into the rec room. I look at her and try to make eye contact. I'm smiling, but she doesn't see because she won't bring her gaze up to meet mine.

"Hi, Stella." My voice is perkier than normal, and I cringe at the forcefulness that it exudes. She brings her chin up slightly and gives me a weak smile.

"Stella, Summer is here to visit with you, as I told you earlier. If either of you needs me, I'll be in my office. It's right around the corner," Lisa says.

"Thank you. I appreciate it." I say the words out loud, but they sound foreign, as if I'm not saying the right thing. I watch Lisa head out of the room before turning my attention back to Stella. "Do you remember me?" I ask, internally reprimanding myself as the words escape my mouth. *Of course, she remembers you, you idiot. It was just a few days ago.*

Stella gives me a single nod but doesn't offer much else. The look on her face is soft, not angsty like I imagined, not like how I looked and felt at that age.

"Do you want to sit? We can chat for a bit," I say, hopeful, gesturing toward the couch.

She stares at me for a moment, taking me in. I know what she's doing. I used to do it, too. Hell, I still do. She's sizing me up, judging my character, wondering if I'm worth her time. I give her a gentle smile and relax my shoulders, desperately hoping she will see *me*. My eyes scan her over, checking her well-being, I suppose. She looks well-rested and clean. Her hair is the same as it was when I saw her on the street, in a sleek ponytail. Her shorts are whitewashed and rolled up a bit. Her T-shirt hangs off her shoulders and is cut short to show her belly button. White Converse are untied on her feet.

"Can we sit at the table?" she asks quietly.

My spine straightens at the sound of her voice. "Of course. Sure." I'm so surprised that she's willing to talk that I have to work to not stumble over my words. We make our way to the table in the back against the windows. She sits down at one of the wooden chairs, and I take a seat next to her. As soon as we sit down, she grabs a piece of paper and a pencil from the storage bins along the wall and begins sketching on the paper as I watch, unsure of her comfort level with me.

"I wanted to come and check on you," I offer. "I've been thinking about you and wanted to make sure you were doing OK." She doesn't look at me but continues to sketch. I lean back in the chair and tap my pointer finger on the table. "So, you're an artist, I see," I say, carefully leaning over just a bit to take a peek at her drawing. Then I lean back again, not wanting to invade her space.

"Why?" The word comes out with wonder; it's not accusatory.

"Why did I want to check on you?"

"Yeah. What's it to you?" She seems like she genuinely wants to know, as if she doesn't understand my motive but wants to.

I shrug my shoulders. "I see myself in you. I felt your fear when you told me you didn't want us to send you back here. I was you…at another point in my life." I don't want to make this about me, so I stop and wait to see how she reacts.

There's a lot of beats in my heart before Stella responds. "I wasn't afraid to come back…I wasn't scared. I just didn't want to." She says this without looking up.

I nod, even though she doesn't see me. I find myself desperate to know her story, but I know part of that is for selfish reasons—to connect, to relate, to help. But I don't pry. I don't want to be another annoying adult in her life who says they want to help but doesn't really. I had enough of those growing up. More than anything, I want Stella to trust me. Leaning over the table, I grab a piece of paper and a pencil, and I begin to doodle—a picture of the night sky. I'm not an artist, and I don't know how to draw many things, but I'm trying to connect.

I look at Stella in my peripheral vision and notice her doing the same to me, glancing over in my direction while not lifting her pencil from the paper, it moves in steady waves across the paper. I glance down at what she's drawing, pausing my pitiful attempt at art, and my mouth drops. The image on her paper is stunning—a meadow of sorts with a forest behind it. She's shading the sun as we speak.

"Wow, you are an amazing artist," I say, and I hope she hears the sincerity in my voice.

She allows a smile to break through her sad exterior. "And you're definitely not," she replies jokingly, and I let out a laugh.

"No, I definitely am not," I say, holding up my picture of stars. "I guess I should just stick to singing."

Stella takes the picture from my hands. "Can I keep it?"

My brows furrow in confusion, but I muster a nod. "Sure." The word comes out in a whisper. I hand the paper to her, and she looks at it like it's holding a secret that she's desperate to know.

"So, you're a singer?" she asks, placing my drawing on top of hers.

I shrug my shoulders and smile. "I am. I sing over at Two WhisKEYS, right by where I first met you—" my voice trails off as I worry about triggering her, but her face is solid, unaffected. "I practically live there," I say, laughing, if only for my own amusement. "I live with the owner, actually. His name is Kash. Working there has basically become our entire life. But I'm OK with that." I feel myself rambling, and Stella looks interested in what I'm saying.

"You live with the owner? Is he, like, your boyfriend or something?"

Rolling my eyes playfully, I respond, "No, he's not my boyfriend." *But I wish he was.* "I also sing at open mic nights around here and sometimes in LA," I add.

It's interesting to think about what my idea of *making a living* has become since moving to California. I moved out here to pursue my songwriting, to put myself out there, in a sense. I have done that—honed in on my talent and written a bit, but not nearly as much as I should. I've made my living by working at Two WhisKEYS, and for now, I am OK with that.

"Is Kash the guy who was with you that night when you found me in the alley?"

I nod, looking at her sincerely. "Yes, that was Kash."

She wiggles her eyebrows at me, and I let out a boisterous laugh.

"Anyways!" I say, through the laugh. "What else do you like to do?"

"I read a lot," she says, glancing behind me. I turn to see where she's looking and notice a large bookshelf filled with books. "I think I've read all of those. Some of them more than once." Her voice is quiet now, as if she's connecting her reading with something that may be sad.

I used to read to escape my life and drown out the horrors that surrounded me. I know all too well the feeling of reading a book multiple times—for comfort, for reprieve. After Ms. Harper, my third-grade teacher, gave me a copy of *The Lion, the Witch and the Wardrobe* to keep, I treasured the copy, reading it so many times that the pages frayed and the spine became a bit mangled. I still have it, though, safe in my memory box.

"Reading is amazing. I read a lot, too. And when I was younger, I read multiple books a week. It was my saving grace."

Stella stares at me, her eyes darting to different parts of my face, taking me in. I know the drill. I created it, it seems. Her mouth opens as if she is about to say something, but she quickly closes it. I don't push her. I see that it's going to be about little steps with her. I have every intention of being there for her in any way she needs me, but there's no rush.

"I think I want to go take a nap," she says softly without looking at me.

I nod. "OK. I'll let you go." We both rise from our seats. She takes the materials we were using, puts them back in their designated spots, and gathers up the two papers we drew on, pulling them close to her chest. "I would like to visit you again if you're up for it."

She stares at me again, seemingly questioning my sincerity or maybe my motive, but I don't falter under her intense gaze. Instead, I give her a warm smile.

"OK," she simply says before turning on her heels and walking swiftly out of the rec room. I hear her feet on the stairs as she makes her way up to her room. I'm frozen for a moment as I try to gather my thoughts, and eventually, I force myself to move and head toward the door to sign out. Lisa makes her way from the back of the house as I exit the rec room.

"Heading out?" she asks joyfully.

"Yes, thank you for allowing me to come and visit," I say, grabbing the pen from the podium to fill in the time.

"She's a sweet girl, but she's in a lot of pain. Did she open up to you at all?"

I shake my head. "Not really. But that's OK. I just hope to be able to be a friend to her." Lisa smiles and nods as I glance at my watch for the time. "Am I allowed to take her out of here to do something sometime?"

"Sure, it just has to be planned in advance, and we have to know where you're going and be able to contact you," she says. "You know…policies and things."

"Right. I get it. Thank you. I'll see you soon, I hope." I adjust my bag across my body and wave, heading to the door.

"Have a great day, Summer!" Lisa says with an odd pep, as if the sad souls she's in charge of protecting aren't, in any way, affecting her.

CHAPTER 11

Kash

I OPEN UP THE massive windows in the bar, letting in the remaining western sun as it's just begun its downward descent. Outside, the lighting is just how I like it—a glow wraps the beach and the pier in a golden light that you have to see to believe. The white sand of Santa Monica Beach glistens in the rays, and the specks of surfers out on the waves look like moving shadows in the light. I'm bopping along to the music I have playing through the speakers at a louder decibel than necessary, but I'm in a musical state of mind.

We have two guest musicians coming in to play for the first set tonight, and Finn and Diego have the night off. Jimmy and Summer will be doing the second set, which I'm thrilled about. It's been a while since they've played together, and I know Summer is looking forward to it. She told me this morning before I left the apartment that she couldn't wait to sing. As I hurriedly ate breakfast and gathered my things to leave for the bar, I worried that she might think I was rushing out to distance myself from her. I didn't mean to be cold, but maybe a small part of me was itching for some space. I have yet to bring up the unfinished conversation we started the night Jimmy's phone call interrupted us. I don't know why I am so apprehensive to bring it up, but approaching this conversation with her, the one that I'm desperate to have, is proving to be next to impossible.

Tonight.

I'm going to do it tonight. I have to stop waiting around for the words to magically escape my mouth.

I'm shaken from my thoughts by a strange man standing outside the bar. He's looking up at the sign, squinting to see past the reflecting sunbeams shining off the windows. He's dressed nicely, a little too nicely for Two WhisKEYS—gray dress pants and a white button-down shirt tucked in. His tie is purple, and his dark-rimmed glasses give him an air of sophistication. I head closer to the windows as he adjusts his messenger bag. He reaches for the front door and pulls. Finding it locked, he puts his hands up to the window and peers in. He sees me and waves, a look of relief flooding his face.

What does this guy want? My curiosity is piqued as I slide the deadbolt left and pull the door open.

"Can I help you?" I ask, a pleasant smile on my face.

"Yes, hello, my name is Jasper." He extends his hand for mine, and I mirror the gesture. "I'm looking for Kash." He takes out a clipboard from his bag, glancing down at it. "Kash Holden."

"That's me." I step out onto the sidewalk, and my hands find their way to my pockets. "What can I do for you?"

"I'm from *Entrepreneurs of the Future,* a magazine based in LA, but we're distributed nationwide. We are pretty well-known."

I can tell the last part is added to make it sound prestigious. I know of the magazine. I give him a nod, letting him continue. "The office is doing a spread next month about young business owners—specifically those who moved from another state to start a business in California."

"It sounds like you're looking for someone exactly like me, then," I say with a nervous laugh, unsure of how I feel about this.

"Yes, actually." Jasper gives me a desperate smile. "Can I talk to you about doing an interview? It would be very basic, as this will be part of a multi-person article." He pauses and waits for me to say something, but I don't. I want to hear more first. "Someone from the magazine would come and do a sit-down with you, and they'd bring one of our photographers. They will ask you some questions and take a few pictures. The spread will be launching in our online and print series next month, in May."

As I cross my arms across my chest, I take my gaze out to the ocean for a brief moment before looking back at Jasper. "Can my business partner be part of it?" I ask.

Jasper looks confused and glances back down at his clipboard. "I was unaware you were in business with someone. That wasn't in the notes I was given."

I chuckle, mostly to myself. "Her name is Summer. We do this together." The words come out naturally, my head gesturing to the bar—to the *this*.

"Oh. OK. Yes, I think that would be fine. Let me leave you with my card, and we'll be in touch. Can I pencil you in for sometime next week—just to get something on paper?"

"Sure," I say, placing my foot up on the edge of the flower bed and leaning into it.

"That is fantastic, Kash. This exposure will be great for your business."

My business is doing great without this article, but I smile at him anyway. "We'll be in touch then," I say, reaching my hand out again to shake his once more.

"We will," Jasper says before turning on his heel and heading back toward Ocean Avenue.

"What the hell…," I softly say. The words come out under my breath and then a smile sneaks out, and I shake my head. Apparently, *Entrepreneurs of the Future* is interested in me, and that's pretty cool, I guess. I head back into the bar to continue getting things checked off my list before the night gets going.

I'm behind the bar, leaning over the shellacked top, flipping Jasper's business card in my fingers, when Summer makes her way in through the back door.

"You look like you're deep in thought," she says, approaching me.

I smile at her and lean forward, card in between my index finger and forefinger. "This happened today."

Summer takes the card from my hand and eyes it, her forehead scrunching in confusion. "Jasper King?" She looks up at me and then back at the card. "*Entrepreneurs of the Future*? Who is this? What is this about?" she asks curiously.

I fill her in on Jasper's visit, and while I talk, the pride that shows on her face warms me inside. When I'm done, she bites her bottom lip and exclaims, "This is amazing, Kash!" She jaunts down the length of the bar through the swinging door and jumps up for a hug.

My face is buried in her hair, the scent igniting something inside me. "I'm glad you're thrilled because I said I'd only do it if my business partner could also be there…and that's you." I pull away from our embrace to gauge the look on her face.

She looks confused and lets an uncomfortable laugh escape. "Business partner? I'm not your partner, Kash."

"But aren't you?" Maybe she isn't on paper. I took out the loan. But in all other ways, this is just as much hers as it is mine.

She shakes her head slowly. "I'm not sure I follow you."

"It's no big deal, Summer. I just want you there with me. Is that OK?" I try to remain lighthearted, but she seems so taken aback by my suggestion that I begin to feel uncomfortable.

"It was you and the stars there that night that I manifested this place, Summer. It's you and me here every day. It's you and me putting in the hard work. It's you and me putting soul into the bones of this place. Please, just do the interview and photo shoot with me?"

She lets a true smile shine through, one that lights up her whole face. She wasn't uncomfortable, I realize now. She didn't trust what I was saying. She didn't believe it.

Tonight's the night. I'm going to tell her how I feel, finally—up in our spot on the balcony once we are home. I will not talk myself out of it this time.

"Kash?"

"Sorry, what?"

"I asked when this is happening?"

Summer pulls me from my racing mind, and I quickly offer an apology for zoning out and then fill her in on the few details I have, telling her that we're tentatively scheduled for next Wednesday before opening. I tell her that I'll know more about what it will entail once I reach back out to Jasper later this week.

"Wow." She shakes her head in euphoric disbelief. "Congrats, Kash. This will be great." She squeezes my forearms and slides her hands down to meet mine. We hold each other's hands for a moment, and my pulse escalates just slightly. She gives my hands a quick squeeze before letting go, backing up, and heading to the kitchen.

I smile to myself. She's right. This is going to be great. I need to stop pretending that this isn't really freaking awesome. I slam my hand on the bar in excitement and let out an audible whoop.

"Oh yeah, Kash? You feeling this?" Summer says from the back as she peeks out from the door to the kitchen, giving me a flirty look.

"Yeah! I guess I am!"

She does a celebratory yell before letting the door to the kitchen swing behind her.

It's time to get ready for the night.

⸻

By seven thirty, the bar is already just about at full capacity. Chairs have been turned to face the pianos as the husband and wife performers, Calvin and Talia, get ready to entertain. I have been observing them while they set up. They have great chemistry—smiling and laughing together, subtle touches, and winks. If their musical chemistry is anything like this, they're going to be amazing. Summer saw them perform at an open mic night she sang at last month. She waited until they were done to tell them they had to come and play at Two WhisKEYS, and so, here we are.

The low hum of background music that plays for dinner fades out, and the magical sound of the live piano takes over the space and captivates the entire room—patrons snap their heads toward the stage, rallying with applause. Calvin and Talia's first song is "California" by Phantom Planet. I let out a boisterous laugh and throw my head back. So cliché but so perfectly matched with the atmosphere.

"They're great!" Nel says as I walk by the bar.

I stop in front of her. "They are amazing," I respond with a smile.

Nel continues serving the couple sitting in front of her, and I glance over to Summer, who is mixing a tequila drink.

"You ready for tonight?" I ask.

"You have no idea!" she practically shouts with excitement, beaming.

I smile at her. I'm so proud of Summer. The way she's transformed over the last two years is nothing short of amazing. She's gone from being insecure, shy, and unsure of her potential—to now—accepting that she has something amazing to offer the world and allowing herself to share it.

"You have a little ice cream right here," I say, pointing at my own cheek, letting a soft smile form. Summer recoils, her cheeks blooming in crimson. She smiles, but it's definitely one stemming from embarrassment, not happiness. She wipes her cheek with two of her fingers and takes a meek lick of her ice cream cone.

"You know, I'm still full from dinner. I don't know how much of this I'm going to be able to eat," she says, laughing.

Her laugh. It's like a melody—musical and sweet. I look at her; her shoulders slumped as if she is trying to hide the entirety of her soul from me. I'm never going to stop building her up. I'm determined for her to realize what she's hiding from herself and the world.

"Why are you looking at me like that?" she asks me softly.

I look down at my feet. What was I looking at? Oh, I was memorizing your face. I was just falling in love with you. That's all. *"Oh, sorry, I was just making sure you got it all," I say with a wink.*

Summer stands tall behind the bar, her shoulders back, showing me—and the little world we've built here—the real Summer James.

"I can't wait!" I say. "Jimmy was here so early tuning up that guitar."

Summer laughs. "I got Talia to agree to stay for the second set and play piano for me and Jimmy. I thought it would add a little extra."

I'm impressed with Summer's drive to make her music perfect. "Does she know your songs? Or are you doing all covers tonight?"

"I gave her the sheet music. We are doing two of my songs and the rest covers." She shrugs her shoulders.

"I'm looking forward to it." I gently slap the bar top. "I'm going to check how the kitchen is holding up."

"Sounds good," Summer responds.

It's nine o'clock when Calvin and Talia end their set and say goodbye to the audience. They get a loud response, so I make a mental note to have them back soon. The buzz and energy of the bar have increased as the drinks flow and the patrons settle into the vibe within the walls. It feels like home.

As I peek outside the open windows, I see that the canvas outside has transformed. Darkness is blanketing the outside, and the moon shines silvery over the ocean. The lights inside are romantic—the ambience is one of my favorite things about the evenings here. It reminds me a lot of Sullivan's, and I smile at the memory of that place as it flies through my mind. I pull out my phone to take a picture from the corner of the bar, trying to get as much of the dining room in the shot as I can. Looking down at the image, I see perfection. Dim lights, candles on the tables, dark wood, and happy customers. I put the image into a text to Maverick and add a message.

Thinking of you guys! I type before hitting send.

A few minutes later, I get a reply from Mav:

It looks great, buddy! We miss you guys—I see Summer must be singing tonight. Have fun!

With his text comes a picture—a selfie of him making a funny face, with Silvia and J.J. smiling on either side of him. I let out a loud laugh before going back to the picture I sent to look again. In it, you can see Summer on the top right side, adjusting her mic stand, a look of peace on her face.

With that, I head toward the stage to introduce the next performers. "Hello, everyone. We are back for set two with our very own Summer James." The crowd claps, and when it quiets, I introduce Jimmy and reintroduce Talia. Then, the music begins as I make my way off the stage and toward the windows. Leaning against the wall, out of the way of guests, I settle in to watch for a minute. Their first song is "Love on Top" by Beyonce, and it's the perfect start. The crowd roars as the intro plays, and Summer instantly engages with the audience as she sings.

When the next song begins, I make my rounds, checking in with patrons and seeing if anyone needs anything. I spend the rest of the evening doing what I love most about my job—meeting new people and conversing with regulars.

And listening to Summer sing.

———

It's two in the morning when Summer and I walk through the door of our apartment. We are both wide awake from the high of a great night. Summer is elated, as she tends to be after singing a set, and she puts the teapot on the stove.

"Do you want a cup?" she yells to me from the kitchen. I'm in my room changing into more comfortable clothes.

"Sure! Thanks."

We take our mugs out on the balcony and sit in our usual seats, mine, the wicker chair on the right, hers the one on the left. Getting comfortable, Summer puts one leg up on the ottoman and one arm behind her neck. Our mugs of tea sit on the table, steaming. I'm the complete opposite of Summer's cool and collected demeanor right now. My insides wretch with anxiety about the things I need to get out. I stretch my leg out onto the patio table and sink into the seat, looking out toward the ocean.

"You guys were amazing tonight," I say, breaking the pleasant silence.

"Thanks, Kash. It was so much fun. My heart is bursting." Her face beams under the moonlight.

I give her a small smile and sit up, leaning my elbows on my knees.

"Summer…," my voice gets stuck in my throat.

"Yeah?" Her body turns slightly in my direction. She looks perplexed at my tone.

"I don't know how to say this to you. But it's been eating me up inside, and I can't keep carrying on as if it's not rattling me every day." I'm rambling, and Summer looks petrified. I realize she's probably going straight to some awful scenario—assuming that I want her to get her own place or something. I shake my head, a motion—to myself—to get to the point.

"What is it?" she asks, whispering the words. I can hear the fear in her small voice.

I pull out my bun and run my hands through my hair, an anxious habit. I put it back up and try to relax my shoulders.

"You're doing that thing you do when you're nervous," she says. I look at her, wondering what she means. "You messed with your hair that night you told me you were moving to California. You messed with your hair when you said goodbye to everyone on your front lawn back in Austin. And you mess with your hair whenever something goes awry at the bar." Her voice seems sad, as if she's anticipating something that will break her heart.

"I am nervous."

A breeze whips through our little space, bringing with it the briny smell of the ocean, mixed with the subtle hints of chamomile from our teas, steeping, untouched on the table.

"What's going on?" Summer asks me with an anxious look on her face.

Breath, I tell myself.

"The other night, before Jimmy called, we were talking about feeling like something is missing sometimes. Do you remember?" She just nods. "Summer, for me, it's you. It's you that's missing from my life." I sit back in the chair again and glance at the sky briefly before looking back at her. She's staring at me, but I can't read her face.

She reaches over the arms of our chairs and gently grabs my forearm. "I'm right here, Kash."

"No, that's not what I mean."

She leans forward, her elbow on her knee, and her chin rests on her fist. "What do you mean?" she asks, the words hitching at the end.

I abruptly stand up and lean over the balcony before turning back to her, linking my fingers behind my head. "I've never felt about anyone the way that I feel for you, Summer. If I could get you to crawl into my heart and see what I see and feel what I feel for you, you would understand." My shoulders slump. I'm failing at this. I can't even find the words to tell her how I feel. As I sit back down, I glance over at her. Her dark eyes are wide, and her shoulders are moving up and down as if she is having trouble taking in a steady breath.

"I don't know what to say," she says, sounding defeated, which is not—at all—how I was hoping she would react.

"You don't have to say anything." Now, I sound defeated, too. I let a moment pass to gather my thoughts. But she is the one to break the silence.

"You mean the world to me, Kash," she states. "I feel more connected to you than I have to anyone else in my entire life." It sounds like she's trying to let me down nicely. "I'd be lying if I said there was never a time when I've hoped for us to be something more than what it is right now." Hope flickers within reach as I listen to her words. "But I need you. I need you in my life for always. I can't wreck this by letting you in too close to my heart and then end up shattering it to pieces—to the point where you leave me and I lose you forever." The tears are sliding down her face, the pain in her words is actually audible, and my heart aches for her.

But my emotions, my desperate need for her to understand what I'm saying, takes over. "I am not your parents, Summer. I am not the Brickmans either." The words come out harsher than I intend. "I'm not Dan, I'm not Meg, I'm not Piper…" my voice trails off, as I suddenly feel like I went too far. I don't want frustration to take over. She just stares at me, looking hurt. "What I mean is—I'm not going to leave you the second the going gets tough. Haven't I proven that to you?"

Her tears are mostly silent, but she—seemingly unwillingly—lets a small sob escape. "Since I met you, everyone has always made eyes at us—wanted us to be more than what we were. But not us—not you and I. We were just *us*—something unexplainable." Her words sound shaky. "And now it can't be that ever again," she whispers. "You crossed this invisible line. You told me how you feel, and now we can't ever go back." She runs her hands through her hair as my shoulders slump. "I can't be who you want me to be, Kash. No matter how much you believe that I'm worthy of love, the reality is that I'm just not there. Sometimes it feels like I never will be, no matter how hard I try." She wipes away her tears with the sleeve of her sweatshirt.

My head hangs with defeat. Words aren't going to change her mind right now. Though it breaks my heart that she feels this way about herself, I know Summer, and she's an ever-evolving being. She has learned to love herself in spite of her past. She's now able to physically carry herself with confidence and acceptance, something she once couldn't even dream of doing. I have seen it with my own eyes. She did that, even when she thought she couldn't—she learned to love *Summer*. But she isn't ready to let someone else love her.

It's too soon.

I should have known that.

I can't just tell her. I have to *show* her.

CHAPTER 12

Summer

Nel's words linger in my head as I lie on my bed, tears dripping off my checks onto my pillowcase. *You break his heart every day.*

I groan quietly, aggravated with myself for pushing Kash deeper into a corner and further away from me. Living in this false state of equilibrium with him, I was carrying on like there wasn't this undeniable connection between us. And now it's out in the open, and I've ruined it. I struggle to fall asleep, but sleep must come because I don't want to miss my appointment with my therapist in the morning. An appointment that, it seems, has come at the perfect time.

"Wow, Summer. This is a lot to grapple with, I'm sure." The look on Janie's face is calm and nonjudgmental.

My shoulders slouch as I listen to the hum of my fan and the noise machine. I always have them on for my Zoom sessions with Janie to block out my voice so Kash can't hear me and so I don't have to watch what I say. It doesn't really matter today because Kash was gone before I even woke up. I'm sure I know the reason for that.

I'm finding it difficult to wrangle a response, and Janie gives me time to sit in what I just laid on her—the fact that Kash confessed his feelings for me and I shunned him away. I look up at the screen, making eye contact with her, and she continues.

"I see what your first reaction was to him saying this, but what is your reaction now? After having slept on it? I want you to take a minute. Think about it. What are your true feelings?"

I attempt to settle my restlessly beating heart before I speak. "I feel trapped inside my own body. I can't let him in—not in the way that I want, and it's killing me…to be a prisoner of my own soul. It's like this one situation is a roadblock from all the progress I've made up until this point. I know how I feel about him, but I'm too scared. Too scared that if I take the leap, he's going to disappear into the abyss, and then I'll be without." A stubborn tear makes its way out, and I swiftly wipe it away.

"Disappear like who?"

"Everyone!" It comes out angrily, but my feelings aren't toward her, and so I apologize.

"No, Summer. I know this is not aimed at me. So let yourself feel."

I wait a few beats before I continue. "Last night, when he was telling me how he felt, it was like I was back in my old house. And then I was in the Brickmans'. Or couch surfing in Piper's shabby apartment. In the span of sixty seconds, I had traveled to the places where everyone I'd cared about had left me, and then, I was back again—back sitting in front of Kash, fearing that if I opened this door to him, he would slip through my hands. Just like everyone else has done my whole life." I lean back in my chair and put my face in my hands. "I'm a mess." The words are jumbled as they fall out between my fingers.

Taking my hands down from my face, I suddenly spot my Post-it stuck next to my mousepad on my laptop.

Summer James, you are worthy of goodness. I pick it up and hold it in my hands before turning it over to show Janie. She grins at me. The tears begin flowing out like a river, and I can't stop them. Janie lets me sob.

When I seem to have reached the end of my tears, she speaks—offering me some homework. "I want you to consider writing a letter to the younger version of you—to little Summer. I want you to forgive her, love her, and tell her it's going to be OK. Do you think you could do that? You don't have to show anyone, but do it for yourself—to get the feelings out and see where the words take you in your healing journey." I nod, unsure if it's something I'll be able to do but willing to try.

Janie and I finish up the session with some closing thoughts and some areas for me to focus on. When we both log off, I shut my laptop. As I take a seat at the edge of my bed to regain my equilibrium, I attempt to process the last hour, finding it quite difficult to wrap my head around this new territory I have entered. I emerge from my room and find that the apartment is eerily quiet. My head is beginning to pound from lack of sleep and caffeine. In the kitchen, I open the fridge and find a breakfast of eggs and bacon wrapped in cellophane and a glass of black coffee, with room for milk and ice. I smile to myself and pull the plate and cup out.

There's a little note on the plate. *Good morning, Summer. I hope you have a good day. I'll see you later at the bar. –Kash*

Relief washes over me like a wave. He isn't going to make this weird, and neither will I, if it's the last thing I do.

Jasper King is a nervous type; I can tell from the second I lay eyes on him. I watch him from the barstool, where I'm perched as the photography crew sets up a few lights. The interviewer sits at a table, and Kash and I will join him once they're ready. We'll snap a few pictures—some inside the bar and some outside with the sign. I'm still taken aback that Kash wanted me to not only be here but be a part of the interview, and I'm trying not to overthink it.

When they're ready, Kash and I pull out the dark wooden chairs and have a seat with the interviewer. As we sit, I steal a glance at Kash. There is pride etched in his features—a humble pride that comes from a man like him—a man who had a dream, a man who worked for the dream and then came out where he wanted to be. A small smile spreads on my face, a gesture mostly to myself, allowing my own pride in him to ignite.

As we wait to begin, I feel his knee brush against mine, and with the contact comes a flush of warmth throughout my body. The urge is strong to take his hand in mine underneath the table, but I don't. Instead, I wring my hands together nervously in my lap.

"Hi, I am Reed," the man at the table states, not taking his eyes off his laptop. "I just need to get a few things set up here, and then we'll be good to go." He taps a few buttons, adjusts his recording device, and shifts his body on the chair while Kash and I sit unmoving in our own seats, waiting to see what will be asked.

Kash turns his gaze toward me, and our eyes meet, causing the air in the room to shift, it seems. I smile, my eyebrows raised, trying to use my expression to tell him this is exciting without using words. I gently squeeze his knee for a brief moment. Maybe to calm his nerves…or mine. He returns the gesture just as Reed is ready to begin.

The interview is simple and quick, and now we're heading out to the front to take a few pictures. I'm standing, fiddling with my hands and waiting for someone to give me direction on where to look and how to stand. I think about the interview. Kash shared about our conversation outside my apartment back in Austin and how, after that, he was determined to make this dream come true. "So, you just decided right then and there that you were going to move to California and open a bar?" Reed had asked, beaming a smile. Kash had looked thoughtful for a moment, like there was more to the story. He looked that way because there is more. But I knew he wasn't going to open that door—not to this stranger who would be putting his words out for anyone to see in a few short weeks.

"And what brought you here, Summer?" Reed had asked—a simple question with a not-so-simple answer.

"I went my whole life believing a narrative that was based on other people's incorrect perceptions of me." I looked at Kash for a moment, who was hanging on my every word, and then looked Reed right in the eye. "When I finally found someone who saw me for who I was and what I was capable of—well, I had to take the leap. Moving here to take this on with Kash was the first time I'd ever done something for myself. It was the first time that I didn't let fear decide my future." I finished my sentence with a single nod, and

Reed smiled endearingly at me as he began to take the interview in another direction. I allowed my shoulders to relax.

I move a rock around with my foot, making thin lines in the sand that has blown up onto the walkway.

"OK, put your arms around each other and give me a big smile," the photographer yells with gusto as Jasper stands anxiously to the side, watching.

As I huddle in with Kash, I smile at the photographer. Not a forced one for the camera, but a real one—a soul-warming smile, the Two WhisKEYS sign hanging above us, the waves crashing to the left and Kash to my right. The flash goes off, and I'm blinded by it, taken aback by the utter euphoria.

Walks to The Girls Home have quickly become therapeutic for me. As I make my way down the sun-beaten sidewalk, a brand new—intricate—watercolor set and other assorted materials tucked snuggly under my arm, a sense of purpose settles in my soul.

Last week, I got permission to take Stella off the premises, and we went to the beach. I watched her, mostly out of the corner of my eye, studying her reactions and movements. She didn't smile—not once—the entire outing, and the first hour of the adventure brought only one-word responses from her. She had her backpack with her, and when she opened it up to pull out her sketch pad, I got a glimpse of a book inside, a book I used to love when I was her age, *Tuck Everlasting*. It gave me pause…taking me back to the way my childhood books felt in my hands during the many different times I read them throughout the years. In my childhood home. At the Brickmans'. In my shabby, ground-level apartment. The pages becoming a bit more worn with each passing year. There were so many times when those stories saved me, and I couldn't help but wonder if they were saving Stella, too.

"Have you read any of that book?" I had asked her, nodding toward her open backpack.

She took her gaze to me, studying my face for a moment, before flipping her sketch pad open. "Yeah," she said softly, her voice carried away by the ocean breeze. "I'm actually rereading it right now."

Her expression seemed to warm slightly, and I turned toward the ocean, a sense of connection strengthening inside me.

The afternoon was spent reading, drawing, and standing ankle-deep in the water at the shore as Stella was uninterested in going any further into the waves.

I got her an ice cream at the colorful truck stationed at the end of the pier, and we sat and ate it—quietly—on a bench.

"Have you ever tried watercolors?" I thought to ask.

"Not since I was really young."

"No, not those Crayola ones," I said, shaking my head. "They have sets with, like, thirty different colors and shades. I bet you would like them."

She didn't respond right away. And when she did, there was sadness in her words. "I haven't painted with any kind of paint...not since...," her voice had trailed off, and her lower lip trembled, but only for a second.

I certainly wasn't going to pry. My intentions with her are not selfish, and I didn't want to come off as being nosey. I simply want to give her what I always needed when I was her age: a safe place to be herself. I put my hand on her knee.

"Maybe I should paint again," she finally said, staring out at the ocean. I couldn't tell if her choice of words was a way to take the conversation away from the heaviness that had settled over her.

"If you feel up to it, maybe it would be good for you," I said softly.

She nodded before taking a meek bite of her ice cream. "I think I really want to."

And so, here I am with a fresh set of amazing paints for her.

I ring the doorbell, and Lisa lets me in. When Stella comes into the foyer, she offers me a smile that I treasure. "Do you want to sit in the rec room?"

"Yes!" I respond. "I brought you something." My eyes widen with delight, and we make our way to the big table in the back against the windows, taking a seat beside one another.

I place the large palette on the table and push it toward her. "Open it."

Stella unclips the tiny silver latch that holds the case together and gently lifts the top up before laying it flat, its contents exposed. A little gasp escapes as her mouth falls open, her eyes scanning over the vast variety of colors and shades and the assortment of brushes in all different sizes.

Almost impulsively, as if without thinking, she leans over and wraps her arms around my neck. "Thank you," she whispers.

I hug her back and smile over her shoulder through my own emotions. "You are more than welcome."

After the hug, she reflexively retreats back to her reserved demeanor. But the gesture feels like progress for her, and for that, I'm grateful.

On my walk home, I can't help but feel like the afternoon healed me some. Reaching Stella has become my mission; whether it takes a month or a year, or more, I don't care. The more I'm around her, the more important she becomes to me. I see it, ever so slightly, the slow and steady way she is warming up to me. She's guarded and protective of her heart, and the way I see it, that's a strength. She doesn't let anyone in; she doesn't want to be hurt. But I'm determined to help her learn to trust someone who truly cares.

I glance up at the sky, squinting into the late afternoon sun. At sixteen years old, I was so much a mirror of how Stella is, and my insides ache—still—from time to time when I process particular events in my past. But young Summer would be proud of where she is; I'm finally starting to see that.

And I think it's time for me to listen to Janie and do my homework.

Dear little Summer,

I'm sorry that you endured all that you did. I'm sorry you held the weight of the world on your shoulders and that you were unsure of your worthiness. It wasn't your fault that you felt unloved. It wasn't you. It was them. I'm sorry that you didn't love yourself. But I love you. You are funny and kind. You are smart and brave, honest and good.

If I could tell you anything, I would tell you that it gets better. You will feel better. You will heal. Your heart will mend. You will see the light in the world, and it will be bright. There will be hard days, but you will find worth and joy in living—in seeing the good that surrounds you, especially in the little things.

I promise you, little Summer, that I will let someone love us—even the broken pieces—because we both deserve that.

I know that now.

Love,

Summer

CHAPTER 13

Kentucky

MAY

THE WOMAN'S HEELS CLACK along the sidewalk as she walks swiftly in the direction of the office building just up ahead. Her mouth is set in a frown, a natural position for her face these days—leaving her toxic home early in the morning and heading to a job she despises. She glances at her watch and sees that she has a few extra minutes before she needs to get settled at work for her meeting at nine thirty. She turns into the convenience store to grab some more coffee and something to eat in between meals, anything to delay the inevitable and dreadful trip up the elevator to the twenty-second floor where her desk rests in her seemingly beautiful office with floor-to-ceiling windows. *Seemingly* is the key word here because what is so great about a pretty office, really, if it's all an illusion?

The woman forces her spine straight and her shoulders back as she steps over the threshold of the store. She smoothes out the already perfect blonde hair that's set in a sleek low bun with a middle part. Everything always has to be just so because who knows who she'll run into at any given moment? A tiresome ideal instilled into her by her mother.

The woman's mother has been driving her crazy lately—needling in her social life, meddling in every aspect, really. A ruse for being interested in and concerned about what she is up to. But in all honesty, her mother only asks questions to see if she can find out how often her daughter spends time with the husband who left her.

The woman walks up and down the aisles before picking up some sliced almonds and a package of raisins. She strolls by the media rack and mindlessly grabs some of the business magazines she and her boss like to look through before heading to the checkout.

The air outside is mild for May, and the woman looks toward the sky briefly, allowing the sun to warm her face. She inhales a deep breath while pulling open the heavy glass door and enters the building. She rides the elevator up to the twenty-second floor, her briefcase on one shoulder and the plastic convenience store bag hanging loosely from her long, slender fingers. The elevator doors slide open, and she steps out, poised and elegant—painting a forced smile with absolute precision—just as her mother taught her.

She pushes through the door that leads to her office. The air is still and stuffy, having been shut all weekend. The woman turns on the lights and the overhead fan before taking a gentle seat in her chair at her desk, turning on the monitor to her Mac desktop computer. As it springs to life, she hears her phone vibrate in her bag. She ignores it at first, assuming it's her husband. When the vibrations continue, she stalls before reaching into her bag and seeing multiple messages on her phone. One from her friend, Brielle, one from her husband, asking her where she put the leftovers from breakfast. *In the fridge, of course, you mindless dumbass,* she thinks to herself. And there are two texts from her father.

Mornin, sweetheart. She can hear her father's southern drawl as she reads the words, and she softens a bit.

Your brother is going to need us to head over there for dinner this week. He needs our support, hon.

She stiffens again, huffing an annoyed breath and rolling her eyes to herself. She loves her father, but his ignorance regarding her brother is getting frustrating. Her father can't seem to see the truth about him, nor does he make her brother take ownership, which continues to pick at her last remaining nerve. She contemplates a response, wondering if ignoring it would just be easier. But she can't. Of anyone who's texted, she can't ignore her father.

I don't know, Dad. I have a busy work week.

She stares at the wall, waiting for a response. Her father won't stand for it. We need to stand by him. *We are family*, he keeps reminding her, nearly every day. What she would like to say is, *What about Mom? She was once part of the family unit, and now you don't ask about her.* But she doesn't say that. Because she doesn't care either way that her father doesn't speak to or ask about her mother. She wouldn't either if she were him. Hell, she barely speaks to her as it is—unless she's riddled with guilt.

She sees the gray text bubbles appear and disappear, and she knows that her father is annoyed and trying to figure out exactly what to say to make her change her mind.

But she won't change her mind. She can't. Her brother is a monster. Her father is the one who first sat him down and reamed him out for things that he had done. She was proud that her quiet, passive father had done the right thing. But as the years have passed, the only thing her father seems to do now is make excuses. She's uninterested in being a support system for her brother as he prepares to go to trial for the charges set against him. She would rather continue pretending she was the only child in the family.

With that thought comes a memory that rattles her—of a past that she keeps tucked neatly away. If she doesn't think of it, it becomes make-believe…a figment of her imagination, not something real or tangible.

Finally, her father decides what to say, and her phone rattles on the desk, causing her to jump away from her nagging thoughts.

Come on, Claire. We need to put our own feelings aside and be the rock that he needs. He's family.

He says *family* again, as if he needs to assure himself, too.

No, Dad. He doesn't deserve it.

Her father quickly responds. **There isn't even proof. We can't abandon him.**

Claire smirks and shakes her head, furiously typing back.

You and I both know that you're just trying to make yourself feel better. You are just trying to save someone—anyone—in the family to make yourself feel better about what happened to us.

She slams her phone down on the desk and heaves a loud sigh, running her hands over her slick hair. She picks up the convenience store bag and puts the snacks in one of her drawers. She pulls out the magazines and places them down on the corner of her desk. She hears another message come in—from her father, she assumes—but suddenly, she's uninterested because what she sees on the cover of the magazine quiets her breath, halts it all together. Her eyes widen as her shaking hand picks up the magazine that rests on top of the pile.

"Summer? Is that you?" The words come out in a jagged whisper as she feverishly flips through the magazine to find the cover story.

When she finds it, her eyes scan the pictures and the words in awe. She quickly reads the whole article, and then her eyes go back up to the top, and she reads it again slowly, word for word. When she's done, she leans back in her chair and holds the magazine idly in her lap. She can't believe it. She smiles to herself and places her hand over her heart, knowing deep down that the universe tilted and Summer flourished. A tear escapes, and then another. She doesn't bother wiping them away. She can't pinpoint how she feels—part of her feels full and proud, but the other side of her soul feels broken, and she can't quite figure out why.

She looks back at the article and shakes her head again in disbelief. *At least one of us made it out*, she thinks to herself. Even if it was the least likely of all.

CHAPTER 14

Kash

"T HIS IS INSANE," SUMMER says, flipping through the magazine, awe written in the expression on her face. "I'm so proud of you." She leans back on the couch and looks at me.

"It really is amazing," I respond. "And I'm proud of you, too! This was a team effort." I tap her knee gently, a friendly gesture.

We both sit in comfortable bliss as we each flip through our own copies for a moment, soaking in the feeling of being on the cover of a prestigious magazine.

"There is just so much heart within the walls of Two WhisKEYS," Summer says, breaking the silence. "I didn't think it was possible to recreate the vibes we had at Sullivan's, but we did. And it's almost stronger. Don't tell Mav I said that." She winks at me, looking a tad guilty for expressing the thought.

I let out a laugh. "Yeah, it's home there, isn't it?"

She nods, and we hold eye contact for what feels like minutes. I can't read the look on her face, but I know her well enough to know that she has something to say. I cock my head slightly to the side. "What's up?" I ask, inviting her to share what's lingering on her mind.

She shrugs her shoulders, as if to say she isn't sure, but then she immediately starts talking. "Remember that conversation we had on the balcony last month?"

"Yes." The word barely escapes my mouth.

"I've been thinking a lot about the things that I said—about being so afraid to lose you. I know that it comes from my past and things that have happened to me." She pauses for a moment, and I am frozen in my seat, my breath suspended in my lungs. "I…," she stutters a bit before taking a frustrated breath. "What about you, Kash?" she whispers.

"What do you mean?" I ask, my brows furrowed.

"You lost your dad when you were so young. And your mom lost the love of her life. You had to watch her in pain while you were also hurt. How are you not afraid, too?" She sounds desperate for answers, as if I have the secret to uncovering the mystery of healing from pain and fear.

But I don't think I do.

My shoulders slump, my elbows rest on my knees. I let my head fall, looking down at the floor.

"I don't know, Summer." My words sound defeated. "I know that's not what you want to hear, but I don't think I have an answer."

She nods, and a sorry smile sneaks onto her lips, her eyes glossing over. It's quiet for a moment before I speak up.

"All I know is that I don't get anything out of being afraid. I came to that realization somewhere along the way." I look up at her, and she's leaning forward, ready to absorb everything I say.

"Yes, I could lose it all in the blink of an eye. Any of us could. You and I should know that better than anyone, right?" She nods, her lips trembling. I shuffle closer to her and wipe a tear from her cheek, allowing my hand to rest there gently for a moment. She leans into my hand and closes her eyes. "I'm not afraid of losing you," I whisper. "At least not anymore." She opens her eyes wide, and a steady stream of tears is making their way down her cheeks, much to her dismay. She uses her sleeve to wipe her nose. "I'm most afraid of never getting the chance to have you entirely." She continues to cry, and I don't want to overwhelm her, but I have so much more to say. "You know I would never hurt you, right?"

She sighs, and it sounds like defeat. "I want to know that," she says. "But how am I supposed to trust that when anything can happen? Everyone in my life up until now is gone!" She is starting to panic, and I'm not interested in getting my way, getting her to understand me right now, at the expense of her mental health.

I stand up and extend my hand to pull her up. I pull her into an embrace as she wraps her arms around my waist. Her head settles into my chest, and I rest my chin on her head. I gently rock us back and forth. "Yes, everyone from before is gone. But it's not fair to you to allow them to keep controlling your life, Summer. Your *family* loves you. We are all still here. We never left you. We will never leave."

She pulls away and looks up at me with red eyes. "Thank you, Kash." She sounds exhausted, and I know this is the end of the conversation for now. And that's OK. "I know that I need to let go of the fear. It weighs me down and festers inside. I know it's what I need to work on. And I will…I am."

I smile at her and tap her nose. "I know."

"I'm going to go take a shower," she says, backing up out of my space. "And then I'm going to call Farrah."

"I think that's a great idea," I smile as she walks to the bathroom. I'm glad she's going to call Farrah. It's a healthy decision to make when she's feeling a bit low.

It's almost time to head to the airport to pick up my mom, who's flying in. So, I go to my room to get changed.

CHAPTER 15

Summer

"I'M GOING TO GET my mom from the airport," Kash yells through the apartment. I'm sitting on the balcony with the door open, FaceTiming with Farrah and Junie. "Bye, Farrah!" he adds.

"OK!" I shout. "Hold on, Farrah. I need to ask him a quick question before he leaves," I say as I walk through the door to avoid shouting. "What are the plans for tonight? If you and your mom have plans alone, that's fine. I just wasn't sure." I smile meekly, still feeling a bit reserved from our conversation earlier. I also don't want to impose on their time.

"We don't have any plans. I think I'll let her get settled, take her down to the pier, and then maybe to Jimmy's for tacos," Kash says, gathering his keys and phone and putting them in his pockets. "But you should join us, too."

"Sounds good. I might go visit Stella, but I'll be around," I say as he waves goodbye and heads for the door.

I turn my attention back to Farrah, who has put the phone down. I'm staring at the ceiling of her house, listening to Junie shriek with happiness. "Hey, I'm back. I was just saying bye to Kash. He went to pick up his mom from the airport."

She picks the phone back up, slightly out of breath, a piece of her auburn hair blocking one of her eyes. She blows it out of her face and plops dramatically down on her couch. "That's awesome that she's coming to visit!"

"I know! I'm looking forward to meeting her in person, not just on FaceTime," I respond. "Anyway…," I say, drawing out the word and implying that I have something to say, and Farrah catches on quickly.

"Spill it," she says dramatically, pulling the phone closer to her face.

I roll my eyes. "Don't be spastic, Farrah."

"Summer. What is it?"

"Kash basically confessed that he has feelings…for me." My stomach twists itself into a knot, and I struggle to calm the sensation.

Farrah's eyes widen, but the rest of her expression remains calm—as if to not overwhelm me, or send me into a tailspin, I'm not sure which. Then, a small smile breaks on her face, and she blinks—once—dramatically. My forehead falls to my hand, and I let out a groan.

"And?!" Farrah's patience has worn thin, and she's clearly ready for me to spill whatever news there is to share. But I'm not sure what to say.

Yes, the person I love feels the same. YAY! But I can't do anything about it because I'm too scared.

No, I can't say that. I'm sure everyone is tired of hearing this *same old Summer* nonsense. Hell, I'm even sick of it.

"And...," I drag the word out. "I don't know what to do about it." My voice sounds defeated, and my shoulders slack. I look into the phone and into Farrah's caring eyes. "The things I told you *not* to do two years ago...to not push us into anything...all of that is still relevant. It's like I haven't grown at all. At least that's how it feels some days."

"Oh, Summer. Your journey is just beginning. You know that. Don't overthink this." She sounds flippant, and her words give me pause. I do overthink basically everything I do, especially when the stakes are high, and with Kash, they most certainly are. "What's the worst thing that can happen?"

"We cross the line, and everything gets ruined," I say sadly.

Farrah gives me a warm look. "Is that it, Summer? Or is the worst thing you letting Kash go and him moving on to find someone else? Isn't that the most tragic scenario here? You depriving yourself of happiness for the sole reason of letting fear win?"

Her words wrap around me like vines, inching their way up and around the crevices, causing goosebumps to form all over my body—the meaning and truth behind what Farrah is saying settles deep into the crevices of my heart. It's as if a lightbulb has just gone off. And with any luck, it will stay; the words will linger. They will help me change the narrative I've created for myself. I look at her and allow myself to cry.

"I wish I could hug you right now," Farrah says through her own tears.

"Me too," I manage to get out. "But you helped—just like you always do."

———

I lean down and glance beneath my bed, my eyes darting to the different storage containers until I find the one I'm looking for. I slide it out and pull the top off. Inside the container rests an array of objects—pieces of memories—stored away for safekeeping. The little box Kash had given me before he left Austin for California is in here, too, but the trinkets I've saved outgrew that little box, and a bigger storage place became necessary. I smile to myself as I quickly riffle through the objects before I grab the one I'm in search of—my tattered copy of *The Lion, the Witch and the Wardrobe*.

When Stella told me she was a reader, I immediately thought of this book. It saved me from so much darkness when I was younger. Wherever there were words on paper, I would go—especially to this book. I figured parting with it now was worth it, if it meant letting someone else feel its comfort. The book rests on my legs, and I move my hand slowly over the cover—the memories flashing like bolts of lightning through my mind. But, I stay in the present.

I am here.

I am OK.

I manage to avoid traveling back in time to a place I don't care to visit. The book saved me then, but I don't need it anymore. It's time to part with it.

As I place the cover back on the box, something catches my eye, and I pick it up—a small chuckle sneaks out.

"But it HURTS," I whine through a pitiful laugh. Nel is keeled over, her head past her knees. She shoots her body upright again, but her head falls back, her beautiful face turned up to the sun, her mouth agape with

hysterics. She clearly cannot find a way to get air into her lungs. I fall down in the sand in defeat, and I start hysterically laughing, too.

The beauty of it is that nothing is really that funny—it's one of those moments where pure happiness has taken over the space between friends, and you couldn't stop laughing, even if you tried. I had heard about these moments, but my experiences with them were few and far between.

"I can't breathe," Nel labors, falling down beside me in the damp sand. "What managed to hurt you oh so badly?" she says, playfully shoving my shoulder, and sighing dramatically through her laughs.

"THIS!" I say dramatically, holding up a large seashell with jagged edges. "And look, I'm bleeding," I say, holding up my foot as bright red blood mixes with salty water and cascades down the arch of my foot, falling around my ankle. "I'm going to attract sharks," I grumble before looking over at Nel, and that does us both in again as fits of laughter escape our lungs. I put my hands over my stomach to stifle the pain there—the beautiful ache of laughing until your stomach hurts.

My thumb glides over the soft pink and white shell before I gently place it back into my memory box, careful not to break it any more than it already is. I have yet to find a perfect seashell while living here, but this one reminds me of myself—a little bit smooth, a tiny bit rough—broken but beautiful.

With the object I came for safely tucked under my arm, I slide the box back under my bed and head out to see Stella.

The air is warm and dry as I step out of the apartment and head right toward The Girls Home. Brown, dry brush scatters the sidewalk, the greenery showing the effects of the drought we are in. I look up at the sun and smile, pulling my sunglasses down from my head. Anxious to get there and see how Stella is doing, I keep a quick pace.

When I arrive, I walk up the brick walkway toward the door to the massive house. I ring the familiar doorbell and wait for someone to come and let me in. Lisa opens the door again and greets me happily.

"Just sign in like last time. Stella will be right down," Lisa says as I use the pen on the podium to scribble my name on the line.

"Thanks," I say, adjusting my bag to the side. A moment later, Stella is making her way down the wide staircase. Her blond hair is in a French braid, and her face is bright, her cheeks slightly rosy, her blue eyes wide and cautious. She's carrying a sketch pad and pencil. "Hi, Stella," I say, unable to hide my enthusiasm.

"Hi," she says shyly.

I roll onto my heels, awkwardly moving my body. "Where do you want to sit?"

She shrugs her shoulders. "Outside?"

I smile. "Sure. Lead the way."

Stella turns on her heel and heads down the hall that leads to a large kitchen. The glass door next to the refrigerator brings us out to the backyard. It's beautiful, and I take in the surroundings as I look around the large space. A few huge Ficus trees are sprawled in the yard, casting shade throughout. Picnic tables rest beneath the shade, and a lanai, sprinkled with lights, rests close to the home. The patio has a large outdoor dining table where I imagine the girls hang out and eat. It is very homey, completely different than I expected.

Stella takes a seat on one of the couches under the lanai, and I join her, choosing a chair next to her. She pulls her legs up onto the couch cushion and rests her sketch pad on her legs. She starts to draw, and I observe her. Every few seconds, her eyes glance over at me, her mouth remaining in a neutral line. I give her a few moments to get settled and comfortable before I say anything.

"I brought you something," I say, breaking the silence.

She adjusts her body, not seemingly excited to learn what it is, but she also doesn't look completely uninterested.

"I don't know if you remember from the night that we met, but I had shared that I'd had a tricky childhood." *Tricky? Really, Summer? That's how you will describe it?* "Actually, that doesn't explain what it was like. It was a horrible childhood. Yes, horrible is a better word." Stella seems amused by my discomfort but not in an unkind way. It's like she finds my frazzledness endearing. "Anyway, I used to read a lot back then, and there was one book that I turned to, always, without fail. My third-grade teacher gave me her copy to keep, and I just couldn't believe it. I read it…over and over again."

Stella looks at me, curious. "What book?"

I smile at her and pick up my bag from the ground. I unsnap the button and lift the flap, reaching in to grab the book. Pulling it out of my bag results in a tugging sensation in my heart. I know that I want to give it to Stella, but there's a longing inside me as I part with the only proof I have of a happy memory from *then*.

"This one," I say, handing it over to her.

She reaches out and gently takes it from my hand. I watch as her eyes scan the cover. "I haven't read this," she says quietly.

"Well, I wanted you to have it," I offer. "This book really helped me through some hard times. But I don't need it anymore. I want you to have it. And I hope it will allow you to feel some magic, like it did for me."

"Am I a little old for this?" she asks curiously.

I shake my head and lean forward, my elbows on my knees. "We are never too old for a little magic."

Stella allows a smile to break through, and there are a few moments of silence as she flips through the tattered pages of my beloved book. "What was so bad about it?" Her words alarm me at first, and I look at her closely but don't respond. Though the question is simple, the complexity of the answer is anything but. "About when you were young…what was so bad?" She pauses for a second before adding, "Sometimes I feel like no one could possibly have it as bad as me." She chokes out the last few words, and I'm barely able to hear them. "How bad was it?" It sounds as if she's desperate, trying to climb into my head and see what's in there, anything that will make her feel a little less alone.

The memories are knocking—flying to the forefront of my brain with aggression—and I steady them with a deep breath and some quick self-talk. This, right here, isn't about me, and I have to remember that. I want to help. I want Stella to feel connected. I don't want her to look at me and see a grownup still wrecked and broken from a past that's long gone. What hope would that give her?

"It was bad, Stella."

And so, I tell her about it. I tell her about the day that I was taken from my house and about the Brickmans. I tell her about the death of my dad, the loss of my momma.

I tell her about Jason.

I tell her about Piper.

And the drugs.

And the sleepless nights.

And being homeless.

The loss—the loss of absolutely everything that I held dear.

About how the stars were my only reprieve.

After I've given Stella the background she was curious about, her eyes are unblinking, and she is leaning toward me in full attention, as if she is trying to catch the words I'm saying in her hands. Neither of us speak for a few moments, just sitting in silence, looking at each other.

Then Stella speaks. "I knew you were someone I could trust."

"When we first met outside the restaurant?" I ask.

She shakes her head. "No, the first time you came here." I nod, but my eyebrows furrow in wonderment, curious about what she means, or what I did to make her trust me. "Because of your pitiful attempt to draw stars." Her eyes are flooded with fresh tears, but she doesn't wipe them away.

"I don't understand," I say.

"My mom named me Stella because she said I was a star." My heart seems to stop entirely; my eyes are unblinking. Stella continues, "My parents immigrated here from Italy when my mom was pregnant with me. They were young, only twenty, and their families had disowned them when they found out they were going to have a child out of wedlock. I was born, they said, only days after arriving in the United States." She stops and takes a breath, her glance being pulled toward the Ficus tree, its leaves rustling in the gentle breeze. I sit, unmoving, patiently waiting to hear more. "I came out fast as anything, Dad told me. And my hair was so blond, it was white. My parents had dark hair and eyes, and there I came, looking like this." She smiles, gesturing to her features. I smile at her. Her next words come out in a whisper. "My mom said I was the light of their lives. A bright star amongst the darkness."

My hand comes up to my mouth, a gesture made to suffocate the incredible urge I have to sob. I take another deep breath, and I get up and join her on the couch, facing her, letting her know that I'm here—to be her friend. "Where are your parents, Stella?" I ask with care.

She looks at me with sorrow etched onto every surface of her face. "They're gone," she chokes out.

"Where?" I ask.

She begins to cry softly, her hands covering her face. I rub her back gently and give her all the time she needs. She lifts her head and looks up, pointing her index finger toward the sky. "Up there," she whispers.

My heart sinks to the furthest reaches of my gut, breaking into a thousand pieces, and I cringe at her pain, feeling it deep in my bones. My arm slides around her, not expecting or needing her to give me any more details but wanting her to know that I'm here for her. "I'm here," I say. "You don't have to go any further. But I'm here."

It's silent for a bit; the only sounds are the birds in the trees and the low hum of cars passing on the surrounding streets.

"I begged them to let me sleep over at my friend's house," she says, sounding distant. "It took all of my energy and tricks to get them to let me go." I nod, listening intently. "There was a fire at my house that night…and they didn't survive. They didn't get out in time." She's sobbing again, and I just hug her and rock her body against mine—back and forth. "If I had been there, I may have been awake. I could have warned them. I could have saved them." She barely gets the words out, but I hear them, sad and gut-wrenching.

"It's not your fault," I whisper into her hair. "I know it feels like it is, but it's not. You'll see that someday, even if it's hard to believe that right now. I don't want you to carry that on your shoulders. I will help you. OK?" I pull away and encourage her to look at me, to understand exactly what it is I'm telling her.

A smile pokes through, barely, but it's there, amidst a trembling lip. She glances out into the lawn before letting her head fall. I don't say anything, giving her a moment and letting her process our heavy conversation. "Thank you for telling me about what happened to you," she eventually says. "It makes me feel a little less alone."

I smile warmly at her. "What do you say, I sign you out one day next week and we spend some time together? We could go to the beach again if you wanted, or if there is somewhere else you would want to go, just let me know."

"Sure," Stella whispers. "Thank you."

We stand up, and I give her a big hug, wishing, more than anything, that she can feel how much I care.

CHAPTER 16

Kash

T HE *BEST OF REBA McEntire* isn't my cup of tea, but it's Mom's favorite, and the playlist I made for the drive back from LAX to Santa Monica isn't disappointing her in the slightest. Glancing over in her direction, I see that she's leaning forward slightly, her eyes studying every little thing we pass. A hint of a smile pulls at her mouth, and a far-off look rests in her eyes as she hums to the beat of the music.

"You OK, Mom?"

"Huh?" she says, turning her face toward me. "Oh, yes. Of course, darling. It's just slightly odd, you know?" She glances back out the window.

"What is?" I ask.

"Well, it's been thirty-five years since I've been here. As I look around, it almost feels like I've traveled back in time. Things seem as if they haven't changed one bit, though I know they have." Her voice rests in a state of disbelief, sounding awestruck. I smile,

136

staring out ahead at the freeway. "It's strange. Your father's been gone more than twenty years, but since walking off the plane this morning, I've never felt his presence more than I do here." Her voice fades off as she turns back to look out the window.

"I know what you mean," I say. "I was never here with him, but I have to say, being in California makes me feel like he's with me, more than I ever felt him when I was in Texas." Mom nods in agreement. "Are you nervous about being so close to where you guys met? Are you worried about how you're going to feel?"

"No, hunny." She pats my knee in assurance. "Maybe I worried about that when you first moved out here, but I'm ready now."

Reba sings to us for the rest of the drive back to the beach, and the terrain changes from city to hills to ocean until we arrive in front of my apartment building about an hour later.

"The traffic here is the devil's work," Mom says as she shuts the passenger door and flattens her hair down before placing her sun hat on her head.

I laugh out loud. "Yes, Mom, it is, but we made it. Let me show you my place before we check you into the bed and breakfast down the street."

"Is Summer here? I'm absolutely thrilled to finally meet her."

We head toward the stairs. "She's not home now," I say. "She's visiting with a friend, and then we will meet her for tacos over at our friend's restaurant."

"So impersonal, meeting her at a restaurant." Mom smiles at me, but I can tell her words hold truth.

"Then you don't know this restaurant," I say through a laugh.

Jimmy Buffet's "Margaritaville" is coming in through the speakers as Mom and I enter the restaurant. I've shown her my apartment, the beach, and Two WhisKEYS, and she's been delighted to see where I spend all my time. But the look on her face when we walk inside J's Tacos is different, and I can't quite place why. Her eyes are squinting as she glances around, looking completely bewildered.

"What is it, Mom?" I ask.

"I'm not sure. This place is familiar. I feel like I've been here before, but I can't quite figure out when." I just smile at her, knowing she has never been here—it wasn't a restaurant when she was last in California. "Just a feeling I have," she adds, seemingly reading my thoughts. As she continues to look around, she spots the picture wall and begins to make her way toward it.

"Take a look around. That wall is awesome. See if you can find Bill Clinton," I say with a laugh. "I'll find Summer."

I glance toward the back of the restaurant and see Jimmy and Summer sitting in chairs where the live entertainment usually plays. Jimmy's teaching her some strings on the guitar, causing a smile to play on my lips. As I approach them, Summer looks up and sees me, and she beams and waves, gently placing the guitar on the stand and getting up to greet me.

"Are you learning a new trade?" I ask, hugging her.

"I guess," she responds with a sly grin. "Where's your mom?"

"She's here!" I say. "Come on. I'll take you over to meet her. She's enamored with this place. She's over there looking at the picture wall." I turn around to see her studying a photo.

"Like mother, like son," Summer says, smiling.

I laugh, and we make our way over to the wall.

"Hi, Jacqueline!" Summer's voice—startling and unusually loud for her—makes me jump. Her excitement is endearing and sweet.

My mom turns on a dime, her warm smile shining at Summer. "Darling…," she says, trailing off, almost as if she's lost for words. She reaches her arms out, inviting Summer in for a hug, which she accepts. As they end their embrace, my mom takes Summer's face in her hands and looks at her disbelievingly. "Such a doll on the screen, but look at you! You are gorgeous, love."

Summer's shoulders slouch, and she blushes, tucking a stray piece of hair behind her ear. She smiles and compliments my mom, too.

"I'm trying to find Mr. Clinton," Mom says through a chuckle. "Kash here tells me he's somewhere on this wall."

"Oh, he sure is," Summer replies. "But you're on the wrong end of the wall." She nods her head to the left and guides my mom over to where the former president's picture resides for all of time, it seems.

Following behind them, I admire this scene of these two special women in my life together unfolding before me. "You know, there are more famous people on this wall besides Bill, Mom."

"And people who aren't famous whose stories are probably just as interesting." As Summer says this, she looks longingly at the wall, her eyes darting around among the pictures.

"Wait…all of a sudden, you care so deeply about my favorite wall in all of California?" I ask jokingly. "All those times you made fun of me, and here you are—agreeing." I cross my arms across my chest, grinning at her.

"I guess, maybe, you were on to something." Summer winks at me, and the three of us continue to gaze at the wall until Mom utters something I can't quite make out. It sounds as if the breath is suspended in her chest.

"Mom?" I say. "What's wrong?"

"It can't be…," her voice fades out as her hand, shaking, lifts to meet her trembling mouth.

I take a step in her direction, placing my arm on her shoulder. "Mom," I repeat.

She extends her index finger forward, pointing to the wall, and I cast my eyes in the direction she's pointing, feeling Summer do the same on the other side of my mom. My eyes dart all over, trying to land on what she's seeing, but I have no idea what she's pointing at; the sepia tones of the faded pictures mean nothing to me—not really.

I look back at her, my eyebrows furrowed. "What is it?"

"It's—" she sets about explaining but is interrupted by Jimmy coming over to introduce himself.

"Well, hello there, Kash and…" Jimmy begins, my mom with her back to him, her behavior still confusing me.

"Jimmy," I say, "this is my mom, Ja—" my voice fades as my mom turns slowly around.

"Jacqueline?" Her name escapes Jimmy's mouth in a rasp of emotion. "Is it really you?" His brows furrow as he steps closer to her, and now I have no idea what's going on.

My eyes are pulled to Summer, who looks as equally confused as me—her shoulders shrug, her eyes are wide, looking at me as if to say, "*What is happening?*" Then, I look at Mom, and tears are streaming down her face.

"Jim? Jimbo Clarence? Is it really you?" Mom's voice wavers as a knot of anticipation grows in my stomach.

"Jimbo?" I mouth the name discreetly so only Summer can see me, and she shakes her head unknowingly.

What the hell is going on?

Jimmy and my mom join in an embrace, and for a moment, it's as if the earth has frozen on its axis and time is standing still. I'm not sure if any of us are breathing. I haven't blinked in what feels like minutes.

"What is going on?" Summer's words are low, almost a whisper, but they break me from the trance.
"You guys know each other?"

Neither one of them responds, but I hear my mom stifle a sob before letting out a heavy sigh.

Eventually, they pull away from one another and turn to Summer and me. Jimmy takes two steps toward me and puts his hand on my shoulder. His mouth quivers, and his eyes are wet with emotion. "I knew there was a reason why I loved you beyond measure," he says, barely able to get the words out.

"Wh—" I start to ask what is going on again, but Jimmy quickly interrupts.

"You're Chewie's boy," he whispers, his hands shaking as he raises them to bring me in for a hug.

"What? My dad's name was Gavin."

Jimmy chuckles and shakes his head. "No, he was Chewie. That man looked like he walked off the set of *Star Wars* every time he skateboarded down the pier or came out of the ocean with his surfboard under his arm. We all called him Chewie—even your mom did." He turns his head and smiles at her, and she returns the gesture, her eyes puffy and red.

Jimmy walks over to the picture wall and, without a second glance, pulls a tattered photo from the spot where it, most likely, has rested for decades. He approaches me with the little faded rectangle and lifts it up, handing it to me. "That's me…and your dad, Kash."

I suck in a sharp breath and hold it in my lungs, taking the picture gently from Jimmy's outstretched hand. I study it—Jimmy looks the same as he does in most of the pictures from that part of the wall—the photos from the seventies. He's fresh-faced and youthful—tanned skin and water-soaked hair. Beside him stands my father, a thick mop of dark hair on his head and a beard that makes him unrecognizable to me—it's not how I remember him. My ability to pinpoint the emotion that I feel right now is proving to be a challenge, but I'm in complete awe with this serendipitous turn of events. I run my hands through my hair and let out the air that's been held in my lungs with a loud force. Summer approaches me and reaches her hand up to my shoulder; I look over to see her eyes glistening with emotion.

"This is amazing," she whispers.

"It is," I say through my own emotion, turning toward Jimmy and my mom.

The four of us take a seat at an unoccupied table in the back of the restaurant. Jimmy leaves and brings us some glasses of water and a bucket of beers on ice. He sits down on a chair next to my mom, the creases around his eyes deep from a smile he can't seem to contain. He pats my knee and gives it a gentle, fatherly squeeze.

"You have his eyes, son," Jimmy manages to get out. "You have his eyes." He says it again, but this time in a whisper.

I smile at Jimmy, but there aren't any words I can find that seem worthy of this moment.

"When I found out Chewie had died, I began talking to him every night, praying he was in a better place. Telling him I missed him." We all look at Jimmy, waiting for him to go on. He shakes his head with a smile. "For a while there, the lights in here would flicker, you know." He taps his finger on the top of the table, leaning back in his chair. "I had just opened this place, and I knew those damn lights shouldn't have been flickering." He lets out a lively laugh. Though I am smiling, I otherwise feel frozen in my seat, hanging on Jimmy's every word as he looks up at the lights. "When he left to move to Texas with you, Jacqueline, he told me he would be back. That he would see me owning my own restaurant on the beach one day. He believed in me more than anyone else on the planet. I guess the lights flickered from him. To show me that he was there. That he had come back to support me."

All four of us grow quiet—the only sounds are the soft tears of my mother and the background noise of the restaurant.

"Your lights always flicker a bit in here, Jimmy," Summer finally says softly.

Jimmy looks down at the table. "They hadn't, though, hunny. Not in years. Not until you two showed up on my strip of sand. And they only flicker when you're in here, Kash. I never thought anything of it until now. Your dad's been trying to tell me that he's here, but I didn't have my eyes open to it. I hadn't put it all together. I kept thinking maybe I just needed to change the bulbs again." He winks at me.

"I guess it all makes sense now, right?" Summer says. "The reason you've always been so drawn to that picture wall was more than just curiosity."

I look over at the wall again. "Yeah, it does make sense now, doesn't it?" I say the words, but it doesn't seem to make sense at all. It seems miraculous and nearly impossible. I shake my head and sit up straight. "But actually, no. How is it possible that I could be in Texas, living my life, and end up right here, unknowingly connecting with my dad's old friend, looking at pictures of him on a wall without even knowing it?" I don't mean for it to, but I know my voice sounds a bit agitated. I just can't seem to get a grip on this new reality.

"It's OK to be confused or blindsided by a turn of events, Kash," Summer pipes up. "Sometimes, I wake up and sit on our balcony, and I can't seem to grasp how I ended up here, even though Southern California has called to me my whole life, for some unknown reason."

Jimmy watches her talking and nods his head as if he might add something, but he doesn't at first.

My eyes stare into Summer's, and her gaze holds mine without flinching. "So are we just all accepting this as an unexplainable coincidence?" I look at each of them for a moment, a look of bewilderment on my face, but no one responds. "Summer wanted to be here her whole life, and then she meets me, and I also have an unexplained calling pulling me here, and we share those thoughts with each other, and then I come here and find my bar, which coincidentally just so happens to be right next to yours, Jimmy? Right next to a restaurant where there's a picture of my dad hanging on the wall?" My brows knit together as I shake my head in confusion.

"Coincidence, son? No." Jimmy's words are confident. "There's no such thing." He leans close to me again and squeezes my shoulder.

My mom moves her chair closer to me and puts her hand on my knee. "Jimmy's right, hunny," she says. "And if you're happy here where your path led you, then it seems like you should thank your dad—for guiding you right to your destiny."

Thanks, Dad, I say in my head. *For continuing to guide me from wherever you are.*

I glance over at Summer, who has fresh tears in her eyes. She nods once at me and smiles. I want to believe in what they're saying, so I attempt to make their thoughts my own. "I guess you're right," I say to both my mom and Jimmy. I say that I agree, but I'm not sure I do.

We all stand up and embrace. And as my pulse comes back down to normal and my heart warms, gazing at three of the most important people in my life, the lights in Jimmy's place, undoubtedly, flicker once, and then flicker again.

We all let out an audible gasp. "See, I told you," Jimmy says. "Coincidences? There's no such thing."

I can't say for sure if I've ever given much thought to fate and its place in my life until now. But ever since I found out about my mom and dad's connection to Jimmy, *fate* is all I can think about. I've found myself going back and overanalyzing every decision I've ever made, wondering if it really wasn't all coincidence, but instead a plan of cosmic proportions.

I was tormented by decisions of which college I should go to, ultimately deciding to stay in my home state, where I met Maverick, who gave me a job at his bar when he opened it. A job that ultimately awakened dreams within me to perform more and eventually open my own bar. A job that brought me to Summer, who inspired me to go after what was calling me.

Since this new discovery, I've also attempted to map out the paths that led Summer here, too, using the information I have.

Her childhood obsession with the ocean that, in time, turned into an obsession with California specifically. Which is a little strange given that she'd never been to the ocean before.

Her journey from Kentucky to Austin, which seemed to be a case of divine intervention. And her recovery in Austin at Champlain Bridge led her directly to Farrah, who introduced her to Maverick and, in turn—thankfully—to me. Our paths never crossed until we were in our thirties, but when I sit and map it all out, I can't help but think about how incredibly miraculous it all is. How our traumas—and our dreams—brought us together and then brought us both here to this beautiful spot near the sea.

I'm interrupted from my thoughts when Summer and my mom return to our beach chairs from their walk. "We found a lot of shells that I can take back to Texas with me!" my mom says, showing me her loot.

"Nothing whole, though," Summer adds, smiling but with a hint of disappointment hidden in her face. My mom looks at her, puzzled. "It's the strangest thing. Since I've been here, I have yet to find a shell that is completely intact." Summer gently takes a shell from my mom's hand and examines it with a furrowed brow before carefully handing it back.

"Oh, it's not a problem, dear," Mom says. "They are all still so beautiful, and they'll remind me of being here. That's all that matters."

Summer puts her arm around my mom's shoulder and looks at her lovingly, a gesture I appreciate. "You're right," she says.

"Mom, you have two days left. What do you want to do before you leave?" I ask.

She looks thoughtfully at me but doesn't answer right away. She shrugs with a smile, seemingly unsure, but then answers confidently. "I kind of just want to walk the pier tomorrow. I want to ride the Ferris wheel and have seafood with you guys," she beams, not asking for much at all.

Summer and I exchange glances. "Done and done," I say.

It's Monday, our day off, and Mom left yesterday. Her visit was perfect, and I'm thankful that she was able to see where I live and how well I'm doing. A lot came up during her four-day visit—things that were so monumental to both me and my mom.

We spent her last day and a half doing exactly what she wanted. We rode the Ferris wheel twice and walked up and down the pier for hours, stopping for fried clams and cut mango with chili flakes. Mom got both a Santa Monica sweatshirt and a T-shirt, all in the name of having a souvenir for any type of weather in Texas. We watched the sunset on Saturday night while drinking glasses of white wine on our balcony, where the conversation led my mom to share that she thinks that Summer and I are holding back from one another. Summer did that thing she does when she's embarrassed, tucking her hair behind her ears, looking down at her feet, and blushing. The conversation didn't go down a rabbit hole, as my mom, thankfully, got the hint that it wasn't in Summer's comfort zone.

I was sad to say goodbye to Mom, but she promised to come out more often, and we settled on that promise. She went back to Texas with a part of her heart mended; I could see it written across her face as I dropped her off at the airport, serenity where there once was restlessness.

Learning about Jimmy's place in my dad's life has caused quite a stir among us; there's certainly no denying that. Jimmy can't seem to avoid the tears that brim his eyes the instant he's in my presence, and then, the only reaction I can muster is to pull him in for a hug, hugs that usually linger for much too long. But it just feels right. So, for the last week, that is what he and I have done over and over: he gets emotional, and I give in to the urges to just pull him into me.

Summer and I find ourselves shaking our heads frequently, unsure of how, exactly, to wrap our heads around this new development but, at the same time, feeling undeniably ecstatic about the comfort it has provided us both with. Comfort in the possibility that something completely out of our control could have this profound of an impact on all of our lives.

This morning, Summer and I enjoyed a quiet morning of free time, and now, we're heading over to The Girls Home and to hang out with Stella since she's out of school. We're planning to take her off-site to do something fun this afternoon.

When we arrive at The Girls Home, we climb the few steps up to the front door, and Summer rings the doorbell, looking over at me with a sweet smile. She's already so well-versed in this process of visitation, and that warms me. A woman named Lisa opens the door and invites us in, and Summer signs the book on the podium by the door.

"Are you still planning on taking her off the premises today, Summer?" Lisa asks kindly.

"Yes, if that's still OK with you," she responds, placing the pen back down on the wooden ledge above the notebook.

"Absolutely. She will be thrilled."

Off the premises.

Those three words sound so cold, so constricting. I stand with my hands in my pockets, a friendly smile on my lips, but I feel so out of place—while Summer looks completely at home—as if the act of transferring guardianship for the day is second nature, no big deal. I'm a little taken aback at the magnitude of our responsibility for taking Stella. But as Stella, meek but seemingly thrilled, comes down the stairs, I watch Summer—mesmerized—as she embraces her. Thankfully, one of us feels comfortable and knows what they are doing.

"You ready to get outta here?" Summer asks with a wink.

"Definitely," Stella responds, giving me a shy wave.

"Hi, I'm Kash," I say, reaching out my hand. "Is it OK if I tag along for the fun today?"

Stella looks back and forth to both of us and shrugs. "Sure."

After saying goodbye to Lisa, the three of us head back out the door into the warm ocean air. Summer told me on the way over here that she wanted to take Stella to the outdoor roller skating rink over in Venice. We head toward my truck, which is parked right outside The Girls Home, and climb in.

"Were you the one who was with Summer the night I was hiding out by the beach?" Stella asks as she shuts the door and buckles her seatbelt in the back seat.

I look in the rearview mirror and let a smile spread across my face. I try to look approachable and nice, not wanting to make her feel uncomfortable. "Yes, that was me. It's great to see you again." I glance over my shoulder at her before putting the car in drive and pulling away from the curb. "Who's ready to spend ninety straight minutes watching me fall on my ass?" Summer laughs, and Stella allows herself to chuckle. I count that as a win.

We cross over into Venice and soon arrive at the rink. As we pile out of the car, I take in the scenery. The hills to the east spread across the landscape as far as I can see, and to the west, the ocean is glistening under the high sun. The outdoor rink, decorated specifically in eighties decor and paint schemes, is just ahead, the music echoing out into the parking lot. What an idyllic place to spend a fun afternoon.

"Have either of you been here before?" Summer asks. "I didn't even know this place existed."

"No," I respond, and Stella shakes her head in agreement. We make our way in synchronized steps toward the entrance.

After we have rented our gear and laced up our skates, we head out onto the rink. It takes me a few minutes to get my bearings, and when I do, I glance over at Summer, and she's glaring at me—her arms out in a steading stance, her legs all but shaking as she moves with very little grace across the rink.

"You said you were going to be spending the majority of the time on your ass, Kash." She begins to slip but catches herself. "You lied," she adds through clenched teeth.

I kick my head back and laugh. It's been a while, but I played youth hockey as a child—a lifetime ago—and apparently, wheels and blades aren't too different.

"Well, I haven't been on skates of any kind since I was nine. I guess it's kind of like riding a bike." My wink does little to warm her. I chuckle to myself as she attempts to mix in with a crowd of people with varying degrees of experience. Taking my gaze to the left, I see Stella holding onto the wall, fear and uneasiness etched into her expression. I make a judgment call to head toward Stella and give Summer some space to get her footing. I approach Stella and lean against the wall next to her.

"A little unsure?" I question lightly.

She makes a face as if to say *you think?,* and I respond with a single nod and a small smile, looking out toward the skaters. A gust of wind blows in our direction, causing Stella to gasp and grab the wall tighter, her knuckles turning white.

"I used to play hockey," I tell her. "It was a lifetime ago, but I remember the first time I stepped onto the ice." I move away from the wall and face her. "It wasn't pretty." Stella allows a laugh to escape, and I continue. "But my dad told me that I was always going to be watching from the sidelines if I never stopped being afraid to fall."

I didn't play for long, only two years. Hockey was something for me and my dad to do together, and when he was gone, so was my desire to lace up. Mom tried, for years, to reignite my passion for it, but she couldn't have known that she was attempting to win something that she'd inevitably lose. There was no going back for me, no matter how hard she tried to convince me.

"So, if we don't follow my dad's advice, you might be glued to this wall for eternity." I wink at Stella, extending my hand, hoping she'll take it and ease herself away from the security of the wall. A moment passes before she lets out an exacerbated exhale and takes my hand, shakily moving away from her safety net. "One foot, and then the other," I instruct. "Smooth and steady. Don't try and walk…just glide."

"Easy for you to say," Stella says, her tone brightening a bit.

I shrug my shoulders. "Everything new is hard at first."

Stella and I take thirteen minutes to go around the rink one time, but she's getting better with each passing moment. Once we make it back to where we started, we catch up with Summer, who has also made noticeable improvements.

"Not so bad once you get used to it," Summer admits, smiling now. "Look at you, Stella!"

Summer glides—clumsily—over to us and reaches out her hands, and we all join together for a slow lap around the rink. It crosses my mind that if one of us goes down, we all will, but I don't harp on that unfortunate image. We make our way around a few times before sitting down on a bench just outside the rink for a break. I head to the concession stand to get us fresh lemonade that we sip from soggy paper straws.

It's quiet for a few moments before Stella breaks the silence. "Did you judge me that night? That night you found me?" She's looking at me, not at Summer, and I immediately feel guilty.

I hadn't really engaged with her that night, certainly not in the way Summer did. Summer had been adamant about being the one to approach her, as I stood a good distance away, my arms crossed in a worried stance. I can only imagine the impression I was unknowingly giving off. I wince, my eyebrows knitting together, taking a measured breath and giving myself a moment to gather my thoughts before I respond.

"Absolutely not. I'm sorry if you thought that I was judging you." She takes a sip of her lemonade, her eyes darting in Summer's direction briefly before looking back at me. She nods. "I guess I didn't know what to do, so my reaction was to keep my distance. I guess, subconsciously, I believed Summer would be better at connecting with you than I would. I'm sorry if I made you feel bad."

"You didn't…not really," she says. "I didn't care then." She takes another sip. "I just didn't want you thinking about that now…now that we are hanging out together." She shrugs her shoulders nonchalantly.

I gaze out over the rolling hills, and a tight smile splays my lips. My heart aches for Stella, just as it did for Summer in the past, when I was learning about all she'd been through. But if I've learned anything from Summer, it's that pity isn't welcomed in situations such as these.

"I'd never judge you, Stella." My words come out light, and I hope she believes me.

"Thanks," she mutters quietly.

"Shall we do a few more laps around the rink?" I ask, getting up from the bench and wiggling my eyebrows at them.

Stella and Summer both roll their eyes playfully but rise from the bench to join me.

"Let's do this," Summer says, moving toward the rink tall and proud, like a giraffe that was just born.

The sun has lowered slightly, inching closer to where the sky meets the sea—turning from blue to a mulled tangerine. As we make our way around the rink a few more times, I can't help but feel grateful again for where I am—the place where I was pulled to make my dreams a reality.

"What's this, Daddy?" I ask, holding out a faded picture in my little hand.

"Oh, that's the Pacific Ocean, Kash. You know that. I've shown you these pictures over and over again." Dad ruffles my hair, sending me a warm smile with a wink.

"I know. But tell me again."

He pulls me up onto his lap, my hand still holding onto the faded picture like my life depends on it.

"This right here," Dad says, pointing to the large lifeguard station, "is where your mom and I sat one night after everyone else had left the beach. We watched the waves crashing on the shore and listened to them, too." He shifts me back on his lap slightly, getting a better grip around my waist with one hand while using his other hand to point to different parts of the picture. I sit, listening intently to everything he says. "Do you remember where this picture was taken?" he asks me.

"California," I whisper, staring whimsically at the photo.

"That's right, my boy, California." He gives me a soft smile, and I smile back at him. "It's my favorite place in the world, buddy. Do you know why?"

I shake my head, eager to know the answer.

"Because it's where all my dreams came true." He takes the photo gently from my hands and looks at it as I look at him. "It's where I found your mom, and it's where I found myself." His eyes begin to grow glossy as he takes a breath and whispers the next part. "It's where you came to be." He taps my nose softly.

"California is for dreamers, right, Dad?"

"That's right." Dad places me on the floor in front of him and puts his hands on my shoulders. "You'll see it someday, Kash—you'll see the place where the sun sets, just like in this picture. And when you do, it will change you—in a good way—if you let it."

The orange and purple hue of the horizon startles me, looking exactly like the one in that photo from my childhood memory and the same image I see every night when I look out over my balcony or out the window at Two WhisKEYS. I feel a hand on my shoulder and know it's Summer's.

"You kinda just drifted away from us back there," she utters softly, moving her hand from my back to the ledge of the rink, where it settles on top of mine.

I smile but not in her direction, continuing to face the water. "Sorry."

"No need," she replies. "I get it." She bumps me with her hip, which causes her balance to become off-kilter. I help steady her, and we both laugh before turning back toward the setting sun. "Are you OK?"

"Better than OK." I say the words, and truly mean them. And I know, for certain, that my dad was right—California has changed me…for the better.

"Good," Summer says. "I hate to say it, but we better get going. We have to get Stella back."

"Yeah, let's go find her." I scan the rink and see her heading in our direction.

"Do you mind if I stay for a bit at The Girls Home? I want to talk to Lisa about doing some volunteer work there if I can. Singing or playing guitar or whatever she needs." She shrugs her shoulders, her expression light, hopeful.

"That's such a good idea!"

"I'll just walk home after."

"I can always just swing back and get you."

"Thanks, but it's only a twenty-minute walk. It'll be good for me to get some more steps in." She winks my way as we approach the entrance to the rink, Stella coming up right behind us.

"OK, if you change your mind, you can just text me."

"Sounds good." We take a seat on the bench and begin unlacing our skates.

"You got pretty good, Stella!" I say.

She laughs and rolls her eyes. "I wouldn't say *good*."

"We both *improved*," Summer adds, also with a laugh.

"Let's come back again soon," I say to both of them.

Stella looks at me like a deer in headlights, and the expression startles me. I wonder if I said something wrong. I eye Summer, whose expression is calm and at ease. "He's being serious," she explains, knowing exactly what to say.

Stella smiles shyly, tucking a stray hair behind her ear. "OK. If you guys want to."

"Absolutely," Summer and I say in unison.

We walk back to my truck, knowing for sure that we'll be sore in places we didn't know existed tomorrow.

***

Dinner is made, and it's staying warm in the oven by the time Summer arrives back home over an hour later. Roast chicken and pan-fried summer vegetables with feta mixed in. Feta is the way to Summer's heart. She smiles at me as she walks through the door and places her bag on the floor.

"It smells delicious in here!" she boasts as I wipe my hands on a dish towel and beam at her.

"Hopefully, it tastes just as good," I laugh.

"Are you as sore as I am?" Summer chuckles, grabbing a glass from the cabinet and filling it with water. She places her glass on the table and stretches and moans at the pain. "If I already feel this sore, what's tomorrow going to feel like?"

I laugh. "Yeah, roller skating is no joke. There's a spot on my hamstring that hurts, and I honestly didn't know that a muscle existed there."

"Seriously, we're never doing that again." We laugh, and I fill our plates with the food and bring them to the table.

Summer takes a bite and moans in delight. "Why is warm feta so good? It should be illegal." I shake my head and smile, looking down at my plate. "What?" she asks, her mouth full.

"Nothing. I just love how you love feta."

She covers her full mouth with her hand and laughs. We eat for a few minutes without talking, just enjoying the meal and the lull of the jazz music playing in the background.

"I was talking to Janie yesterday," Summer starts, and I look at her with intention, wiping my mouth with my napkin. Summer pulls a piece of chicken off the leg with two fingers, placing it in her mouth before continuing. "She was asking how my songwriting has been going. And if I'd made any progress with producers picking up my songs at open mic nights and stuff."

"What did you say?"

She thinks for a moment. "I told her that I'm really at a standstill. I told her I haven't been able to write lyrics for a while now."

"Do you think you've been working too much at the bar?" I ask. "Do you want to take some time to focus on songwriting? That is your dream, right?"

She stares at me intently, and I'm curious about what she's thinking. Just like I always am. She looks down at her plate. "By the end of my session with her, she had me believing that I can't write because I'm not hurting anymore."

My eyes widen, and I lean over the table. "Wow. That is an interesting perspective. How do you feel about that?"

"It's tough to figure out. I guess it's good and bad. If that's true, then it means I'm doing well, but it also means my creative outlet might have dried up. It means I'll have to work harder to get inspired." I nod and let her go on. "I talked to Lisa just now when I dropped Stella off, you know? About volunteering there to sing and play instruments with the girls. And she asked if I ever considered being a musical therapist."

"Not going to lie; I don't know much about that career, but that sounds like it might be a good fit for you."

Summer smiles shyly and moves the vegetables around on her plate. "She told me a little bit about it and gave me the business card of someone she knows who teaches courses on it." She reaches down into her bag and pulls out the card, handing it over to me across the table.

I look at it, turning it over to read both sides. "This is really interesting, Summer. What do you think? I don't want you to give up dreams, but it sounds like something meaningful to consider, no?"

"That's exactly the word. *Meaningful,*" she says, pointing at me. "I've always wanted to make a difference. I just didn't know how. I thought maybe my words, my songs, could do that. And maybe they still can, if a muse ever brings poetic lyrics back to my brain. It just isn't happening right now. Even when I try." She's talking fast now, and I listen, focusing on every word. "Doesn't hurt to consider it, I don't think."

"I don't think so either. Why don't you take a few days off from the bar next week and do some research? Make some phone calls?" I try to encourage her.

"I think I will do that." Her smile is warm, and the excitement in her eyes thrills me. "I'm going to start visiting the girls two mornings a week during the summer and then see how it goes from there. That may give me a little taste of what a job in that field would entail."

"That sounds like a great plan!"

"You don't mind if I take some time away from the bar?"

"Absolutely not. We have plenty of help, and you know Finn and Diego—even Jimmy—will help if we need them." I reach my hand over the table and place it on top of hers. "I told you that the bar is just as much yours as it is mine. But you taking some time to explore a possible new passion? That's important. And I fully support it."

"Thank you, Kash. So much." Summer jumps up from the table and comes to me, bending down and wrapping her arms around my neck. I can feel her warmth, which stirs a warmth in me. I push the longing away, rubbing her back like the friend I need to be. "You are the best."

I smile at her. "No, you are."

My admiration of Summer was not a slow-burning, unexplainable series of events. However, I wouldn't explain it as instantaneous, either. It's difficult for me to put into words my feelings for Summer. The feelings don't seem to make any sense; they are emotions I have never experienced before. When I try to put my feelings into words, I can't. I struggle to make them tangible. I have a hard time understanding it myself, much less explaining it to someone else. All I know is that the women I dated before I met Summer were shallow—one-dimensional—and the rate at which I'd become disinterested alarmed me.

I blamed my past…my fear of getting too close to someone and then losing them. It made sense, having watched my mom suffer such a huge loss in her life. But I understood the pain I experienced from losing my father—that was my experience. Seeing my mom struggle to cope, losing the love of her life…I couldn't grasp the severity of it because it wasn't my life. It was a different kind of relationship. But even though I didn't fully understand her pain, I was still fearful of loving and losing, for many years.

Eventually, that reasoning didn't feel real anymore. It didn't feel believable. It's almost as if I used it as an excuse for not connecting with them. But the truth is that I just wasn't able to see myself with any of those women.

As I've grown into myself and have accepted my loss, the reality of my dating life has become crystal clear. Now I know what I want—and what I don't want.

I knew Summer had depth the moment she walked into Sullivan's that first night I met her. I don't know why or how I sensed it, but I did. I was drawn to her, but at the time, it didn't feel like love or even lust. It was something I couldn't—and still can't—explain.

Our friendship blossomed like a flower as we nurtured it with the utmost care. And as she slowly let me in, I was able to bear witness to all the layers of Summer James.

Silas told me one night before I left Austin, "You can't save her, man."

I glared at him, frustrated with his words. Save her? She didn't need saving. I knew that with 100 percent certainty because I was watching her save herself, right in front of my eyes. But one thing I knew then (and still know now) is that there is no rushing with her. It's not a game to be played and won. My feelings for her are the closest I have come to love. I've admired her strength, and it's only grown as time has inched by.

It's hard to always know if you are getting to know an authentic version of a person. But I consider myself blessed to be able to understand Summer the way I do and know her so intimately, always seeing her for who she is. Every single layer.

I know her like the back of my hand, and learning her has been the most amazing adventure. There's a line on her face that creases when she's planning out the order of her words before she says them.

There's a tone in her voice that elevates when she can't contain her excitement.

The sound and depth of her sighs tell me exactly how she is feeling.

Her strength.

Her heart.

How lucky am I to know her? The truth of it is not lost on me.

CHAPTER 17

Summer

JUNE

I DON'T KNOW WHEN *it happened—when the bottle went from slim and made of glass to wide and plastic with a thick handle, but as Dad makes his way into the kitchen through the dented screen door that leads in and out—to and from our backyard—I notice the large plastic bottle hanging from his limp fingers, only two inches of liquid sloshing around at the bottom.*

There's hot rage emanating from his pores as he stumbles into the kitchen, his feet shuffling on the faded linoleum floor.

He hiccups.

I hold my breath.

The stool beneath my feet suddenly feels unsteady as my knees tremble, my upper body leaning over the sink to clean the crusty plates Dad and Momma have left around the house.

My senses are on high alert as I feel Dad stalk up behind me. The words that spew from his mouth are words I hear all too often:

You're worthless.

You're a waste of space.

I wish you were never born.

Words that once hurt me but now can slide off my armored heart like rain on a window.

The words—those I can shake.

But not the fist.

So, I'm gone—somewhere else in mind where the breeze blows, and waves crash along the shore, and gulls screech overhead. I'm gone to where my heart can feel joy, even for a moment—a moment that isn't real, but it feels like it is, and for now, that's enough. This is how I save myself.

Kash places a brand-new handle of vodka up on the shelf behind the open ones. The windows at the front of the bar are wide open, letting in the smell of brine and the sounds of the shore.

As real as can be…right at my fingertips.

I realize I haven't heard a thing Kash has said.

"Hmm?" I manage to utter.

"You weren't listening, were you?" he asks without judgment, a dimpled smile brightening his face.

I look at him apologetically. "Lost in a daydr—actually, a day…nightmare might be a better word for it." I let out a hefty sigh and place my elbows on the bar.

"Old memories?" Kash asks, ripping open another box of miscellaneous items that need to find their homes behind the bar.

"Yeah," I say, holding on to some heaviness. "Under the right circumstances, a glance at a handle of alcohol can do that to me." I place my forehead down on the bar and try to shake the feelings brewing inside. I sense Kash walking away from the task at hand and making his way over to me on the other side of the bar.

When he reaches me, he gives my back a gentle rub. "Being a bartender must really suck, then." He tries to make me smile, and it works—a little. "It's been a while, hasn't it?" he says softly, calming my nerves. My skin reacts to his touch, tingling and warming, my heart picking up speed.

I lift my head and give a small nod. "They flash in sometimes—the memories—but it's brief, little snippets that I can acknowledge without spiraling into darkness. But, I guess, sometimes they take me a bit too far. Like just now." I turn my body toward Kash, my shoulders slumping. "But I have been recalling happy memories, too." My tone is sprinkled with hope.

Kash smiles. "Do you want to talk about it? The good or the not-so-good memories?"

My heart warms a degree—the gratuitous feeling spreading through my bones. I wonder how many times I've relived a traumatic moment with Kash's help. It's more than I can count. He's been there—every time I have needed him—his calm spirit and gentle encouragement helping me through. In an effort to give more attention and energy to the happy moments, I beam a smile at Kash. "Remember that time you tried to t—"

He shakes his head and throws it back, letting out a hardy laugh, cutting me off and finishing my sentence, "Teach you how to surf?"

Our eyes lock, and the laughter erupts deep down in my belly.

"Why are you singing?" I ask Kash as he floats atop his surfboard right next to me. I'm on a borrowed board that looks massive underneath me. He's so close, and I have no idea how I am ever going to peel myself away from the security he gives me and actually ride a wave in.

"You look terrified," he says, winking at me. "Figured I could soothe your nerves a bit." He glances briefly at my hands, and I draw my eyes

down to them—they're clutching the side of the board with all the strength they can manage, and my knuckles have turned a ghostly white.

"I'm not scared," I respond unconvincingly.

"Ok, big shot," Kash says endearingly, getting into position on the board. "Lay down then, and get ready, just like we practiced on the sand."

I take a deep breath and shakily lift my legs out of the water and onto the board, lying on my stomach. Kash gives me a single nod, one of encouragement, and I return the gesture with a nervous smile.

"Here comes a good one, Summer. Go for it. I'll be right next to you." Kash glances back over his shoulder, and I do the same, not really knowing what I'm looking for but trying to follow Kash's lead. "Go, go, go!" he yells, and I watch him paddle his arms. I do the same, but with less grace and more anxiety. He jumps up and begins to cruise toward shore. I cruise as well—contently on my stomach. I miss the ride—the wave curling under me and on its merry way, leaving me in the dust. But I remain on my stomach, letting the following waves push me—slowly—into shore where Kash is standing next to Finn.

I struggle off the board and onto the rough shoreline, a wave almost knocking me under as I squirm to pull my bathing suit strap up. I huff a dramatic breath and manage to get myself and the board up and out of the wet sand. "Kash, I said I didn't want you to invite anyone else. No one needs to see me learn how to do this," I say, annoyed.

"Oh, I was here on my own accord, Summer," Finn says with a look of pure pleasure on his face. "And learn how to do what exactly? Boogie board like a toddler on four different waves?" His tone is jovial and good-natured, but I glare at him for a moment, feeling a bit embarrassed. Kash's eyes widen, but I can see the effort he's exerting trying to stifle a laugh. I glance out at the water and envision the sight the two of them must have seen as I made my way to shore, and I lose it. I glance back at the two of them, the three of us laughing so joyously that my insides

hurt, and my ears ring with the sound of wheezing laughter. We all fall onto the sand and take deep breaths, gasping for air between laughs.

"I think I'll stick to what I'm best at: admiring the ocean from right here on the sand," I say with a sigh.

"You can always try again," Kash adds, hopeful.

"Isn't that the truth," I respond, not taking my eyes off the waves.

"That was so funny, Summer," Kash says, laughing. "Little disappointed you never gave it another go." He winks at me, and I shake my head and glance down at my hands.

"Surfing's not my thing." I shrug my shoulders and hope I don't sound like a quitter, but surfing *really* just isn't my thing. "But the laughs made it all worth it."

The look on Kash's face warms. "There was a time, not too long ago, when you didn't know if you would ever be able to let go and just laugh wholeheartedly. And now look."

I reach out and place my hand atop his. The emotions his words provoked in me make it hard to gather my thoughts. *Thank you.* I mouth the words because that's all I can manage, but I'm confident Kash knows I mean it.

"I'm playing tonight. Did I tell you that?" Kash asks me as he moves behind the bar to finish unpacking the inventory.

"No, but that's great. More than one song this time?" I ask, smiling. Kash loves to jump in for songs with Finn and Diego, but he hasn't been playing as much as he used to, and it makes me a little sad. The dream was for him to own the bar AND play at it. The first part of the dream seems to be taking precedence as of late, and I've missed seeing him up there, playing his heart out.

He looks thoughtfully at me. "I'm playing a few songs." He gives me a nod while cleaning up the empty boxes. "A few new covers

I've been working on," he says, adding a wink. The flop in my stomach is a welcome surprise—a splinter of a giddy feeling I've always denied the chance to break through—a desperate attempt to try and protect myself. I steady my breathing, deciding not to think too much about the little butterfly knocking around on my insides.

———

After leaving the bar earlier to take a midday break, I went to see Stella for a bit. We sat outside under the lanai, chatting and drawing. I had brought ingredients to make sweet tea, attempting to make it like my dear friend Barb does back in Austin. Stella had puckered her lips at the first taste, the sweetness overpowering her mouth. We both laughed as I added more tea to the glasses in an attempt to mellow out the sugary taste. The visit was a good distraction from my racing thoughts this morning, and I was thrilled to see Stella in good spirits, smiling and joking with me.

Now, I'm heading back to Two WhisKEYS. The air outside has taken a turn; the weather is predicted to bring in some much-needed rain to the area. The drought has caused the grass to become brittle, and the hills behind Santa Monica look as if they're begging for a drink. As I walk into the bar this afternoon, clouds have cascaded the skies, and a thin layer of fog sprawls out over the ocean. I inhale the humid air and pull it all the way into my lungs, cleansing my insides. It's time to prepare for the night.

When the evening is in full swing, the bar is beyond crowded, and there are three of us serving drinks: Nel and I—like always—and Finn has joined us out of necessity. Though we're always busy, tonight is extra busy. The wait for a table is over an hour, and the bar is packed three rows deep. Nel, Finn, and I are high-fiving, hip-checking, and ringing the bell for solid tips, and the energy surrounding us is palpable. Kash hasn't performed a whole set in a long time, and maybe that's led to the steady increase of people coming in through the door.

The locals love Kash. They adore him, really. Tonight, he's been up there on the piano, dueling with Diego, and the crowd has been so loud, my ears are ringing. But I love it. I love this place. I snap a picture of Kash up there performing and send the photo in a group text to Maverick, Silvia, Farrah, and Silas. **Look at him go!** I say in the message.

"Diego is going to take a quick break," Kash announces into the microphone. "Let's give him a round of applause." The crowd cheers as Diego does a quick, shy bow and hops down the risers, skipping steps as he goes. He heads into the back, most likely to catch his breath, towel off, and chat with the cooks. "Don't hate me," Kash says playfully to the audience. "But I'm going to take the energy down just a bit with a ballad." The crowd doesn't boo; they yell even louder, thrilled to have Kash perform a solo, I'm sure. I know I am. "But don't worry. Once Diego takes a breather, we'll be back with all the energy, taking your requests." He adjusts his microphone and shifts on his bench. He glances at the bar and scans it, looking for me, I'm sure. When our eyes meet, he flashes me the smile I love. The one that shows his dimple, the one that melts me. "I dedicate this song to someone very special in my life. I hope she likes it."

He keeps his eye on me, and it feels like my stomach has fallen to the farthest reaches of my body. The flutter of my heart in my chest is dizzying. Nel gives me a light pinch on the hip, but I don't even turn to look at her. I can't. My eyes are set on the stage.

The initial notes begin, and my body freezes at the sheer beauty they produce, erupting feelings inside that surprise me. I glance around the bar, and all eyes are on Kash as he takes the tone down from *rowdy* to utterly peaceful in four seconds with his magical fingers. I inch my way to the end of the bar, as far left as I can go, attempting to get as close to the stage as possible.

This song.

He hasn't started singing yet, but I know what it is. "Make You Feel My Love" by Adele.

He sings the first line, and his beautiful voice, raw and smooth, cuts through the room with ease and brings goosebumps to my arms. I glance down the bar for a quick second, wide-eyed, with my mouth partially agape. There isn't a single person waiting for a drink. Everyone who's sitting at the bar is turned toward the stage, watching and listening in complete awe. I turn my head back to the stage and listen to the lyrics. The melodious sounds coming from the keys invite tears to my eyes. Kash's hair is up in a bun, pulled away from his face, which is speckled with beads of sweat, his cheeks flushed with color. His eyes close as he sings, feeling the song deep in his bones like he always does.

But this time, it's different.

It's like with every word he sings, he's speaking directly to me. It's as if the lyrics were written specifically for him to sing to me.

The song is about to end, and I feel like time has stopped. I can't hear anything except the sounds of the instruments and Kash's voice. I'm in such a trance that it's as if we are the only two people in the bar—Kash and me. My heart feels light, as if I could float right off the ground. My hands are shaking, and I feel unsteady, as if the floor has dropped out from underneath me. When it's over, Kash takes a bow, and the crowd stands, clapping and screaming for him. His voice moved everyone, not just me. But it was more than his voice that touched every fiber of my soul. It was the words he was dedicating to me.

Me? Am I dreaming this right now? I suddenly need air, and lots of it.

"I'll be right back," I say to Nel as I run off, not giving her a chance to stop me. I know the crowd will begin to gather at the bar, but I just need one second to bring some fresh air into my lungs. My chest feels so tight. I walk swiftly out the front door, and the heavy sea air hits me, causing me to gasp and suck it in fast. I feel an emotion coming to the surface. It's a good emotion, but the overwhelming nature of it is unsettling, and my fight or flight senses are triggered, even though I know I don't need them to be. It's just a habit, a learned response. My breaths are coming in short, rapid bursts, which is a sign of a feeling I am all too aware of: fear. My body is trying to protect me. So, though a positive emotion is present, my mind's natural reaction is to be frightened. I sit down on the curb and try to take slow, steady breaths, but the thick air makes it hard to breath deep. Even the air feels unsteady; I can feel the storm brewing outside, and also inside of me.

I start to think about leaving, going to a place where no one can find me, not to run away, just to think. Clear my head. Make it all make sense. I'm afraid of everything I'm feeling right now. But an equally big part of me wants to open the door and let all of Kash in. Right into my heart.

The door to the bar opens, and before I see who's coming out, I know. I know it's him, and my stomach churns with anticipation. *What should I say? How do I react?*

I get up from the curb where I'm sitting, my hands on my hips. I begin to pace, fighting the urge to run, to save myself from the discomfort I'm feeling. I know running won't help. But the fear is getting to me. I'm torn between staying exactly where we are in our relationship, in this state of utter limbo, and sharing everything that's on my mind, all my feelings out on the table. This fight within my own head is driving me mad, and I begin to walk swiftly in the direction of the water. I try to stop myself. I try to convince myself to turn back, to go the other way—into Kash's arms. But fear wins.

"Summer…," Kash's voice fades into the thick air as he follows behind me, his footsteps close at my heels.

I reach the edge of the pier, my lungs tight and screaming for relief as I suck in every last bit of heavy air surrounding me. Then I feel it, the first drop falling from the sky, landing heavily on my face like the tears I want to shed. My insides rattle with the wind blowing forcefully off the water.

"I don't deserve you!" I shout at him over the sounds of the storm, my voice breaking as my emotions erupt, my soul aching for him but feeling completely unworthy.

His face looks pained, like he's hurting for me. "How can you say that?" His words are loud over the wind, but as they come out, they are strained, like it took all his effort to get them out. It's as if he is gutted. "It's always been you, Summer." He sounds defeated, as if he's losing me, watching me drift away with the storm.

I take a breath, quick and ragged, as the skies open up and drench us with sheets of water. The rain invites my tears to finally come, and with them, sobs escape me, and I'm unable to control it. But I don't have any more time to grieve my inability to let him in because in a millisecond, Kash is directly in front of me. There isn't any space between us. His wet hands gently grab my jaw, our noses touch, and his eyes look into mine. Water streams down both of our faces, our hair clinging to our skin, our chests rising and falling in exasperated bursts.

"Let me in, Summer." His words are desperate; his eyes are begging.

I open my mouth to speak, but I'm unable. Kash's lips crash into mine, and everything inside me lightens—the weight of every single trauma, every ache—it's all numbed by his embrace, and I melt. My arms rise up to his neck and wrap around it. I reach up on the balls of my feet, desperately attempting to get closer to him. Kash feels me relent and moves his hands to wrap them around my waist, lifting me off the ground, as the storm rages around us. I wrap my legs around him, and we continue to kiss hungrily as if pulling apart would be the end for us.

I am his lifeline, and he is mine.

The downpour was brief, and as it settles into a light drizzle, we pull away from each other and look up at the dark, starless sky. A comfort settles within me—not one that comes from the vast expanse of darkness, but from the arms wrapped around me.

<hr>

We stay up much too late, sitting on the balcony sipping stale, room-temperature champagne that we found abandoned in a kitchen cabinet after closing up the bar. "To celebrate," Kash says with a grin as my skin ignites with a warm sensation—goosebumps spreading to places I didn't know they could appear, like my eyebrows and my forehead. I feel tears brimming in my eyes, and my huge smile is causing an ache in my jaw that I welcome happily.

We aren't sitting on our normal chairs, but rather, we're squished on the tiny wicker loveseat—an air of endearing awkwardness settles in the crevices our limbs have formed.

Is this real? Or am I dreaming? It feels strange for Kash to be holding me in this way. Something pulls at the part of my brain that wants to deny me the luxury of being loved, that feels worthy of love, making me second guess this new reality.

But his fingers gently caress my bare arm, causing very real chills to tickle my spine, and I allow the sensation. He smells like the bar, mixed with the sweet smell of the fresh rain that soaked his long hair while we stood together on the pier.

Our conversation comes in waves of whispers, audible laughter, comfortable silence, and the soft lull of Kash singing into my hair.

"So, you're ready to date me?" he asks with a small chuckle.

I smile, though he can't see the gesture because of how we're sitting. The word *date* doesn't seem like it fits our situation—it sounds cheap and juvenile. Memories of the dates I've been on in Santa Monica come flooding back. My night out with Jesse, who talked about himself all night, showing me his recent headshots that he was using for auditions in LA. Or the guy named Aiden, who asked me out at the bar while I was working. He was nice but slightly pushy, and that kind of personality trait would never mesh well with mine. I know myself well enough that I didn't let that one go too far, or for too long. Lessons learned long ago that when your instincts are telling you something—good or bad—you better listen to them.

I stare out the barred windows of my ground-floor apartment, scanning the street for signs of him. He said he'd be here an hour ago. I let out a huff—toward no one but my pathetic self—back to waiting for someone to follow through on their promises to me. I glance at my clock on my microwave, which hasn't worked in months. The club money I earn is going to more pertinent things as of late—things I have deemed more important than a microwave.

Food.

Clothes.

Drugs.

I met Lex at one of my friend Piper's parties. I'm not completely convinced that Lex is his real name, but I never found a good enough reason to question him. He's tall and broad, his frame overpowering me, and much to my dismay, he reminds me of my father. The way he slurs his speech when he drinks, the way his footsteps sound when he's angry…the way he attempts to erase his wrongs with saccharine sweet words.

I stop scanning the street and look up at the sky out the window and see the moon, crescent in shape, surrounded by the stars. I find the brightest one and give it a soft smile. I wonder how many other people are looking at the same stars right now. I wonder who else is desperate for comfort. It can't just be me. Can it? The loneliness of it all settles into my heart, causing an insufferable ache that I can never seem to mend. I look down at the floor, my shoulders slump in defeat.

An aggressively loud pounding on my mangled and dented apartment door rattles me to my core. He's here…finally. But by the tone of the knock, I'm not so sure I want to let him in now. I shuffle to the door, my breath caught in my throat. I unlock the deadbolt quickly and pull the door open to see a disheveled Lex on the other side of the threshold. His hair is a mess, his knuckles—red and raw. The mark under his right eye is sure to begin swelling at any moment. My shoulders slump as I open the door wider, allowing him to stumble in, almost knocking me off my feet. He heads directly to the couch.

"You're an hour late." My voice comes out assertive, and it surprises me. "What the hell happened to you?" I stare at him, realizing it doesn't matter one bit how late he is when he's in this condition.

"Ugh, Summer," he groans with annoyance. "Chill out. Don't be such a bitch." He covers his face with his arm. "Get me an ice pack."

I glare at him, anger burning my insides. When I don't answer right away, he removes his arm, looking at me impatiently. "Please," he adds condescendingly, hoping—I'm sure—that the word alone will appease me. Against my better judgment, it does.

I walk to the freezer and take out the only ice pack, the one I have for occasions such as these. As I reach for it, my own yellowing bruise on my forearm seems to scream at me. I toss the ice pack on his lap and land on the couch next to him. I sit back against the sagging, flat cushion and stare at one spot on the wall until a single tear makes a track down my face.

Lex sees it. "Oh, Summer, come here. I'm sorry," he says, putting his arm over my shoulder. But I know he doesn't mean it.

He caresses my hair indifferently for a few moments before he stills completely, his snores growing loud in my ear.

I get up to put the ice pack back in the freezer. I'm sure I'll need it soon, and I'll want it to be ready. I head to my bedroom, grabbing one of Piper's trusty pills from under my pillow. I swallow it dry and lie staring at the ceiling until sleep washes over me in restless waves.

I turn my smile so Kash can see it. "I'm more than ready to be with you, Kash."

CHAPTER 18

Summer

JULY

"**S**TOP BITING YOUR NAILS," Kash says, glancing over at me from the driver's side, a sweet smirk pulling on his lips.

I abruptly pull my hand from my mouth and roll my eyes, letting out an annoyed sigh. "Well, where are we going?" I ask, a nervousness evident in my voice.

It's been three weeks since Kash and I braved the storm as we embraced on the pier that night—the storm that put an end to the California drought and an end to my drought of a loveless life. Three weeks of undeniable peace. Three weeks of butterflies in my stomach and getting to know each other on a whole new level as we walk this delicate line that we've willingly crossed—all the while hand-holding…and heart-holding, too, I guess.

"It's just a leisurely day in LA," he says, winking.

"There's no such thing," I reply, letting a little more playfulness come out. A day in LA will not be leisurely—at least, I can only assume this to be true from my other excursions into the city. But I trust Kash, so I relax my shoulders against the back of the passenger's seat and glance out the window at the dry brush passing by in brown and green blurbs.

Kash begins to hum along to the song, and I open my mouth to sing the lyrics to "Landslide" by Fleetwood Mac. I get one whispered line out before I notice that I'm holding my breath for a moment, the lyrics seeping into my soul and bringing up a memory that isn't jarring but rather a simple reminder of the life I left behind.

"Can you turn the music down?" Claire says, staring at her reflection in the mirror, brushing her golden strands just so. "I hate this song." The last part comes out in hushed annoyance as she pretends not to want to be heard, but in reality, she wants me to know that she despises me and everything I do.

I roll my eyes to myself and turn down the volume knob on the stereo that rests on top of my desk. "You could put headphones in, you know," she says, disgusted.

I don't respond. I'd rather just pretend that she isn't in the room. I force myself to just focus on the song and the melody. It reminds me of Momma. I picture her smiling, the sun glistening off her hair in the backyard while this song plays through the open kitchen window. It's easier to imagine her like that instead of being buried under soil and grass. I wipe the lone tear discreetly from my cheek before abruptly turning the music off and storming out of the room I share with Claire. To where? I don't know. Nowhere feels like home in this house. I only feel a reprieve when everyone in the house is asleep and I can creep out onto the roof to be with the stars.

I roll the window down halfway and feel the wind between the strands of my hair, and I close my eyes. I can almost feel Kash smile in my direction, and my mouth turns slightly up at the feeling of his gaze upon me. His hand gently squeezes my knee as the song echoes around us. The unsavory feeling of this memory lingers in my mind, threatening to take me from the moment, but I don't let it steal my peace and serenity completely.

I can't.

I won't.

But I can't get rid of it completely—I can't ignore it. Acknowledging the times before *this* has been part of my healing. Acknowledging and releasing the past has allowed the heaviness to fall from my shoulders. But it's been an upward battle, one that has proven to be worth it over the last year. I place my hand over Kash's and let myself just *be*.

I allow the song to form a new kind of memory.

———

I take a seat on a plush couch that rests against the glass wall of the rooftop bar we decided to try. I'm giddy with an excitement that I can't quite get a handle on. A shiver runs through my body even though it's ninety degrees. This place is beautiful—the potted plants and splashes of color on all the furniture feel so warm and inviting. Hollywood stretches out in all directions below us, the white sign displayed on the mountaintop just to my left. I glance toward the bar where Kash is grabbing us some drinks—a glass of rosé for me and a gin gimlet for himself. He begins heading back to our table, and we make eye contact. He flashes a genuine smile, creating creases next to his eyes—a look that melts me to a puddle. His biceps are flexed, showing off his tattoos, as he carries both our drinks and takes a seat next to me. He sets the drinks down on the table and reaches up to put his hair in a bun. "It's freaking hot," he says.

I smile and pick up my glass. "Cheers," I say. "To us."

"To me and you," he replies, our glasses clinking together.

Kash pulls his sunglasses down to shield his eyes from the bright midday sun and relaxes into his plush seat. For several minutes, we sit in comfortable silence. I close my eyes and tilt my head toward the sun, letting its rays warm my face. It feels good. Kash and I break the silence at the same moment.

"Wait until you—" he says, but he stops when he hears me talking at the same time.

"I really want to do something special for—oh, sorry, you go first," I say.

He smiles, showing me his dimple and his white teeth. "No, yours seems important. You go."

I smile back at him and begin again. "It's Stella's birthday next week. Maybe we can take her out to do something fun and then head to Jimmy's for dinner. She loves Mexican food."

Kash doesn't say anything at first. He just looks as if he's admiring me, which causes me to blush, and I nervously tuck a loose strand of hair behind my ear.

"You are something else," he says, taking a sip from his tumbler.

Giving him a questioning look, I ask, "What?"

"You are just so thoughtful. I love how you have taken Stella under your wing. I'm sure she really appreciates it."

I shrug my shoulders. "I really like her. I don't know if it's because we have similar stories…similar types of loss, but it comforts me to know I can be there for her. Like I wish someone had been there for me."

Kash nods. "I know," he says quietly. "And you're definitely doing that."

"I'm happy to do it. Now, what were you going to say?" I ask, taking a sip of my drink that's now covered in condensation from the heat.

He beams again. "Oh…yeah, that. I was just going to say—wait until you see where we are headed after this. You're going to love it."

"There's more?" I ask through a laugh. "We already sat on the Friends couch and did a million other touristy things this morning."

Kash shakes his head. "Those are all things we should've already done since we moved here, but we haven't gotten around to."

"So, are you going to tell me? Or…," I trail off, looking at him with anticipation.

He looks at me as if he's contemplating what to do next, mischief playing on his face. "Drink up," he says. "Let's go now. I can't wait."

A flutter of excitement jumps around my insides as I take a few hurried sips, eager to get to where we are going.

Kash parks the truck in a metered spot, and I look around, wondering where we are. I spot a sign up ahead, *Griffith Observatory*, with an arrow pointing in a direction my eyes follow. Up ahead is a long path surrounded by green grass. The path leads to an enormous snow white building with three dome shapes on top with a flat roof in between. I try to take in the surroundings, my brows furrowing in wonder. When my eyes meet Kash's, he beams, his left hand on the door handle.

"You ready to *really* see the stars, Summer?"

CHAPTER 19

Kash

THE SUN IS JUST starting to set—exactly how I imagined this part of our day going. I want Summer to see the stars more clearly than she ever has before. Growing up, the stars were her only reprieve from the life that broke her. Allowing her to connect with them on an entirely new level was my motivation in bringing her here.

She walks next to me, her hand in mine, and I can tell she's excited and also a bit surprised. As we make our way down the path toward the building, I decide that it doesn't look like a building that belongs in Los Angeles. It seems otherworldly and out of place. I'm thankful to be experiencing it for the first time with Summer.

"It takes my breath away," she says, seemingly to herself. I agree with her, but mostly because of the excitement of what's waiting for us inside the building. I know, deep in my bones, that this will mean something to her.

We walk in stride, Summer picking up her pace in anticipation, I assume.

Inside, we explore the exhibits, learning about space and the universe. We learn about tides and moon phases, eclipses, and star paths. Summer absorbs it all; each exhibit we enter seems to bring her a new sense of peace. Watching her experience the different rooms, the photographs, the lighting, and the information—it all amazes me.

"Thank you…so much," she says, turning toward me and taking both my hands in hers. Her eyes have a sparkle in them, a glimmer that's always there, but right now, it's shining a bit brighter. Her cheeks are flushed. She goes up on her tippy toes, and I instinctively lower my head to reach hers. Our noses touch, and she closes her eyes, sighing softly before placing a gentle kiss on the corner of my mouth. She wraps her arms around my waist and settles her head on my chest. We stand there, embracing lovingly, in the middle of the moon exhibit, as droves of people pass us on either side. But it feels as if it's only the two of us here.

"Are you ready to go outside?" I whisper into her hair.

Summer nods, a euphoric smile on her face. I take her hand and lead her as we follow the signs to the terrace outside. Once we step out into the thick open air, we head toward the edge of the balcony to look out over the cityscape. We've been here almost two hours, and since our arrival, the sun has set completely, and darkness has taken over the night sky—darkness amidst the city lights. Los Angeles is aglow with the awakening of nightlife, and the expanse of space that's visible up here makes it hard to feel the ground beneath my feet.

Summer leans over the edge of the wall and looks down and then up at me. "I feel like Jasmine. I don't know why." She laughs playfully. "I feel like Aladdin is going to come floating by on his magic carpet and take me for a ride."

I raise my eyebrows and smile before I start singing "A Whole New World," and she joins in singing Jasmine's part. We start to dance, and I twirl her around as we sing, and a little audience gathers. I give her a final twirl and pull her into me, her back against my chest. I rest my chin on her head, and we gaze out into the night again. The city smog is lit up from the lights. I feel Summer's head tilt up higher into the sky.

"I can't really see the stars," she says, a little disappointed.

"Let's find a telescope," I say, guiding her around the terrace to locate an unoccupied one. We walk for a minute, finding one located just past an archway. I adjust it a bit and invite Summer to have the first look. She smiles, takes it in her hand, and places her eye on the lens. It's silent for a moment, as if time is suspended. I gather air into my lungs and hold it there, my cheeks filled to the brim.

A few moments later, she pulls away and turns to me, her eyes wet with emotion.

"Are you ok?" I ask, smiling.

I used to sit on the roof of my borrowed home and talk to the stars at night. Her words about the past float into my mind.

A sob escapes her mouth, and she opens it as if she wants to say something, but her lips start to quiver. I move my body closer to hers and pull her into me, rocking her back and forth. I look up at the sky, recalling a time in Austin when Summer and I had laid on a blanket, staring at the stars. We figured out that we both used the brightest star to connect to the love we'd lost long ago—her mom and my dad. As she pointed up to her star, her finger ever so slightly brushed against mine, letting me know that she appreciated the bond that was forming between the two of us.

Recalling this moment now reminds me of the love I have for her. It reminds me of how it started, where it began to flourish and grow into something that couldn't be tamed. That was the first time I had envisioned myself being able to love someone wholly, having never been able to imagine it until that moment with Summer beneath the stars. Up until then, I'd been fearful. Afraid to love and lose. Afraid to end up like my mother, who had loved and lost so heartbreakingly.

When I bared my soul to Summer, I told her that I wasn't afraid. And I was being honest. Because I wasn't scared of what had happened to my mom anymore, not in the slightest. I was most afraid of never having Summer, never getting to love her the way I longed to, just as I'd confessed. There is nothing to fear now. I need to be sure she understands the depths of how I feel. I pull her gently away from my body, and with my thumb and forefinger, I tilt her chin up so her gaze can meet mine.

"Summer, I need you to hear me, loud and clear." Deep breath. "I know this is an emotional and moving experience for you. At least that's what I assumed it would be when I decided to bring you here. Seeing the stars, your safety net, so clearly, is both beautiful and heart-wrenching, I'm sure." Another deep breath. I'm looking right into her eyes, and she's looking, unblinking, into mine. "I want this to be a moment you won't forget. A moment in time that heals you, even if it's a small, tiny piece." She wipes her tears, takes her own deep breath, and allows a smile to break through with a single nod of her head. I place both my hands on her cheeks and move my face just slightly closer to hers. "I love you, Summer. From here on this earth to where the stars burn." My voice is low as I look deeply into her eyes, making sure she hears every bit of truth. Making sure she feels it. "I love you with everything I am."

She begins to cry, and I guide her head to my chest, smoothing her hair and desperate to soothe what aches in her soul.

CHAPTER 20

Summer

I SLAM MY LOCKER *shut and begin making my way to the cafeteria. There's no one waiting for me there, this much I know, not after the weekend I just had. A weekend that ruined me. Meg's mad at me because I made her leave her car at the party because she was drunk. And Dan is livid at me because he found out (through photographic evidence that I can't deny) that I made out with a random guy named Zack. He's done with me, and I really can't blame him. I'm not even going to attempt to mend that relationship.*

I cross over the threshold into the lunchroom, and the buzz of social interaction fills my ears. I look around, hoping to see Meg before she joins Dan at our usual table. I'm sure I'm not invited to sit with them today—I'm sure I'm shunned to the furthest reaches of this rectangular room. I see Meg in the line at the soda fountain, a paper cup in one hand, a straw in the other.

"Meg," I say, approaching her. She turns in my direction, and the annoyance is evident on her face. She rolls her eyes and turns away, filling

her cup. I roll my eyes back, though she doesn't see. She's being completely unreasonable. I shouldn't be punished for trying to keep us safe and out of trouble. "Hey, just talk to me for a second, please," I say. "I'm not going to apologize for insisting that we leave your car at the party, Meg. I still think it was the right choice. I can deal with it if you need some time to get over it, but please don't treat me like chopped liver. We're friends…teammates. We are supposed to look out for each other. Right?"

Meg's shoulders slack as she turns again back in my direction. She lets a smirk escape before opening her mouth. "I left the picture in the back of Dan's car on purpose." The smile on her face isn't meant to be friendly. "Yup, Summer. I sure did," she adds, her voice rising. I want to melt into the floor, but I stand my ground, no emotion on my face. "At first, I was going to do it just because it was your fault that I was grounded, but as I sat there waiting for you and Dan to pick me up, I started to realize that you had done that to MY friend. Dan is my friend, and you did something horrible to him. He deserved to know. So, I decided that I would help him find out the truth about you." She takes a sip of her drink. "You thought someone like him could love you, huh? But you ruined it just like you ruin everything in your life."

I open my mouth to speak but snap it shut. I have nothing to say.

Meg steps closer, her eyes narrowing. She gets close enough that I can feel her breath on my face. "Your own parents didn't love you, Summer. What makes you think anyone else will?"

A lump forms in my throat as tears brim my eyes. I take a tiny, ragged breath while Meg steps backward, out of my space, before turning toward our table and swiftly walking away, her hair swaying as she walks. I let out a breath and quickly exit the cafeteria, desperately trying to suffocate the sobs bubbling inside. I reach my locker and rest my back against it before sliding to the floor, letting my head fall to my knees.

Meg's right, and truth cuts deeper than any knife.

"Did you hear me?" Kash's gentle voice brings me back to the present. He holds my cheeks—wet with tears—softly in his large hands. I reach my own hands up to his face and do the same, leaning my nose against his and closing my eyes.

Kash loves me. All of me. And though I've known this for a long time, hearing him say it out loud solidifies it in my heart. "I heard you," I whisper. "Loud and clear."

He wraps his arms around me, and I feel his love deep in my bones. "I didn't know someone could love me the way you do," I say. "But I know that you do because you've *shown* me; you've made me *feel* it for as long as I've known you. I knew you loved me before you just said it. I could have gone the rest of our lives together with you never even saying it because you show me every damn day that it's always been me." I turn and point to the telescope. "Looking through that lens a few minutes ago did something to me. Seeing the stars that clearly, it reminded me of when I let myself believe that I loved *you.* When I came to that realization—actually quite a long time ago—it was like seeing for the first time in my life. And looking at these stars tonight with such clarity gave me the sudden urge to tell you how I've felt." I wipe a tear. "But you beat me to it." A laugh sneaks out.

The smile on Kash's face warms me. "Summer—"

"No, it's my turn," I say, cutting him off. I take his hands in mine and look him in the eyes. "I love you now, and I loved you then. I know I wasn't letting you in; I couldn't. And I'm sorry about that, but getting to where we are now is worth the time it took, don't you think?"

Kash starts to say something, but I continue, cutting him off. "I don't think of it as wasted time anymore, Kash," I say. "I think of it as time that was needed to make it just right. Time I needed to heal. Time you needed, too." I burrow myself into him, exactly where I fit best. "I love you, Kash. Always."

It's been a week since Kash and I went to the observatory. And a month since I've slept in my own room. It's Monday, our day off, and I should be sleeping in and catching up on rest, but I can't. It's Stella's birthday, and we have a whole day planned for her, and I can't wait. But also the way that the sun is coming in through the blinds and cascading across Kash's sleeping face melts me into a puddle, pooling right under his arm.

It's my new favorite sight.

My favorite spot.

I nuzzle in closer—carefully—not wanting to wake him. My breaths are coming in slow, measured waves as I sync them with his. It's like we're one, and imagining a time before we were this way is hard to muster. Kash and I have talked at length about not regretting the amount of time it took for us (or me, rather) to let go and just be together. We have no regrets. I believe that wholeheartedly. Because without rushing it, we've learned how one another ticks—who we are at the core. The good, the bad, and the downright ugly. We both have healed immensely since moving to this corner of the world. Me, with my responses to triggers, and Kash, with his acceptance of the monumental loss of his dad. And Kash has taught me the most important lesson I've learned thus far: fear creates more fear, and with that comes more loss. Had I continued to be fearful of losing him, I would have never truly seen him for who he is to me. If he had continued to be fearful of ending up like his mom, then there would still be a wall between us, literally and figuratively.

But the wall is down now. And looking back at the roads that led us to each other, it all seems so amazingly mapped out to perfection. Like each coincidence and act was mere happenstance, planned precisely so we'd land right here where we are now. Jimmy's explanation of this comes to mind, and I smile to myself.

I feel a laugh bubbling in my belly, recalling a text I got from Farrah last month—the one I got just mere minutes after I posted a picture of Kash and me on my Instagram account.

Um, is there something you're not telling me?

When I didn't answer immediately, another one came in.

Summer. Text me right now. I know you have your phone…you JUST posted a picture.

I had barely finished reading the last word when the familiar sound of an incoming FaceTime call sounded on my phone. It was Farrah. I answered it, and apparently, the look on my face gave away everything, as evident by her shriek.

"You can't post a picture like that, with your head tipped that way toward Kash, and not think that I wouldn't know what was going on," she had said, causing a laugh to erupt from me.

Since Kash and I first met, she has always been the one to love *us* the most—the *us* she knew was there and hoped we'd eventually let flourish and grow. Never pushing. Never forcing (well, maybe a little at times—from the goodness of her heart) until it happened on our own accord—exactly as it should have.

"What's so funny?" Kash rolls over onto his stomach, facing me, his voice hoarse from sleep.

I cover my mouth with my hand. "Sorry," I whisper, kissing his nose.

"Why are you whispering? It's just us here, and you already woke me up." He winks, and we both laugh.

"True." I turn over onto my back, looking up at the ceiling, my head nestled into the crook of his shoulder.

He rests his head on top of mine, and we lie—as one—a tangle of sheets and limbs. I have learned that there's no need to talk in moments like these. Moments that have become the highlights of our hectic lives. Lately, these mundane moments with Kash have been feeding my soul. And I wouldn't have it any other way.

"You're my favorite, Summer," he whispers into my hair.

I smile into his chest, my cheeks aching with love. "Now look who's whispering." I look up at him, beaming, and his eyes squint with a smile that moves me, causing creases at the corners of his face. He leans down and places his lips on mine with the utmost gentleness, and then I'm lost to him.

Maybe it's too much, taking Stella to Disneyland for her birthday, but she deserves it, and Kash agrees. So, here I am, packing my backpack with some sunscreen and my sunglasses. I'm so excited that I can't help but smile to myself. I slide my black sequined Minnie Mouse ears onto my head and beam at myself in the mirror. It's going to be a fun day; I can feel it. I grab Stella's matching ears and T-shirt and head out into the kitchen.

"I'm ready," I announce, unable to hide my enthusiasm.

"You sure are!" Kash says through an endearing laugh.

"I would say this is false advertising," I say, pulling at his shirt. It's charcoal gray with a picture of Grumpy the Dwarf on it. Grumpy is not a word that describes Kash in the slightest.

He shakes his head, smiling. "It's all I could find."

"I could have gotten you one to match Stella and me."

He gives me an *oh please* expression, causing me to giggle. A T-shirt with the original Disney princesses isn't really his style, I guess. Though, knowing him, he would wear it if I asked him to.

"Are you ready to go get the birthday girl?" Kash asks.

"More than ready!"

We wait out front of The Girls Home for Stella to come out. I asked Lisa to bring Stella out to the truck so we could surprise her out here with all our Disney garb on. I'm so excited that I can't control my body movements. I bounce on my heels, waiting for her to come out, her headband in my hand.

Kash puts his arm around my waist and bends down to place a kiss on the top of my head. The gesture sends goosebumps across my skin.

The door to the building swings open, and Lisa and Stella step out.

"I hope you guys have a fabulous time," Lisa boasts, walking over toward us with her clipboard so I could sign Stella out.

"Thank you!" I exclaim. I glance at Stella, a goofy smile on my face. She seems a bit uneasy. "Do you know where we are going?" I ask.

"Let me guess. Disneyland?" For a brief moment—barely a millisecond—fear is written on her face. But as fast as it showed up, it's gone, replaced with a meek smile. I'm sure Kash didn't even notice, but I sure did. A pit forms in the hollows of my stomach, but I ignore it, telling myself it's nerves or something of the sort.

"Yup!" I hold up her headband and take a step toward her, placing it gently on her head. I place my hands on her cheeks. "Happy birthday," I whisper.

We walk through security with what seems like the rest of the state of California. *Why is it so crowded?* I attempt to shake off the sudden onset of social anxiety and take a deep, cleansing breath. I glance at Stella and Kash as we all adjust our bags and sunglasses after the security line.

"Ready?" Kash asks us.

"Let's do it!" I say, my excitement causing Stella to roll her eyes in good fun.

The melody of "Zippity Do Dah" plays somewhere in the distance; the sound of it invites a feeling of nostalgia to take over me. It's odd because it isn't one of my personal memories but more a longing for something that I wished would have happened but never did—a day filled with making memories with my family.

The smell, too, has an instant effect on me, and I suck air in through my nose—deeply—if I'm trying to leave an imprint on my mind, an impression that will never fade. The scent is like popcorn mixed with cotton candy and fried dough, but that isn't all. There's something else intertwined in the scent that I can't quite place. Disney Magic, I guess.

As we follow the crowd of people all headed toward the main entrance, I welcome the fluttery feeling inside my belly. I've heard people say that Disney is for children of all ages—that the kid in you comes out to play when you're here, even if you're 100 years old. In my mind, I give a gentle knock on the door to the past—*Come on, little Summer. This is for you.*

Stella's gaze is scanning all the scenes around us, and I hope she isn't overwhelmed. "Have you been here before?" I ask her.

"Once," she replies absentmindedly before pointing to a snack cart. "Can I get you guys a Mickey ice cream?"

"Sure," I start. "I mean, yes, but this day is on me, Stella." I smile at her, wrapping my arm around her shoulder. She looks bashfully at me but gives me a nod before the three of us head toward the snack cart.

We haven't been inside the park for more than five minutes when a glob of ice cream lands on my shirt. I roll my eyes, wiping it with my napkin, making it look worse, not better.

"That's so Summer," says Kash, his mouth full of ice cream. We all laugh at that, and though I'm annoyed to already have a stain on my shirt, I just can't seem to let it bother me. We're in DISNEYLAND!

"What ride are we going to go on first?" Kash asks, pulling out the paper map from his back pocket.

"Can we go on Space Mountain?" Stella asks, wiggling her eyebrows. "I was too afraid last time I was here."

I want to ask her more about that time, but my instincts are telling me to let it be, so I do.

"Let's do it!" Kash exclaims, pointing to the spot on the map. I glance over his shoulder, reading the word Tomorrowland across the section where his finger is. Kash looks up and scans the park. "Looks like it's this way." He points to the route, and we begin our journey to Space Mountain.

The sign in front of the ride informs us that it's a forty-five-minute wait. My shoulders sink until I hear someone coming up behind us celebrating that it's *only* a forty-five-minute wait. I don't do theme parks, let alone Disney, so I just didn't know. *Perspective.*

"Is that too long?" Stella asks. "It's totally fine if you want to find a different ride."

"Forty-five minutes? That's nothing," Kash says, flicking his hand at her, dismissing her concerns. "We can have a lot of Rock Paper Scissor tournaments in that amount of time."

Stella's expression is one of pure gratefulness, and though I'm not surprised by Kash's positive perspective, I am appreciative.

As we wind our way through the waiting area, we laugh and joke and play our game. Finally, we're very close to getting onto the ride, and my adrenaline spikes. The dark tunneled area we walk through makes it look like we are actually in some sort of space continuum, and it ignites a childlike excitement deep inside. I feel Kash's hand make contact with the small of my back, and I glance up at him, his smile warming me. "This is so fun!" I say, unable to hide the thrill building up the closer and closer we get to the spaceships. Once we get to the front, we each get into our own lines so we can sit in the same ship. I'm in the front, Stella's in the middle, and Kash is in the back.

We soar through the dimensions of the ride in under five minutes, every minute of which I'm screaming through a goofy laugh. I hear the shrieks of Kash and Stella behind me ebb and flow as the spaceship dives down and heads back up toward the stars. My head rattles with the jolts, but I don't care. Who knew that screaming and laughing with reckless abandon could be so healing?

The ride parks, and we exit the car, all of us laughing and holding onto each other as we regain our footing on solid ground. Once we're back out in the sunshine and heat, we share our thoughts on the ride.

"That was so fun!" Stella says, and the way her face lights up, the way I'm watching her walls crumble just a tad bit right before my eyes, makes me a bit emotional.

"Wild!" I say. "But my head feels weird." I reach my palm up to my forehead but laugh away the slight dizziness that lingers from the ride. I take a sip of my water. Kash and Stella do the same.

"Want to do something a little calmer next?" Stella asks.

"Sure thing, birthday girl," Kash responds, pulling out his map again. It's become slightly warped from his pocket already, but he unfolds it and scans it. "Here. Take a look, tell us where you want to go next." He hands the map to Stella, and her eyes dart around until she lands on something that has caught her eye. She extends her pointer finger to Adventureland. When I look closer, it seems like she is pointing to a specific ride.

"Jungle Cruise?" she questions.

I shrug my shoulders. "Sure! Let's head over there."

We all adjust our bags before getting on our way. The walk over to Adventureland is an adventure in itself. We pass in front of Sleeping Beauty's castle and pose for cheesy pictures in front of it. For a moment, I just stare at the large structure long and hard, all of my senses working at once. Music plays around us, and the sounds of laughing children—with the occasional crying ones—is the constant background noise, everywhere we go. The growing strength of that smell I just can't place—it's captivating. I feel a tad bit guilty for the joy this trip is bringing me because it's for Stella, but I can't help it. I'm sure she doesn't mind sharing the joy with me.

We arrive at the entrance to the Jungle Cruise, and it only has a twenty-minute wait. We consider ourselves lucky, and we acknowledge our good fortune as we wait in line. I glance around at the scenery—it's as if we've been transported to an actual jungle. The lush greenery and sounds of running water and tropical birds singing make it extremely difficult to grasp reality. Disney sure knows how to do make-believe. I smile at nothing in particular as we inch our way closer to the water's edge and the boats we'll soon be boarding.

"Watch your step as you get on board," the Disney cast member says as we get into position to step over the threshold into the boat.

"Excuse me," a woman beside us says. "My daughter is afraid to sit near the water. Do you want to sit in our row?" She's talking to Stella, and Stella is about to respond, I see her mouth open, but the woman continues. "Or you can sit with your parents; no big deal, just thought I would offer our window seat!"

There's a person in front of us who will get the window seat in our row, and I thought it was a nice offer. Until I see the look on Stella's face, and then, my stomach grows sour. "They're not my parents," she spits out, climbing into our designated row.

The nice woman looks taken aback, but it can't be anything compared to the way my insides feel. I'm not offended by the tone Stella used. I'm heartbroken for what I know she's feeling in her heart right at this very moment.

"Sorry," I mouth to the woman before climbing into the boat next to Stella, Kash right behind me. We sit in our row, and he gives my knee a gentle squeeze, but I can't bring myself to look at him. I don't want to risk upsetting Stella even more. Instead, I look at her. She's looking out at the water over the shoulder of the person sitting next to us. I let her be. Because I know what's happening to her right now; she's gone somewhere, somewhere she can't take me to, at least not yet. I'd know that look anywhere, and I see it reflecting in the one eye I can partly see: a distant, dazed look that a person only gets when they've gone somewhere else in their mind.

CHAPTER 21

A little girl named Stella on her 7th birthday

"YOU CAN SIT ON *your mom or dad's lap, sweetheart," the driver of the boat says, causing the little girl to beam. The driver could sense the child was apprehensive about the ride, maybe unsure about the water and what may lay beneath it. "But I promise I won't let anything bad happen to you." The woman winks at the little girl, and the family of three climbs aboard. The little girl sits on her dad's lap before gaining the courage to slide off and put herself right against the window. She looks out at the trees and down to where the boat cuts the water as they pull away from the dock. Only seconds. That's all it takes for the child to gain confidence that comes from the security of her family unit.*

She squeals and points to all the things she sees, both the mundane leaves on the trees and the amazing colors and sizes of the animals they pass.

"Mommy? Daddy?" The little girl's sweet voice causes her parents to turn to her endearingly. "This is the best birthday ever. Can we come here for every one of my birthdays forever?" Her voice is hopeful.

Her parents laugh, and her dad pulls her in closer to him and kisses the top of her head.

"Oh, darling. We will most definitely take you back here," her mom starts. "But do you want to know a secret?" The little girl nods her head, a desperate need to know. "Disneyland is more special when you don't see it all the time. When you let years pass and you come back, it's like magic all over again."

"Oh. Ok. Let's wait a million years then," the little girl says, sounding very serious.

"Well, we don't have to wait that long," her dad says, laughing.

The little girl looks thoughtful. "OK, how about ten years? How old will I be on that birthday? Forty-nine?"

Her parents smile at her. "Ten years sounds good," her mom says, leaning over and placing her hand on her cheek. "You won't be forty-nine. You'll be seventeen, and I know you'll be the most beautiful birthday girl then. Just like you are now." The little girl nuzzles into her mother. "I love you more than all the dolphins in the sea," she whispers into her daughter's hair.

CHAPTER 22

Summer

"PLEASE, WATCH YOUR STEP as you exit the vessel, and have a magical rest of your day."

I'm a little unsteady getting off the boat, though not for the same reason as I was after exiting Space Mountain. Stella didn't move a muscle on this ride, and she needed a nudge from both me and the person sitting next to her to wake herself from the trance she was in and get up from the bench.

"You OK?" I ask her, taking a sip from my water bottle. I don't want to intrude into her thoughts, but I want to make sure she's alright. She nods without making eye contact.

Kash has learned a lot about traumatic memories from dealing with me, and I watch him to see how he reacts—he's calm and collected, as always. "Stella, places like this can be overwhelming for anyone. No matter what, you say the word, and we can be at the car in fifteen minutes." He doesn't ask questions. He doesn't pry. He gently lays out how easy it would be for us to bail. No questions asked.

Stella sits down on a bench and stretches out her legs, her hands tangling in her lap. She pulls her sunglasses down from her head, and I see her lip quiver, just for a moment. I know there are tears building behind the tinted lenses of her glasses, and my heart aches for her. We give her a moment. I sit next to her on the bench and take my eyes out to the crowds in front of us. People are bustling around, strollers swiftly pass by as families rush to make it to shows and rides. Mickey Mouse balloons speckle the air in a variety of colors, grasped by tiny fists. It's a heartwarming sight for anyone watching. I glance over at Stella, and I know that it doesn't matter—not really—how heartwarming something looks when the image is tainted by whatever is going on behind the scenes of a traumatized mind…a painful memory will ruin everything. My desperate need to help her boils under my skin. Knowing how trauma works makes me want to save her from it, but I know that it isn't possible for me to do that. She has to do the work. But I will do whatever I can to let her know that she doesn't have to do this alone.

Against my better instincts, I take her hand in mine. I don't want to overstep, but I would have done anything for someone—any-one—to show that they cared about me when I was her age. To my surprise, she gently squeezes my hand and doesn't let on that she wants me to let go. So, I don't. I wrap my arm around her shoulder and pull her close, allowing her to rest her head on my shoulder. Kash says he's going to run and find a bathroom, and I just send him a nod.

"I'm not going to ask you what's wrong, Stella. But I just want you to know that I'm here for you."

"I know." Her words are barely a whisper, coming out as a tiny squeak. "I'm so glad to have met you."

Relaxing my shoulders feels like work, which tells me that I must have been tensing them much too long. Her knowing that she can trust me, that my intentions are good and I care about her, makes me feel a little better. It gives me hope for her. Hope that I never had for myself. "I can't even tell you how happy I am to have met YOU."

"I don't want to leave. Not just yet," she says, sitting up straighter and turning toward me.

"No? OK."

She shakes her head, looking around at the commotion going on near us. "I don't want to end this trip here on a negative note. You went completely out of your way for me, and I don't want you to think I'm not grateful, I am, I just—"

"Stop, Stella," I interject. "We didn't do this for you to be grateful." I put my hand on her knee gently. "We did it to celebrate you—to have fun. If that isn't happening, then it's time to go." I give her a soft, encouraging smile.

Stella's face lights up as she opens up her arms and leans in for a hug, which I gladly accept. Pulling her into me feels natural, and I hug her as tightly as I can. "And I'm starving. Can we find food?" I laugh. "And go on the teacups?" She looks at me, hopeful.

Kash returns from the bathroom, balancing three Dole Whips in his hands. The atmosphere has completely changed in the ten minutes he's been gone, and Stella and I gladly take the Dole Whips from his hands. "We were just saying how we had to find something to eat," I say. I take a bite of the frozen treat, and my eyes widen as the creamy pineapple taste explodes in my mouth.

"Is this for real?" Kash says, looking at the cup of ice cream in wonderment.

"We have only eaten ice cream today," Stella says, laughing.

"True. Maybe we should grab some sustenance after this," I say, even though I don't really care. I'm just happy. "Stella wants to go on the teacups."

"Let's do it," Kash announces.

We spend the rest of the afternoon getting dizzy on rides after waiting in ridiculously long lines, taking pictures with characters, and buying souvenirs that we absolutely do not need. It turned out to be a beautiful day, and as we make the drive back to Santa Monica, I start to crave Jimmy's tacos, a real meal after snacking all day.

"Is it OK if we take you for a birthday dinner at our friend's restaurant?" Kash asks Stella as he glances in the rearview mirror. I turn around in the passenger seat to see her looking a bit bashful. "If you aren't up for it, we can drop you off first."

"Is it too much?"

"Absolutely not! That was our plan all along," I insist. "But if you don't want to, that's OK, too. It's been a long day." I smile at her.

"No, I want to." She grins at me before looking at Kash in the mirror. "Thank you."

"You deserve it," Kash says. With that, I look at him, studying the way his tattoos sway under the flex of his forearm while he holds the steering wheel and lets go to take a swig of his water bottle. *You deserve it,* he just said. I know that she does. But the fact that Kash has grown to love Stella just as much as I do brings a tear to my eye. I smile to myself. *How lucky am I?*

"Still Standing" comes through the car speakers, and Kash turns it up in excitement. "I love this song!" I know Stella and I are in for a show, so I take out my phone and record Kash singing with his beautiful voice. After a moment, we're all singing, and when it ends, Kash has a dreamy look on his face as he focuses on the road.

"What's up?" I ask him.

"That song reminds me of Silas. Remember when we used to play it all the time at Sullivan's? People would go nuts!" There's happiness in his voice, mixed with a sense of nostalgia—a longing. "I miss him." And then sadness trickles into his tone.

Along with a wink emoji, I send along the video to Silas, accompanied by the words **miss you**.

Reaching over the center console, I take Kash's hand in mine as my own memories flutter around. I think about all the times he and Silas would duel the song, and I'd be behind the bar, watching and admiring as our dreams began to simmer. Dreams that didn't seem possible, not then. Even imagining a time when I could express myself through music seemed fleeting—a wisp of a thought that certainly didn't seem possible. It seems like a million lifetimes ago, really.

I push my hair behind my ear as the song ends, and the roar of the audience fills the space. The patrons love that song. The regulars and tourists all request it, almost every night, and it never gets old. Kash and Silas get up from their benches and meet in the front of the stage to take a bow before their set break. A surge is about to take over the bar area. Farrah scurries behind me, helping some customers who snagged the last two bar stools at the bar. I need to get my head out of the clouds—it's time to serve a million drinks.

The lyrics to "Still Standing" float through my head, stuck there after the performance. I hum it—loudly—while pouring tequila into a tumbler of ice, adding a lime wedge to the side, and sliding it to the person who ordered it. I add it to their tab before going to assist someone else. I look up to see that Kash has made his way to the bar, sweating and smiling.

"How'd we do?" he asks, though I'm not sure why he would ask. He knows he's talented. He knows everyone always enjoys his performances.

I smile back. "Unreal." I grab a tumbler and make him a vodka soda, sliding it over to him. "That last song is going to be stuck in my head all night."

He winks at me and places a ten-dollar bill in the tip jar. "That's just the way I like it."

Kash makes his way back to the stage, and I watch him—maybe for a moment too long because Farrah catches me and playfully shakes her head. She won't say anything; she knows better than that. But I know what she's thinking. Because it's exactly what I'm thinking: Kash has a grip on me, and I'm not sure what to do about it. The feelings frighten me, so ignoring them seems like the best option. Therefore, I will do nothing. Nothing at all except pretend it isn't true. Best friends can grip you in ways that you weren't expecting. That makes sense. I'll stick to that reasoning.

I'm torn from my thoughts by the lights being dimmed again, signaling that Kash and Silas are back on stage, and a new song begins to take over the place. A grin takes over my face—a smile for the life that's turned out to be mine. A life I never thought I deserved. But I'm here. Still Standing.

We pull up to our apartment and invite Stella in to see it. I offer her a change of clothes if she's interested, but she's not, so I stay in my sweaty Disney clothes, too. She looks around our place, and I'm not sure what she's thinking, and I don't ask. I just let her glance at the magazines on our coffee table. She walks to the door that leads out to our tiny balcony and looks out at the ocean. "Wow," she mutters, barely audible.

"Yeah, it's peaceful," I say. We stand quietly looking out for another moment until Kash comes out of the bedroom changed into fresh clothes.

"Ready?" he asks, and we head out the door and walk to Jimmy's.

We step into the restaurant, and the familiar smell of spices and the sounds of the bar flood my senses. My stomach growls, and I smile at Stella, who looks thrilled to be in an establishment with food. We walked a lot today, and though we tried what seems like every single snack Disney offers, we never carved out time for a sit-down lunch.

"Kash! Summer!" I hear Jimmy's warm voice before I see him. "And hello, my dear," he says, approaching us. He sticks out his hand to shake Stella's. "It is wonderful to see you again." It warms my heart the way Jimmy remembers her but doesn't make her feel uncomfortable about how they first met. "I'm so glad to have you here on your birthday!"

Stella smiles but looks down at her feet, her shyness on full display.

"I saved you all the best table in the house." Jimmy leads us to our table, toward the back, closer to the bar, with a view of every part of the restaurant.

There is so much to look at in here, and Stella can't help but stare at all the knickknacks, photos, and decorations: surfboards, the tiki hut bar, brightly colored artwork, and speckles of sand—just how Jimmy loves it.

"Do you want to look at the photo wall?" The excitement in Kash's voice causes me to laugh.

"Sure." Stella shrugs and walks over with Kash to look at the famous wall.

I take a seat at the table that Jimmy has set up for us. "How was your day?" he asks me, taking a seat in one of the chairs beside me.

Leaning back in the chair, I cross my legs, sighing with exhaustion. "Jimmy, I'm getting old. Disney made me tired."

He pats my knee, his rheumy eyes glistening at me above his soft smile. "My dear, you'll never again be as young as you are right now. Soak in all this life has to offer you."

Classic Jimmy. Preaching his wisdom to anyone and everyone who will listen. And I will always do just that. I lean forward, resting my elbows on my knees. "You're right." We share a moment just sitting together, sharing pleasantries, until Kash and Stella come back to the table.

Jimmy slaps his knee and gets up from the table. "What can I get you all to drink?"

"Can I order for you?" Kash asks Stella, and she shrugs her shoulders, smiling. "She has to try your Raspberry Lime Rickey, Jimmy." He claps his hands together. "And I'll have one, too."

"Make it three," I add.

"Coming right up!" Jimmy says, walking toward the bar.

"You are not going to be disappointed in that drink," Kash says, passing out the menus. "He puts cream in them. I know it sounds weird, but it's good. I promise."

"He's right. They are delicious," I agree, looking over the menu, even though I have it memorized and already know what I want. "Anything look good, Stella?"

"So many things look good, but I think I'm going to get the beef burrito bowl."

"Good choice," Kash says. "We should get an appetizer too. Mexican Nachos?"

"Definitely," I respond, shutting my menu.

"What are you getting?" Stella asks me.

"Spicy shrimp tacos with Mexican street corn."

"Oh, that sounds good." She looks perturbed and glances over the menu again.

"Get the bowl," I assure her. "You can get the shrimp tacos next time." She holds my gaze, looking grateful. "Besides, everything on Jimmy's menu is amazing."

We sip our drinks and pick at our nachos, talking about the day's adventures. We laugh a lot, and before we know it, Jimmy is delivering our meals. The aroma from the steaming plates permeates the air and causes my mouth to water. The light green secret sauce from my tacos drips off the shrimp and onto the plate, and I groan. It can't get in my mouth fast enough.

Jimmy pulls up a chair from the table beside us. "Mind if I sit with you?"

Kash takes a big swallow before giving Jimmy a look that says *you're kidding, right?*

"Of course, Jimmy," I say, my mouth full.

To be an observer of our table, we'd look like a little family—mom, dad, daughter, and grandfather. Though it's not exactly the truth, the word *family* is accurate. Jimmy has taken on this fatherly role in our lives, and his connection to Kash's dad still mesmerizes us. Especially Kash, who still has a hard time accepting the truth for what it is: miraculous. Stella has become so much a part of my life that it feels as if losing her would form a gaping hole in my heart. I sit at the table, half listening to the conversation. I'm soaking in the feeling that's come over me, a feeling I've grown accustomed to over the last two years but something I'm still amazed by: unconditional love.

A look comes over Kash, one that causes his eyebrows to furrow, and I force myself to tune back into the conversation.

"And I'm sorry for the mood I was in on the Jungle Cruise." Stella takes a sip of her drink and moves food around on her plate with her fork. "My parents took me on that ride on my seventh birthday. I knew we'd gone to Disneyland, but my memories didn't really become clear until we got on the ride." All three of us listen intently. She stops for a second, and I notice that as Stella takes a breath, I'm holding mine. "That day with my parents, on that ride, we had talked about going back to Disney in ten years…on my seventeenth birthday." Her voice grows soft, and it sounds like she may cry. My mouth drops—ever so slightly—hearing what she just shared. It all seems so unbelievable.

"Stella—" I start, but I'm lost for words at first. I put my hand on her back as her head falls slightly. "I'm sorry I put you through that." I feel bad. Though there was no way for me to have known about this, I still feel terribly guilty having been the reason for her flashback—the one that made her so incredibly sad.

"Don't be sorry." She turns her head toward me. "There's no way you could have known. I didn't even know. But it was a happy memory. It seems like recently, all I can remember is the night they died. I envision them scared and suffering. It's like my mind is blocking out all the good stuff. I'm happy to have remembered a joyful moment from my childhood." The words don't match the heartbroken look on her face, but I know what she's trying to say. I know the complicated nature of a memory.

She has something else on her mind, I can tell, something else to say, but she remains quiet. "What is it?" I ask.

She shakes her head slowly, not opening her mouth at first. But we give her a moment, and eventually, she starts talking again.

"Something led me here that night you found me." She's looking at Jimmy now. "I don't really know what to say; I can't explain it, not really. It was like my feet were being guided here, to this very spot. And now, it scares me to say it out loud, but…," her voice chokes, and she raises her hand to her mouth as a sob escapes. Jimmy reaches out his hand and rubs her back.

"What are you afraid of, Stella?" I ask. "We're here for you."

"I'm afraid I let myself get too close to you."

My heart crumbles into a million pieces because I know how she feels.

Fear. Fear is what lingers for people like Stella and me…and even Kash. When you lose everything that means something to you, it's the fear that takes root in the fibers of your being. It's fear that holds you back from living. It's fear that hinders you from connecting. I can't tell her not to be afraid, but I can show her, though, that she doesn't have to be. Not with me. Just like Kash did. He told me, but he also showed me, and eventually, I learned to trust.

"Oh, sweetie. If anything, I want you closer," I say, hoping that she understands what I mean—that I desperately want her to let me in as much as she wants, that I want to be there for her in every possible way.

I stand up and pull her into an embrace. Barely a second passes before Kash stands and wraps us in his embrace, and Jimmy joins in—a pig pile of love. By the time we pull away from one another, my eyes are as wet as Stella's, and even Jimmy is wiping a tear. We all sit back down in our chairs, picking up dirty napkins to wipe our sopping faces.

"You know, Stella, you aren't the only one drawn to this little spot by the ocean," Kash says, and we all turn to face him.

He tells her the story about how his parents met and spent time here and how he always felt pulled to California, to this little stretch of sand where Venice meets Santa Monica. He tells her about his strong connection to Jimmy when he first moved here, the inexplicable force to be near him, only to find out almost two years later that he was his dad's best friend. He tells her about the picture on the wall and how they made the connection when his mom was visiting. Jimmy confessed to always being drawn to Kash, too.

And then, Kash starts to tell her about me. How I, too, was called here by some unexplained force. He searches my face briefly, trying to look for anything in my expression that's telling him that I don't want him to delve into that part of the story. But I want Stella to know everything. I want her to know that even if she can't fathom love, it's real. I nod at Kash, telling him it's OK to go on.

And so, he does. I skimmed the details with her that day in the backyard of The Girls Home, but this is different.

He tells her about how I would go to the ocean in my mind anytime I was being hurt as a child and how that ocean became the Pacific Ocean as I grew up, and then it became California. How the images in my dreams, my escape, transformed from a fictitious place to a place that was very real. How it called to me until I listened to the voice and came to this place. He tells her how I came here for me, listening to the voice that I had begun to recognize as my own.

And he is right about all of it. Though I loved him when I came to California, I didn't come to follow Kash. I came because I loved *me* and the pull toward the West Coast wasn't something I could deny any longer.

"And here we all are," Kash says, smiling, emotion peppering his words. "It's all such a—"

"Don't you dare say it," Jimmy says.

"Coincidence?" Stella says with a smile, finishing Kash's thought.

Kash takes my hand, and Jimmy speaks up. "No, my dears," Jimmy's voice is adamant. "I've told you before, and I'll say it again. And you hear me this time. There's no such thing, don't you see it now? This here is fate." We all exchange glances. "Do you hear me?" We nod. "There's no such thing as coincidence. Happenstance had no part in bringing you—us—together. It's destiny, is what that is."

I look at Kash. He's smiling, but his eyes are saying something more complex, but it's an expression I can easily read. He can't, for the life of him, understand how Jimmy made his way into his life in this way. He wants to, but it's difficult. We've talked about it at length—losing his father has hardened his opinion on the concept of *things happening for a reason*. Because there's no fathomable reason that his dad should have been taken from him at such a young age. But here Jimmy is, bringing it up again, how we all were pulled here on purpose. And I believe Jimmy. But it's easy for me to believe it. I hope someday Kash, too, will accept it for what it is because it's unimaginably beautiful.

The bar has gotten increasingly louder, but it's as if it's just us sitting here. I mouth *thank you* to Jimmy because it's really all I can muster. And he just gives me a single nod of his head and his signature smile. He always knows exactly what to say in any situation. But what he just told us is medicine for the hard things all three of us have held onto for far too long, things that have festered, difficult things that, unfortunately, wreaked havoc on all of us. But not anymore. Jimmy's words are a way to explain why and how we all ended up as intricate pieces in each other's lives. His words give a gentleness to the harsh realities we've each faced in our lives.

It's beautiful, truly, to be able to see life through Jimmy's eyes. A shiny perspective on an otherwise cloudy image.

"I think the birthday girl needs a dessert," Jimmy says, getting up from his seat. "And a candle to blow out." He leaves us briefly, and I reach each hand out to grasp Kash and Stella's. There are no words left to say, not really. Jimmy's were enough in this moment, and I think we all agree on that. I can tell because they look as content as I feel on the inside.

We sing happy birthday to Stella, and her cheeks turn a crimson red, but her smile beams brightly behind the flame on her lava cake. She blows it out, and I'm curious what she wished for, but I don't ask. I just soak in her glee, thankful that the day turned out even better than I could have imagined.

CHAPTER 23

Kash

AUGUST

Now that we've been together for a while, I don't feel pressure to impress Summer. I just want us to have fun and make memories. But when I was invited to a formal event for restaurant owners, I couldn't pass up the opportunity for us to get dressed up and have a proper date. Since Summer and I solidified our relationship, we've been making memories I'm already treasuring. Frequently, I find myself smiling while alone in my office doing paperwork, my lips spread up into a wide curve, thinking about the images of her rolling her eyes at me playfully or pushing up her sleeves and rubbing her hands together as she prepares to make something adventurous for dinner on Monday nights.

For months now, we haven't worn anything besides casual clothes you'd wear at the beach. I'm really excited about this chance to get dressed up, and as I sit on my couch, my knee bouncing with anticipation, I can't take my eyes off of our closed bedroom door.

She's been in there—alone—for over an hour getting ready. Just before I left the room fully dressed and ready to go, she stood there with her towel wrapped around her, hair falling over her shoulders in dark, damp waves. She looked at me longingly, but behind the lust was a discomfort that I couldn't wait to ease when she was dressed. I know she's nervous about the event; getting dressed up isn't comfortable for her because she doesn't feel worthy. It's my job to ease her nerves, and it's a task I'm most certainly up for.

Eventually, a goofy smile spread over her face. "Well, aren't you handsome," she said.

I approached her, taking her face in my hands. "And you are the most beautiful woman I have ever seen." My words were strong but quiet, and she looked at me as if she was desperately trying to believe the sentiment.

She shook her head, tucking her wet hair behind her ears. "Get out of here," she said, amusement in her words. "I need to get ready."

So, now, here I sit, impatiently waiting for her to emerge from the bedroom. My legs, which have become quite restless, force me to stand, and I straighten my suit jacket. It feels strange on my body—entirely too constricting—and I already long to get back here and change.

I mosey over toward the sliding door to the balcony, stuffing my hands into my pockets, unable to cease the pacing that has taken over my body. I'm looking at the ocean when I hear the bedroom door softly open. Without even a moment's thought, I turn, instantly unable to hide my anticipation.

Chill, dude.

There's no chilling.

"Wow." The word comes out strained and breathless. Summer is stunning, and she appears in a way that I have never once seen her before. Her hands are crossed in front of her, her shoulder slightly curled forward in an effort to hide the discomfort that lingers, I'm sure. I can tell she doesn't feel like herself. Ever since she walked into our apartment with the dress in her hands last week, she has made it clear that even being in its presence feels awkward. She borrowed the dress from Nel's sister, and it's red and hugs her body. It sparkles under the recessed lighting overhead; the shine catches my eye as she slowly moves her body. The vision is making breathing nearly impossible. I swallow, and the motion feels like effort.

"So?"

"So…," I say as I run my hand through my hair. "I'm speechless." I take wide, quick steps toward her and pull her into me. I feel her melt into my embrace, and we rock—slowly—side to side. I inhale her scent, and it's one that I can't place. I feel her hands slowly caressing my back, and she lets out a soft sigh. I pull away and lift her chin with my finger so that her gaze meets mine.

"I'm quite the catch," she whispers. And I laugh.

Though she still has the tendency to pull into herself, to shy away from attention, she now has this confidence about herself that's quiet but fierce. The front-row seat I have to watch her evolve still amazes me.

I pull her back into me, and we settle in like we're slow dancing, but there's no music, so I make my own, softly singing the lyrics to the song I sang at the bar, the one I dedicated to her the night we started this journey. The lyrics speak strongly to our story, and soon, we're both singing, our voices blending together as if they were made to do just that.

"Remember when we first danced together at Farrah's wedding?" Summer asks.

"How could I forget?"

"I hadn't ever danced on a dance floor until that moment." Emotion fills her voice.

"Yeah, I know." I kiss the top of her head.

"There were so many things I had never experienced until I started facing my past." She pulls away and looks up at me. "You have been a part of so many of my firsts."

I smile softly at her and wait a beat before speaking. "And it's my honor." I gently kiss her forehead.

Time seems to sneak by at a speed that I can't quite fathom. We dance under the dimmed lights of our living room, and we sit on the couch, stroking limbs and the soft skin of cheeks, sharing conversation in soft voices, barely above whispers.

Summer sighs and sits up abruptly, reaching for her phone on the coffee table. "What time is it?"

I look down at my watch. *Oops.*

Her shoulders slump. "We missed it." For a brief moment, she seems disappointed. But the sentiment is quickly transformed into something different.

I beam at her, my smile reaching my eyes. "Time flies when—"

She cuts me off. "When you're truly happy."

Jimmy's lesson hangs in the air—a gift that shows up when you least expect it. Wisdom that never falters.

I slip off my suit coat and toss it in a heap on the couch before sitting back down. Summer and I inch closer together again.

She rests her head on my shoulder and allows a chuckle to escape. "I spent all that time getting ready to just sit here in our living room looking like this. Do you think if we hurried right now, we could sneak into the event?"

If I know Summer, which I think I do, she doesn't care about this thing we were going to, but she feels bad about it. I can tell.

"I don't care about missing it. And the getups we have on don't have to be completely wasted." There's a hint of mischief in my voice, and Summer stares at me with curiosity.

"What are you thinking?" she asks, smiling.

"We're going to be the most overly dressed people who have ever performed at Two WhisKEYS." I take her hand, and we make our way to our home away from home.

"Let's sing 'Time of My Life,'" I say as we round the corner that leads to the entrance.

Summer looks at me, and a displeased expression spreads over her face. "I've never performed that." She shakes her head.

"Yes, you have."

"Kash." She rolls her eyes. "Yes, OK, I have. You're right." A loud, nervous laugh comes out. "In our kitchen once while we cooked."

I smile at the image, pictures of the life we're creating. "Then you're more than prepared." As we approach the door, I let go of her hand and pull the handle, motioning for her to go through first. She stares at me for a moment, a small smile playing on her lips, before she takes a step over the threshold, and I follow closely behind her.

The ambience is perfect: a dim glow lights the space, and the brightest lights shine over the stage. The noise is comforting, and every seat in the house is taken. The bar is crowded, but everyone looks like they are enjoying themselves. It looks like a typical Saturday night, and I'm proud of the way the staff has held their own without me here.

It only takes a heartbeat before I hear Nel shriek over the sounds of conversation and the music that plays through the speakers during the set break. She comes out from behind the bar and strides over to us, on a mission.

"It's over already?" she asks, taking Summer's shoulders in her hands. "Look at you, Summer! Oh my God."

"We missed it," Summer laughs.

Nel's eyes widen, and then she wiggles her eyebrows at us causing us all to laugh.

"We thought we'd stop by and not waste this opportunity for the world to see us like this," I say, gesturing to our outfits.

"You both look unreal," Nel says, shaking her head. "You have to sing a song!"

"Oh, don't worry. Kash is *insisting* that we strut up on the stage looking like this," Summer says dramatically.

"As you should!" she responds, turning back toward the bar. Summer and I head to the stage to talk to Finn and Diego, who have returned to the platform and are tweaking their instruments.

Finn and Diego happily allow us to take the stage before they start their second set. Finn announces the surprise as we take the stage. Summer looks like a natural all dressed up, even in the extremely high heels she has on. But I know she's using all her effort to keep her balance and not fall over.

"Hi, everyone." Her voice booms through the space, shaking me from my thoughts. It surprises me a bit that she took it upon herself to speak first. But I love it. "Kash insisted we stop by in these ridiculous outfits," she laughs, and the crowd claps and cheers. "He also insisted that we sing a duet that I've never actually performed. So, enjoy!" She laughs and looks at me. I shake my head at her.

"Let's do this," I say, nodding to Finn to get the music started.

And then, we perform the way that we always do, Summer and I, like our lives depend on it. We sing like our voices were made to only ever sing together as one. Summer smiles at me, a genuine smile, and I know that she's thinking—just like me—about the time we sang this in our kitchen and she ran into my arms as I lifted her up in the air, just like in the movie. She laughed, and so did I, and we both fell in a pile on the floor of the kitchen…laughing until our stomachs ached with a sweet soreness that you have to experience to understand. A sensation that, according to Summer, means we must be perfectly content.

When the music ends, we embrace, and I kiss her cheek. "That was awesome," she whispers breathlessly in my ear.

"It sure was."

We bow, and with the gesture, my heart is full. The night isn't at all what either of us were expecting.

It was so much more.

Jimmy keeps saying it was destiny, not a handful of coincidences, that brought us all together. He inferred that we are all connected by an invisible string—brought here to this exact space at this exact time by some cosmic intervention. At first, it seemed too difficult to comprehend. It didn't make any sense. And I still feel that way. But it's beginning to be a bit easier to believe because nothing has proven it wrong yet. I want to own the words wholeheartedly; I want it to make sense. And I feel myself inching closer to accepting it. I'll get there eventually—I hope.

A warm wind whips around my shoulders, shuddering me from my thoughts. I pull my ankle up behind me, stretching my hamstring, as I stare out into the sea, as if it's the first time I've seen it. How can it be that I've been here almost two years but each time I really sit and look at it, the ocean feels new somehow?

I glance down at my watch—it's 6:57 a.m., and the air already feels hot. The heat wave we've had these last three days has put the temperature almost at 100 by the time it hits midafternoon. I think today calls for a pre-opening swim. I smile to myself. What a day: Breakfast, some housekeeping at the bar, a swim, get ready for opening at four thirty this afternoon. I'm excited about the lineup for tonight. Summer and Jimmy are playing the first set, and I hope Summer will be brave enough to play the guitar. She's been practicing a lot with Jimmy and also on her own. She sounds great, and I think she's ready to perform in front of people. I'm not sure if it's as perfect as she would want, but I hope she just lets go and takes a leap with this one. It will be fun to watch.

I climb the steps to our apartment two at a time, unlock the door, and push it open. I'm surprised to see Summer tying her shoes. "Hi!" she says joyfully. "I'm getting a late start this morning. Is it already scorching out there?"

"It's getting there," I reply. "Did you sleep OK?"

"Yeah, I was just too comfortable to get out of bed. But I made you breakfast. It's in the microwave. I'm going to go for a walk. See you at the bar after? A few new shipments came in yesterday."

I lean in and place a soft kiss on her lips. "See you there," I whisper. "Thanks for breakfast. Have a great walk." And with that, she steps out the door, and I'm alone, and our tiny apartment suddenly feels much too big without Summer.

———

"This next song is one I've been working on with Jimmy here," Summer announces into the microphone, winking in Jimmy's direction. He smiles down at the ground while taking his bass guitar off his back and placing it on its stand. He grabs his acoustic guitar and hands the other acoustic to Summer. Yes, I'm so glad she's going to play. They each grab a stool from off-stage and take a seat in the middle, adjusting their straps and instruments. "Bear with me," Summer chuckles into the microphone, and the audience laughs along with her. "Jimmy has been teaching me how to play guitar, so no one is allowed to judge! I'm new at this." The audience begins to clap and cheer. When the crowd lulls, I see Summer scan it until she finds me standing toward the back. She beams at me, causing heads to turn in my direction. "This is for you, Kash," she says just before she begins to play.

It's difficult to take my eyes off Summer, her fingers strumming the strings with ease as if she has been playing her whole life. Jimmy plays beside her, looking at Summer with wet eyes and the smile of a father, a look of pride. But if I know Jimmy, the pride is not in himself—in his ability to teach her—but rather, it's pride in her...for overcoming the difficulty of learning a new instrument—and for her innate ability to produce music so beautiful that it could make anyone stop in their tracks.

Summer sings the lyrics to "I'm Yours" by Jason Mraz, and I hang on her every word; her soulful voice cascades throughout the entire place, causing goosebumps to form on my skin. I glance around at the patrons, who all have their eyes glued to the stage. I can almost guarantee they all have goosebumps, too. When the song ends, I clap until my hands hurt and wait until her eyes meet mine. Her smile reaches all the way to her ears, and she lifts her fingers in the shape of a heart toward my direction, which causes a resounding "aw" from the audience. I place one hand on my heart and point at her with the other. She winks before jumping into the next song.

I'm heading back to the bar to check on things, and as I walk that way, my eyes land on Nel taking care of a woman I can't place. I make my way over to introduce myself like I always do, and as I get closer, I can see that the woman has a copy of *Entrepreneurs of the Future* in her hand, the one with my face on it. I stifle a groan. So many people have been coming into the bar with that magazine—some of them wanting a taste of my famous whiskey, some wanting to take me (or Summer) on a date, others wanting tips and advice on how to start their own venture.

Though I appreciate the support, it's not in my nature to boast. I don't really like the attention. I'm not comfortable talking about my successes—especially when the most important thing I've accomplished can't be seen by anyone else. What I see as my most successful accomplishment wouldn't be important to anyone who reads that magazine. My success is measured by the connection I feel with my dad…and by the honest and true connections I've made with the people in this community. I don't mean to groan when I spot this woman, but I don't feel like talking about myself right now. I want a solid night with locals, sipping their drinks and savoring the music.

A warm breeze comes in from the open windows as I approach the bar and with it comes a heavy scent of the ocean. The breeze grounds me, reminding me of what's important.

I walk behind the bar as Nel turns around to grab a bottle of Grey Goose from the shelf, along with a martini glass. "Hey, Nel, how's it been back here?" I lean against the back end of the bar, facing the people sitting at it.

"It's been steady…great as always," Nel says, mixing a vodka soda.

"How lucky are we to work here?" I ask, smiling.

"The luckiest," she responds through a grin, placing the dirty martini down in front of the patron I don't know. And I know she's not just saying that because I'm the boss. This bar is a great place to work. It's Nel's home, too.

Just as I'm about to gather the energy to introduce myself, the woman beats me to it.

"Um, excuse me," she says over the music. "Are you Kash?"

I swallow my annoyance before I respond. "Yes, I am." I put my hand out to shake hers, and she takes it, her limp hand resting in mine for only a brief moment. "Welcome to—" I start, but she cuts me off.

"And that's Summer who was singing to you just now?" She shyly nods her head toward the stage. And all I can manage is a smile. "Are you dating her?" she asks quietly.

"Yes, sorry, I'm not available to—"

She cuts me off again. "No, no. That's not what I was asking." She looks down at her hands resting on the bar.

"Oh…uh…," I falter. I am at a loss for how to respond to this person because I'm not sure why she's here. I steal a glance in Nel's direction, who has her eyebrows knit together and a look of unease spread across her face as she glances at Summer on the stage. "So, how can I help you?" I glance down at the magazine lying in front of her beside her untouched martini.

Something just doesn't seem right, but when I look at this woman, she seems harmless enough. My eyes meet hers again, and my stare must give off the vibe that I'm impatiently waiting for some kind of explanation because she takes a breath and straightens her spine. She opens her mouth as if she's about to speak but snaps it shut again, pursing her lips.

"Did you have a question about this or something about the bar?" I ask, pointing at the magazine.

The woman scoffs but not rudely; she almost seems like she's coming undone. Her eyes gloss over as she takes her gaze back again toward the stage where Summer's singing, this time without the guitar. The lyrics escaping her mouth fill the space, blocking out the sound of my breathing and the sound of my heart beating as I stare at this stranger, trying to figure out what exactly she wants.

"Do you love her?" she asks, barely audible.

"Excuse me?"

"I said…do you love her?" Her eyes bore into mine with intention, her words seeping out through clenched teeth.

"Do you know Summer or something? Or are you related to Stella? Who are you?" I don't want to sound unhinged, but I feel the curiosity bubbling into something much more protective than wonderment. I'm suddenly worried.

"I don't know anyone named Stella," she says, shaking her head slowly. "But, yes, I know Summer." She pauses for a moment, taking a shaky sip from her glass. "Or, I knew her before—I knew her a lifetime ago, it seems."

Leaning closer, I glare at her. "Who. Are. You?" I ask again, making it clear that it's the final time I'm asking. If she keeps this up, I'm asking her to leave. My protective instinct for Summer begins to take over. She knows her from *another lifetime?* From what I know about this *other lifetime,* I don't want this person in my bar.

"Are you Piper?" I ask before my tone rises. "Is your name Piper?" My voice is demanding now, and it doesn't feel like my own when it reaches my ears. "Are you coming here to take something from Summer when she's at her best? Is that what you want? To come back from her past, the one she's tried so hard to get away from—to the home she's finally made—and ruin her safety?" A few people—regulars—sitting at the bar glance my way with concern in their eyes.

"Kash—" Nel places her hand gently on my shoulder, and I brush her off, not wanting to be touched. "Where is this coming from?"

Honestly, I don't know how to answer Nel. I look anxiously up at the stage to Summer, who's none the wiser, or so it seems. She's smiling and talking to the crowd as I stand here, unable to catch my breath. Hearing this person speak of Summer's other life has brought out a side of me I didn't know existed. The woman stares at me with wide eyes.

"Piper, you need—"

The woman cuts me off and puts her hands up defensively. "I'm not Piper," she whispers. "My name's Claire...Claire Brickman. I—"

It's my turn to cut her off. "Oh, I know who you are. Get the fuck out of my bar."

CHAPTER 24

Summer

A BEAD OF SWEAT trickles down my temple, and a euphoric feeling—the same one I always get while singing—takes over my soul. The loud, whistling crowd warms my insides, and prickles on the back of my neck rise and linger as I take Jimmy's hand and we bow together. The crowd grows even louder as Jimmy places a hand over his heart, squeezing my hand tightly with his other. I send a closed-lip smile his way before pulling him in for a hug. "Thank you," I say into his ear.

He shakes his head at me. "You're a great student." His eyes fill with tears.

"You're such a softy," I joke.

He laughs loudly as he heads for the stage stairs, and I head to the microphone.

"Thank you, everyone." My voice fills the space as the noise from the crowd lingers but begins to die down. "Singing for you is my most favorite thing." The crowd whoops again. "We'll take a little break and then—" I stop mid-sentence as my eyes catch a glimpse of Kash; the look on his face is not one that I see often, if ever. I squint my eyes for a better look while simultaneously finishing my sentence, "Finn and Diego will be performing the next set…get your drinks refilled with Nel and get back to your seats. You don't want to miss their show." I try to make my voice sound natural, and the audience claps again and begins shuffling toward the bar. I clip my microphone into the stand and move it out of Finn and Diego's way. They won't need it. The guitar Jimmy's been letting me borrow is placed behind the pianos; all the while, I never take my eyes off Kash.

Nel puts her hand on his shoulder, and he rejects her gesture. *What in the world?*

I make my way to the stairs, taking my gaze in the direction that Kash is looking. I see a woman, not a regular from what I can tell. Only the side of her face is visible as she faces the bar, her hands twisting in her lap. Her shoulder-length blonde hair falls just so, blanketing her shoulder.

As I approach, Kash backs up from the bar and knits his fingers behind his head, beginning to pace. He angrily throws his dark hair into a bun, his jaw twitching and clenching as Nel approaches him again. The blonde woman is swiftly walking away, and my eyes bounce from her to Kash as I arrive at the bar. The woman turns her head, looking over her shoulder, and our eyes meet. She stops, her shoulders sink as my mouth drops.

Claire.

The point of her nose, the exact shade of her golden hair, the thin line of her pursed lips—it's all the same. She's exactly the same as I remember her from the last time we laid eyes on each other. Time has aged her, but barely. Her youthful face shines through—a mirage, a trick of the mind, toying with my emotions. Is my mind playing a trick on me? Why in the world would Claire be in this bar, all the way in California? Did she come to haunt me?

"Summer…," my name comes out of her mouth. I don't hear it, but I know that it does because I can read her lips. The noise from the bar and the increasing sensation of water—or wind—rushing through my ears drown her out. I just can't believe that this is happening.

"Summer…do you hear me?"

*I pull my hood off my head, letting out an exasperated breath. "Yeah."
I sit up on my bed. "I mean…no. What did you say?" I allow a yawn to sneak out, even though I'm well aware Claire will take offense to it—the yawn symbolizing my complete disinterest.*

Claire rolls her eyes in the way that she does, and I widen my eyes, contorting my expression to one of blatant annoyance.

"You know, you don't always have to be so hostile."

"What are you talking about?" My voice begins to rise. "You were talking to me, but I was zoning out, and I didn't hear you. And then you rolled your eyes at me. So, who's the hostile one?" Claire turns her back, attempting to ignore me. "So…," I drag out the word, waiting impatiently for her to say whatever she felt the need to tell me. "Are you going to say it?"

She whips her head around to face me, her blonde hair floating through the air dramatically. "I said," she begins, moving her head with a slight tick, showing her attitude. "Actually, forget it. It's about Trevor, and what do you know about guys?" She laughs, trying to make a joke of her comment, but I don't smile.

I don't smile because she's right. What do I know about guys? Nothing except that I can't hold onto one, especially the good ones. Dan flashes through my mind briefly, and my heart sinks to the bottom of my stomach.

"What's going on with Trevor?" I ask, but I don't care—not in the slightest.

She looks at me expressionless. There was a time in our lives when Claire longed—so desperately—to be my sister, for us to be comrades, for us to share secrets behind our bedroom door, for us to be as thick as thieves. We were young then, in junior high, and I never had the heart to tell her that it would never happen. So, I didn't tell her, but I certainly showed her—with my actions— that I would not ever let her in. Eventually, she punished me for that, turning her back on me completely by spreading a rumor that I was in a secret relationship with her brother. She never admitted it was her who started the inferno that spread through our home and our school like wildfire. But it was her. I know it was. As I sit here, cross-legged on my bed, staring at her, processing all that's gone on between us, I'm not at all shocked with the realization that so much time has passed since the rumor was started, and our relationship is as sucky as it is.

"He wants to go out with the hockey team tonight instead of hanging out with me like he promised. Do you think he's cheating on me?"

My eyebrows furrow. Does she really want my opinion? "Well, Trevor's a loser, so…," I say as I lean back against my headboard.

"Helpful, Summer, really helpful." She turns her back to me, and I see her reflection in the mirror as she applies her lip gloss with precision. "I figured you would have an opinion since you're a cheater, and it takes one to know one. Isn't that what they say?" She lets a small laugh escape at my expense.

I roll my eyes, but she doesn't see. Dan, again, flashes into my head, and I wince at the memory of what I did last year. The night that I attempted—for the umpteenth time—to dull the ache inside, to fill the void, by making out with a stranger at a party. Meg taking the picture and giving it to him. Me with no boyfriend and not a friend in sight. I brush away the memory; no need to wallow in mistakes that can't be changed.

"So, are you coming to Jake's with us then?" I ask nonchalantly, pretending she didn't just dig right into my soul. I open my paperback and flip to the page I'm on.

She scoffs. "With you and Jason? No, thanks."

OK, I mouth the word but don't voice it, arriving at page 211 of my book.

"I'm hanging out with the girls." Her words are flippant, meant to cut me, I'm sure, as she knows that I don't know what it's like to have a group to refer to as the girls, at least not anymore. "Don't you think it's a little pathetic that Jason is your only friend? He has his own thing going on now with college. Don't you think you should find some new friends?" It's senior year. A little late for that now. I think this, but don't say it. I read the same sentence in my book over and over.

"Summer," she calls my name, but I don't look up from the book. I'm turning inward, the way I always do—loathing my life and everything it has become.

"Summer...," Claire's voice now sounds older than the voice from my memory.

She stands frozen in her spot, and I take a step closer to her, cocking my head to the side slightly, still wondering if what I'm seeing is reality. As I glance over to the bar, I see the look on Kash's face, and his expression startles me as it's not one I recognize. Annoyance? Maybe. Defeat mixed with anger? Possibly. He begins to make his way out from behind the bar as a crowd gathers for refills. We don't have time for Claire—we have customers to serve.

Just as I think this, Finn, Diego, and Jimmy make their way behind the bar to help Nel.

The last time I saw Claire was the night that changed the trajectory of my whole life, the night that my *only friend* took advantage of me, taking every last bit of dignity I had. That night was the last night I slept in that bed in our shared room. By the time the sun set the following night, I was homeless, falling and falling deeper into the darkness.

I glance down at my feet briefly—at my tattered Converse—before lifting my eyes toward Claire—her entire being is the epitome of *put together*. My trauma response is strong as I feel utterly inferior, as if I'm still eighteen…still a foster kid…still not belonging to anyone or anywhere…with no family of my own. But as quick as the feeling emerges, I swiftly straighten my spine and soften my jaw. I push that negative self-talk out of my brain.

This is *my* home.

This is *my* safety.

I am OK.

Summer James, you are worthy of goodness.

I am NOT the sum of my past.

I feel Kash's hand on the small of my back. "I told you to leave," he spits out to Claire; his voice is angry, words inching out through clenched teeth. I turn my head in his direction, taken aback by his tone.

I place my hand lightly on his arm. "It's OK." The words come out hushed, but I know he heard me. "I'm curious, actually, why she feels the need to traipse into my life now." No anger in my words, no resentment. I'm able to shake off the complete sense of lacking that used to define me and replace it with reminders of what is true now in my life. The glossy floor beneath the soles of my shoes, the ocean just beyond Claire's back, the love of my chosen family protecting me—these are beacons of proof that where I am now is home. What I left behind is anything but that.

Kash, Farrah, Nel, Jimmy, Silvia, Mav—they are my family. This woman, who was once my "sister," is not my family. She holds no place in my heart. I don't need to be anything more than the real Summer James. I don't need to prove myself in order to be loved. I am good enough.

"So, Claire, what *are* you doing here?"

She purses her lips, seemingly stifling her rising emotion. I raise my eyebrows and feel Kash shift his weight beside me. I'm well aware that he doesn't feel good about this. I know he wants (or needs) to protect me…because I know him. And he knows me. All of me. All of me now and all of me from my time with Claire. He knows what I've been through, and he hates this. I can feel the tension coming off of him. I turn toward him. "Go behind the bar and help them." I nod toward the crowd waiting to be served as Nel, Finn, Diego, and Jimmy hustle behind the bar.

Kash's eyes dart to every part of my face, gauging my expression, most likely trying to decide if I'm being honest with him. His face looks pained. I know he tried to get her out before I saw her, and I don't want him to feel bad or like he's failed me.

"I'm good." I try to assure him. "You *know* I'm good." I say those four words so only he can hear them and add a wink. "Go."

He glares at Claire and hesitates for a moment. I briefly smile, though I know it's not the time or place to do so, but Kash's demeanor is so out of character, and I can't help but think that it looks good on him. He shakes his head at nothing or no one in particular before turning on his heel and heading toward the bar.

I look back at Claire. "What are you doing here?"

"Can we go somewhere quiet to talk?" she asks.

"I'm working." Her shoulders slump again in defeat. "Claire, you found me. After all this time, sixteen years, I think—you found me…somehow. You come to my place of employment and expect me to drop everything—" I put both arms out to emphasize the crowd, "and just leave to go and talk to *you* after all this time? Did you think I was waiting for you to show up at my doorstep? Because I can assure you, I wasn't."

Claire looks heartbroken, but I don't let it phase me. I can't. My arms instinctively go up to my chest and begin to cross, but I force them down. I don't want her to think I'm uncomfortable in my skin. "We are adults now, Summer. Can't you just give me a chance to say my piece?"

I can't help it. My arms cross, and I leave them there. And in all honesty, it's a better place for them to be than idle at my sides, ready to take a swing at her. "I don't owe you anything, Claire." I shake my head at her slowly in disbelief at her audacity.

"No. I know, I know," she responds quickly, trying to save herself, I'm sure. "I'm just saying, we were like sisters. For seven years, we shared a room. Shouldn't we reconnect? Mend our friendship?"

"You seem to have a selective memory. How quickly you've forgotten what you did to me during those seven years." I take a step closer to her, though I'm not entirely sure why. "The last time I spoke to you, you made fun of me—scoffed at me—for everything I had lost. I went, emotionally damaged, into the night, having no idea what I was up against. Not until it was too late." I struggle to contain my emotions, but I try. "And then my only friend—your brother—took advantage of me when I was at my weakest. He raped me, and, well, you know what happened after that." I glare at her, unwavering. It seems as if she's unsure of what to say in response. "Oh, were you unaware of what Jason did? Did you believe the lies your *mother* spewed and your father didn't do anything to stop?"

"I…I—" Claire bows her head in defeat. I allow her to stutter until she finds the words she wants to speak. "I found out eventually. A few years ago."

"And what? Your regret has festered since then until you gathered the courage to come and find me?"

"No, I—" She loses her words again, and in turn, I lose my patience.

"I want you to leave." My words are final.

Her face falls, but she nods once before tucking a magazine, our magazine, under her arm and digging in her bag, pulling out a card. I don't care to ask why she's holding our edition of the magazine. I don't care in the slightest. "I'm here until the day after tomorrow. My cell is on that card. If you change your mind, text me. If you don't, I understand." I take the card from her hand without saying anything. "You have a beautiful voice." She offers a weak smile, but when I don't return it, she quickly takes it back, her face becoming unrecognizable to the cold one that I remember from when I was younger. Her expression is pained, a bit lost.

Without taking my eyes off of her, I tuck the card into the back pocket of my jeans. She gives me a quick wave with a sad look on her face before turning around and walking out of the bar. I watch until she's made her way past the windows I love so much, until I can't see her anymore. Only then do I relax my shoulders and turn away from the ocean view. I turn to look for Kash, and I'm not surprised to find him pulling me into his embrace the second I turn toward the bar. I allow myself to relax into him.

Everything is OK.

I flip the rectangular card around in my fingers aimlessly, hoping—with desperation—that some sort of clarity will hit me and I'll come to a decision on what to do about this Claire situation. At first, I thought my decision was obvious: I would watch her walk out of sight into the California evening, and I would go on living my life. Turns out my emotions, my curiosity, and—much to my dismay—my anxious thoughts are sending me into a tailspin.

Kash pushes a steaming mug of tea across the bar. "Compliments of the kitchen." His smile eases the tension that's settled in my shoulders, and I pull the mug closer.

It's two thirty in the morning, and the bar has long been emptied, all but the two of us. The lights are on but dimmed, and the place is sparkling and immaculate, ready for tomorrow. I take a gentle sip from the mug and sigh.

"Thanks, Kash." He gives me a questioning but soft look. "I know you were trying to protect me by avoiding what inevitably ended up transpiring." I pause, shaking my head slowly. "But I'm beginning to think that this is something that needs to happen. Facing another part of my past. Another step in my journey of healing."

He nods, taking a moment before he speaks. "It wasn't enough when you went to Kentucky to confront Cassie and Greg before you left Austin?" His question is non-judgmental; a curiosity lingers in his words.

"No, it was. At the time." I take another sip, feeling the warm tea travel down my throat. "But seeing her face tonight…well, it opened a door I didn't know needed to be opened. And I realized there are some things that need to be dealt with behind that door." Kash leans over the bar and takes my hands. I look at him for a moment before continuing. "When Claire showed up, I felt bad about myself," I admit. "It was only for a second, but—" I swallow the lump in my throat. "But the feeling was so strong that I realize that I should use this opportunity to face a person who did me so wrong when I was younger. If I let her fly back to wherever she came from without facing her, I'll regret it. I know I will."

"I think that's a wise choice." I don't know if he believes what he's saying. I think, deep down, he would rather me carry on without ever seeing or talking to a Brickman as long I live. But that's because he doesn't want me to feel pain anymore. I nod, agreeing with him. "Do you want me to go with you?"

I study his face, thankful for the offer, but I need to say no. I shake my head. "No, but thank you. I appreciate the support, but I need to do this on my own—without you holding me up. I need her to see me as who I am now. That I have become a strong, independent person in spite of who I was before."

Kash walks out from behind the bar and meets me at the stool I'm perched on. He pulls me into his chest, and I settle in there, feeling his warmth. "But I will let you carry me home and take me to bed," I say into his neck, my voice sounding muffled, but the sound of my smile is actually audible.

"Done and done."

I gave Claire particularly clear instructions on how to get to the lookout spot I determined was an appropriate place for us to meet. It's not a place I go often, if ever really, so if things go awry and the space is ruined for me, oh well. I walk up the battered, wooden steps toward the smell of the briny ocean mixed with the aroma of fried food coming from the food truck just off the sandy path. The stairs ascend to a clearing that overlooks the ocean. There are benches, picnic tables, and pastel Adirondack chairs scattered throughout the space.

My eyes scan the area until I spot Claire sitting in a light pink chair, an empty blue one next to her. She's facing the water, her hair in a sleek, low bun. Attempting to calm the racing of my heart, I force one foot in front of the other, reminding myself as I walk that this is my territory. This is my home. And I have grown. I have healed. I have people in my corner now. There is nothing to be afraid of.

"Hi," I say, pulling the chair a bit away from Claire but turning it more in her direction. I sit down, placing my bag on the sand beside me. I sit on the edge of my seat at first, slightly uncomfortable.

Claire straightens up in her seat. "Summer…hi." She sounds surprised to see me. "I wasn't sure if you'd show up."

"Well, here I am."

"Yes. Here you are." She looks at me with an expression I can't read. It's like she's in awe of me, which seems odd. "So, how have you been, Summer?"

I stare at her wide-eyed. I don't want to talk about myself, not even a little bit, but I guess that's the point of this—to be an adult and meet her halfway. It can't be a one-sided conversation. Though, all I really want is to hear an apology or something of the sort.

I turn my head to the sea and pull the salty air into my lungs. I tell Claire about my life here and what my days consist of. I hesitate to tell her the details that make my heart sing. I want to leave out the pieces that she doesn't deserve to know, the things I don't believe she is privy to. So, I tell her some things without going into too much detail. I tell her about the bar, my singing, and I tell her briefly about Texas, leaving out the parts of my life where I was lost—homeless and buried in pain. I don't even want to hear that part again. At least not right now. My entire spiel takes only a few minutes. Claire is looking at me intently, absorbing all I have to say. When a moment of quiet passes, she smiles without showing her teeth, her eyes growing glossy.

"What about you?" I ask. "How are you? And—" I swallow hard, not wanting to say it, but I do. "Your family…how are they?" Not that I care.

She studies me again, and I shift in my seat, attempting to get comfortable, but it really isn't possible in this situation. "How long do you have?" she says through a pitiful laugh. After I don't respond for a moment, she sighs, looking out toward the ocean, her hands twisting in her lap like they were last night at the bar. And then she begins talking. Once she starts, it's like the floodgates have opened, and she can't stop. And there's nothing for me to do but listen.

CHAPTER 25

Claire

I DIDN'T KNOW THEN, at eighteen years old, that my soul had been spoiled to the point of rot. Summer had been gone just over a year, and Jason had moved out of state for his sophomore year of college. I had been an only child for a year. A blissful year. A year of suckling at my parents' guilt for all it was worth. Guilt that I didn't comprehend until much later, but at the time, it didn't matter. I was the pride and joy of the Brickman household. I could do no wrong. Even when I did, it didn't make a difference.

My senior year had been everything I'd wished it would be. Driving around listening to burned CDs with my friends, sitting in basements—sometimes sipping, sometimes pretending to sip—the beers that would be handed to me, getting home after curfew but not getting in trouble. And then there was Trevor Bayview. Being on the arm of the most popular guy in school didn't hurt, landing me the title of prom queen and other useless accolades that seemed dire at the time. If there was a red flag flying in my direction in any area of my life, I was a professional at ignoring it.

I was growing into a carbon copy of my mother, and, looking back on it, Cassandra Brickman was the last person I should have wanted to embody. My smile was fake ninety percent of the time, and I practically invented the resting bitch face for the other ten percent. I couldn't be bothered with things that I deemed *beneath* me. I wasn't phased with the problems of the world, or the problems of the people around me for that matter. It was my year to shine, and no one was going to get in my way. The space that opened up on Summer's side of the room was a constant reminder that what I'd wished for so passionately in the fifth grade—a sister—was just a little girl's silly plea to the universe. At seventeen, I was grateful she was gone. It didn't phase me like it should have how she was there one day and gone the next. Mom said she went to another foster home, and that explanation was enough for me.

What I should have done was give a shit. But when you look back at the life that's long gone, there isn't much to say about the mistakes you made, is there? There wouldn't be any lessons in life if we all just made the right choice in the first place. But I at least wish, in hindsight, that I was a more decent person, that I took after my father more, flaws and all.

When Trevor cheated on me with the editor of the school newspaper at the end of senior year, people thought that was the end of us. Trevor, I assumed, was trying to make himself seem more distinguished, more serious. Editor of the school newspaper versus the cheer captain? He told me, after I found out, that, of course, we would be breaking up before college. He was going to Northwestern with a hockey scholarship, and somehow, that made him more distinguished than anyone else in our grade.

"It's time for me to smarten up, don't you think? Take things seriously," he had said to me as we stood against his car in the school parking lot.

"Who are you? Warner Huntington?" I asked, my arms crossed at my chest. He gave me a questioning look, having zero clue who I was talking about. Apparently, *Legally Blonde* wasn't a movie he had memorized like I had. I huffed, annoyed (actually heartbroken), and stomped away, trying to be brave like Elle Woods but actually feeling like a weak loser.

Turns out, Trevor's interest in poised seriousness didn't last. It wasn't long—only a few days—until he came crawling back to me. And I took him back before even a full week had passed. That decision is probably my biggest regret. That one act of forgiveness started a chain reaction, the catalyst to all the other times I gave him the benefit of the doubt after that. Turning him into the perfect guy became a task I desperately tried to complete, to mend, to mold. A project, if you will. Just like my mother would have done. Eventually, everything he did annoyed me—the way he breathed when he was falling asleep, the way he grunted when putting his shoes on, the way he never knew where the damn leftovers were.

Or I should say the way he *breathes*…the way he never *knows*. Because that's the present tense, and I married Trevor. However, it's also true that, presently, I'm planning my exit from being a Bayview. Though, I don't really want to go back to being a Brickman either.

I went off to college at the University of Chicago to study business. The location intrigued me for no other reason than it was close to

Northwestern, close enough to keep an eye on Trevor. I spent four years doing what seemed like a normal college experience. I joined a sorority and made friends based solely on close proximity. Connections loosely held together by linked elbows while stumbling down dark roads late at night on our way to this party or that social, and nothing more. Nothing deep. Nothing real.

I had that false sense of happiness, a delusion that warped my thinking for far too long. A lie I let my mother instill in me as truth: *If it looks like you have it all, then you must.* She never actually said those words to me; she didn't have to. She showed me. I knew how to paint my face just so—with lots of makeup and fake expressions—so that I could control everyone around me. Dormmates, sorority sisters, resident directors, professors. I found ways to get the best dorm rooms and a free pass any time we got caught drinking on campus. I knew how to finagle a better grade. A grade I most certainly didn't deserve.

"What are you going to do in the real world, Claire?" my sorority sister, Janine, said one night while we all were drinking champagne and getting dressed for a toga party. "Have an affair with all your bosses?" That elicited cackles from the seven girls in the room. I glared at Janine with a smirk on my face. I knew I shouldn't have told her the extent I'd gone to to pass my economics class in order to graduate and land the job I was hammering for. *Keep it locked up,* my mother always said.

"Poor Trevor," Shayla added, retying the knot in the back of her toga sheet, her words insincere.

Not poor Trevor. Trevor was fine. Tit for tat. Over and over again. That's the way it was with us. Whether it was newspaper editors or hockey groupies up at Northwestern, I always found out. *Tit.* And then I would retaliate, if the chance ever arose, with professors or TAs or Starbucks baristas. *Tat.*

You may wonder why on earth I didn't just break it off with him. And I don't know why, not exactly. All I do know is that it seems that I was addicted to the insatiable need to *win.*

Win what? The answer is elusive, if I'm being honest. A mystery, even to myself. Our relationship put me on the map in high school. That, mixed with the unimportant lessons I was subconsciously learning from my mother about poise and perfection, control, and power, all created a drive inside me that took over.

Trevor was being scouted by professional and semi-professional hockey teams throughout college, and knowing this created a fantasy in my mind. A crystal clear image of what my life would be like if that happened and we were still together. The fantasy had nothing to do with my pride, or my love, for Trevor. It had nothing to do with Trevor at all, actually, except what he could get me. It became a selfish plot that began to tangle in my mind, a challenge I desperately needed to win, like all the others I'd conquered prior. I wasn't going to watch Trevor rise to fame with another woman on his arm. *Over my dead body.*

He was injured badly just before graduation. Severe tears in his MCL and ACL led to surgery, which he was told did not have to be career-ending for him. But the tears in his knees led to tears in his passion. He swiftly slipped into a cycle of resentment and self-loathing. A caring girlfriend would've been strong through the pain. Held up their partner until they got on the other side of it. But my resentment grew, too, until I didn't have a handle on it.

I believed that he'd pull himself out of it eventually. I guess I put the responsibility all on him and assumed the sweet reward of fame would be enough to lead him back to reality.

It didn't.

When the smoke cleared and the prospect of playing professional hockey became a faded dream, I found myself still at Trevor's side. I was working in advertising at a partner company of my dad's business. When college ended, I started there right away, putting all my energy into it, hoping to inspire some drive in Trevor as well. And I did, if only slightly.

He got a job at a local news station, doing sports reporting on a small scale. He also began volunteering at the community college in Louisville, helping the hockey team.

We were twenty-six when we got married. And that's when I knew I had made a mistake. Trevor was unfulfilled with the path he'd taken after his injury. And me? I, too, was unfulfilled. The love I thought I could create for us from our faulty foundation ended up not being love at all. Not in the slightest. Our union is the opposite of love. I wish I could say that I don't know how I got here…but I do, and I need to own that. We, Trevor and I, didn't begin as *young love*. We began as an opportunity for me to rise through the ranks. I was spoiled. I was materialistic. I was desperate.

And I have to admit that I'm not sure I ever knew what love was until now, not really. I've never witnessed love like I did last night at the bar. Being envious of Summer is not something I ever imagined possible. But I am.

I never told anyone about the night that I saw her on the streets all those years later, sitting on a curb in downtown Louisville. I was looking for Trevor. He had stormed out, and I assumed he was drunk somewhere, meeting up with old high school friends to bounce from strip club to strip club. My car inched up and down the dark streets, peering into every establishment, unsure of what I would do if, or when, I found him. But then I found her instead.

She looked so utterly sad, as if her face could never possibly brighten again. As if she would be sad for all of eternity. My car slowed to a crawl as I got closer, but I couldn't bear to look any longer. Why was she there? What had happened to her? It was the first time I'd questioned everything my mother had told me about Summer's departure. But I still didn't question it enough then. I know that now.

I never told anyone because I was embarrassed that I was even in that part of town that late at night in the first place. I was too afraid of what it would do to my reputation if anyone knew that I was there. And that trumped any desire to bring up the fact that I'd seen Summer alone on the street.

From that point on, I began questioning everything my mother said. I didn't realize I was doing it, at least not at first. But the inexplicable truth of my life and family became more clear as time went on. The loose threads that were barely holding us together began to fray so easily that before I could even understand what was happening, there was no seam left to cling to.

When Jason first got put on extended leave at his job for sexual harassment a while back, I was appalled. *My brother did what?* But when we sat around the table for a family meeting, the tight-lipped expression on my mother's face and the exhausted one on my father's seemed to show me that they were not at all surprised by the accusations. Jason had stormed out of the house after voices were raised. About what? I couldn't say. I had zoned out, confused. After he left, I excused myself to the kitchen for some water, and some air.

The walls between the kitchen and the dining room muffled his voice, but I could still make out the anger in my dad's words. I stood still, my whole body tense, and my shoulders practically touching my ears, as I held my breath and strained to hear every word the two of them muttered.

"I knew she was telling the truth," he said, hissing through his teeth.

Mom didn't respond right away, and though I couldn't see her, I just knew she was rolling her eyes at his expense. "You can't help yourself, can you, Greg," I heard her blurt out angrily. "You always have to bring Summer into the mix."

A loud bang sounded, most likely my dad's fist on the table. "You have issues, Cassie. Deep issues. The fact that Summer showed up here a few months ago, saying what she said, and you have no remorse for what that child went through…in OUR HOME."

"She is a grown woman, Greg. We need to move on," said my mother.

"No, she is a grown woman now. But not then. We were supposed to protect her. She was just a child. And the fact that you have zero regard for the negative impact we…or should I say YOU, had on her disgusts me. I should have stood my ground against you when I had the chance." Dad's tone turned to one of defeat, and my shoulders slumped as I let out the breath I didn't realize I'd been holding in.

I walked back into the dining room through the swinging kitchen door, and both of my parents straightened their spines and gave each other sideways glances as I took my seat. I wasn't about to let this conversation that I'd overheard go without finding out what the hell they were talking about. "So, Summer showed up here? When?"

My mom took in a labored, annoyed breath. "Yes, dear, she was in the area." Her voice raised an octave as she glared at my father. "Right, honey? She wanted to say hello." Her smile, the painted-on one, was shiny and fake as plastic. Inwardly, I cringed, reflecting on the traits that my mother had passed on to me, and I didn't want them anymore. Instead of being poised, instead of pretending that everything was OK, I allowed the rage to build inside me, my eyebrows furrowing, my heart racing. I couldn't figure out why the feeling was so strong, but I couldn't fight it.

"What. In. The. World. Happened?" I asked, my eyes glaring into my mother, each word coming out as its own sentence, slow and deliberate.

Mother flicked her wrist in my direction, dismissing my demands for the truth as a frivolous curiosity. "Nothing," she insisted.

My dad rolled his eyes. "It wasn't nothing," he deadpanned, sitting back against his chair, crossing his arms across his chest.

"Dad? Please?" The words to my father came out much weaker than the ones I sent in my mother's direction.

He leaned forward, his elbows on the table, and opened his mouth to speak. No surprise to me, my mother attempted to quiet him. "Greg." His name came dripping out of her mouth like a warning.

But, to my surprise, he ignored her. "Yes," he began, "Summer showed up here a few months ago. It seemed to me that she was attempting some sort of closure. She had strong words to say to your mother and me." He paused there, most likely waiting for the wrath of my mother. He scanned my face for something, but I wasn't sure what. He cleared his throat before continuing. "She accused Jason of raping her at a party the night before she left our house." My body stiffened at the admission. More accusations of abuse by my brother that I just couldn't fathom. I nodded, just once, hoping he'd continue, that he'd give me all the information that had been kept from me up until now. "She said he'd raped her, not that she came on to him, which is what he accused her of the night it happened. She said he'd told her that no one would believe her, so there was no point in her telling anyone." He paused, and I let out a breath that caused an ache in my chest. She was right about that. No one would have believed her. But as my father filled me in that evening, I *did* believe it. Without a doubt. Dad continued. "And when she woke up the morning after the party," he shrugged, "your mother called Social Services to have her removed from our house. But before she could be shipped off to God knows where, she ran away. And your mother and I didn't do enough to look for her." He glared at my mother, but she seemed unphased, her chin lifted as if she was attempting to convince herself that she had the upper hand.

The memory of Summer sitting on the curb that dark night, looking heartbroken and pained, like the world had chewed her up and spit her out, played in my mind, and my heart crumbled into tiny pieces. The feeling I had inside was a new feeling. Empathy, sorrow, selflessness.

"So, what you're saying is, you did nothing with this information that Summer brought to you. You didn't bring it up to Jason? You didn't try to mend what was broken with Summer?" My words were accusatory. I knew that they were, but I just didn't care. "And now he's gone and done it to other women?"

My mother rolled her eyes and made the noise she makes with her tongue that has always driven me crazy, as if the word gaslighting had a sound.

"No, Mom, I won't let you turn this into nothing. I won't let you ignore the truth and make the rest of us feel like we are the crazy ones." By the rest of us, I meant my father and me, but also, I felt a loyalty to Summer in that moment that I'd never felt before.

Then, it was my mother who stormed out, almost knocking her chair down in the process. And so, there it was: Dad and me against Jason and my mother. A breath came out of my mouth in a short, loud burst as I pulled my hands through my hair. The sheepish look on my dad's face sickened me for a brief moment. It was as if he wanted me to feel bad for him, but after all I'd learned that night, all I could fathom was that my sorrow was only for Summer. My guilt. My shame. We had all done wrong by her, and imagining her out there, alone in the world, broke a piece of my hardened exterior.

"Mom is insufferable," I said to my father in disgust.

He opened his mouth like he was going to say something, possibly defend her but thought better of it. He pursed his lips and looked down at his hands on the table. I'd had enough and got up from the table, grabbing my purse. I headed for the door and to my car and back to my pitiful husband without so much as a goodbye to either one of my parents.

The months that followed were filled with family meetings that I didn't attend. I would slowly find out what was going on from text messages. Dad had hired lawyers to help Jason get out of the mess at work, which did seem to help. But when local news stations began covering the story of the mishappenings of a "well-to-do" business-man in town, other women began coming out of the woodwork to share their stories about Jason. Currently, as I tell you this he awaits trial for his actions. I don't care what happens to him. The family is trying to save face, but I hope he gets what he deserves. It won't take away the pain that all these women, including Summer, felt and still feel, but at least he'll be held accountable. The trial has been delayed countless times, and each time it is, I am broken, knowing the system is inevitably designed for people like my brother and my family to thrive. But I will continue to pray that there is some redemption…anything for these victims.

My parents divorced last year, not too long after I learned of Jason's long list of wrongdoings. I watched their marriage crumble under the pressure of the court stress, but it didn't take long for me to understand that it wasn't just the issues with Jason that caused their union to end. It was my dad's realization that Mother wasn't the person he wanted her to be, and most likely, she never was. It pained him. I could see it in every move he made, in every facial expression. As if just existing was excruciating. He wanted her to be better. But she is who she is. And though he's softer than her, it didn't compliment her hardness. Their opposition wasn't an attraction, apparently, at least not anymore.

With all the realizations and skeletons that came out of the closet, I began to pull away from my family. If anyone still gets my attention, it's Dad, but even that is minimal. And though I favor my dad more at this point, the fact that he won't make Jason take responsibility, won't make him face the accusations without the lion of a lawyer he's paying for, a lawyer who will undoubtedly help him get away with it, sickens me.

As my parents' marriage ended, I began to accept the fact that mine also was done. I tried, for a brief time, to mend it, but I quickly learned that you can't mend something that was never whole to begin with.

The house I grew up in was sold to a young family, and as I drove away for the last time, watching the lattice outside my childhood bedroom fade out of view in the rearview mirror, I hoped that the ghosts within the walls of the house wouldn't claim that family, wouldn't sink their teeth into their souls. I prayed that the promise of a happy family life with white picket fences and pretty flower boxes wouldn't cloud the new family's visions, that it wouldn't make them forget what was important, like it had for us.

Seeing Summer at her bar, glowing from the inside out, proved to me that I've had it wrong all along. I'm more than ready to take responsibility for my own actions and for what they have done to others. I can't blame my family anymore for the way I turned out. I'm a grownup. It's time I acted like one.

CHAPTER 26

Summer

"**I** TOLD YOU TREVOR was a loser." Claire laughs, but it sounds awkward and uncomfortable. "It's one of the last things I said to you, Claire." I watch a couple walk hand in hand to the fenced ledge, waiting for a beat before continuing. "While you poked me about me not having friends and criticized everything I did, I sat and took it, like I always did." I shake my head, not looking at her. "I was, and still am, a good judge of character. I could have predicted everything you just told me about Trevor. And your entire family, for that matter."

"You *are* a good judge of character, Summer," Claire whispers into a gust of wind that whips off the shore. "So, can you see that I'm sorry? Can you see that I've changed?"

There isn't a part of me that thinks she's truly changed. Not enough, at least. Maybe she's starting to. Maybe she's finally realized that the way she lived, the way she treated others, was superficial at best. But changing takes time. It takes work. I would know. It seems to me like this visit is nothing more than an attempt to clear her guilty conscience. I hope that I'm wrong. I really do. I hope that she finds peace in these changes she's attempting to make.

"What do you want from me?" I ask her. I'm genuinely unsure of her intentions.

"I needed to see you. After I saw you on the cover of that magazine—" She shakes her head in disbelief, it seems. "I felt this urge to know that you were OK. To know that you were happy. I needed to see it for myself." She gives me a half smile through her bubbling emotion. "I was hoping we could reconnect. Rebuild our relationship. We were like sisters, after all."

I glare at her, trying to find just the right words to respond. "You just spent thirty minutes telling me how you've been a conniving person for the last sixteen years since I've seen you, that you saw me alone on a street, sad, and you were too proud to help me." She opens her mouth to interrupt me, but I put my hand up to stop her, not aggressively but I'm not done speaking. "The fact that you think you can show up in my life, now, after just a few months of soul searching, and ask for my forgiveness, to ask for me to let you in—it shows just how much this attempt at redemption is more of a necessity for you than it is for me." She looks at me sadly but doesn't respond. "I'm beyond happy for you that you're getting to the point of realizing the truth after all this time. It gives me a little hope, knowing that people like you can at least try to change. To grow. I hope that you find happiness. I hope that you find what you didn't even know you needed. I really do, Claire." She smiles and reaches over, placing her hand on my knee. I move my leg out of the way. "But you will not be a part of my life." I shake my head slowly. "You will leave and go back to Kentucky tomorrow. And that will be it. You will not contact me ever again." My words come out soft, but I know she can tell I mean them. I'm not trying to sound tough or intimidating. I just want her to know I mean what I'm saying.

It's cathartic to know that the life I thought I'd had no place in, the family that always made sure I knew my place as a guest in their home, the family I yearned to be a part of, was actually just an illusion. I was the only genuine one, the only one who was whole. The way they made me feel about myself was all a lie. And now, I live my truth.

"Do you really mean that?" Claire asks, her voice wavering.

I nod, sure as I've ever been. "Yes, Claire. Thank you. Thank you from the bottom of my heart for being honest with me and helping me see the truth even clearer than I've been able to over the last few years. But I love myself too much now to let you into my heart."

She looks out over the ocean, her chin quivering. "OK." The word barely comes out. "Can I give you a hug before I leave?"

"I don't really see the point in the gesture. We were nothing to each other before this, and we will be nothing to each other going forward." I believe I've made it clear that I'm done with this conversation, and I'm grateful when she nods and moves her body to get up from the chair. A tiny sob escapes as she waves and turns to head back down the sandy path.

Relaxing into the chair, I turn to face out toward the ocean. Turns out I didn't ruin this spot for myself. If anything, it has instantly become a new favorite place. A place where I proved that my strength is unwavering now. *I am worthy of goodness. I am not the sum of my past.* And as I make my way down the beach path toward the street, I'm startled at first to see Kash idling in his truck on the side of the road.

"Need a ride?" he yells through the open window, smiling enough to show his dimple.

My shoulders relax, and I smile back as I pick up the pace, heading toward his truck. "Didn't I say I didn't need you to come with me?" I ask lightly as I climb into the passenger seat.

He tilts his head, still grinning. "I know you didn't *need* me." He puts the truck into drive and pulls away from the curb, placing his hand on my thigh. "But I thought you might want to get some ice cream."

And that's the way of Kash. How he always has been: allowing me the space to do the hard work myself, but then always being there to make the darkness a little brighter.

September is well underway when I get a text from Joey that alarms me. It's Sunday morning, and Nel and I are sitting on a secluded stretch of beach just north of Santa Monica. We both have to work tonight but decided to get bagel sandwiches and iced coffees and to sit in the sand for a bit before we have to go in. My phone vibrates in my beach bag, and I ignore it at first, but when it vibrates a few more times, I reach in to grab it, surprised to see three texts from Joey. "What the hell," I mutter to myself. I glance at Nel, who definitely didn't hear. She's bopping to the music coming from our portable beach speaker.

Have you talked to Farrah in the last few weeks? Does she seem off to you?

One minute later, another text came through.

I don't know if it's a postpartum thing or something else, but she's reminding me of other times when she was depressed. I'm worried.

Sorry to bombard you or worry you with this…hope you're doing OK…

My stomach lurches, feeling like it's sunk to the farthest reaches of my body, taking my heart along with it. "Nel, I'll be right back. I just gotta call a friend."

She shields her eyes from the sun with her hands and looks at me. "You OK?"

I give her a weary look but manage a weak smile. "Yeah. Just got a weird text from Farrah's husband. I want to make sure everything is OK."

"Alright, I'll be here if you need me." She sounds concerned but lets me walk off. I quickly call Joey, and he answers on the first ring.

"Hi, Summer."

"Joey, what's going on?"

"Have you talked to Farrah lately?"

"Yeah, all the time…," my voice fades off as I try to recall anything different about her mood the last few times we've talked. "I haven't noticed anything off, Joey." I try to sound hopeful and reassuring, but it's hard to feel confident when I'm so many miles away, when I haven't seen Farrah in person in almost two years, when one or both of us is always distracted when we're talking. My heart sinks again. I feel like I've failed her and Joey.

"No? OK, that's good. She has been crying a lot, Summer. She's dazed so often and won't let Junie out of her sight. She won't even let her mom watch her, or my parents. So, we haven't had a lot of time to connect." The sound of his deep breathing fills my ear. "I don't want to fail her. I'm just not sure what to do right now."

"Joey, you're not failing her. You're doing everything right. You noticed a change, and you're acting on it." I look out over the ocean, trying to gather my thoughts—think of a plan. But before I can say anything more, Joey speaks up.

"I think she needs to come see you." His words aren't a question. He isn't asking me. He's telling me, and it's obvious from his tone.

"Yeah?" I try not to sound excited. Seeing Farrah would make me so happy. And apparently, it's what Joey thinks she desperately needs.

"Yes. It would have to be all of us, though, because she'd never go without Junie. And I want her to have a break to catch up with you. If I come, I can take care of Junie and give you guys some time to connect." It's like he already planned this out and he just called to warn me that they were coming. Not that I need a warning. "What do you think?"

"Yes, Joey, you all can absolutely come for a visit. I think that would be amazing for her, and me, if I'm being honest." I relax my shoulders a bit.

"Yeah…yes…definitely." I can hear him doing something in the background, but I'm not sure what.

"I think you should have her get in touch with her therapist, even if she insists she's fine."

"I have been trying." He sounds defeated. "But I'll keep at it."

"It's going to be OK, Joey." I'm well aware that he doesn't believe me, but I know that it's true; he's clouded with worry, and I'll do anything I can to help him…and her.

"Let me call you back tonight, and we can finalize a good time for you to book flights and stuff," I say as the excitement of seeing my best friend and her family starts to sink in.

"Thank you, Summer."

"No need. But seriously, don't stop pestering her until she agrees to see her therapist. You could even call Champlain Bridge. I'm sure they would be more than willing to help."

Just saying the name of the place that saved me brings up a bout of emotion that takes me by surprise. I met Farrah at Champlain Bridge when we were both in the process of finding light in the infinite darkness. They were so integral to my healing journey. They gave me my best friend. They gave me Janie. If there is a reason to believe in hope, it's that place.

"Yes, you're right. I am going to call them as soon as I hang up with you," Joey says, sounding relieved.

"OK, I'll talk to you tonight. Bye, Joey."

We hang up, and I head back to Nel, and as I do, plans begin to form in my mind, plans that I'm determined to execute. Kash has been bringing up memories from Texas a lot recently, recalling funny times and being 1000 percent nostalgic. It's impossible to even count how many times he's said how much he misses Silas and Maverick—over and over again.

When I get home to get ready for work, Kash is already at the bar. He had texted me while I was at the beach, letting me know he was heading in early to polish the floors; the text made me laugh and roll my eyes. The already glossy floors at Two WhisKEYS do not, in any way, need to be polished. But that's Kash, and I do love him for it.

I take a shower and sit with my hair wrapped in a towel and another wrapped around my chest. I pull up the calendar on my phone. Today is September 23. The bar is having a Halloween Extravaganza in three weeks. If I could get all, or at least part, of the Texas crew here for the party as a surprise for Kash, I'd be crowned queen in his eyes, I know it. Since Farrah and Joey would already be here, I think having our Texas family together again would be amazing for her. I text Joey first, throwing out the idea to him before I reach out to anyone else. He texts back immediately, saying he thinks it's a great idea. He'll talk to Farrah, and I'm going to text the rest of the group. Joey and I make plans for him, Farrah, and Junie to fly in on Friday, October 18.

I text Maverick, Silas, and Silvia, knowing that it might be next to impossible for them all to come unless Maverick closes the bar down for a weekend, but I try and remain hopeful. Because this would be such an amazing surprise, if I can pull it off.

Hey, guys! Joey and Farrah are coming to visit Oct 18. The bar is having a Halloween Party on the 19th, and I would LOVE to surprise Kash with a visit from his favorite people. What do you think???

I tap my fingers on the coffee table, eagerly waiting for a response from any one of them. It doesn't take long before Maverick responds.

Seriously, Summer? I can't shut the bar down, and I can't keep it open with us all gone like that.

My shoulders sink in defeat, but I don't even have a second to think of a response before he sends another one.

Just kidding! Did I tell you I relinquished some control and hired an assistant manager? This is a great idea. We miss you guys…a lot.

Relief floods me. This just might be possible.

Then Silas sends a message:

I taught someone "Still Standing" last week on the piano, and it reminded me of Kash. Let's do it!

I let out an audible screech and lie back against the couch. Thinking about how sad Kash was when we heard that song on the radio on our way home from Disney melts my heart. He's going to see his best friend in person for the first time in years. And so will I. It is happening. Everyone's hearts are going to fill up again by being together.

Do we have to dress up? Silvia's text makes me laugh.

Yup! I respond. It will be amazing!

We text back and forth a bit longer with promises to share updates on flights and plans. We agree not to drop a single hint to Kash.

There's a giddiness that's building and an excitement that's difficult to control as I finish getting ready for the night. Visions of a surprise family reunion in October take over as I tie my Converse and leave our apartment, humming as I go. My, how times have changed.

The sun blares above me, scorching the grass along the walkway that leads up to The Girls Home. I jog up the steps and ring the doorbell. The guitar Jimmy lent me lays across my back. I've been coming here every Monday afternoon when the girls get back from school, playing some songs and teaching a few of the girls who are interested—not much, just a few notes. Having them jot down the thoughts in their heads—feelings that may be hard to understand—is also a habit I have been trying to instill. I've been spinning my own set of dreams for this place—dreams of getting a couple of instruments to leave here for those of them who want to practice.

Recently, I started taking online classes to help me get a degree that will allow me to work in musical therapy. I do most of my work in the mornings when I get back from my walks. I've started with some gen ed classes, and soon, I'll move on to some psychology courses.

At first, it was hard to come to the realization that my original plan, the reason I moved here in the first place, to be a songwriter, kind of fizzled out. I felt like a failure. But maybe it was a stepping stone to what I was really supposed to be doing…helping others.

Volunteering with the girls at the home has been filling a hole in my heart. I watch music touch the lives of these girls, some of whom seem as lost as I once felt. It really does make sense for me to be doing this after all the trauma I've been through…and it feels great to be able to say that.

Lisa opens the door, and I step inside. "I should get you your own key at this point," she says through a bright smile.

"I do feel like I'm home here," I say, shifting my guitar and my bag—which is filled with things for the girls—into a more comfortable position.

I quickly sign in at the podium and walk myself to the rec room where some of the girls, including Stella, are sitting.

"Hey, Summer!" Brianna says, getting up from the couch and clutching her little tattered notebook. "I need you to check out these lyrics I wrote this week. I need to know what you think." Her eyes sparkle with a youthful glow.

I smile back at her, placing my hand on her shoulder. "I'd love to see them." I sit down on the couch. "How have you girls been this week?"

Madison speaks first, her full head of curly dark hair falling over her shoulders. "I got detention today, for no reason except that I spoke my mind." She laughs.

I roll my eyes playfully. "Stay out of trouble," I scold, throwing a pillow at her. "But also, never stop speaking your mind." I wink at her, and her expression warms. "I brought you each a present," I announce, reaching into my bag. I pull out the new notebooks and pens I got for them. We do a lot of writing and reflecting when we work together, and I thought these would be a nice gift. Each book has a personal note I wrote for each girl. I start passing them out, glancing inside first to make sure each girl gets theirs.

They take turns giving me quick hugs and thanking me as they read their personalized notes and flip through the crisp, blank pages.

"I'm going to play a song. If you know the words, sing along," I say, adjusting the strings just a bit. I start playing "Home" by Edward Sharpe and the Magnetic Zero. It doesn't take long before most of the girls are singing the lyrics, Brianna's voice the loudest and most in key.

Stella's face is void of emotion, and I don't take my eyes off of her. When the song ends, she gets up abruptly and heads swiftly toward the kitchen.

"Um, OK, girls," I start, trying to quickly think up a plan. "I want you to reflect for a moment about what these lyrics mean to you and jot some thoughts in your new books. You don't have to share this with anyone. It's just for you, so be as honest as possible." I get up from the couch. "I'll be right back."

Stella's sitting at the table when I enter the kitchen. She's fiddling with the notebook I got her. It's pretty, with a gold spiral ring and a picture of two dolphins on the front. "You OK, Stella?" My voice is soft. She doesn't say anything for a long moment. I don't want to pressure her to open up, but I want her to know that I'm here for her. "You don't have to—"

She cuts me off. "It's the dolphins." Her tone is heavy; it sounds like there's a lump forming in her throat. I open my mouth to speak but can't find words that make sense. "Dolphins are a sign…from my parents." Her mouth quivers. "My parents used to tell me they loved me more than all the dolphins in the sea. My mom loved dolphins. She said it's partly the reason why she loved California. There were no dolphins in Italy where she lived." She allows herself to smile at the thought of her mom. "I always see dolphins when I need them the most." She wipes a stray tear quickly, trying to hide it from me. "But it took me off guard just now. Because I didn't feel like I needed them. I didn't ask for a sign. But I got one anyway. It shook me. That's all."

My eyes are wide. I can't help it. I swallow hard and force myself to take a breath. "I don't want to say sorry. Because deep down I feel like this is a good thing. But you seem so sad…so I feel like I need to apologize." My words don't make sense.

She smiles at me, timid and soft, beneath glistening eyes. She wipes her tears again and reaches out to me. I quickly take her hand in mine. "You don't need to apologize," she says. "I guess I was just trying to make sense of it. Why? Is it a sign? Or is it just a coincidence?"

"You remember what Jimmy said, don't you? There's no such thing."

***

September bleeds into October, and before I know it, I'm waiting outside the airport for the crew, idling in Kash's truck. I've been following their flight and planned to park and meet them at baggage claim, but I couldn't get my act together. I had to make up a story about why I needed to take the truck for a few hours. Not that he cares when I take it, but my anxiety about spilling the beans made it all the more difficult to play it cool. The story I landed on was that I had to visit the main campus where I'm taking my classes to drop off some paperwork and sign up for a few extra credits. He bought it without question. Because, of course, he would.

LAX is swarming with people when I arrive. I get out of the truck and lean against it, looking at my phone for the time. It's 3:49 p.m. They should be out at any moment. My stomach is swirling with excitement. It just doesn't seem possible that I'm going to see Mav, Silas, Farrah, Joey, and Silvia. And I'm going to meet Junie in person for the first time. It doesn't feel real.

"Summer!" I hear my name being yelled off in the distance, and I scan the area for familiar faces. I see them all heading toward me with their luggage. Farrah starts to run, and I do the same. My cheeks ache from the huge smile on my face. We collide into each other; she swings me around, and then I swing her, her auburn hair wrapping around me.

"Farrah!" I say, pulling her face into my hands, emotion in my words. "It's really you."

"In the flesh." We just stare at each other.

"Summer, dear!" Silvia's voice warms my heart, and I pull away from Farrah to greet the others.

"Silvia!" I hug her tightly, smelling her signature scent.

"I missed you so much, darling."

My eyes are so cloudy I can't see straight. I jump into Silas's arms. "Braids are looking fresh," I say, giving one a tug.

"You look great, Summer," he responds; his familiar British accent is like music to my ears.

Maverick hugs me so tight that he picks me up off the ground. "My pride and joy," he says in my ear. "How are you, love?"

"I'm so good, Mav. So good." His smile is so authentic. And so is his love and belief in me. He trusted me when he didn't have any reason to. He's seen me go from the lowest of lows to here, where I am now, and he looks at me like a big brother would look at his little sister who's all grown up, with pride and awe.

I hug him again, and while I do, I see Joey over his shoulder, and in his arms, it's her. My little Junie. A chubby-cheeked, button-nosed little love with auburn ringlets, just like her mom. "Hi, Joey, I do love you, but this little one right here, I need to hold her…right this second." Joey laughs and gives me a side hug, handing Junie to me. She reaches out her arms to me as I take her from her dad. She places her fat little hands on my cheeks, and I let out a joyful sob. "Hi, my love," I whisper. She rests her head on my shoulder for a brief moment, and I relish in it, smelling her baby scent and trying to memorize it as best I can. She begins to whimper a bit, and I hand her back to her dad.

"She's definitely tired from traveling for the first time," Farrah says, rubbing her baby's back. "She was so excited to meet her aunty!" She embraces me again, squeezing me as tightly as possible.

"I'm so excited that you are all here," I say through tears. "This is just a dream." I look around at all of them, here, in the flesh, and I want to pinch myself. I could not be any more grateful for these people I call my family.

"So, I have to go rent a car," Joey says.

"Me too," adds Maverick. Between all of them, they are renting two cars for the weekend.

"I confirmed that they will have the correct car seat in it," Farrah says to Joey. "Do you mind if I ride with Summer, Joey?"

He looks at her surprised, probably because she is insinuating that she's fine leaving Junie to ride in a strange car on a strange highway without her. "Um, yeah, of course, babe."

She turns and beams at me. "We can catch up!"

"Amazing! We'll meet at your hotel," I say to Joey.

"Sounds perfect." He gives Farrah a kiss, and Farrah squeezes Junie before climbing into the passenger seat of the truck.

"I can hang out with you guys at the hotel for a bit, but then I gotta get back so Kash doesn't get suspicious!" I say, laughing.

Everyone takes off in the direction they need to go, and as I drive off, my heart is as light as a balloon.

My hands are fidgety in my lap, shaking and twisting, as I glance out the window of the big van. I place my hand over my racing heart and allow myself to smile as the shore passes by in blurbs of blue and green, a watercolor display of perfection.

"You OK?" Farrah asks.

I turn to see her soft smile directed at me. I nod once at her before looking back out to the ocean. We're about to pass it completely, so I don't want to miss it. I hold my breath as I stare at the horizon without blinking. I touched the ocean for the first time yesterday, and it was like the dark parts of me were eclipsed with light for a brief moment. For a moment, I could breathe. For a moment, I was light as a feather. And now, twenty-four hours later, I have a sense of relief inside, like the feeling didn't completely go away after that experience. It's hope—that's the feeling inside. Though it's been foreign to me for such a long time, I'm embracing the feeling.

"We can always come back, ya know?" Farrah says, sensing my sadness as the scenery outside quickly changes to dry brush and dirt.

Farrah. My new friend.

"Yeah, I know," I whisper. I hadn't realized until right now that I was utterly nervous to see the ocean for the first time. In my head, it was this sacred place that saved me over and over. What if it didn't live up to the hype? What if it let me down?

But it didn't.

It was the complete opposite. Seeing the ocean—feeling it—saved me. The experience gave me healing. It gave me the truth. It gave me a friend.

"So, can you tell me about yourself, Summer? Can we be BFFs?" Farrah's energy scares me a little, but her sweetness wins out, and I smile at her.

"Yeah. Sure, let's be friends." I laugh, and she takes my hand.

Our conversation on the long drive to Austin surprises me. Someone like me doesn't tend to open up, and I don't in the van, at least not completely, but I disclose enough to shock myself, and the way Farrah listens, the way her eyes invite me to open up, it's all without judgment. It's all out of love. And though we just met, I already know what's to come for us: a trusting friendship like I've never experienced.

We fill each other in on the way back to Santa Monica on little life things, mostly the mundane—things we already know about each other since we talk almost every day. I want to get to the heavy stuff, the stuff that's been scaring Joey, but I want to give her my full attention when that time comes. Driving on the freeway doesn't feel like the right spot. "What do you think about going and sitting at the beach for a few minutes before I drop you off at the hotel?" I ask, giving her a sideways glance.

Her shoulders slump as she sighs and takes her gaze out the window. "I know Joey called you."

The air in the truck turns tense, and I force myself to gather my thoughts. I let a moment pass, contemplating my next words.

I don't want to overstep. I don't want to make her uncomfortable, but like she has done for me in the past, I need to be there for her. "Yes, he did, Farrah." My voice is soft and gentle.

Her exhale is loud. "OK. Let's stop at the beach." She forces a smile, telling me I know she doesn't want to get into this. But I don't care. I've been there—the place of denial, the place of avoidance. It's my turn to be on the other side.

After I park the truck, we stop and get iced tea at the little food truck on the edge of the road that leads to the lookout where I sat with Claire. I decided on this spot because there's little to no chance that Kash will see us here. We're away from the pier, and he doesn't have his truck—I do—so it's not like he'll be driving by. He'll be around the bar, probably getting some work done, some last-minute things for the party tomorrow.

I choose a seat away from where Claire and I sat when we were up here, and Farrah takes a seat next to me. "Wow, it's really beautiful." She takes in the scenery. "I can't believe you live here." She smiles, but there's sadness in her voice. She covers her mouth with her hand, and her shoulders start to shake. I put my hand on her arm, but I hold back from saying anything yet. She knows I'm here. This is all on her terms. "I miss you, Summer. I knew that I would when you left originally, but it's harder than I ever imagined."

I nod, not taking my eyes off her face. "I know," I say softly. Because I do know. I miss her terribly, too. But I guess I'm just realizing, here in this moment, that it's different for me. Since I came somewhere new and started over—chased after new dreams, discovered love, found happiness—because of all that, it's a bit easier for me. Because the pain of leaving was worth it for all the beauty I've discovered. And I know I didn't *lose* Farrah. Things are just a lot different now. But for her, not much has changed. She's a mom now, but besides that, everything else is the same.

She stares at the waves for what feels like an eternity, and I barely breathe, waiting for her to say something, even if it's something that breaks my heart. "I have been in a dark place, Summer," she says. "Not all the time. Not every day, but when it hits, it's just too much." Her head falls into her hands. "Everything is overwhelming." She shakes her head. She looks incredibly sad. I continue to rub her arm. "I can't explain it, but I get overcome with the strongest emotions, especially about Junie. I'll take her foot in my hand and kiss it, telling her how much I love her, and she giggles. And then I just start crying because her tiny little foot is never going to be that small again. Ever. She grows, Summer, so fast, and it's like I can't catch her. I can't stop it." Her voice breaks, and the sound of it tells me that her heart is also broken.

I suck in my lips, holding back my own tears, trying to be strong. "When this happens, are you able to tell Joey how you're feeling? Right in those moments?"

She doesn't respond. It's as if she doesn't hear me. "No one warned me." She wipes her tears.

"Warned you about what?" I ask softly.

She turns to look at me, her face raw and red with emotion. "That having a baby would cause me to lose a part of myself. And I don't mean I don't have time for myself, or that I forgot who I am since becoming a mom. No, that's not at all what I mean. It's like she came out and took part of me with her, and so the thought of losing her, or something happening to her, crushes me. It makes me unable to function at all. Just looking at her breaks me." She pauses for a moment, and she looks like she's trying to collect herself. A gust of wind blows a tendril of her hair. "I'm afraid of losing her. I'm afraid of something bad happening to her. I'm afraid of missing things, even the tiny, stupid, mundane things. The worry is suffocating. I don't know how else to describe it. Time goes by so fast, and the desperate need to stop it, to keep her just as she is, it's a battle I'll never win. And it depresses me. There. I said it." She sits back in the chair and runs her hands through her hair.

For a moment, I feel inadequate as her friend. I don't have any experience with bearing and raising a child. Hell, I didn't even have a positive experience of being raised. But then I remember something Jimmy said to me a while back. I move to the edge of my seat, facing her. I ask for her hands, and she gives them to me. "My friend Jimmy said something to me recently that really made me stop and think. He said that time is time. It's not fast or slow. It just is—no matter what. He said that if you feel like time is going by fast, you should consider yourself lucky because you have something worth enjoying in life, something that's worth trying to grasp with all your might, even if it's impossible." I hope my words aren't making her feel worse. She's looking at me with furrowed eyebrows. So I take a breath and continue. "He basically was saying that no one has ever stopped time, and the second you quit trying to stop it is the second your life begins." I'm looking straight into Farrah's eyes, praying that she hears and understands the sentiment in the words, the same way I did when Jimmy first said them to me.

A hint of a smile forms at the corners of her mouth. Then, I can see her teeth as her smile widens. She sobs. I get up and pull her into a hug, rocking her slowly. "Time is time," she whispers into my ear. "It's hard for me, Summer, but I'm going to remember that." Tears continue to fall from her eyes in streams. After a few minutes, we sit back down, settling into our chairs and gazing out at the ocean, content to be together after all this time.

A few minutes later, she breaks the silence. "I have been going to therapy twice a week. And I walk—outside—every day. It really does help. I think being with my best friend again unleashed some extra emotion I had stored up." I nod. "Joey was right to worry. I'm glad he cares and noticed something was off. And I'm so glad he called you. Truly, I am. I don't ever want him to be fearful of my safety the way he was years ago, right before you and I met." She shakes her head at the memory. "I don't want to waste my time with Junie by crying over every little thing. I don't want to miss things because I'm feeling this way. I know I need to live in the moment and let time do its thing. It's one day at a time, though."

"It sure is," I say, feeling those words deep inside. "When we talk on the phone and FaceTime, I want you to feel comfortable opening up about whatever is on your mind. And I want you to feel like you can cry. Even if it's just to cry about a piece of Junie's hair falling out. I don't care what it is." Her head falls into her hands again, and her shoulders begin to shake. "OK, are you laughing or crying?" I ask. Her head tips up toward the sky, her mouth agape with silent laughter. "Oh my God. You already cried about a piece of her hair falling out, didn't you?!"

"Yes," she wheezes, and then I lose it. We both laugh uncontrollably, just like old times. Though this has been a heavy conversation, this is us. It's how our friendship started and how it will always be—real and authentic, the most genuine love there is. We aren't afraid to have deep and important conversations, and because of that, we know all the parts of one another. There is no judgment, only acceptance. Grateful isn't a strong enough word for how I feel about her and our friendship.

I drop Farrah off at the hotel with the rest of the group, and I stay for a bit, stealing a piece of pizza they got from one of my favorite places right off the pier. "No one is allowed to leave this building until you're on your way to the party tomorrow," I warn them before heading out of the hotel. "You have a pool, a restaurant, everything you need."

"OK, OK! We will see you tomorrow, dear," Silvia says. "With bells on."

I wave and turn on my heel, heading back to the truck and back to the apartment to get changed for work. I can't stop smiling. By the time I stroll through the doors of Two WhisKEYS, my cheeks ache from the grin I can't wipe off.

CHAPTER 27

Kash

OCTOBER

"M ONSTER MASH" PLAYS THROUGH the speakers as I glance around the dimly lit dining room. Everything is set for the big party tonight, and the decorations are absolute perfection. Orange and white lights hang from the bar and the ceiling. Skeletons dressed in funny costumes are stationed around the room—my favorite is the cowboy. Every table is decorated with pumpkins, and there's a stack of hay bales and pumpkins greeting guests at the front door as they arrive. Black witch hats are suspended from the ceiling, as if they are floating above us. I smile. Two WhisKEYS's first annual Halloween Bash is about to commence, and I could not be more thrilled—and proud—of what has transpired here since we opened a few years ago.

Summer spent what felt like seventeen hours—but was probably more like forty-five minutes—painting my face into a creepy skeleton. I slicked my dark hair back away from my face. I'm performing tonight, and I don't even want to know what this getup is going to look like the second I start sweating on stage. But—oh well—it's all in good fun.

The back door opens and slams shut, and a second later, Summer makes her way into the dining room. She's the female counterpart to my ensemble, and she looks perfectly the part: a skeleton with a crown of flowers on top of her loose, long hair, which she rarely wears down. "Look at you," I say, beaming.

She laughs. "We are the best looking bunch of bones I ever did see." She approaches me, and I open my arms, but she nixes my plan. "Can't mess up the makeup," she tsk-tsks.

"Of course not." I squeeze her arms instead when I'd much rather kiss her, but I don't dare. "The place looks amazing." I want her to know that she did an unbelievable job. She glances around the bar, looking pleased with her efforts. "It looks like you hired someone. Honestly, it looks professionally done."

She shrugs it off like it's no big deal, but looking around, I know that's not true. Our bar has been transformed. It looks like a new joint that just popped up on the strip. All of the regulars who bought tickets are going to be floored when they step inside.

The vibe's going to be different than it usually is, and I'm amped to see how the night unfolds. It's more of a family-friendly event, mostly because we wanted Stella to be able to come. We sometimes have families that come in from the beach earlier in the afternoon when we first open, but it's rare to have families after six o'clock.

"Guys—" Nel comes in from the kitchen, looking ecstatic. "I brought dry ice!" She's carrying a stack of large bowls and some boxes. She heads to the bar, and Summer and I meet her over there to check it out. "I'm making some spooky punch that will be SMOKING—literally!"

Nel is beyond thrilled about this, and I can't help but get excited with her. "It's certainly going to be the best party this pier has ever seen."

Summer is popping a bottle of champagne, and the cork goes flying across the length of the bar area, causing her to squeal. "This calls for a toast," she says, beaming. I smile back at her, agreeing. She turns and takes three flutes from the shelf along the back of the bar and carefully pours the champagne into each glass before passing them out to Nel and I. Then, she lifts her own. "To new traditions and…old friendships." She winks at me, and we clink glasses. "It's going to be a night to remember."

I can't help but think that Summer looks a tad unhinged. And old friendships? Who is she talking about? Though my brows have knit together in confusion, I continue to smile at her. Summer's real teeth and the ones painted on beam at me, and all I can do is let out a loud laugh. "To tonight, our first Halloween party." I lift the glass to my lips, taking a sip, the bubbles exploding in my mouth.

Nel puts her glass down and claps. "This is going to be epic."

At exactly four o'clock, I open the door and all the windows, the salty air, my favorite scent, making its way into the room. I watch the Ferris wheel for a moment as it slowly makes its way around. Everyone looks decked out and ready to party as they make their way toward the bar. Soon, the whole place is abuzz with chatter, and Halloween songs are playing through the speakers. Summer made an excellent playlist: "Addams Family," "Monster Mash," "Spooky Scary Skeletons," and so many other great tunes. And I'm performing, too. But, if I'm being honest, my heart isn't really in it. I'd rather be mingling, chatting it up with all the guests. But I gave Finn and Diego the night off to come enjoy the party, and I think it will be good to break up the Halloween songs, so

I guess I'm singing. Maybe I can convince Summer to make an appearance with me. But a low-key performance is the plan for tonight, and that's fine by me.

Nel is hard at work, mixing a drink as I make my way to the bar. She opens her eyes wide, smiling and calling me over. She stirs the ladle in the bowl that's smoking with dry ice. She pours the maroon-colored drink into a plastic tumbler and passes it over to me. "Try this," she says. "I made it special for tonight."

Bringing the cup to my lips, I take a sip, and it's delicious. It tastes like fall, if fall had a taste. Cranberry, maybe with spices, and a smooth rum finish. "Rum?" I say. "Nel, we are a whiskey bar. What will the townsfolk have to say?" I wink at her, a grin on my skeleton face.

"I can't take you seriously with that makeup on, Kash." She shakes her head and laughs, her own makeup crinkling under her wide smile. Summer did her makeup, too, crafting her into a scarecrow with a creepy pumpkin-like face. I swear, Summer needs to rethink her career choices again. She has quite the talent.

"It's really good. Can you fill me up with another cup? I'm going to deliver it to Summer." I glance behind me, scanning the bar for her. It takes me a minute, but I eventually find her talking to Cade and Millie Bedard, some of our regulars. They're wealthy retired lawyers who love a good whiskey on a Wednesday night, their preferred day to come in. They've treated us like gold since we opened. "Actually, give me three, Nel. I'm going to bring a few over to the Bedards, too."

"I'll be back for mine," I say. "And get out from behind there, Nel. People can serve themselves. That's why we made everyone pay upfront. So we could enjoy the party, too. Isn't Rob coming?"

"OK, OK," she says, clearly having a hard time peeling herself away from the bar. "Yes, he'll be here in about thirty minutes. He had to go home and give Sienna a kiss after his shift before coming." A warmth spreads across her face as she talks about him. I know it's hard for her to deal with his schedule, but she does it with grace and pride.

"Awesome," I say. "I look forward to hanging out with him."

With that, I turn and make my way over to Summer and the Bedards. "Compliments of our talented bartender," I say, passing out the cups to Cade, Millie, and Summer.

Cade takes a sip and gives me a questioning look. "Rum?"

"That's what I said! But it's so good. Enjoy."

Millie lets out a distinguished laugh.

"Oh, Kash, I was just joking," Cade says, winking at me. "We were just telling Summer here that we hope this party becomes a yearly installment."

Gently pulling Summer into me, I smile at her. "I agree, Mr. Bedard. I think we'll have to make this a yearly thing."

"Mr. and Mrs. Bedard, will you excuse us? We need to check on the food table," Summer says, her voice sounding overly sweet.

"Why are you acting so weird?" I ask as we walk away.

She rolls her eyes. "Sorry. Sometimes the Bedards make me insecure." She laughs, clearly hearing how ridiculous that sounds. "They're too rich or something." We both let out a cackle. We're just regular people, and the rich customers can be intimidating sometimes; I'll give her that.

"OK, but you're acting weird in general," I say, giving her a look.

She turns to me, giving me a smile that creeps me out with her makeup. "What? I'm fine. Let's go mingle." And with that, she saunters toward Stella and the crowd that's gathered by the snack table. I shake my head lightheartedly and follow her.

The snack tables we set up…or should I say, the ladies set up—because it was all Nel and Summer—are immaculate.

"These look so real!" Stella says, running her fingers over the cobwebs displayed on a piece of driftwood on the table.

"Well, I collected them from the alley out back," I joke.

Stella rolls her eyes at me, shaking her head as she plucks a piece of handmade candy right out of an intricate skull that rests on the table. The candy and festive cupcakes came from our friends in town, and everything looks fantastic on the table. If this display can't get someone in the Halloween spirit, nothing can. I start to envision Christmas parties at the bar before I stop myself to live in this moment right here. Because it's perfect.

"So, don't you think you should get on the piano and play something?" Summer asks me. It's six o'clock, and she's probably right, but she's giving me that creepy smile again, and I can't help but laugh.

"Yeah," I sigh. "You're right. What should I start with? I didn't practice anything festive." I sigh, reminded how much I don't feel like performing.

Summer is quick to give her opinion. "Easy. 'Still Standing.' You've been talking about it for months. And you haven't played it in a while." I give her a questioning look, and she begins to talk fast, making me question her motives. "You won't even have to concentrate. It will just come out without even thinking," she says. She's acting really strange.

"Okayyy." I drag out the word, then put my fingers on her chin, lifting her face for her eyes to meet mine, trying to center her and calm the hysteria that seems to be bubbling. "Why are you acting crazy?"

She smiles, showing both sets of her teeth. "No reason."

My eyebrows furrow, but I can't help smiling. I'm 1000 percent skeptical of this woman that I love. On the other hand, I also know Summer so well that I should know not to question. "I'm going up to the stage now," I say, nodding my head to the skeleton staring at me with wide eyes.

With all the preparations, I didn't think ahead enough to plan a set. That wasn't the priority. But Summer's suggestion is a good one; doing a song that's ingrained in my memory, one that is so comfortable for me, is a good choice. I sit down on the bench in front of my piano. I press a few keys, checking for a good sound, which it has because I already tuned it up this morning. Looking out into the dining area, there are no eyes on me like there usually are. Everyone's engrossed in the party, which was exactly what we wanted.

I pull the microphone down to my mouth. "Good evening," I say, my voice booming throughout the place. "I hope you're all having a great time tonight." The place erupts in cheers and whoops. "I'm going to interrupt the Halloween songs and play something live, a song that means a lot to me. I hope you enjoy it." The crowd continues to cheer as I get situated. I don't know what's holding me back, but it's as if I don't even want to play, like I just want to walk down the steps and just *be*. Enjoy my party. But I can't. I've already committed. So, I relax my jaw and my shoulders, and I start playing the first notes of the song, and I get a bit more comfortable, ready to sing the first line.

My mouth opens in anticipation to sing the first line of "Still Standing," but it's not my voice that comes out. This wasn't my part when we used to sing it at Sullivan's, so I begin to think I've lost my mind because I'm hearing Silas's voice instead of my own. But I'm not crazy; I'm not the one singing. Someone else is. Where is that voice coming from? I look frantically around the bar, trying to find it. As the chorus is about to start, I see him.

Silas.

He's coming out from the kitchen, a microphone in his hand. I yell so loudly that my throat scratches as I get up from the bench and run down the stairs. Silas finishes the last line of the first verse, and the urge to sing the chorus with him like we always used to takes over, but I can't. The lyrics are mixed up in my throat, entangled with emotion that I'm having a hard time stifling. We embrace each other so tightly that we almost tip over. I grab his face in my hands. "What the hell are you doing here?" I'm sure the crowd is confused, but I don't care.

"We missed you," he says, smiling so big that his eyes are squinting. "And Summer, she's pretty amazing. She set this up so we could all surprise you."

I glance toward the snack table to see Summer holding her hands to her face, her eyes smiling at me. "We?" I say, confused. Silas points to the kitchen door, and I take my gaze in that direction. And there they are: Silvia, Maverick, Farrah, and Joey holding Junie. "No way!" I exclaim, running over to them. We all join in a huge group hug as Summer reaches us. For the first time in years, we're all together again under one roof—my roof. The surprise astonishes me.

"OK, boys," Summer says as she breaks us up. "We'll catch up after, but the crowd is waiting for an explanation," she says, bringing us back to the present and ushering us toward the stage.

Silas and I take the steps two at a time onto the stage, and I sit down on my bench and address the crowd while Silas gets situated at the other piano. "So sorry, everyone," I say into the microphone. "But I just got the surprise of a lifetime. This here is Silas, one of my best friends. We used to play together every night back in Texas, and man, have I missed him!" The crowd cheers. "We're going to try this song again. It was one of our favorites to perform together, so I hope you enjoy it." I smile at the crowd before adjusting my microphone again. I nod at Silas, and the piano notes begin taking over the space.

We perform the song better than we ever have. I can't even manage to stay sitting. I'm up off the bench, singing my heart out, sweat surely ruining my skeleton get-up, but I don't care. Not in the slightest. This is what truly performing is to me: feeling it in my bones and experiencing it with someone else who feels the same. We're at the last part of the song, singing together, when I make eye contact with Summer. I send her a smile and a wink. She looks elated and oh so proud of herself for pulling this off. I'm proud—and absolutely grateful.

Silas and I end the song and hug again before turning to the crowd and taking a bow. Though they don't know Silas, I can tell they feel our connection. It shows in their cheers. "Sorry, everyone. I planned to do a whole set, but I have some people I need to catch up with. So, you'll have to deal with the festive playlist Summer put together." I say it with a laugh, and it elicits chuckles from the crowd. I click my microphone in its stand, and we head down to meet the group at the bar.

"You!" I say to Summer, pointing my finger at her endearingly. She laughs and jumps into my arms.

"I can't believe I didn't tell you accidentally! Especially yesterday when they got here. It was so stressful! But it worked. It was perfect, wasn't it?"

"If you didn't have an extra set of teeth painted on your face, you'd be getting the biggest kiss right now."

"Later," she says with a wink.

A song from *Hocus Pocus* begins playing, and the party is back in full swing, like it was before Silas and I sang. Everyone seems to be having a great time. "Looks like this party is running itself. Let's go to the back office so we can catch up," I say to the group. We head back there, and as we settle into the room, I'm again overwhelmed with the fact that my favorite people are here and taking over my office right now.

"I gotta hand it to you, Kash," Maverick starts. "We've seen pictures and videos but being here in person is absolutely unbelievable. You have done an amazing job."

I smile and put my arm around Summer. "WE have done it." Summer leans her head against my shoulder, beaming.

"Yes, of course," Silvia says. "You both have just absolutely shined since coming to California."

"And they've fallen in love. Why is no one talking about that turn of events?" Farrah wiggles her eyebrows. "It's all just so beautiful." She claps her hands together, and then everyone stares at Summer and me with stars in their eyes.

"How long are y'all here for?" I ask, purposely changing the subject. Not that I don't love talking about me and Summer's story; I just know she hates to be the center of attention.

"Just until Tuesday morning," Maverick says. "I gotta get back to the bar. You know how it is." He slaps my back lovingly.

"Oh, I sure do." I look at the group endearingly. "We're closed on Mondays, so let's do something fun."

"It's already planned," Summer says, taking my hand in hers.

Of course it is. The best surprise I've ever had is turning out to be better than I could ever have imagined. "So, are you all planning on hanging out at the bar tomorrow? What's the plan?"

"Well, yes and no," Summer starts. "I'm taking Silvia and Farrah around town in the morning, maybe driving up the coast a bit to see the view on the way back down PCH. You should take the guys down to the beach to play volleyball or give them a surfing lesson or something."

Silas rolls his eyes. "I'm a musician, definitely not a surfer." He lets out a boisterous laugh.

"You can just take a dip in the Pacific Ocean," I say. "Man, I still can't believe y'all are here. Get in for a group hug, everyone."

"Oh, dear, you haven't changed one bit, Kash," Silvia says as we all embrace again.

"OK, we need to go back out there," Summer announces. "I need to find Stella. The poor thing probably has no idea where we went."

We make our way back out to the dining room where Diego and Finn have taken it upon themselves to perform for the crowd. The dance floor is filled with people in their costumes dancing to "Brown Eyed Girl." I glance around and see Stella dancing freely with her friend from the group home, Brianna, whom she invited to come with her. Seeing her enjoy herself and look so free from pain brings a smile to my face. I grab Summer's arm and point in her direction. Summer's shoulders relax, and her smile looks peaceful, as if Stella's contentment is hers as well.

I never imagined Two WhisKEYS being a place where annual Halloween parties would become commonplace, but after tonight, there's no doubt in my mind that a tradition was created within these walls this evening.

———

Time and distance haven't changed the dynamic between this group one bit. As I look down the long table where we sit at Sunnyside Up Cafe, I find myself smiling, the muscles in my shoulders slack and at ease. Being with them has settled something inside my heart that I hadn't realized was haywire.

Our table is in the far front corner of the restaurant against the windows. Beyond the glass, all that can be seen is sand and water. It's nine thirty in the morning, and the beach is already crowded with sunbathers and families frolicking in the water, the sun inching its way into the blue California sky. I still pinch myself that I live here sometimes.

Summer's hand slips into mine as Silvia tells us something that's made Summer excited. I slide back into the conversation, pulling myself away from my daydreams—from my gratitude.

"I need more information!" Summer squeals. "Why have you not said anything to me until now?"

A wide smile spreads across Silvia's face, and Maverick chuckles. "Oh, it's nothing, really," Silvia responds, flicking her wrist.

Maverick shakes his head. "I beg to differ! Those two have twinkles in their eyes for each other, and they have no problem letting us witness it all night at the bar," he says through a laugh. "Spill the tea, Silvia!"

Silvia rolls her eyes in jest. "Lenny is a great friend." The table goes quiet, everyone's eyes on her. She glances at us before breaking out in a laugh. "OK, fine! Lenny is my main squeeze!"

We all break out into a laugh, and I glance at Summer; the expression on her face is one of elation.

"Lenny is one of our new servers at Sullivan's," Silvia informs us. "And he is my cup of tea, if I do say so myself."

Maverick cuts in. "It is pretty adorable."

"This is so exciting," Summer says, and Silvia nods.

"Well, no need to rush us to the altar," Silvia jokes. "Let me just enjoy the man for a second, will ya."

"Well, please keep me in the loop. I'm a little disappointed that I was on the outside of this," Summer says lightly, taking Junie from Farrah's arms and placing her on her lap. Junie squeals and bangs her little chubby hands on the table, causing us to turn our attention to her and smile. Why are babies so cute?

Though Summer FaceTimes with Farrah and Junie every week, I'm a little taken aback at the connection between the two of them. It's hard to build that when you aren't in person and you only talk on the phone, but their bond is real; Junie looks to Summer with a familiarity that is undeniable.

"What a treat this has been," Silas says through a mouthful, flicking a braid over his shoulder. "It wasn't long enough, but the fact that we were all able to come here and be together at one time is quite thrilling, no?"

"Yes, quite thrilling indeed," Maverick adds, mocking Silas's British accent. We all chuckle.

"It was the best surprise to see you all here," I say, agreeing with Silas, my best friend who's actually sitting across from me.

"We are family," Farrah adds. "No matter what, we are there for one another. We can never forget that."

A sweet silence spreads across the table, and we all take one another's hands.

"I love you all so much," Summer says, emotion in her voice.

The murmur of *I love you* cascades around the table. When the bustle dies down, Junie takes Summer's cheeks in her hands and yells, "I lub you!"

Summer's lip trembles. "Ohh!!" is all she can muster as she pulls the sweet baby into her chest.

The moment—this brunch—settles into my mind, a core memory forming: family, friends, love, and the waves.

CHAPTER 28

Summer

NOVEMBER

Evenings in Santa Monica have an air about them that effortlessly seems to say: *Come. Enjoy. Relax your shoulders. Take a breath.* And I do just that as Kash and I walk hand in hand down Ocean Avenue on our night off. The sea rumbles and roars to our left, the bustling streets to the right are filled with people who look calm and at ease, their laughter lingering in my ears. It's a perfect night. The sun is setting, casting a soft pink hue in the sky. As dusk nears, the soft lights from the stores and restaurants shine out onto the sidewalks. I cherish these walks through our town—always—each and every time.

We cross Ocean Avenue and make our way to the other side of the street, on our way to meet up with Nel and Rob. Rob has a rare weeknight off, so Nel and I arranged a double date. We walk down a wide alleyway lined with twinkle lights that leads us to an outdoor patio with a rustic bar. Soft jazz music plays and mixes with the lull of the conversations, providing a perfect ambiance. The sound comforts me; it reminds me of Two WhisKEYS.

"Hey, guys!" I hear Nel's voice rise over the noise, and I turn in her direction, a wide grin appearing on my face. As we weave through the tables to reach them, I'm giddy with excitement.

"Hi, Rob!" I say, reaching my arms up for a hug as he stands to embrace me. "So good to see you again so soon after the Halloween Party!"

"Same to you, Summer!" he responds. "It's wonderful to see you both."

Kash and Rob give each other an endearing handshake as we take our seats around the table.

It's nights like this, so perfectly perfect, where I sometimes find myself zoning out, a dopey smile glued to my face, my cheeks growing sore and stiff from the permanent position of my mouth. I'm incredibly grateful for where I have landed, and sometimes, the euphoria of the truth mesmerizes me. I find myself unable to grasp how I got here. How I built this amazing life for myself, out of nothing but a dream. Nothing but hope.

I feel Kash's hand on my knee, and I relax my jaw as I turn to look at him. His cheek rests on his fist, a sparkle in his eye. He mentally brings me back to the table, knowing all too well what I was just doing. He's been there when I was removed from the present, paralyzed by fear. And he's here now when I detach from the here and now momentarily. He doesn't say anything, but his hand on my knee reminds me of the space he occupies in my heart.

"Have you two tried that new axe-throwing place over in Huntington Beach?" Rob asks.

"No, not yet. I heard it's fun, though," Kash responds.

"It kind of freaks me out," adds Nel.

"Everything freaks you out, Nel." I laugh, breaking a piece of bread off and popping it into my mouth. "Sharks, earthquakes, and now throwing axes." I wink at her.

Nel's hands go up in defense. "Whoa, whoah. If you aren't afraid of earthquakes, there's something wrong with you." We all laugh at that. "If we were at the bar and the ground started to shake, I would hope you—my best friend—would protect me with all your bravery." She smiles wide and takes a sip of her wine.

Best friend. Bravery.

The words swim around the table like wisps of smoke tickling my senses.

I never really thought of myself as brave. And even though our current conversation is lighthearted and doesn't really mean anything, to me it does.

And to be at a place in my life where I have a few great friends, a few *best* friends? Being reminded of that certainly helps me remember how far I've come.

At least I have Piper—the thought swims through my head as I trudge down the dirty side street in downtown Louisville, past the club where I once worked before I was let go—on account of being unreliable—toward Piper and Benji's apartment. I hate Benji. He's frightening, but Piper is my only friend, so I have learned to deal with him. I never want to go over there—not really—but unfortunately, it's become a necessity now.

Because where else would I get my drugs? And at least going over there gives me some human interaction since I don't have any now, ever since I finally separated myself from Lex.

As I shuffle my feet down the street, I can't help but wonder if our paths will cross tonight. The possibility is high since I met Lex at their apartment. Where—through my whiskey goggles—I chose him to warm my bed.

I hold my breath, taking the steps to the second-floor apartment two at a time. When I arrive at their door, I'm out of breath. I steady my racing heart, tuck my hair behind my ears, and push it open.

Music thumps, shaking the floor, and smoke hangs like smog—thick and vile. But it doesn't bother me. There are worse things. Things that make my skin crawl. Things that make me worry.

I scan the living room for faces that I recognize. But I don't see anyone. Not at first. Not until my former coworkers catch my eye. I see a bartender I worked with, but for the life of me, I can't remember her name. And a gaggle of strippers stands around the tiny kitchen table, Piper at the center. She does a double-take when she spots me, and I can't quite read the expression that's spread across her face. It's almost like she spotted a ghost. She purses her lips and heads in my direction.

"Hi," I say, mustering up excitement that is virtually non-existent.

Piper grabs my forearm and pulls me into her and Benji's room. "What are you doing here?" she asks. Her voice sounds both angry and sympathetic, as if she can't figure out her emotions.

I search for the words to answer her—her question catching me off guard. "Uh, I'm always here."

She rolls her eyes. "Benji is pissed at you. You haven't paid for your share of drugs in like…six weeks." She glances at the door, and I follow her gaze, suddenly nervous for my well-being. "Didn't you get my text?"

I shake my head. "I don't have a phone anymore." My voice sounds pitiful, but I can't control that.

Piper's shoulders drop, her face looking as if she almost feels sorry for me. But she quickly covers it up by crossing her arms over her chest. "You need to leave."

"What?" I ask, panicking. "But what about me and you? We're best friends. We've been that way for so long. We've been through so much together." My eyes begin to water as memories of us at various homeless shelters scurry through my mind's eye. We only had each other, and now she has no problem dropping me. "I don't need more drugs. But I don't want to lose you as a friend."

She doesn't say anything right away. And I'm left to wonder if she believes those words that just came out of my mouth because she doesn't answer. And I certainly don't believe them, at least not the first part. We stare at each other, and I contemplate my next move. I hear Benji's voice in the hallway, and my heart seems to be beating in my throat.

He enters the room, his presence taking over the space as if he's a bear sizing up intruders in his den. "Summer, get the fuck out. We're done with you. Haven't you gotten the message through your thick skull yet? And Lex is on his way. I really don't feel like dealing with that drama." He shakes his head in annoyance.

My breaths are coming in short, nervous bursts, my eyes darting over Piper and Benji's faces. Piper narrows her eyes, and her face turns cold.

"OK," I whisper, willing my feet to move toward the door. I have no choice. It's time for me to go.

I walk back through the smoke-filled living room and out the door, only looking back once to see Piper with the group of dancers again, laughing and unharmed, while my heart crumbles to heap on the floor of the dingy apartment. Outside, my body lowers itself to the curb as if in slow motion, as if I don't have control over my limbs. I sit there outside of Piper's apartment building for an amount of time that I can't even begin to estimate. A minute? An hour? More? I don't know for sure. All I'm certain of is that the weight of everything feels incredibly present, sitting directly on my shoulders and pulling at my mouth. It all feels so sad and so heavy. I'm not sure if I will ever smile again.

A sip of red wine accidentally goes down the wrong way, and I choke on the burning sensation as I ground myself back in the present. I glance across the table at Nel, my real friend. My amazing friend. An honest, loving, and sweet soul who has never wavered. I'm sitting at this table surrounded by people I adore with solid, healthy relationships that flourish and bloom while being watered and tended. I'm so grateful.

Austin wasn't a fluke. My wonderful friends from Texas—my family—came into my life when I needed them the most, and they're with me—still—no matter the distance. And I did it again, here in California—built relationships that mean the world to me. I did all of this even though there was once a time when I was convinced that I was unworthy. But now, I know and believe it with all of my heart—I am worthy, *worthy of goodness.*

Kash and I stop at the pier on our way back to our apartment for an Italian ice. We take a seat on the ground, right in the middle of the hustle and bustle of the evening.

"That was a nice dinner with Nel and Rob," Kash says, taking a bite. I smile and nod, thinking about the amazing food and company. "You OK?" he asks. "You've been kind of quiet all night."

I look at him, swallowing a bite of the cold, lemony ice, my face serious. "I need to ask you something," I say, my voice soft. His expression grows worried. "I've been trying to figure this out for so long, and I really just need to ask." I pause, sighing dramatically.

"What is it?"

I take my gaze down the length of the boardwalk before turning back to face him, holding my pained expression. He places his hand on my leg, a look of concern on his face. "Kash…," I say, trailing off.

"Yes?"

"Is this the place where Jessica Simpson filmed the music video for 'I Think I'm in Love With You'?"

The air around us goes silent for a moment. It's as if we're the only ones on the pier. My mouth curves up to a huge smile, and Kash throws back his head and lets out a loud laugh. I chuckle, too. "Because it's been really driving me crazy trying to figure it out," I add as Kash puts his ice cream down and stands up, pulling me into his arms and swinging me around.

Our foreheads touch, and he places a gentle kiss in my nose. "Oh, we are for sure performing that song at the bar soon," he says, his face filled with joy.

"Promise?" I ask, leaning into his mouth and kissing him with intent, as the world spins around us.

We walk home hand in hand, and my whole body feels weightless, my breaths full and deep.

"How are the girls at the group home doing in their music sessions?" Kash asks.

"I can't even tell you how much I adore them," I reply, shaking my head in disbelief. "Some of them started off with such tough outer shells, but now that they've allowed me into their trust spheres, I can see so much of their light!" I hear my own excitement, so I know Kash can feel it, too. "Everyone is so unique; each one with different interests and talents. Even the ones who aren't musical are comfortable sharing those things with me."

"That's incredible," he responds.

"Yeah," I say, nodding. "Between my volunteering there and the classes I'm taking, I know I've found something I'm truly passionate about."

We approach our apartment, and Kash stops out front, taking his eyes to the stars. He motions for us to sit on the stairs. "For old times' sake?" he asks, hopeful.

I beam at him, remembering how we used to do that at my old apartment in Austin. We take a seat on the concrete step, still warm from the sunshine of the day. Kash extends one leg out, and I lean back on my elbows.

"Do you remember the night we sat on the steps outside your apartment one night and made a wish under the stars that we would go after our dreams?" Kash looks at me, peace in his expression, and I smile at him, placing my chin on my knees and wrapping my arms around them.

"Of course, that memory is etched in my mind," I say softly.

"I think your new dream suits you perfectly."

I sigh. "Me, too." Turning more toward him, I continue. "At first, I thought that I had failed my dreams, not continuing to pursue songwriting with vigor. But I trust myself. And I know it's not a failure. I just didn't know what I was called to do. I didn't know then. But I know now. And writing songs was a step that brought me closer to my true passion."

"I'm so proud of you, babe," he says, pulling me close.

"I'm proud of *us*," I say. "Letting go of what was holding both of us back looks really good on us."

Kash chuckles, and we sit, embracing each other, in sweet silence for a few minutes, gazing up at the stars.

"I really would love to raise money for The Girls Home," I say, breaking the silence. "And get them some instruments that would help them hone in on their talents and interests." I sigh. "Something to think about, I guess."

"Definitely. You'll come up with something," Kash says. "I believe in you." He squeezes my shoulders. "Now, can I take you home?"

"Yes, please," I reply, my voice suddenly soaked with exhaustion.

CHAPTER 29

Summer

DECEMBER

T HE RADIO IS STATICKY, but I finally find a station that's audible enough and plays Christmas songs. "Jingle Bells" comes through the speakers, and I gleefully sing along as I make my handmade ornaments out of construction paper and wire that I found in the garage. I begged Momma for a real tree this year, hanging on to hope so tightly that this would be the year she would say yes. But, of course, Dad would have nothing of it, claiming he would be the only one to water it and clean up the pine needles. Even I, at seven years old, knew that he would never be the one to do that. It would be me. But I couldn't carry a huge tree home, and I didn't have any money. So I carried the little artificial tabletop tree up from our basement and made my own decorations for it since I couldn't find the box of ornaments my momma had sworn was down there somewhere. I place the final ornament on the little tree, smiling at my accomplishment—my little piece of Christmas spirit.

"Summer! Turn that fucking music off! I'm sleeping, girl!" Dad's screams make me jump, my joy fizzling to nothingness as I turn the volume down with shaking hands. It was good while it lasted, I guess.

"Have Yourself A Merry Little Christmas" plays softly through the speakers in our apartment. Kash hums the tune as he hangs up an ornament. I smile at him from the couch, my legs tucked under me, a steaming mug of tea warming my hands. The smell of pine—a real tree—is thick in the air. Placing the mug on the coffee table, I get up to fill the jug I've been using to water the little evergreen. When I come back into the living room, I see Kash sweeping up some rogue pine needles that have fallen on the floor.

"I got it," he says, taking the jug from my hands and climbing on all fours under the low branches. I watch him, not surprised at his effort but moved by the subtle ways he takes charge without being overbearing—the way he gladly does his part. He stands back up, places the jug on the coffee table, and exhales a deep breath. "Come here, babe."

He holds out both arms, and instantly, I'm wrapped inside them, my head nestled in the crook of his shoulder. We begin swaying to the song. I know the song is going to end soon, and I don't want it to. I want to stop time right here where we are. I want our apartment to always be this way, glittering with white lights and smelling like a magical forest.

But if I've learned anything this year, it's that time is time. My role is not to freeze it; it's to enjoy it. Relish in the little moments like these—the flames from the cinnamon candles flickering, casting shadows on the walls that mirror the movements of me and Kash.

The song ends, and Kelly Clarkson's "Underneath the Tree" starts playing. Kash takes my hand and spins me as the melody picks up the pace. We dance as if there is nothing else in the world more worthy of our time. When the song ends, Kash holds me close, resting his forehead on mine, his eyes glistening as he looks deep into mine. "Merry Christmas," he whispers.

"Merry Christmas."

The week before Christmas, Kash and I take Stella to the pier for the Christmas at the Sea Festival. It's chilly for California tonight—fifty-one degrees—and Stella and I are both dramatically wearing winter hats and down vests. I link arms with Kash and hold Stella's hand as we walk underneath the large arch at the entrance to the Santa Monica Pier. The place is decked out to the nines: lighted trees decorate the entrance, wreaths hang from every light post, and there's a huge wooden sleigh with an artificial Santa and eight reindeer. I force Stella to take a selfie with me in front of it. She rolls her eyes but smiles, and I know she loves it. Deep down, she's happy.

As we walk along the pier toward the Ferris wheel, musicians play festive tunes on guitars and ukuleles, the holiday spirit swirling around us as the waves lap along the shore below us. Sure, white Christmases might be pretty cool, but this? This is what I've been dreaming about my whole life.

"Oh, Stella, let's make some homemade ornaments," I almost squeal when I see the craft table.

"I'm gonna walk over here for a bit; no crafts for me tonight," Kash laughs as he separates from us for a moment.

Stella and I sit at a little craft table to make our ornaments. And just like that, I'm seven years old again. But this time, I have more than just construction paper and wire to use. And I use every single one of the supplies available.

Just as we finish up with our creations, Kash walks up, holding three hot chocolates, melted marshmallows swirling on the top.

"Thanks for inviting me, guys," Stella says, blowing gently on her steaming hot cocoa.

I exchange glances with Kash. "No, thank YOU for agreeing to hang out with two old people on a Saturday night," I say jokingly, but I do actually mean it.

"Hey, who are you calling old?" Kash laughs, giving me a playful jab in the ribs.

Stella looks down at her feet, smiling. "There really isn't any place else I'd rather be tonight."

I'm shocked at her honesty—and her vulnerability. I put my arm around her, and we continue walking as we sip on our festive drinks.

As we enjoy the evening, we taste homemade cookies from a bakery around the corner, decorate ceramic Christmas trees, skip along the pier to the sounds of the music, and Kash even asks to join in with a street band singing "Have a Holly Jolly Christmas." This night could not be any more perfect. When we drop Stella off at her home, she hugs us both intently. "Thanks again," she says, pulling away.

We say our goodbyes, and as Kash and I walk away, Stella stops us. "Wait—Summer?"

"Yes?"

"Um. I have something for you." She pulls out a folded piece of notebook paper from her pocket and hands it to me, sucking in her lips—trying to be brave, it seems.

A puzzled expression cascades my face. "What's this?"

"A few months ago, when you were here working with us...the day you gave us those notebooks?" I nod, swallowing the pang of guilt that rises as I remember the dolphins. "You asked the girls to write down what that song 'Home' meant to them while you came and looked for me. Do you remember?" I nod again. "Well, that night, I did the assignment. I ripped it out. I want you to have it." Her voice is soft but sure. I take the paper from her hand and start to open it. "No. Wait until you get home—please."

"OK," I say, pulling her in for one more hug. "I will. And I'll call you tomorrow, OK? And we'll pick you up on Christmas Eve, and you'll stay with us for the weekend; sound good?" These plans were already made; I just wanted to reinforce that they're happening. Stella beams, and Kash and I turn to leave, heading back toward our apartment. Kash takes my hand. I can't wait to get home and read this note.

Dear Summer,

There is no home when you lose your parents, is there? It's like you're just floating—aimlessly—through the abyss, with no place to sink into the soil to grow even a single sliver of a root. There's no warmth. There's no light. There's no glee. My feet move because I force them to; I smile because maybe, if I fake it, it will become real. I'll be happy if I convince myself that there's no other way to survive. I have tried all that. Nothing works, and it's easier to just accept that fate.

You know what I mean, don't you, Summer? It's why I've grown so attached to you. I've known since the second I met you that you understand me—wholly. I'm not happy that you were hardened by your life and what happened to you, but I am grateful that we—because of fate, not coincidence—had stars that aligned with one another.

You feel like home to me. I don't need to share a house with you to feel that way, though. Just knowing that you're there, always, is enough for me. Thank you, from the bottom of my heart, for giving me some semblance of a family for Christmas. I love you.

———

I wasn't prepared at all for what Stella's note would do to me. In the weeks that followed, a purpose was calling out to me, and as loud as it was, it was impossible to ignore. But, at the time, I wasn't sure what to make of the feeling brewing inside. Now that some time has passed, things are starting to come together. And as I sit here waiting for Janie to join our Zoom session, I realize that things that once seemed pixelated and mixed up, like a beautiful kaleidoscope, are now becoming a little bit clearer day by day.

I see that Janie is joining our call, and I straighten in my chair and shake myself from my thoughts.

"Hi, Summer, how was your Christmas?" Janie asks, her smile welcoming.

I let out a dramatic sigh. "It was amazing."

"Tell me about it," she insists, so I do.

On Christmas Eve, the three of us—Kash, Stella, and me—ordered Chinese food and watched holiday movies until way too late. Stella found a recipe for Italian cookies, and her only request was that we make them—from scratch. So, we did. Stella was a natural in the kitchen, keeping a dishrag over her shoulder at all times and sticking her tongue out in concentration, like she does when she sketches, as she placed the icing and sprinkles meticulously on the cookies. They turned out amazing, like they came from an Italian bakery. This gave me pause, wondering if Stella had memories of baking them with her mother. The whole time, she looked elated and at peace. Watching her was heartwarming. How amazing that she could allow herself, at such a young age, to find joy amongst immense loss. I've learned a lot from her.

We made rich hot cocoa from scratch and drank it until our stomachs ached, and we lay in a heap together on the couch. I woke up just before sunrise, curled up on the couch next to Kash, Stella on the other side of the sectional asleep under a fuzzy blanket, her face lit by the warm lights of the Christmas tree we'd left on. We had to jump through a lot of hoops to have Stella stay over at our apartment, but I would have done it a million times over, and the vision I woke up to on Christmas morning made everything worth it.

As day began to break on Christmas morning, I quietly got up from the couch and went to the kitchen to get the coffee started and put out some muffins on a plate to bring into the living room, a little snack to hold us over until we made pancakes. I softly sat back on the couch with my book and a cup of coffee, planning to read until Kash and Stella woke up. But it wasn't long until they both rustled awake. We hung out on the couch, sipping coffee and eating fresh blueberry muffins for what seemed like hours, and I was fine there in heaven. I would have stayed there with them all day if they'd let me. We gave Stella her gift, a beautiful art set and sketch pad. She held it close to her chest, a look of gratitude spread sweetly across her face. We gave her some clothes and a few paperbacks as well, and when she was done opening her presents, she swiftly got up and went into the spare room where her bag was. A few minutes later, she came back with two wrapped boxes. She handed one to each of us, and Kash and I exchanged curious glances.

"You didn't have to get us anything," I said.

"Yeah, you absolutely didn't," Kash added, though he, of course, looked thankful.

Stella shrugged her shoulders. "I know I didn't have to," she said. "But I really wanted to."

Kash unwrapped his package to find a framed photo she painted of the inside of Two WhisKEYS. "I used all watercolors," she informed him, beaming. Kash seemed to be unable to find the words to thank her, but he pulled her in for a hug and I watched Stella smile in his embrace.

When it was my turn to open my gift, I carefully peeled off the pretty holiday wrapping and pulled it out, my breath catching in my throat. It was a special edition copy of *The Lion, the Witch and the Wardrobe.*

My eyes snapped up to meet hers. Though my vision was blurry through the tears, I could see her smile.

"I know how much that book means to you," she said. "But I also know you wanted me to have your copy for keeps. I thought this was the next best thing."

"I love it," I whispered, getting up to embrace her. "Thank you. So, so much." I held her face in my hands and let our foreheads touch. I didn't say it out loud because it most definitely wasn't true for Stella, but it was the absolute best Christmas I'd ever had.

"Wow, if that isn't exactly what you needed, Summer, I don't know what it is. What a beautiful holiday you had." Janie's validation makes something that's felt impossible to believe feel a bit more real.

I peel the sticky from my computer screen and hold it up to the camera so she can see it.

Summer James, you are worthy of goodness.

I'm lost for words as I choke on my emotions. "Do you believe it now? Have we mastered the mantra, Summer?"

I crinkle up the Post-it and dramatically toss it in the trash, laughing through my tears. I nod, letting my head fall into my hands. "Yes," I say. "There's no way not to believe it now."

CHAPTER 30

Kash

FEBRUARY

"**D**AD, ARE YOU GOING *to make it back in time for my game?"
I hate that my voice sounds desperate and not like the big kid
I've been trying to act like lately.*

*Dad looks at me with love and pride, placing his hand on my shoulder.
"Have I ever missed a game, Kash?"*

I look down at my feet. "No," I respond softly. "But—"

*"I know. My meeting is farther away. But I'll be there in my usual seat
before you even take the ice."*

"OK," I say, and I think I'm finally convinced.

*"My old friend Jimbo used to say, 'If you love it, do it as hard as you
can.' Can you do that, buddy? Can you put your all into this game?"*

*I nod. Dad's always using his old friend's sayings to teach me lessons.
I always wonder if he's a real person or just someone my dad made up.*

*When my team takes the ice to warm up for the last game of the season
and I scan the bleachers behind our team bench and he's not there, my*

fears are realized. It alarms me because Mom's not there either. I move smoothly across the ice—my stick in hand—but my eyes aren't focused on the puck or the goal. They're darting all over the arena, desperately hoping to spot them coming in to take their seats. But they don't.

It doesn't cross my mind that something tragic has happened, something life-altering. I'm only nine. I don't mean to, but all I can think about is that Dad is my good luck charm. And if he isn't here, then how will we win?

And we don't.

After the game, I sit on the bench, listening to our coach tell us how hard we worked. That he was proud of us for overcoming a lot throughout the season. But the words fall on deaf ears, mine and my teammates. Because losing doesn't feel like a lesson worth learning right now.

I blame myself. I didn't feel like I was doing my part during any of the three periods. I felt disheveled and lacked focus.

But I also blame my dad. It's his fault that I couldn't focus, and as my coach drives me home, I glance angrily out the window as the lights on the street pass by in quick, blurry movements.

When I arrive home, I see Mom's car and a police car in our driveway. But not Dad's.

I sit up straight as I possibly can as my stomach sinks to the furthest reaches of my body. I look at my coach, and he purses his lips at me. "I'll walk you to the door, buddy," he says. But I barely hear him. His words are muffled and strained. I walk to the door, my legs feeling like they're lead, like I'm dredging through mud.

I stare at the doorknob, willing myself to reach up and grab it, turn it, and push the door open like I have a million times. But I'm paralyzed. The act of breathing feels too difficult.

I swirl my cup around, the water forming a funnel, spinning and spinning, much like my mind.

If you love it, do it as hard as you can.

I suck in a breath through my teeth and lean back on the barstool. I look up from the cup, appraising everything in front of me, a dream that has come alive right in front of me.

I did this.

I built this business with my hands, a labor of love. It's what I wanted, and I did it. I put my all into this space, and I can say with all honesty that I found something worth fighting for. It took years, decades really, but I finally found the strength to do what my dad had told me to do the night he died—to put my all into what I loved. Through the years, I've tried to find sparks that would ignite me. The sports, the clubs, the girlfriends, anything that would help me feel a sense of purpose and connection. Nothing ever seemed to fit, though—not really.

Not until I found music did the puzzle start to come together. When I found the people in my life who guided me to where I sit right now. I glance around the bar—at every nook and cranny—and a warmth spreads through me. It all seems to make complete sense now, the parts that were missing sliding into their perfect spots.

I shake my head and run my hands through my hair.

I am happy.

I am whole.

I did it.

My spirits are high as I get up from the stool and head back to my office. It's time to start getting ready for the evening. It's going to be a great one.

I told Summer to invite everyone from The Girls Home to an event tonight. She thinks it's a little anniversary event to celebrate

Two WhisKEYS being open for two years—well, a little more than that, but it was the best thing I could think to tell her to derail any suspicions. Because this night is not an anniversary celebration. It's a fundraiser for The Girls Home.

Summer has wanted to do this for a while now, but between her classes and working, she hasn't found time. And I thought this was a great way to show her how much I love her and how much I will always be there to support her and her passions.

Jimmy has been just as much a part of the planning as I have. "Anything I can do for my girls, I'll do," he'd said to me a few months ago when I brought it up. I'd only smiled at him, unable to find the words to express my gratitude.

The plan is that Summer, Stella, Lisa, and the rest of the girls from the home will show up thirty minutes after the event actually starts. If Summer has gotten wind of this shindig, she hasn't let on, and I can't wait to see their faces when they walk through the door. They're all going to a late lunch that I planned with Lisa as a bonding experience for the group. Lisa knows what's going on, as I needed intel on exactly what would be best to have brought in for the girls. I needed her input to make it perfect. After they're done with their lunch, they're heading over to the "anniversary party." Summer insisted that she skip lunch with everyone, adamant that I'd need the help, but I assured her I was fine.

In the meantime, my whole staff has decorated the place. They've arranged the tables in such a way that accommodates the raffles we have going on and made the appetizer tables look welcoming and ready for the delicious food we're serving. Everyone has helped with everything I've asked of them; the whole production has been a team effort. Jimmy left his restaurant to his assistant manager, and he hasn't stopped moving since he arrived, helping with every little thing.

"Where do you want the raffle prizes?" Jimmy asks me, his hands full with a basket.

"On that table," I tell him, pointing to the one set up on the side by the wall. Jimmy nods, heading over to the table.

"Who's playing tonight?" he asks, positioning the basket until it looks the way he wants it to.

"Finn, Diego, Calvin, Talia, and a few other local artists who've volunteered," I respond. "And a few music stores in town donated instruments for The Girls Home."

"That's amazing, Kash." Jimmy looks moved, and it causes pride to expand inside.

The money raised will all go directly to the home. Lisa has plans to use it for music lessons, art supplies, new bedroom sets, updated appliances, and experiences for the girls to have outside of the home. I can't wait to see how this town—our community—pulls through for this fundraiser. In thirty minutes, the wait will be over.

At 3:25 p.m., my hands are starting to sweat; the anticipation is giving me all sorts of jitters. People have been pouring in through the doors for the last half hour, and the party seems to be coming alive. Any minute, the guests of honor will arrive.

Nel comes up behind me and hands me a glass of water. "Take a breath, Kash." Her smile is warm, and the gesture causes me to relax my shoulders.

"Is it that obvious?" I ask with a laugh.

"Oh, yeah." She rolls her eyes with a little laugh.

I take a sip of water and glance out the large windows, looking for the group. And as my gaze reaches the beginning of the pier, I see them. I quickly turn and jog to the back of the bar and hop up on the stage. Grabbing the microphone, I clear my throat, and the gesture is enough to get the crowd to quiet down. "Hi, everyone. Thank you so much for being here. I will be back up here in a bit to fill you in on the night, but right now, it's time to gather and face the door. They're arriving any second."

The crowd begins to scurry around the room as I place the microphone back on the holder. I jog down the steps, head toward the door, and stand beside Jimmy.

"This is amazing," Jimmy says, his eyes glossing over.

"Well, let's get to the end of the night before we start with the praising," I joke.

He shakes his head slowly and squeezes my bicep. "This is what life is all about, and don't forget I said that. Helping people and doing what you love? There is nothing more fulfilling."

My eyebrows furrow at his words, at the serendipitous vibe he has that never ceases to amaze me. As if he had been placed on this earth for the sole purpose of guiding me.

I reach out my arm and give him a squeeze like he did for me and then pull him in for a hug. "Thank you—for everything," I say as we embrace. "I couldn't have done this without you." And as the words come out, I'm not so sure if I mean this event or life in general. But it doesn't matter. I mean the words, no matter how you look at it.

"Well, I'm not going to be here forever," Jimmy says lightly. "I need to do all the helping while I can."

"Can you stop saying that," I say through a smile. "You better be here forever."

"Well, I—" Jimmy is cut off by the commotion at the door.

The girls are here.

The door opens, and a hush spreads over the whole dining room. I hear a laugh escape from Summer, but she's holding the door open for the girls and hasn't seen what's beyond the threshold yet. I see Brianna and Stella walking in first with their arms linked, confusion clearly written on their faces. They stop short and laugh, turning around to face Summer. The other girls shuffle in, hesitation in their steps and looks of confusion on their faces as well.

Summer finally makes it in, and everyone in the room yells surprise. Her mouth drops, as if it's unhinged from her jaw. "What is this?" she says, scanning the crowd until she finds me. I don't provide much of an explanation. Nothing but a smile that hurts my face.

Lisa walks in last, looking elated and beyond grateful for the turnout. Summer waves to familiar faces as she makes her way over to me. When she reaches me, we embrace. "What is going on?" she asks, her voice muffled.

"It's a fundraiser for the girls." I pull away from her, looking into her eyes as they begin to pool with fresh tears.

She bites her bottom lip. "Are you serious?" Her words are a whisper, and she looks around the room as the noise is picking up and everyone is bustling around the room again. The rest of the girls make their way over to Summer and me.

"Everyone is here for you guys," I say, and I fill them in on what the event actually is; not an anniversary party but a party for them.

The girls squeal with excitement and head off to get some food.

Lisa's expression is ecstatic. "I can't believe how many people are here," she says, breathless.

"It is amazing, isn't it?" I respond.

"Wait, you knew about this, Lisa, and you were able to keep it a secret?" Summer asks in awe.

"I did," Lisa beams. "Isn't this so kind of Kash to put this together for us?"

"It sure is," Summer brushes my arm and smiles at me, the look of love shining in her eyes.

My parents taught me about acts of service by the way they treated each other. Making special dinners for no other reason other than it was a Wednesday. My dad taking my mom's car to be detailed out of the blue. Notes left in steam on the bathroom mirror. Little things that were, in fact, big things. I clearly understand the driving force of such acts. The impact it's having on me right now as I watch Summer's heart being mended a little more in this very moment is what it's all about—actions speaking much louder than words.

The afternoon starts off with a bang, and the first hour is busy; people bustle around checking out the raffles and learning more about The Girls Home. Excited energy is palpable in the air—the atmosphere is filled with hope and light.

About an hour in, Jimmy finds Summer and me, and Stella is beside him. "So, I have a secret," he whispers to us. Summer and I exchange glances and wait for him to continue. "Stella here came to me a while back. She asked me to teach her a song so she could play it for you, Summer." I look at Stella, her eyes growing wide. "Now, it wasn't the plan to play it here today, but I think now is as good a time as any, wouldn't you say?"

Stella swallows, panic taking over her face. "Um. I can't. I can't sing. I only know the guitar strings."

"See, that's the thing," Jimmy says. "I've also been teaching Summer the same song. So, you both can go up there and play it together." He's never looked prouder.

"The Carole King song?" Summer asks. "From *Gilmore Girls?*"

"That's the one."

Summer and Stella stare at each other blankly, but only for a moment. Because after a beat, they both smile. "Are you up for it?" Summer asks her.

Stella's eyes widen. "Let's do it," she says, a shy grin slowly creeping across her face.

My eyes are glued to them on stage as they prepare for the performance. Jimmy is assuring Stella, who looks utterly terrified. Summer is tuning up the guitar. She's comfortable on stage with the instrument now, but I assume she's feeling the dreadful pre-performance jitters in her stomach because she's most definitely worried about how Stella is feeling. She has the tendency to take on the emotions of others, especially those she loves.

When it looks like they're ready, Finn grabs the microphone. "Everyone, we're going to get a special performance from our very own Summer James and one of our guests of honor, Stella." The crowd cheers. "I expect the tip jar to be overflowing," Finn adds with a loud laugh. He exits the stage, trots down the stairs, and heads toward the bar.

Summer nods at Stella, who gives her a soft smile, her face growing incredibly pale. The music begins, a bit shaky at first, but they quickly find their rhythm, and I feel the music in my bones. Summer begins singing the words, and they look at each other adoringly while they perform. It's the perfect song because it speaks to their relationship. The crowd is silent; all eyes are on the stage.

My breath catches in my throat, thinking about how Jimmy arranged for this moment to happen. He knew exactly what he was doing. I look around in front of the stage and spot him. He's looking at the two of them performing with the biggest grin on his face, as if they are his own flesh and blood; pride is etched into the lines on his face.

When the song ends, everyone who was sitting stands up, and the whole bar is clapping, a standing ovation. Summer moves her guitar to her back and pulls Stella in for a hug. Stella lets her head fall back and laughs. Summer gestures her hands toward Stella and brings her hands together to clap, inviting the crowd to cheer even louder for her first performance ever. Stella smiles at the crowd, and though bashful, she looks exhilarated.

Hours tick by, the afternoon slipping into twilight as the sky outside the windows deepens to a shade of purple.

"Looks like this will have to be another yearly event," Jimmy says, coming up beside me, his hand on my shoulder.

I smile at him. "Absolutely!" We both glance across the bar at the crowd. "Can you believe this turnout?"

"I can, actually." His voice is soft, and his response gives me pause. Jimmy has always believed in my success. He's always known that I would create a life here and make it a good one—ever since that stretch of days when I came out here from Austin to check the place out. He was walking joyfully past what is now Two WhisKEYS and stopped dead in his tracks, looking as if he was trying—desperately—to place me. I introduced myself, filling him in on what I was doing here. We didn't talk long, mere minutes. But before he continued on his way to his own restaurant, he stared at me for a moment. He chuckled to himself before saying, "I don't know you from Adam, son, but something tells me that you're right where you need to be."

Turns out, he did know me—in a way—and though it is wildly unfathomable, we're all here, living this life we've built together. Call it fate. Call it divine intervention. Call it whatever you want. But not a coincidence. Don't call it that. Because though it took some time, I truly know now, that there is no such thing.

By the end of the night, the three big plastic jugs used for tips are all filled to the brim. It has to be thousands of dollars. I'm not surprised at the generosity, but still, it's amazing.

As I'm loading the jugs into the back of Lisa's twelve-passenger van along with the amazing instrument and art supply donations, Lisa assists me. "I can't take all of this money, Kash." Her voice trembles, and she puts her hands on her hips.

"Oh, you most certainly are taking it all," I say lightly as I shut the passenger door. "That was the whole point." She stares at me for a moment before shaking her head. "You have no idea how much Summer wanted to do this. It's been on her mind for a long time. Her heart has the biggest spot in it for you and those girls. And because of her, so do I. This money does not belong to me. It's yours."

Lisa makes a noise that seems to be the result of stifling her emotions. She pulls me in for a hug. "Thank you," she whispers in my ear.

"I would do it all again tomorrow if I could."

The girls and Lisa head back home, except for Stella. Jimmy promised her a few songs once everyone left. I head back into the nearly empty bar.

Summer sees me enter the door and runs to me, jumping into my arms. "A million times saying it wouldn't be enough," she says into my ear. "But thank you."

Placing her back down on the ground, I respond, "You know there is no need to say it." I place a kiss on her lips, and she sighs into the embrace. "We're a team. It's me and you." She smiles and melts back into my arms—just as the lights flicker.

CHAPTER 31

Summer

APRIL

S PRING IS MAKING ITS comeback, and the sun feels warm on my face. Kash is on my left, Stella on my right, the ocean just up ahead. "We wanted to take you for a walk to talk to you, Stella," Kash says.

Stella nods, looking nervous.

A helicopter seed from the tree floats down in front of us, and I try to catch it but miss as it flutters to the ground. I pick it up. "Have you ever played with one of these?" I ask, peeling back the little stem and exposing the sticky insides.

Stella shakes her head and gives me a weird look. "Played with a piece of a tree?" She doesn't sound rude, just confused.

I stick it on my nose and give her a big, goofy smile. Making Pinocchio noses out of sticky helicopters is a beacon from my childhood, and sharing it with Stella warms my heart. She allows herself to laugh as she picks one up off the ground and peels it back, sticking it on her own nose. She pushes it down hard, making it stick. "It smells like the earth." Kash joins us. We all chuckle. And I let out a hefty sigh.

"Want to sit?" I ask as we approach the benches looking out over the water.

"You're scaring me," she says. I shake my head.

"No, this isn't scary," Kash assures her.

"What's going on?"

"Well, we have been talking to Lisa," I start. "And we think it would be best for you to have a bit more stability. We'd love it if you would allow us to foster you in our apartment." I say *allow* because we want this to be Stella's choice. She can stay at the group home, if she really wants to. Or, she can come live with us. She stares at us blankly. "It could be temporary, to give you a break from being surrounded by so many teenage girls." I let out a nervous laugh, annoying myself. "It can all be on your terms, as much as possible."

She turns to Kash, gauging his expression. He just smiles at her, assuring her that he is in on it, too.

She doesn't say anything for a long while, just stares out at the ocean. Then she turns back to us, away from the water. "Do I have to sleep in that room with all the stuff?"

I laugh so hard, I startle myself. Kash shakes his head and laughs at her little joke. "Yes," he says. "But we'll clean it all out for you before you move on over."

The three of us exchange curious glances until Stella says, "OK. Let's do it!"

Relief floods me in waves. Stella is going to be OK. It isn't too late to save her, to protect her. But, then again, is it ever too late to be saved? I don't think so.

The balcony is where I get all my best thinking done, a habit I learned from crawling out onto the roof at the Brickmans' as a teenager. As I rub my hand over the smooth ridges of the wicker chair, it reminds me of the feeling of the roof shingles under my palms.

I glance up at the sky and count the speckles of light right above me. When I get to the brightest one, I pause for a moment, deep in thought. I'm not sure exactly when I stopped talking to that star as Momma. And I wasn't sure why, either. But now, I know. When I used to talk to her up there, I was in desperate need of guidance—for someone, anyone, or anything to tell me what to do. To tell me how to be happy—how to be fulfilled.

When she was living and breathing on this earth, she couldn't do that for me. I was desperate, for a long time, for her to be the mom I needed. I was desperate for her to save me from my father. Then, I became desperate for her to fix herself so she could get me out of foster care. And after she was gone, I was desperate for her soul to be free so she could walk with me through life. I was desperate to feel her presence, to get a sign, any sign, of her being in my life. But I never felt attuned to her spirit. And I never did get a sign that she was there—not in the way that Stella, Kash, and Jimmy get signs frequently. So, eventually, I let go of that bright beacon in the sky. I had to stop wondering if she was there; I had to quit seeking her out. I love the stars, I swear, I do—even still. But now, when I look at them, what they are is a reminder of how far I've come. I can look up at them with gratitude and hope because they saved me; at some of the darkest points in my life, they were there. Not my mom, but those stars.

The rise and fall of my chest match the sounds of the tide going out. I smile and take a sip of my wine. The ocean, it called me. For decades, it seemed to speak to me somehow, and eventually, I listened—to the ocean calling me home.

CHAPTER 32

Stella

ONE YEAR LATER

THE TIDE IS MENACING today, and watching the waves crash against the sandy shore ignites a comfort inside me that hasn't been there in a while. The roaring sound is cathartic; it's something bigger than me, bigger than all of us. Being here reminds me that life is so much more than the here and now.

It has to be.

It needs it to be.

I look up at the sky, close my eyes, and search for the words to speak to my parents, something that's been impossible for me to do since I lost them. But not now, not anymore.

Mom and Dad, I feel you.

I feel them in the spray of the ocean.

I feel them when the sun warms my face.

I feel them when a shooting star streaks across the dark sky.

I feel them in the melody of the music I strum on my guitar.

When I try new things.

When I fail.

When I prosper.

When they led me to my new home.

I look over at Kash and Summer holding hands a bit down the beach. Summer points out to the horizon, and my eyes scan in that direction, and I see two dolphins playing in the surf. I smile to myself—at the sign my heart recognizes.

It's been almost a year since I moved in with them, into the office where Summer says she used to sleep before she moved her things, and her heart, into Kash's room. They talk a lot about us getting a bigger place, saying that it makes sense for us now since the apartment is really only made for one person. But if I'm being honest, I don't want to move. We've been making it work, and being this close to the ocean is the most amazing thing. And I'm also aware that this was meant to only be temporary.

Maybe I'll be gone soon. Maybe I'll be back at The Girls Home…or I'll go to college, and then Kash and Summer will have the apartment to themselves again, and they'll have their space back. I think they would still keep in touch with me—at least, I hope they will.

They begin to walk toward me, and I make my way in their direction. When we meet up, Kash gently puts his hand on my shoulder. "Beautiful, isn't it?" he ponders. "I'm so glad Summer finally convinced me to give it a shot—coming out here before the world wakes up. It's amazing to have this all to yourself." He glances longingly out at the waves. "And now, I'm slightly addicted to the way it feels at this time of day."

Summer smiles at him and nestles herself into the side of his body. I wonder if she notices that she fits there perfectly, like a puzzle piece.

"We want to talk to you about something," Summer says, looking at me thoughtfully. I can't entirely read the look on her face, but from what I can tell, it doesn't seem sad. I hold my breath as the two of them take a seat in the sand. Kash pats the spot next to him, gesturing for me to take a seat, so I do. Summer turns her body slightly so we're almost sitting in a circle.

"Stella, we love you," Kash begins, and I feel a lump in my throat forming, a flutter in my chest. I don't respond; I just look at them, my eyes darting from Summer's face to Kash's.

"Very much," Summer adds.

A small smile escapes, but with it, a few tears form behind my eyes because I don't know what to expect next. Kash and Summer are newly in love and couldn't possibly be happy with me in their space. I begin to brace myself for the news—that I'm going back to The Girls Home. When I moved in with them, it was to give me some space from the other girls, to let me breathe; that's what Summer had said. It was never a permanent situation, and I knew that from the start. I'm ready for them to bring me back if that's what this is.

"I know what this is," I say. "It's time for me to go back." I try not to sound sad. I don't want them to feel the burden of my pain. That wouldn't be fair.

Kash and Summer exchange a look. "What?" Summer says. "No, Stella."

I furrow my brows at them. "Then what?" I whisper the words.

"I want to adopt you." Summer puts her hand on my leg, and all space and time halts. There's a rushing sound in my ears, and I feel like I might pass out.

"WE want to," Kash adds. "We just aren't sure what the rules are since we aren't married. But this is a *we* thing. We want you to stay with us…forever, if you'll have us." Kash grins in that way he does, and my shoulders relax.

"Are…are you serious? Are you sure?" I stutter the words. "But I'm almost eighteen…an adult, technically."

"Never been more sure of anything," Summer replies with conviction. I believe her. I can tell by the way she says it and by the way they're both looking at me. "And you're still in high school. You have so many years left where you could use some parental guidance."

"OK," I respond, allowing a small smile to show. It feels right because I know that Kash and Summer don't want to replace my parents. And I don't want that either. But I don't deserve to be alone forever. And we have become a family. Maybe an unorthodox one, but a family nonetheless.

"Yeah? That sounds good to you?" Kash says, looking pleased.

I nod happily, and we all stand up. We wrap ourselves into a three-person pretzel, hugging as tight as we can. Kash rustles my hair, and we pull away, looking at one another. I'm in shock, but the happiness I feel can't be described in words.

"Ouch," I say through a laugh, stepping on a shell. I look down, and among the shards of white remnants from the sea, I see one that's intact, one that is whole. I pick it up and examine it in my hand, turning it around to admire the pearly, smooth surface and the beautiful ridges of the outside. "Look at this," I say, holding it up. "It's the most beautiful seashell I've ever seen."

Summer gently takes it from my hand, and her eyes glisten with fresh tears. Is that sadness written on her face?

No, it certainly isn't.

It's complete and genuine peace—a happiness that's tangible. A happiness that you can only feel when you're *home*.

Epilogue

AN EXCERPT FROM THE JOURNAL OF SUMMER JAMES, SOME YEARS IN THE FUTURE

I MUST ADMIT, IT feels sort of strange to be writing this…to be journaling again. To be doing something that once felt like a lifeline but has fallen out of my routine for far too long. But, as I've learned throughout my life, with change come triggers, and it's my responsibility to be ahead of it…to do the work…to continue to heal—no matter the obstacles. And change has come, hurdling us all into a new routine that feels foreign and unbelievably unfair. It pains me to put it on paper, to face the difficult truth.

But I have to accept the pain.

I need to allow the emotions to flow through me and remind myself that the sorrow I feel is better than not feeling at all.

Last month, we lost Jimmy. And with his departure from the physical world, he took with him pieces of all of us. He always used to say, *I'm not going to be here forever,* as if he was preparing us for the day when we would have to walk this life without him. However, nothing could have prepared us for what it would actually be like to be without him. But I see him—I feel him. So, I know he's still here. He has to be.

I see him in the shadows on the beach. I feel him in the gentle breeze that comes off the waves as if he has summoned them to tell us *hello* and *I love you* and *enjoy this moment*. I hear him in the strum of my guitar. The infinite lessons he taught us are timeless gifts that he continues to remind us of, day in and day out.

Much to our surprise, he left everything he owned to Kash. When Kash was struggling to clean out Jimmy's bungalow, his heart weak with sorrow, he was reminded of Jimmy's words. He told me he could hear his voice as if he was whispering in his ear, saying, *Don't cry for me. I'm always here.* And so, Kash gathered the strength to get through the task. But it was far from easy.

We wondered—tirelessly—where Jimmy's family was, if there was any. Where did he come from? Did he have any roots? Why was there no one else to leave his things to but us? He never did talk about a family or any other home but this beach. His only sense of family seemed to be us, a thought that never seemed important until he died, and we were the only *family* to be seen.

I'm amazed at the impact that Jimmy had on Stella, even though they only knew each other for a short time. I guess I shouldn't be surprised because that's how Jimmy was. He could leave an impression on you that would last a lifetime with just one profound statement.

When Stella called last week from college to tell me she had changed her postgraduate plans a bit, she informed me that she would be accepting an art internship after graduation rather than the marketing one she originally accepted. Her voice sounded like she was choking on her words. I asked her what was wrong, and though it took effort, she eventually mustered the words. Words that seemingly came straight from Jimmy's heart. "I can't waste my time doing something that doesn't bring me joy, something that doesn't encompass things I'm passionate about," she said. She had double majored in business and art, assuming she would work in an office building doing marketing or advertising. But the art portion of her major has taken precedence. And deep down in my bones, I know she is making the right choice with that. I smiled into the phone, knowing where she'd gotten the motivation to adhere to those words. It was undoubtedly Jimmy.

When I asked her what her decision was and she filled me in on her plans, a pride built up deep inside me. She'll be assisting in running a program for at-risk youth at the art museum. A positive venture. A ray of hope despite the sadness. Stella is motivated, and I know she'll do amazing things with her talent, starting with this internship. During one of their guitar lessons, Jimmy had told her that her art told a story that wasn't just seen with the eyes but heard—somehow—through the soul. And those words moved her. And I have no doubt that she'll carry Jimmy in her heart forever now, along with her parents.

Jimmy never did tell us about his heart condition. Not until we were about to lose him. As we sat around his hospital bed, we held his hands while the tears soaked our cheeks, and he told us not to cry. "I told you over and over again that I wouldn't be here forever. Did you think I was lying?" His tone was jovial as he attempted to lighten the heaviness, I'm sure. He said he didn't tell us that something was wrong with his heart because, in his mind, there wasn't. He said he had a space big enough there to hold all the people he loved most in the world and that he had a spirit that could light his path even on the darkest days. And he was certainly right about that. Not only did he light up his own life but also the lives of all of us around him.

"Why worry about things you can't change?" It was one of the last things he said before he quietly slipped away from us. "I wasn't going to have you all looking at me differently had I told you about my ticker. Treating me like I was fragile." He smiled at us then as we exchanged glances. "Don't you dare fret over what hasn't come to be. Worry just brings more worry. You have each other. Hold on to the moments and savor them—the good, the bad, and even the downright ugly." He looked right at me when he said that, and it took all of my strength not to sob on his shoulder. I felt lightheaded as I held my breath, desperate to be strong for him. He patted my hand gently. "I'm not abandoning you." He was talking to all of us, but still only looking at me. "I'll just be somewhere else for a while…until we meet again."

He always told us that we were right where we needed to be, that invisible strings had led us to one another. Though the threads sometimes became tangled and other times were seemingly shredded to minuscule pieces, we all picked up our own shards of broken strings and mended them back together, landing us right where we are right now.

He told us—as we watched him slip away—that he wanted us to celebrate his life when he was gone. To sing and dance and laugh, to spread his ashes where the water kisses the shore. And so, that's exactly what we did as Kash sang "Drink a Beer" while strumming Jimmy's favorite guitar in the early morning hours on the beach along the pier. The lyrics made the ache in my chest feel as if it would always be there, that it would never heal. And so, even though we did laugh, sharing stories of our beloved Jimmy, we also cried for all that had been taken from us.

Though I've lost so much in my life, what I've gained is infinitely more meaningful. The most important lesson being that even with its broken pieces, this life is a beautiful one. What I once feared—getting to the end of my time here and realizing that I'd missed out on living—is a thought of the past, not something that holds any truth over me anymore.

A few nights after Jimmy passed, Kash and I sat on our balcony, hollowed out from heartache and grief, two manila envelopes sitting in our laps, our last tokens from Jimmy, we supposed. Neither of us wanted to open them and have his last gifts consumed too quickly, leaving us with nothing left to savor.

Kash ran his hands through his hair and looked at me, his eyes weary and red. "Why does it feel like Jimmy's purpose in life was to bring us together?" he said, his voice trailing off into the night. He got up from the wicker chair and put his hands on the railing, looking out toward the waves. "It's weird, isn't it?" He looked to me for validation. But I could only shrug. If Jimmy taught us anything, it was that we shouldn't think too much about how our lives unfold. Because it always seems to just make sense in the end.

"Does it really matter?" My words were soothing, trying to settle Kash's troubled heart.

He looked at me, his head slowly shaking. I got up and embraced him, caressing his back as he did the same to me. And then, we opened our envelopes. I watched as Kash opened the little clasp and slid out the papers inside, which contained Jimmy's will—all he had to his name was now Kash's. And a tattered skateboard keychain. And a note in Jimmy's messy scrawl that read:

This was your dad's, Kash. He hung this from his belt loop every day as he soaked up all that this place had to offer him. He accidentally left it with me before he left for Texas, and I never got rid of it. I found it recently, and I know you'll find joy in having it. I love you. Please keep living as I've watched you do all these years, with joy and passion in your heart. And take care of our girls. I'll always be with you.

Kash cried real tears for the first time since I've known him, and when I crawled into his lap, it wasn't long before there was no deciphering between his tears and my own. And we stayed that way for a long time, our breaths matching one another's as we listened to the crashing waves against the shore until it felt like it was time for me to open my own envelope. I grabbed it, sitting back down next to Kash on the loveseat. I peeked inside and pulled out the little slip of paper that read:

Summer, never stop looking for the miracles around you.

I smiled to myself, allowing my shoulders to relax as an image of a smiling Jimmy spread across my mind's eye. I peeked again inside the little envelope—something small catching my eye. I reached in, feeling something hard. I took it in my fingers and pulled it out. Looking at the little figure caused the air in my lungs to suspend. I whipped my head toward Kash in disbelief as he brought his hand to his mouth.

A tiny pig with white wings sat idle on my shaking palm. "How is this possible?" I muttered, mostly to myself. I tried to recall a time when I told Jimmy about the recurring phrase from my past—*when pigs fly*—but I couldn't conjure up a memory. Because the truth is, Jimmy didn't know its significance in my life. The way the words once traumatized me—instilling ideas in my head that I was never going to be good enough.

Never going to amount to anything.

Never going to belong.

Never going to be loved.

Until a tiny pig flew with me—miraculously—to California. To this life that I gratefully call my own now. A life where I am loved. A life where I thrive. A life that fulfills me.

Kash took the pig from my hand, spinning it between his own fingers, gazing at it under furrowed brows. "It's such a—"

But I cut him off, hearing Jimmy's voice, loud and proud, in my ear. "Don't you dare," I said, my smile reaching my ears. Kash grinned back at me, wrapping his arm around my shoulders and pulling me close. And together, we whispered the words that Jimmy convinced us to believe, the truth about happenstance: *There's no such thing.*

Thank You

I can't believe I'm writing an acknowledgments section again! My dreams have all come true for a second time and this sequel would have not come to fruition if it weren't for everyone one of you mentioned here.

Christy, thank you for crawling into my brain, AGAIN, and creating a cover that puts readers right into the setting. We all know we shouldn't judge books by their covers, but how lucky am I that I have two books that are worthy of being grabbed just for being utterly beautiful?

Erin, your encouragement, patience and expertise brought the best out of my manuscript once again. I am forever grateful for your willingness to work with me a second time. I hope I made it a little easier this time around!

I am still amazed by the kindness and support I have received from complete strangers while debuting my first book—strangers who have become friends. I can't thank these lovely ladies enough for continuing to love and share about *When Pigs Fly* and *No*

Such Thing over and over again simply from the kindness of their hearts. The messages and constant support are unmatched. It means so much to me. Thank you: @antisocialmomreads @lululovegold @reads_withliz @mamabirdedits @cameadows.

Hil, you may be a "non-reader" but your excitement and the encouragement you continuously provide me warms me up inside! You would make everyone pick up these books if you could. You're always the first person to share updates and posts for these books and I am forever grateful for that. Thank you.

Courtney at A Great Notion Books, thank you for making me feel like a REAL author and hosting me for my first ever book signing. I can't put into words what it feels like to do something so monumental when even the thought of such an accomplishment seemed impossible not too long ago. The experience helped me to remember to keep going with this book—to look at the big picture.

A giant amount of gratitude is extended to my ARC readers! Thank you for your time and the thoughtfulness you put into reading and sharing about *No Such Thing*.

Rita M. and Megan H.—thank you for your feedback on the roughest of drafts. I know how hard it is to be critical during the beta process. I appreciate you so much!

Kayla, what can I say? I don't think I will ever write a book again without you attached to the document from the very first word. Your feedback is top notch and your support never wavers. Ever. I love you so much.

Mom and Dad, thank you for your support and pride in me for finally fulfilling my dreams. I guarantee most of the sales from the first month of *When Pigs Fly* are from your friends on Facebook! Love you!

My babies, thank you for being proud of your mom. I hope you know that your dreams are always within reach.

ML, I'm so grateful for your constant manifestations of me making it big. Where I keep myself grounded, you raise me up. I love you.

To everyone who holds Summer close to their hearts, it's because of you that *No Such Thing* is in your hands. It's your love for her that kept her growing and kept me going until I did right by her…for you. I hope you stick around to see what's next. <3

About the author

Krissy Lanier was born and raised in Massachusetts. She lives there with her husband, Matt, and three children. They have a dog named Memphis and a cat named Joey (after Joey Tribiani). Krissy has been teaching kindergarten for 12 years and recently was inspired to go after her dream of being a writer. *No Such Thing* is her second novel.

When she's not teaching and writing, Krissy can be found at the beach with her family or with her nose stuck in a book. She is passionate about spreading awareness about foster care and Type 1 Diabetes, which she has had since childhood. Want to follow along with her as she works on her third novel? You can find her on Instagram @krissylanier_writes.

www.ingramcontent.com/pod-product-compliance
Lightning Source LLC
Chambersburg PA
CBHW021412010826
48972CB00014B/1596

9 798988 252832